DREAM LOVER

He caught her by the waist as she tried to spin away from him, then he pulled her hard against himself and forced her chin up so that their eyes were locked together. "We can have it all—everything you just described. I want to be with you until the day I die, and I want to spend every day making you happy. I swear it. You believe me, don't you?"

"I don't know. I want to . . ."

He had called *her* eyes inspiring, but *his* were positively spellbinding. The golden flames promised passion and adventure, while the warm brown background spoke of sincerity and unselfishness. It would be so easy to place her heart, and her life, in his hands. His lovemaking was hypnotic and thrilling. She loved him with a passion that could never be extinguished, and yet she feared for him, and for herself . . .

KATE DONOVAN

A DREAM APART

PINNACLE BOOKS
KENSINGTON PUBLISHING CORP.

PINNACLE BOOKS are published by

Kensington Publishing Corp.
850 Third Ave
New York, NY 10022

First Printing: April, 1995

Printed in the United States of America

To my husband, for the encouragement
To my daughter, for the enthusiasm
And to my son, for the ending

Prologue

In the distant past, magicians moved among the inhabitants of North America. Some chose to respect and intermarry with the various tribes of moundbuilders and hunters, while others chose to use their powers to terrorize and dominate. For a time, the most powerful of all North American magicians were twin sorcerers, who wandered into a village of proud and peaceful natives, adopting them as their own. They proceeded to build a series of burial mounds which were also channels to the magical powers deep within the earth. With such power, their descendants might have been able to rule benevolently and without fear of destruction. Unfortunately, the twins were murdered by malevolent lake wizards from the north before the fourth and final mound could be completed. The descendants of the twins could thereafter draw only imperfect power from the existing mounds and eventually were all but annihilated by the lake community.

Two of the mound magicians escaped the wrath of the lakes. The first was the sorceress Kerreya, who had married Valmain, a king from across the "untraveled sea," beyond the reach of the lakes and their greedy slaughter. The second was a sorcerer named

Aaric, who had been sent far into the future by Kerreya's jealous sister Maya to destroy the Valmain kingdom. A battle between Aaric and the Valmain champion was thus inevitable, with the victor emerging as heir to the legacy of the twins, and as avenger of the atrocities of the lake wizards.

History became legend, yet the legend was never completely forgotten. To some it became a soothing bedtime story, while to others it carried a message, or a warning, or a promise of a magical world lying dormant . . . waiting . . .

Chapter One

To the casual observer, the pretty undergraduate in the white peasant-style dress was calm, almost serene, as she sat in the bustling hallway outside Matthew Redtree's office. Mentally, however, the young woman was pacing, all the while berating herself for having ever become involved with a sociology class, even one so innocuously named as *Symbolism in Legend and Myth*.

You took this class for all the wrong reasons and this is your punishment, Molly Sheridan. From now on, stick to science and math. They may be hard work, but at least you know when you've gotten the right answer!

She had been lecturing herself this way for ten full minutes, all too aware that she needed this precious time to prepare for her upcoming molecular biology exam. She couldn't afford to give any more attention to Sociology 105B. Hadn't she dutifully attended every lecture? Hadn't she turned in the final exam one day early? She had even taken the course Pass/Not Pass, rather than for a grade, as extra insurance against complications. What more could Matthew Redtree want from her?

Perhaps it was all a mistake. Perhaps this instructor had sent for her because he had simply misplaced her final exam paper. Or perhaps he had loved it and wanted to congratulate her. The absurdity of this last feeble rationalization brought a reluctant smile to Molly's lips.

While frustrated, she was not truly intimidated. After all, the outcome of this course—barring complete failure—was not going to affect her GPA, and it seemed impossible to fail an assignment as subjective as this one, which had simply required each student to recount and analyze an obscure legend or fairy tale of their own choosing. The examination had been as easygoing as the instructor himself— Matthew Redtree, the gentle, soft-spoken, mystical legend-spinner who had summoned her. When she closed her eyes she could almost picture him, quiet and unassuming, sporting a rumpled tweed sports jacket and an apologetic smile . . .

At that moment the legend-spinner appeared and, to her dismay, his eyes were cool and not at all apologetic. The sports jacket was nowhere in sight and, in its absence, his lean, muscular arms, scarcely camouflaged by an austere white polo shirt, seemed almost menacing. The blue-black hair that had always been neatly groomed now appeared tousled in unruly frustration, but it was his voice that proved to be the real shock—clipped and callous—as he accused, "Molly Sheridan?"

She gave him her most sincere smile and swept by him quickly into his office. "Is this about my final, Mr. Redtree? I turned it in yesterday, right on time. But I always keep copies on my hard drive. I could have one here in an hour."

"Sit down, please, Ms. Sheridan. I have your final right here." The stern-faced instructor waved the document in question ominously. "There are some problems with it. I felt it might help to meet you and talk about it."

"By 'problems,' do you mean problems with the grade, or problems that I have to fix? Because to be honest, I'm on a tight schedule. As I'm sure you are. I loved your class, but," Molly gave her shoulders a slight shrug, "I've got three more exams in the next three days and I have to give them my undivided attention."

"I appreciate your candor, Ms. Sheridan. However, your treatment of this subject . . ."

"Pretty bad?" There was reluctant agreement in her clear blue eyes. "This kind of subjective assignment has never really been my strong suit. I'm more the facts-and-figures type, you know? I'm a scientist."

"So am I. A social scientist."

Molly laughed, then blushed. "Sorry. I thought you were joking."

Matthew Redtree frowned. "Perhaps this exam was a joke to you, too."

She blushed again and stood up, raising her hands in mock surrender. "Okay—here's the truth. I'm not all that proud of it, but here goes. I'm taking this course Pass/Not Pass. So technically I don't need a good grade on the exam. I was in a bind and I figured I could either do my usual—kill myself going through a dozen references, trying for an 'A' on the final—or I could use the legend I was already familiar with and wing it. I figured I could still get a Pass. Are we meeting because you're thinking of not passing me? Because I honestly didn't think it was all that bad. And," she took a quick breath, "I really do feel I learned a lot from your lectures, if that counts for anything."

"We're meeting to determine whether your paper

has any merit," he explained, "which turns on whether the legend you based it on is legitimate."

"You never heard of it?" She sighed, sinking back into her chair and fluffing her sunstreaked shoulder-length curls with absentminded ease. "I was afraid of that. Actually, though, I think I included all the highlights. I mean, the basic legend's there, and then all the stuff about the plague and the champion . . . That's all legend, too, right? Even if some of it's true?"

"True?" He fanned through the pages of her exam paper. "You're saying you believe parts of this fairy tale are true?"

"Well, not truly *true,* I guess. I mean, I don't believe there were sorcerers and sorceresses and spells. But I guess I've always thought the part about . . ." She hesitated. This sounded bad. And she was babbling. She'd better retreat. "No, I guess I don't believe any of it."

"Did you make it up?"

"What? Ohhh! I see. Sorry, I was missing your point. No, this is definitely authentic. It's been told hundreds, maybe thousands of times. Lots of people have heard it."

"All of them in your family, I suppose?"

"Well, yes," Molly laughed. "But you'd have to know my family to know that none of us could have made this up. We're very down-to-earth, if you know what I mean. Not creative writers."

He was plainly not amused. "Is it written down anywhere?"

"Not that I know of, but I can tell it to you. I mean, the rest of the details. But," she paused to shrug, "what's the point? Unless you're planning on not passing me, of course."

"It's a simple question, Ms. Sheridan." His voice

had become a frustrated growl. "Can you document, or otherwise legitimate, this legend? This 'Valmain Legend,' as you call it."

"As I 'call' it?" she repeated slowly. "That's its name! I'm trying to be patient, Mr. Redtree, but it's starting to sound like you're calling me a liar." Her eyes locked with his. "If my great-grandmother were here, she could tell you the whole story and you'd believe it, documentation or not. That's how I first heard it, and I never doubted it! That's all I can say."

"Can you arrange that?"

"What? Oh. No." Her tone grew wistful. "She died when I was four."

"How convenient."

With studied dignity, Molly rose to her feet once more. "I think that's about it. If you want to talk about this any more, talk to my adviser. I'm going to see her right now to drop this class."

"Drop it? That's ridiculous! It's ended. You already took the final."

"I don't want it on my record!" Catching her temper, she repeated quietly, "Talk to my adviser."

"Listen. Don't go." He moved to block the doorway. "You've got an A in this course, if that's all you're worried about, Ms. Sheridan. I just want more details."

"I don't want an A. I just need a Pass. If I've earned it. Either way, I'm through with this course *and* this conversation."

"Please! Just listen." Matthew Redtree ran his fingers through his thick, unruly hair and insisted, "I've been rude. It's unintentional. I've been under a lot of stress."

"So have I. And I still have three more finals to get through. Please step out of my way."

"Listen. Accept my apology. I know it's no excuse, but I'm in a position where, if this legend of yours is legitimate—and I mean that in the nicest way—it could be the one I've been searching for. For years!"

Molly's eyes narrowed. He seemed sincere, but slightly deranged. Was this some by-product of publish-or-perish? In any case, reality was beckoning to her. She had three finals to go, and they were important. This was not. "You need this for your next book?" she guessed.

"Right!" His golden eyes flashed with excitement. "I'm researching legends in which dreaming plays a pivotal role. Will you help me?"

"So you're interested in my legend because the sorceress Kerreya dreamed things and her dreaming made them come true? I see. That always fascinated me, too." Backing a comfortable distance away, she nodded. "Okay. Let me get past my finals and then maybe I can give you some more details. Is that okay?"

"Yes, that's great. But . . ." His smile was wry and apologetic. "Don't take this the wrong way. Is there anyone who can corroborate your legend now, this instant? The older the person, the better."

"Corroborate? You're calling me a liar again?" Molly sifted her fingers though her curls impatiently. "You want proof? I'll let you talk to my grandmother. She lives in Ireland now, unfortunately, but I can put you in touch with her and she can give you all the details. Then you'll never bother me again. How's that?"

"Perfect!" He seemed inordinately relieved as he reached for the telephone. "What's her number?"

"Now?" Molly shook her head, again impatient. "It must be almost midnight in Ireland. We can't bother her now! Anyway, I don't carry her number with me. Couldn't you come over to my apartment tomorrow morning?"

"You're not going to like this, Ms. Sheridan, but . . ." His smile was supremely apologetic. "Remember, we're both scientists. Consider this a controlled experiment. I have to be sure . . ."

"That I don't get to her first and coach her?" Molly shook her head, reluctantly amused. "Unbelievable. You live in a strange world."

"Someday maybe I'll tell you just how strange," he chuckled. "But for now . . ."

"I can adjust. Here's the deal. You give me a C, and you give Grandma full credit for the legend in your new book—she'll love that!—and I'll hang around here and study until, well, probably 11:30 or so, I guess, then we'll go to my place and make the call. Take it or leave it."

"I'll take it. And I'll take you out to dinner while we're waiting. It's the least I can do."

"No way. I've got to study." She spoke briskly, intent upon maintaining a detached relationship. "Actually, I'd prefer if we just set up camp at the library."

"You're willing to spend the next seven or eight hours studying without a break?"

"That was my original plan for tonight, as a matter of fact. For every night until finals are over."

"And you call *my* world strange?" he grinned. "Well, at least I'll get all these finals graded. Starting with your A for the course."

The library was brightly lit and crowded—a tribute to finals week, when day and night blur and procrastinators scramble—but Molly Sheridan was a dedicated student, trained to filter out such minor distractions. Filtering out Matthew Redtree proved somewhat more difficult. He was a *major* distraction, radiating intensity and energy, all of it positive, all of it focused, and, for the moment, all of it focused in her direction.

He had been Molly's all-time favorite lecturer, largely because he had made so few demands on her. One lively textbook and class twice a week—lectures that consisted of his telling of simple, primitive, enigmatic folktales to a roomful of entranced students. Molly had never missed a "session," as she called it, always arriving early and always choosing a seat toward the back of the lecture hall, after which she would slip off her shoes, lean back, close her eyes, and let Matthew Redtree's soft, resonant voice transport her.

He was a cross between a preacher and a therapist, both of which Molly suspected she needed but neither of which she had the time or inclination to seek out, and so she turned instead to *Symbolism in Legend and Myth* and invariably emerged refreshed.

Her eyes had been blissfully closed during the lectures, but now they were open—wary—and she was surprised by what she observed. From the back of the lecture hall he had looked thirty, or older, and slender. She could see now that he was younger—perhaps twenty-eight—and quite muscular. Lean and hard, deeply tanned, with gold-flecked eyes and blue-black hair—while soothingly handsome from a distance, Matthew Redtree was disturbingly sexy at close range and Molly couldn't afford to be disturbed. Not yet. *One more semester,* she reminded herself. *Stay on schedule, Molly.*

She could feel his eyes on her, taking in every movement, and while she tried to remain aloof, she knew her cheeks were flushed. *Concentrate on your work, Molly,* she pleaded with herself. *This isn't the kind of biology they're going to test you on in less than forty-eight hours!*

Matthew Redtree's voice interrupted her self-reprimand. "You're not as tall as I thought you'd be."

"Does it affect my grade?"

"What?" He seemed taken aback. "Sorry. I didn't realize I said that out loud. I just expected you to be taller."

"Expected? From my exam paper? Do I write tall?"

"No," he grinned. "Never mind."

"I'm five foot four—and a half. Without shoes."

"Without shoes," he nodded. "You don't like shoes. I noticed that in the lectures. You're just like the women of ancient Cambrisia. They felt that covering the feet was unnatural—"

"It's in your book." Molly spoke sternly, intent upon discouraging any further discussion of the barefooted, bare-*chested* women of ancient Cambrisia. To his credit, Matthew didn't allow his gaze to move, even momentarily, from her frowning face to the bodice of her lacy white dress. Lucky for him, she decided. This was becoming too complicated for finals week in particular or for Molly Sheridan's orderly life in general. "You're supposed to be grading those exams," she added firmly.

"Do you exercise, Miss Sheridan?" Her petulant sigh seemed to amuse him, and he added impishly, "It won't affect your grade, of course."

"I swim. Every day. Would you also care to know my weight? My shoe size?"

Matthew chuckled. "Are you seeing anyone?"

"If you mean, like a shrink," Molly retorted, "no. But I have the name of a good one, if you'd like it."

He ignored the obvious sarcasm. "I meant, are you dating anyone?"

"I'm too busy—to date *or* to play games. And frankly," her steady blue eyes rebuked him, "I'm disappointed in you. I thought you were a serious scholar."

"Don't be disappointed yet, Molly," he urged quietly. "We'll talk to your grandmother, and then . . . I'll tell you a story that will change your life."

There was something in his tone—a kind of hope mixed with invitation—that was dangerously seductive, but she resisted it coolly, reminding him, "I need to study. We'll talk to my grandmother, and then you'll go away and give me a passing grade. And you'll give her credit for our legend in your next book. That's our deal, right?" She searched his eyes, feeling suddenly vulnerable. "Please?"

"Whatever you want. I promise."

Whatever I want? Molly mused silently, wondering if a man like Matthew Redtree could understand how little—and how much—she wanted from life.

I'm too busy to date or to play games, she had chastised him and that, in a nutshell, was Molly Sheridan. She was busy. She was dedicated. Motivated. She intended to make a difference—to bring something new and wondrous to the world.

Even as a child she had felt a strong pull toward the future, and had always cheerfully sacrificed the present in its honor. Her quiet, industrious nature had manifested itself in every aspect of her life, including her childhood dreams, in which she had amused herself with sewing in a lovely dream meadow that would have tempted any other child to romp and tumble.

My sewing dream, she recalled fondly now. The

simple days. All gone. She was all grown up and
ready, pending one more semester of study, to face
the world that she had benevolently ignored until
now. One more *very* important semester, she reminded herself firmly, and so, reluctantly, she
would benevolently ignore Matthew Redtree and
his gold-dusted eyes.

He was staring again. "How old are you?"

Molly sighed. "I thought we had an understanding."

"You look so young."

"I'm twenty-one." She decided to turn the tables.
"How old are you?"

"Twenty-eight. And I'm six feet tall. One hundred seventy-five pounds. Born and raised in Southern California. I'm a fifth-degree black belt in—"

"That's enough," she assured him. "More than
enough. Believe me." Her shy smile softened the
interruption. "I really did enjoy your lectures, Mr.
Redtree. And your book. It must be wonderful to
earn your living studying a subject that so clearly
fascinates you."

"It's a means to an end," he murmured. "Just a
means to an end, Molly Sheridan."

Don't ask what that end is, she warned herself.
*Study! Tomorrow he'll be gone and finals will be
back.* She returned to her books, uncomfortably
aware of his stare, which was sometimes almost
wistful, but more often resembled some form of
mental dissection. The hours ticked away and a
distracted Molly found herself wondering what her
grandmother—the strident, overprotective Elizabeth Scanlon—would think of Redtree's inquisition, and what she would say! Grandma could be
pretty blunt. Maybe she'd chew him out, long-dis-

tance, for doubting her darling Molly. That would be great.

Thoughts of her grandmother relaxed her and Molly was eventually nodding and yawning. She caught herself, acknowledging Matthew's observant grin with a self-mocking smile. "Sorry. Maybe we should leave a little early? If I don't get a cup of coffee I'll doze off right here." She gestured aimlessly. "I get up early every morning, and I'm usually asleep by ten. It's past my bedtime."

"If you need sleep, you should sleep," he advised. "Don't take caffeine. It's not good for your body, Molly."

"Don't lecture *me,*" she laughed. "I'm majoring in biochem, with a minor in nutrition, and I'm very careful about my diet. Usually. But I'm not a fanatic."

"Well," he admitted cheerfully, "I *am* a fanatic."

"I've noticed."

"I meant about food," he chuckled, "although you're right. I tend to be a fanatic on many levels." Jumping to his feet, he gathered his papers, along with her books and laptop computer, and loaded them all into his worn leather knapsack. "Let's get out of here. We'll go to your place and you can sleep until midnight."

"Food," she corrected, hurrying to keep pace with him, "and coffee. That's all I need. This fresh air will help, too," she added as they emerged from the bustling library into the balmy night and headed toward Molly's humble home.

She liked Matthew Redtree's long, easy strides and confident posture, which were seemingly unaffected by the weight of his overloaded knapsack.

Remembering his mention of some involvement with martial arts, she took a moment to imagine his body engaged in complex, graceful, and deadly motions, then laughed at herself for indulging in so uncharacteristically physical a fantasy.

"Tell me the legend again, Molly," he urged as they crossed at the busy intersection between the campus and the city. "Tell it exactly the way your great-grandmother used to tell it to you."

"Exactly?" She shook her head in emphatic protest. "That would be embarrassing, to say the least. I was just a little girl then—an only child, and *very* spoiled. I'll tell you the legend, but I'll have to leave out most of the sentimental bedtime-story business."

"It won't seem silly to me, Molly," Matthew smiled. "I've gone all over the world, and the most helpful legends—in terms of accuracy and inspiration—are the ones that have been told, over and over, to children by someone who loved them."

Molly nodded. "There was a lot of love involved in this one. When my great-grandmother died, my grandmother—the one you're going to pester—took over the bedtime-story routine. She knew it by heart, of course . . . I guess that's the version I know best."

"Let's hear it." He took her arm as they moved onto an almost deserted side street. "Every word."

"Okay." She drew a deep breath, then recited, "There was a sorcerer with two beautiful daughters who lived in a land where magic flourished. Their most sacred holiday was the day when magic first came to their land.

"There was another land, across the untraveled sea, where the practice of magic had been forbidden from the beginning of time. The land was ruled by

Valmain. The king. My family is supposedly descended from him . . ." Her blush had reappeared.
"I believed it completely when I was a child. Can
you imagine? Anyway, Valmain's kingdom was
being slowly destroyed by a virulent plague . . .
Although Grandma didn't use the word 'virulent'
. . ."

"What word did she use?"

" 'Nasty'," Molly laughed. "A 'nasty' plague.
And because Valmain could find no cure, he decided to try magic but, of course, there was no one
with such knowledge or skill in his kingdom. He
made up his mind that he would travel the untraveled sea—I guess that must have been the Atlantic
Ocean—and he would seek out a people famed for
their abilities to control nature. He traveled many
days and nights, through endless cold and darkness,
until he found the land of the wonderful sorcerer
with the two beautiful daughters.

"The first daughter, whose name was Maya, fell
in love with Valmain and gladly provided him with
a cure for the nasty plague. But it was the younger
daughter—a curly-haired sorceress named Kerreya," she paused to finger her own curls in gentle
self-mockery, "—who won Valmain's heart. When
Valmain asked the sorcerer-father for Kerreya's
hand in marriage, Maya was more furious than anyone has ever been, and she cursed Valmain and his
entire kingdom."

"Slow down, Molly," Matthew urged, his voice
husky with anticipation. "This part is very important."

"Is it?" They had paused under a street lamp and
she studied him carefully. "I thought it was the
dreaming that interested you."

"Maya was furious . . ." he prompted, ignoring her challenge. "Go on."

"Maya cursed Valmain. She vowed that Valmain would experience betrayal as profound and as devastating as the betrayal he and Kerreya had worked against her. She vowed that the kingdom of Valmain would be destroyed by that betrayal.

"But Kerreya pleaded with her father, the mighty sorcerer, for a means of softening Maya's curse, and he gave her a power, greater than that of her sister, to call forth a champion to defend Valmain from the inevitable betrayal. Even though he couldn't cancel the curse, or guarantee that Kerreya's champion would prevail against it, he did provide a chance for Valmain to survive."

"Maya must have been livid," Matthew mused. "What did she do when she heard about the champion that Kerreya and her father provided?"

"I have no idea. I only know that the sorcerer was so distraught over the feud between his daughters, and so disappointed in Maya for her abuse of her power, that he . . ." She hesitated, then waved one hand apologetically. "We've reached one of those embarrassing moments."

Matthew nodded, staring deep into her eyes. "The sorcerer was so disappointed," he whispered, "that he invoked a powerful spell, through which he cursed all of his descendants. He vowed that his power could not be inherited again, except by a descendant who was truly deserving. Right?" He smiled at her widened eyes and reminded her, "It was in your exam paper, remember?"

"Oh, that's right!" She exhaled sheepishly. "But it wasn't as simple as whether they were 'truly deserving.' In order to inherit the sorcerer's magic, the descendant had to be 'strong and pure of heart.' "

Almost to herself, she added, "I wanted to be that."

"It's incredible," Matthew murmured. "Other children dream of being beautiful, or rich, or famous, but you . . ."

Molly backed away, unnerved by the reverence in his eyes. "Don't get carried away. It didn't last forever. As I grew older, my goals became a little bit more practical."

"Strong and pure of heart," he repeated stubbornly. "You radiate those qualities . . ."

"You're nuts." She smiled shyly. "And it's your turn. Tell me a story. We're almost to my place, and I'm all talked out."

They strolled in the moonlight, or rather, as Matthew observed, the half-moonlight, which launched a telling of the legends of the Half-Moon People.

"I remember that from your book," Molly nodded. "They celebrated the nights when half of the moon shone in the sky and the other half shone in their lake. That never made sense to me."

"Huh?" Matthew seemed shocked by such blasphemy. "The half moons represented balance to them. And unity. It's very simple. What didn't you understand?"

"What about all of the other nights? I mean, didn't they notice that when there was a full moon in the sky, there was also one in their lake? And et cetera?"

"Sure," he grinned. "They thought it was very pretty." He patted her arm. "These groups all believed they were special. The most important people on Earth, so to speak. But they weren't dumb. They knew that the other tribal groups had gods and spirits looking out for them also. Lesser powers, they presumed. So, even though every thing in nature was significant, only certain things had significance vis-à-vis one particular group. The Half-Moon People were very concerned with balance. No caffeine, for example," he added mischievously.

"Caffeine 'balances' out my studying. But I agree. It's going to take actual sleep to balance me now."

"Do you dream?"

"Doesn't everyone?"

"Tell me what you dream about," he insisted.

She thought again of her little sewing dream, but dismissed it as childish, declaring instead, "I concentrate on my ambitions. My goals. Not dreams."

"Okay. Tell me your goals."

"I'm a biochem major. I'll graduate after two more courses. Then I'll get my master's. I want to do drug research . . ."

"Drugs?"

"I want to do research. To develop new cures. I'll be a toxicologist, technically, and I'll probably work for some large pharmaceutical group . . ." She noted his frown. "Does that sound overconfident? I've worked hard, my grades are good, my professors have been very encouraging . . ."

"It's not that, Molly. I just have a problem with . . ." He stopped himself, as though unwilling to again appear fanatical. "I prefer natural cures. Herbal medicines. Drug research is somewhat counterproductive, in my opinion."

"Oh?"

"More than any other single problem, drugs are tearing this culture apart. Destroying it."

"I'm not talking about illegal drugs, Matthew."

"*Il*legal drugs," he repeated, a ring of sarcasm in his tone. "You can't legislate morality. They should *all* be legalized and then we should begin the weaning process. We'll never get people off heroin and cocaine as long as we sing the praises of aspirin and codeine and tranquilizers and . . . Uh, I'm sorry . . ."

To Molly Sheridan, this was blasphemy, and she had frozen in her steps to stare at him. *"All* drugs?" she demanded. "You'd get rid of all of them?"

Matthew seemed to choose his next words with the utmost care. "I've been talking too much. I didn't mean to offend you."

"It's fine," she murmured. "You think I haven't been confronted with the ethical side of all of this? To tell you the truth, I agree with you to a certain extent. On the other hand," her eyes were stinging with tears, "I've seen pain, Matthew. *Real* pain, up close and very personal. I'm not sure you have. I saw my own mother in incredible agony, trapped beside me in a car accident . . . I would have given *anything* for some codeine for her, or even an aspirin . . ." Molly banished the image of her dying mother's mangled body and shook her head vigorously, rejecting the sympathy he seemed about to offer, retreating instead into the comfort of their mere acquaintanceship. "Did I mention we're here?" With an artificial smile, she motioned for him to follow her onto a dimly lit porch. "Don't judge me by my apartment. It was advertised as 'furnished,' but that was a gross overstatement. One sofabed. One ugly table. Two rickety chairs." As she pushed the door open her smile grew apologetic. *"Ta-da."*

Chapter Two

She hadn't had many guests, much less a strange man with more than his share of sex appeal, in her modest home, and she flushed as she studied it through newly-critical eyes. White walls, with only a few charts—of the muscles of the human body, and the periodic table of the elements—to distract the eye from the humdrum blinds and utilitarian beige carpeting. "I'm hardly ever here," she explained. "I'm always at the lab, and the landlord made me promise not to paint or nail anything up."

"The plants make it very homey," he reassured her. "I like it, Molly. This," he indicated a steamer trunk that served as a coffee table, "is great."

"It was my grandfather's. I travel very light. Everything I own fits in there, or I don't own it for long." She hurried to the refrigerator and retrieved a pot of soup, which she placed on the stove. "Are you hungry?"

"Hmm? Can I look in here?" Dropping the knapsack on the floor, Matthew opened the trunk and grinned at the contents, which included a baby quilt, some term papers, his legend book, countless photographs and several tattered dolls. Brandishing a huge sewing kit, he teased, "I take it you like to sew?"

"Therapy," she smiled. "I sew when I'm worried. Or confused. I save a fortune on clothes during times of crisis."

"That food smells great."

"It's the garlic," she nodded. "I may have over-done it."

"The more the better. Amazing healing proper-ties." He joined her in the kitchenette. "Is that soup?"

"Chicken soup. Homemade. Don't tell me you're a vegetarian?"

"Hardly. Just the opposite."

"You're a cannibal?"

Matthew chuckled. "I was going to say 'a hunter.' Anyway, I train a lot. I need lots of protein and all. And you," he nudged her toward the dark green tweed sofa, "need sleep."

Contact with his fingertips sent a tremor of curi-osity through her shoulders, suggesting to her that she 'needed' something other than sleep, but he seemed oblivious to her reaction and so she re-minded herself she was too busy for such nonsense and moved to sit on the sofa.

Matthew nodded his approval, taking her place by the stove. "Put your feet up and get some rest. I'll watch the soup and I'll serve you when it's ready. After all, I'm the cause of all of this disruption."

Disruption. Molly had to agree that that was an appropriate label for his entry into her life. Shed-ding her shoes, she tucked her long, bare legs under herself and snuggled into the cushions.

"Now, tell me about your grandmother, Molly. What's she like? Did she visit you often when you were a child?"

"She lived two blocks away," Molly smiled. "I saw her every single day, unless she and Grandpa were vacationing in Ireland. I know I was spoiled, being an only child and all, but it felt so right. My grandparents ran a little Irish import store, and I spent a lot of time with them. My father was—I mean, is—a pediatrician, and my mother was a teacher."

"She was killed in a car accident?"

"Four years ago. That's when everything began to fall apart," she added pensively. "Mom died, then Grandpa had a heart attack, then my father remarried . . . all in the same year. I suddenly hated Boston, and so I applied to school out here, and was accepted . . ." Anticipating his next question, she added, "That's when Grandma decided to move to Ireland permanently. Almost three years ago, and I'm glad she did. She's met a wonderful guy named Brian, and I think they're unofficially engaged, or something, and . . ." She shrugged. "What else do you want to know?"

"Does it bother you that your grandmother's considering remarrying?"

"Pardon?"

"Does it bother you to think that another man will try to take your grandfather's place? The reason I ask is, when you talked about your father's remarriage, you winced, like you disapproved of it."

"Did I?"

"Sure. You said your mother died in agony, and during that same year your father remarried, and you suddenly hated Boston and moved here."

Molly's cheeks were burning with embarrassment and annoyance. "What's your point?"

"He remarried, and now your grandmother's remarrying."

"It's hardly the same thing, Matthew."

"True. It's been four years," he mused. "On the other hand . . ."

She regretted having confided in him—his memory was too good and he seemed to be determined to analyze her, which could only lead to more embarrassment. "Do you suppose we could just drop the subject? It's very personal." Her eyes narrowed slightly. "You aren't planning on asking Grandma personal questions, are you?"

"Strictly Valmain stuff," he assured her quickly. "For example, is she your maternal grandmother? Is this Valmain connection from your mother's side?"

"Right. Mom was my Valmain connection." Molly savored the phrase for a long moment. "If I ever have a little girl, I'm going to name her Kerreya, and *I'll* be *her* Valmain connection." Then she flushed and apologized, "Listen to me! You wanted to know about Grandma, not me."

"I want to hear everything about both of you."

"I'm irrelevant," she objected briskly. "Let's see. Her name is Elizabeth Rose Scanlon. She's a very outspoken woman. Strong-willed. Opinionated. And she adores me, so watch yourself on the phone. Don't accuse me of cheating on the exam."

"I really screwed that up, didn't I?" he groaned. "I apologize, Molly. I know you'd never lie to me."

From one extreme to another, she complained to herself. *He is a fanatic. Now he thinks I'm strong and pure of heart.*

"Just lean back and close your eyes now," he urged. "Try to relax."

"I don't think I have a choice," she confessed with a yawn. "I'm so sleepy . . ."

The nap was blissfully refreshing. As she dozed,

the aroma of the soup mingled with the soft sounds of Matthew Redtree's voice, recounting tales of the Half-Moon People, and the effect was seductive in its innocence. Her apartment, sparse and efficient, was suddenly cozy and safe and ever so slightly romantic. It was all so relaxing—the aromas, the sounds, and then the feel of lips brushing hers, first reverently, then almost playfully . . .

She roused herself, certain that she must have dreamed the contact, and found that her guest was indeed leaning over her, his expression earnest and his voice gently informing her that midnight had arrived.

"Matthew . . . ? Did you . . . ?"

"What is it, Molly?" His voice was filled with concern. "You seem confused. Did you forget I was here?"

"No, I just dreamed, I guess."

"Tell me your dream."

"Never mind." She smoothed her clothes suspiciously. "I'm awake now. I'll make that call."

"Just say hello and introduce me. That's all."

"No secret code?" She was pleased to have a reason to be justifiably annoyed with him. His chuckle further unnerved her and she dialed quickly, gesturing for him to be quiet. When her grandmother Elizabeth answered, the granddaughter said only, "Hi, Grandma, it's me. Everything's fine here. I'll talk to you in a minute, but first I have a friend here, whose name is Matthew Redtree, and he has some questions for you, okay?" Then Matthew grabbed the receiver and began his excited interrogation.

Watching his expression turn from hopeful to amazed over the next half hour, Molly knew Elizabeth was lecturing him, and she almost laughed out loud. She could always count on her grandmother to inject a little common sense into a confusing situation, and she wished Matthew would hurry so that she could get in on the conversation. It had been much too long since the last call. When he finally handed her the receiver, however, his expression showed such urgency and excitement that she couldn't bear to unlock her gaze from his for even one short moment and contented herself with a murmured promise to call her grandmother soon.

"So?" she prompted when she had placed the phone back into its cradle. "Are you convinced?"

"If you only knew . . ." he began, then took her hand and led her to the table. "Sit. Eat." Before she could protest he was serving her a huge bowl of steamy soup.

"Aren't you going to join me?"

"I can't sit," he explained. "When I get this way, I have to pace. It helps me think." The gold flecks in his eyes were dancing. "I've been hunting for this legend for years. My whole life, in fact."

"You're exaggerating," she observed as she watched him commence the promised pacing. "I don't think I've ever met anyone as intense about his work as you are, Matthew. Don't you ever get sleepy?"

"I'm pumped," he grinned. "And I'm grateful to you, Molly. You've been patient, and now," he paused dramatically, "I want to share something amazing with you."

"Tonight?"

"The whole Valmain angle is so classic," he began, oblivious to her stifled yawn. "A king who forbids the practice of magic but turns to it in his hour of need—"

"A classic hypocrite?" Molly interjected with a

weary smile. "Can you believe he dared forbid his bride her practice of magic? Her birthright? He knew she was a sorceress when he married her."

"Can you believe *she* agreed?" Matthew teased in return. "If *he's* a classic hypocrite, *she's* a classic martyr. Or worse. And Maya—the evil sister—was a classic villainess. In fact," he deposited himself into a chair facing her and leaned forward eagerly, "I have an incredible theory about Maya."

"I'd love to hear it, Matthew, but frankly, I'm too tired to concentrate."

"Huh?"

She laughed fondly. "If this weren't finals week . . ."

"Right." Raking his fingers through his hair, he murmured, "Of course you're tired. You need to be rested. I understand completely." Jumping to his feet, he added, "I apologize. I'll get out of your hair and let you sleep. Tomorrow we'll have breakfast together—"

"Tomorrow I have to study all day for a late afternoon exam."

"I know I promised I'd leave you alone after the phone call, Molly, but," his smile was slightly desperate, "I want to see you again. Any time, any place, as long as it's soon."

Molly sighed. "Leave your phone number. I'll call you after my last final." She raised a hand to ward off further protest. "Please?"

He seemed about to argue, then relented, leaning down to retrieve his knapsack and emptying it of Molly's books and computer. "I'll be waiting for your call." Positioning the pack on his back, he straightened and stepped to within inches of her. "Before I go . . ."

Molly's pulse began to race and she backed away

quickly, unprepared for the golden flicker of desire in his eyes. Again she wondered if he had kissed her during her nap, and again she reminded herself that this was an unworkable fantasy. "Good night, Matthew," she reprimanded gently. "I'll call as soon as I have a free minute."

He hesitated, then readjusted the knapsack and disappeared through the door and into the night.

"Forget him," she admonished herself, annoyed at the confusion he had left in his wake. "You need to get some decent sleep and then spend some quality time in the lab. You can live without kissing for a few more months. It's *not* on the schedule." Still, she admitted, he was incredibly sexy, and he could be somewhat charming when they weren't on the subject of legends. And those *eyes* . . .

She had always evaluated potential male companions by a sensible set of criteria: Was the candidate polite? A good listener? Well groomed? Amusing? Intelligent? While Matthew Redtree could have passed any of these tests, it seemed irrelevant. He had bypassed the standard evaluation, going straight for a new set of criteria—how fast did her heart pound when he was near? How easily could she melt at the sound of his voice? How frightened was she of the responses his touch might evoke? How much did she ache for an opportunity to learn more about those responses?

"Cut it out!" she pleaded with herself. "The guy's a self-proclaimed fanatic and a little *too* physical in almost every sense. Just have a cup of tea and *forget about sex!*" She studied the contents of her cupboard in frustrated amusement. Peppermint, chamomile, oolong, . . . which of these could soothe away the after-effects of a subtly erotic student-teacher conference? She probably needed the traditional cold shower, or, more likely, a good night's sleep.

As she began to pack her books and final exam paper into her trunk she caught sight of her well-worn baby quilt and sighed. Was life ever that simple? She was momentarily tempted to curl up under it. If she did, would she have her sewing dream?

It was the fondest of her childhood memories—memories of the simple days, before the accident, when her mother had been her confidante, her father had been her hero, and her pretty, recurring dream had been her refuge. As she unfolded the sofabed she sighed again and wished childishly for a return to those carefree days and comforting nights.

She had dreamed the same scene, night after night, for nearly seventeen years. Herself—barefooted, freshly scrubbed, curly-haired, and tranquil, in a pure white ruffled petticoat and simple sleeveless chemise—sitting in an emerald green meadow positioned amid three grassy hills. She had called it her sewing dream, in reference to the activity that had both soothed and preoccupied her through those peaceful nights.

Night after night her slender skillful fingers would patiently stitch, working an endless silver thread into a length of pure white fabric draped across her knees. The sensation—of being both actor and observer—would engulf her, and she never questioned her actions beyond a slight yearning to know whether the garment in her lap, which she assumed to be a beautiful dress, would ever be completed. Not that it truly mattered . . .

The dream had disappeared with the accident that had robbed her of her parents, with death taking her mother while a new life stole away her father. Now Matthew Redtree had brought back the memories, of both her childhood and her dream, and she struggled to regain the perspective that could shield her on a lonely night.

Unable to sleep despite her weary state, she slipped into bed and reread her final exam. "Not too bad," she thought. "I almost deserve this A. There's tons of symbolism here! The two sisters, Kerreya and Maya—they're clearly good and evil. And I think I'm right that their father is nature. Father Nature? Whatever." She giggled sleepily. "And the first Valmain symbolizes man, and later his granddaughter came along to represent womanhood . . ."

She devoured the story anew, entranced as always by the two sisters, ancient possessors of magic powers, and how the jealous sister, Maya, had helped a handsome young king named Valmain. And how Valmain had then betrayed the beautiful, powerful Maya, marrying instead the curly-haired sorceress, Kerreya. *Maya cursed them,* the exam paper recounted. *Valmain would suffer betrayal, as Maya had. Gentle Kerreya begged her father to remove the curse, but he refused. Instead, he offered Kerreya hope in the form of a second spell—a spell of protection. It could not remove, but perhaps over time could thwart, the curse. Kerreya proclaimed that, whenever Maya's curse threatened destruction, a champion would rise up to defend Valmain.*

Kerreya went back across the seas with Valmain, who loved her greatly but continued to ban the use of magic in his kingdom. While his bride tried to obey, her magic was strongest in her dreams, which she could not always control.

And the sorceress-father of Maya and Kerreya was so distressed by the sisters' feud that he vowed his

*descendants would never again be allowed such pow-
ers unless they were truly strong and pure of heart.
Since that time, the power has been untapped, waiting
for one who is deserving . . .*

"Kerreya," a sleepy Molly sighed. "If only they
had given *me* that name. Such a beautiful, beautiful
name . . ." Her head began to list and she scolded
herself, "You're getting punchy. *Go to sleep.*" Allowing herself one last thought of her handsome,
dark-haired visitor, she made a mental note to call
her grandmother soon to explain, then melted into
sleep.

It had been years, and now suddenly the sewing
dream was back with more intensity than ever!
There she sat, in the same fragrant, grassy meadow,
stitching the same white garment with the same silver thread. As always, the dream figure's appearance charmed her sleeping observer, from the
shoulder-length, sunstreaked curls to the lacy white
petticoat and chemise, to the deeply tanned bare
feet resting in a bed of emerald green grass.

It was a homecoming—simple, beautiful, and
eternal—and Molly welcomed it with almost profound relief. So much in her life had changed, but
this pretty little dream was just the same.

Or was it? As she watched herself in wonder, she
realized one thing was astonishingly different: this
time, she seemed to be finishing her project! Finally,
after so many years! She watched herself stand up
and drape the garment over her shoulders. It wasn't
a dress at all, but rather a long, flowing cape. And
suddenly, she was no longer "watching" herself.
She *was* the dream girl. The dream was real—more
real, in fact, than life itself had been for these long,
lonely years!

She awoke, flushed and trembling slightly with

excitement. *Excited about what?* she wondered. *About a cape in a dream? Matthew Redtree must have brought this on, with all his dream talk. It's probably some sort of sexual fantasy.*

It was certainly a possibility. Hadn't she dreamed of his kiss only hours earlier? Hadn't she wanted him to find her beautiful and desirable? Hadn't there been more than one or two moments of delicious tension . . . ? *No!* she reprimanded herself yet again. She had no time for such nonsense! If she started studying right away, maybe she could still get an A on her next exam.

Across town, Matthew Redtree hadn't even tried to sleep, much less dream. He was busy rereading his notes from Elizabeth Rose Scanlon's tale and wishing he had remembered to bring Molly's final exam paper back with him, or at least to have made a copy. *And* wishing he could kiss her again. The dream girl!

Why hadn't he suspected her sooner! He'd noticed her, of course. Even in a roomful of 150 students, one could hardly fail to notice a pretty, barefoot girl, sound asleep and occasionally shifting contentedly. Always in white clothes—why hadn't he noticed *that?*—and always tranquil, with an aura that Matthew had appreciated instinctively during the lectures. Why hadn't he made the connection? She was slender, her bearing was proud, and the curls were just right—light brown, laced with streaks of sunlight.

In all the years of waiting and searching for her, he had never once imagined a sexual or humorous component to this relationship. Such thoughts would have seemed irreverent—almost incestuous—until now. Yet suddenly it seemed so right. Her mere presence made him feel steadier, stronger, more capable and, in a very real sense, invincible. She was 'pure of heart', and it was a wonder to behold.

And her other qualities! Thick, dark lashes, deep blue eyes, soft, full lips, in*cred*ible legs . . . Not that any of these were of importance, of course, or at least, he couldn't allow them to assume any importance. If Molly Sheridan was the dream girl—and he knew in his soul that she was—then he couldn't afford to allow commonplace urges to overshadow age-old duties.

He chastised himself for having kissed her and vowed on the spot to look beyond the soft curls and firm, shapely breasts that had momentarily seduced him. "Remember her eyes," he counseled himself. "They're brimming with strength, and you're going to need that to battle the Moonshaker's descendant." And so he thought about those eyes, which held a power that could weaken him with their disapproval, but which could then just as easily strengthen him whenever they so desired. Eyes that were a deeper blue than any sapphire, more clear and sparkling than any lake . . .

He still needed a little more information, but honestly had no more doubts. Who would have thought he'd have found these two women through an Irish legend, of all things! The two keys to his long-awaited blood vengeance. The dream girl and . . . *Maya!*

"It's not really an Irish legend, you know, Matthew. It's even pre-Celtic, in a sense. At least, according to my great grandmother, Ireland was once—" Molly caught herself, acknowledging that this would undoubtedly set him off again. She had agreed to a quick lunch in an impersonal coffee shop—he had pleaded so charmingly for a copy of her exam paper—but she was hoping to stay off the subject of her Valmain ties.

"Once what? Tell me, Molly. I promise not to overreact."

She laughed, enjoying this new side of him. Cheerful. Self-deprecating. Maybe she had judged him too quickly. They were definitely having more of those "moments" she had noticed the previous night. "Okay. Here's a test, although as a legend-lover, you've probably already heard this one. All of this is supposed to have happened when Ireland was a much larger island. Before a large chunk—the Valmain chunk, of course—broke off and drifted westward, toward a kind of Celtic heaven called Tir na Og, or something like that. So my legend isn't really an Irish legend."

"Okay. I'm going to let that one get right past me, for now. Just to prove I can. Just to prove that I'm not always a fanatic."

"You already proved it," she observed dryly. "No health food fanatic orders four eggs."

"Eggs," he insisted, "have been part of the healthy diet of every major successful civilization. Our society's preoccupation with cholesterol over—"

"Hold it! You were trying *not* to be a fanatic, right?"

"Right." His eyes were twinkling. "So, how about dinner tonight?"

"I've got to study. But . . ." Her stomach tightened with anticipation. "Maybe . . . If I get through today's exam in one piece, and if we make it an early evening so I can get a decent night's sleep. Last night, I was restless . . ."

"So was I. I kept going over the legend. There are gaps I need to fill out." He paused and studied her. "Is this going to annoy you?"

"No, go ahead. I know it's in your blood or something. What's missing?"

"This Maya. She's the sister, the one you think is evil, right? Do you know any more about her?"

"Let me think. I know about Kerreya. She's supposedly my direct ancestor, although technically, that would make me related to Maya, too, since they were sisters. Maya would be my great-great et cetera aunt." The realization charmed her. "I've never thought about it that way. It's interesting. Maya's descendants would be evil like her, and so the sorcerer's decision to let only pure-hearted descendants have power would have cut magic out of her line—right?"

Her inquisitor was mildly impatient. "Probably. But I want to know about Maya herself, not her descendants."

"I don't know any more. Maybe she looked like Kerreya, you know, curly hair? And she wanted Valmain, so she cursed his kingdom when he married Kerreya."

"Maybe so," he nodded. "And you say his land doesn't really exist anymore?"

"Do any of these legendary places still exist? I mean, as they were then? If they existed at all."

"I'd like to know if the curse won out, I guess," Matthew sighed. "Crazy, isn't it?"

"Actually, no. I think I know the answer, too. I was told it never did. A champion always appeared to save the day, thanks to Kerreya." She fingered a strand of hair self-consciously and added, "I guess the real curse was progress. I made that point in my exam, remember?"

"Oh, you mean that stuff about the champion being a symbol for technological progress? Where'd you get that?" he teased. "It doesn't sound like Great-Grandma."

"Pretty bad, huh?" Molly winced. "I was desperate. But Maya never sounded like a quitter. A woman scorned, you know," she added lightly. "I'll bet she's still out to get my family."

"Don't you find that a little unnerving?"

"You've got that look again," Molly sighed, disappointed by the relentlessness of his absurdities. If she wasn't careful, she was going to fall in love with this fanatic and would be doomed to engage in ludicrous conversation forever, instead of the studying she needed or the foreplay she craved. Shrugging out of the booth, she smiled blandly and announced, "I really have to go. I'll never graduate at this rate. Good luck with the new book, Mr. Redtree."

"Wait!" He caught her lightly by the wrist. "Do we have a date for tonight?"

"I'll call your office if I can make it," she promised, extricating herself from his grasp. "How's that?"

"Better than nothing. I really want to see you again, Molly. We've got a lot to talk about."

Right, she drawled to herself as she hurried away. *In the middle of finals, I'm going to sit around and talk about bedtime stories? I had something a little more adult in mind, Redtree. This was your last chance and you almost passed yourself off as normal. Almost.* Refusing to acknowledge her disappointment, she headed for the library.

Nice going, Matthew, he was berating himself, as

he watched her walk away. *If she's the dream girl, then you're dead! No way is she going to help you.* He thought about sending flowers, but decided it would probably just annoy her. Maybe if he were honest with her. Totally honest. But that was risky. What if she decided he was crazy and took the story to the head of the department? This wasn't exactly his 'dream' job, but it did give him the time and resources necessary to do his research.

Maya. She was the key. Molly Sheridan didn't know many details but maybe her grandmother did. The problem was that their family's legend centered on Kerreya. The wrong sister. It had been Maya, not Kerreya, who had helped a sorcerer named Aaric the Moonshaker murder Matthew Redtree's ancestor so long ago.

Perhaps it was time to go back and talk to his great-uncle, August. August knew more about their half of this puzzle than anyone. If it hadn't been for him, Matthew still wouldn't understand his dream. Not that he fully understood it, even now, but he was ready to guess that pretty Molly Sheridan was the girl who stood in the dream mist holding a spool. And his uncle had insisted that *that* girl would be a source of power. So Matthew needed Molly, who had absolutely no use for him!

Matthew also needed sleep, and welcomed the opportunity to test his latest theory. Would he recognize Molly now? And would that trigger anything? Because, more than anything, Matthew Redtree wanted his dream to change, if even very slightly. The same dream, detail for detail, night after night, since childhood . . . His uncle August would say that that was fortunate—that it gave him time to prepare—that when the dream started to change, the real danger would start.

Matthew didn't *feel* prepared. He had tried. He had researched until his eyes burned. He had traveled thousands of miles and, when his book had become a moderate success on campuses, had plowed every dollar back into his search. Physically, he had done all he could do, mastering the three weapons he carried in the dream—bola, bow and arrow, and dagger—and training on a dozen more, just in case. He had experimented with all forms of martial arts, trying to perfect his skills, following his uncle's instructions to the letter. Still, he did not feel prepared. He had to *understand*. All of the strength and prowess in the world wouldn't be enough if he had to walk into this blind.

Sleep came easily and, as always, the dream easily followed. She was there, as always, in her brilliant white cape and, as always, her face was turned away. She handed Matthew the end of a string from the spool and he walked slowly into the mist. Neither spoke, but their apprehension was apparent. The dream girl held the spool tightly, as though dropping it would be cataclysmic.

Nothing. It was the same. Every detail. The curly hair . . . the proud bearing . . . He would go and see Uncle August soon. If he was lucky, he could get back on Molly Sheridan's good side and bring her along. Maybe his uncle could convince her, gently, the way he had convinced a seven-year-old boy more than twenty years earlier.

Molly was back at the library, trying to concentrate on her studies. Again. And again, Matthew Redtree kept popping into her head. He was absolutely gorgeous, she decided, but gorgeous in a rugged way that didn't usually appeal to her. It appealed to her now, though, and it was keeping her from concentrating.

Until now, she had daydreamed of a charming, calm, sophisticated lover—a distinguished physicist, perhaps, or a dedicated surgeon. When daydream had occasionally slipped into fantasy, she had imagined herself in the arms of a huge, fair-haired scoundrel with a booming voice and a wicked gleam in his eye. Never had she entertained yearnings for a lean, dark-haired athlete with intense eyes and disturbing interests.

Enough! She decided to see him that evening after all, if only to get him out of her system so that she could return to her predictable existence. Either he would seduce her—which she now admitted she wanted—or he would rattle on about sorceresses and curses until she couldn't remember what she'd ever seen in him.

The mere thought of seeing him in less than eight hours made her giddy despite the stern efficiency of her surroundings. She decided to buy something sexy to wear—a skimpy halter dress, or a tube top and tight jeans—*anything* but the soft, innocent skirts and blouses that had become her uniform over the last four years. And she wouldn't wear her usual white. She'd wear black, or perhaps hot pink, with a coordinating shade of lip gloss . . .

Except you don't have time to go shopping because you have to study! She was rapidly losing patience with herself. *Just wear your eyelet skirt and the silk blouse with the pearl buttons and forget the femme fatale act.*

But she could, and would, dab some perfume on a pulse point or two. The rest was up to Matthew

Redtree. With any luck he'd wear his sexy tweed sport coat, and have some candles burning, and champagne chilling, and something other than Valmain on his mind.

Chapter Three

Dinner at Matthew's house in the Berkeley hills turned out to be more than Molly could handle. Every dark-paneled wall bore at least one weapon, each more menacing than the one before. There were bronze Celtic shields and daggers inlaid with semiprecious stones. The workmanship ranged from meticulous to crude, the latter being all the more menacing in Molly's eyes. One ax in particular seemed to be nothing more than a sharp rock forced through a tree limb. Matthew explained proudly that his ancestors had patiently fashioned such weapons while the limbs were still a part of the living tree, allowing the gash to heal for years around the ax head—thus 'cementing' it in place with sap—before detaching the branch and using the weapon.

Molly was unimpressed. "Who's your decorator? Attila the Hun?"

"Most of these are collectors' items. Very valuable. It's my hobby. And they're all disarmed. None of the guns are loaded, and," he added apologetically, "I don't usually bring dates here."

"That makes me feel real special. Thanks, Matthew."

"You *are* special, Molly. You're so special I'm going to tell you something I've never told anyone outside my family."

"If you don't mind, I'll settle for seeing places no other date has seen. I think your secrets would scare me away."

"After tonight," he smiled, "I'm hoping you'll see me as an ally, not a threat."

"Ally?" *What am I supposed to say to that?* she asked herself nervously, moving to the far side of the room and pretending to study a selection of arrowheads.

The most unnerving thing about Matthew Redtree, she decided, was his casual confidence. He behaved as though he'd known her for years. They were strangers who were clearly primed for some form of encounter, yet he was thoroughly relaxed. Why wasn't his heart pounding, as was hers? Why wasn't he stammering, just a bit, or breathing irregularly, or showing some other sign that he was as uncomfortably eager as she?

She sat herself primly in a straight-backed chair, refused his offer of refreshment, and tried to picture him naked, hoping that the old trick would boost her confidence. Instead, it further subverted her and she hastily redressed him, adding an overcoat for insurance, and wondered if he indeed had all of the lean muscles and tight lines she had so generously ascribed to him. *Impossible,* she assured herself. *Even a fifth-degree black-belt hunter can't be that perfect.* Moistening her lips, she glanced toward the hall, wondering about his bedroom, which was undoubtedly decorated with whips and handcuffs, or maybe even a rack . . .

Matthew positioned himself directly before her.

"My secret is a dream. A recurring dream. Have you had that experience?"

She refused to be intimidated. Didn't everyone? "Of course I do. Tell me yours and maybe I'll tell you mine. I should. In a way, I think you inspired it."

The gold flecks in his eyes ignited. "What!"

"Steady, Matthew. I'm kidding. It just so happens I started having *my* dream again after you got me thinking about stuff like that. So?" She smiled with sudden understanding. "You have an interesting recurring dream? That explains a lot. That's why you're so . . . intense . . . on the subject, right?"

"Right. And that's why I'm telling you about it now—so you'll understand me and not think I'm crazy. But you have to promise to listen to the whole thing—the dream and the other information I have—before you judge me. Do you promise?"

"Okay. Unless it scares me," she qualified quickly. "It's not a nightmare, is it?"

"No. It's a warning, or an omen, I think. But listen, and then decide." Taking a deep breath, he began, "When I was just a kid—about seven years old—I began having a dream. The same one, night after night."

"You said it was a warning?"

"I was standing in a kind of mist. There was a quiver on my back, and a bow in my hand. There was also a dagger, and a bola—do you know what that is?"

"No, but . . ."

"Wait!" He disappeared down the hall, returning with a long leather thong connecting two sand-filled deerskin sacks the size of tennis balls. "See this?" Feeding the thong through skilled fingers, he began to spin the weapon and then, with a flourish, let it sail across the room, where it wrapped itself around a suit of armor and brought it clanging to the floor. Matthew's face was flushed with sheepish pride. *"That's* a bola."

"I'll take your word for it," she grimaced. "Back to the dream . . ."

"Right. I was heavily armed. Seven years old and ready for battle, can you imagine? But the battle never came. Instead, I just stood in the mist and waited. But I wasn't alone."

"There was a dragon, right?"

"Cute, Molly." His smile was rueful. "There was a female there. Slender, calm, completely silent . . . I never saw her face, but she was holding a shiny string, and she would always hand the end of the string to me, and I'd always take it so solemnly, like it was a lifeline . . . I'd start to walk into the mist, then I'd wake up."

She didn't need to ask if he was now an adult in the dream. She knew from her own dream that it was an illusion. It looked like the dreamer, whatever the dreamer happen to look like at the time—never seeming to change, but always the person he or she is at that moment.

"My great-uncle August knows a lot about our family's heritage, and when I told him about the dream, he was sure it meant that I was the person our legends said would avenge the murder of one of my ancestors, whose name was Lost Eagle."

"And that's how you became interested in legends?"

"Right. Our legend tells how Lost Eagle and a sorcerer named Aaric, the Moonshaker, both were in love with the same woman, who was evil. Lost Eagle had an amulet that protected him from Aaric's magic, but the evil woman stole it and, after that, Aaric easily murdered him, using the unfair advantage he had from his sorcery. With his dying breath, my ancestor vowed that one of his descendants would avenge him in battle."

"That's amazing, Matthew," Molly cooed. "Your uncle told you that story when you were just a little boy? It must have been so intimidating." *No wonder you're such an intense guy,* she added silently.

"I was lucky to have someone to explain it to me. He made it make sense, and eventually I realized the dream wasn't going to go away. So I started listening to some of the other old guys and their stories. And I asked questions. Then I learned to fight, learned about weapons, and I studied similar legends in my spare time, wrote the book, started teaching . . . But I never fully understood why it was happening."

"How could you understand?" she soothed. "It must have been such a confusion of emotion and information. I'm an adult, and even *I* find it intimidating. I can't imagine being a child and having someone tell me I was responsible for avenging my ancestor!"

"Uncle August explained it in simple terms. He focused on the evil woman who stole the magic amulet that had always protected Lost Eagle. Once Lost Eagle was unprotected, Aaric the Moonshaker killed him."

"And before Lost Eagle died, he vowed that his descendant—meaning you—would get revenge against Aaric's descendants *and* against that evil woman's descendants?"

"And," Matthew paused dramatically, "that evil woman's name was Maya."

For a long moment Molly stared, as stunned by

the expectation in his eyes and tone as by the revelation itself. So that was it. Finally! *Maya.* No wonder Molly's exam paper had shaken him up. Matthew Redtree was *believing* all of this! He *believed* he had an ancestor who had an amulet that made him invincible. That the 'evil woman' Maya who had stolen it, for some guy named Aaric, was the same Maya who had fallen in love with Molly's Valmain. He actually believed every word of it!

She rose to her feet and touched his shoulder gently. "Listen, Matthew. I really think you're putting the cart before the horse, or whatever. You probably heard stories about this Lost Eagle and Maya when you were very young. Four or five years old, maybe. And they inspired you! You wanted to be a warrior like Lost Eagle. You wanted to be the one who avenged him. Even at that age," she added in reluctant admiration, "you loved all this legend business. So you incorporated it into your dreams, and now you can't separate it back out. Maybe if you saw someone who does dream interpretation . . . ?"

Matthew grimaced. "Don't you think I've tried that? Don't you think I wanted to find a rational explanation? Doesn't it mean anything to you that Maya is in both our legends?"

"It's just a name, Matthew! Probably a dozen legends have such a name. There was a whole civilization named Maya, remember? It's a coincidence."

"The Mayan civilization? I agree, that's just coincidence. But Maya and Kerreya were here, 'across the untraveled seas.' And your Valmain came, and somehow *our* ancestors crossed paths. On the same side, against Maya. That's why *you* are in my dream."

"Me? You didn't say anything about that!" She

challenged him with her clear blue gaze. "Come on, Matthew, you said you can't see the female's face. It doesn't take a genius to figure out it's probably your mother . . . Don't you dare laugh! I've done a little reading in my life, too. That string could be a symbol of something very normal, a boy facing manhood, all armed, but not ready to leave his mommy . . . Stop laughing!"

"You're great!" He grasped her shoulders and grinned broadly. "You'd have to see a picture of my mother to appreciate the joke. She was big, with long straight black hair. The dream girl has curly hair, like yours, and she's slender, like you. And her manner is like yours."

"Your uncle filled your head with all of this when you were very impressionable." She shrugged herself free from his hands. "If you can't see that, then I don't know what else to say."

"Don't say anything. Just stand there getting prettier and prettier." He sank to one knee and took her hand, with both reverence and mischief in his warm golden eyes. "It's amazing. Every time I look at you—"

"Cut it out, Matthew. You can't sweet-talk your way out of this. You're only interested in me because your uncle told you your 'dream girl' can give you strength. Right?"

"Right." He rose to his feet and nodded. "And I can give *you* something. A champion. A *Valmain* champion. Do you see?"

"I don't *need* a champion. I need a normal guy. Which *you*, apparently, are *not!*" She paused for a breath, more disgusted with herself for her romantic fantasies than with him for his heroic ones. "Find yourself another dream girl, Matthew. You're very good-looking. There are a lot of women out there who would think this is flattering, but—" She pulled back one instant before his lips touched hers and demanded, "What are you *doing?*"

"I'm kissing you, or trying to," he explained cheerfully. "Just relax."

"Relax? In this chamber of horrors? *Look* at this place." She indicated a nearby weapon-filled wall impatiently. "How many swords does one person need?"

"Actually, that one's a cutlass. Great, isn't it? I just got it. And the one next to it is a sabre."

"They're all just swords to me, Matthew. Give it up." Gesturing dramatically, she declared, as much to herself as to him, "We clearly have nothing in common."

"Would you feel more comfortable at your apartment?"

"Yes. Alone."

"Molly! Give me a break. Make me another deal. Listen." Catching her by the waist, he nuzzled her neck contritely. "I promise to think about what you've said tonight if you promise to think about what I've said. *And* if you tell me your dream."

The tingle was radiating through her shoulders and breasts in tiny, hypnotic waves and she abandoned herself to it for a long, luxurious moment before pulling away and resuming her prim demeanor. "I'll tell you my dream, but only so you can see how silly it sounds."

"It won't sound silly."

"Fine. I've always dreamed I was in a meadow sewing on a piece of white fabric. There was never any plot to the dream, just a restful scene. But last night it changed a bit. I finished the sewing, and the fabric turned out to be a white cape with silver stitching. And I put it on, and it's beautiful, and in the dream I'm proud of it." She had been watching his face and now scowled at the realization that he was about to go crazy again.

"Molly! Don't you see the similarities? What does your spool look like?"

"I beg your pardon?"

"You said you're sewing in the dream. What does the spool look like?"

"I don't know. I don't think there is one. At least, not in sight. Which, of course, means there isn't one at all, and listen to me! I'm beginning to sound like you!"

"Maybe the spool isn't important, then," he mused. "What *is* important is that your dream has started changing. That's a sign that the time for the battle is at hand . . . No, don't interrupt." He was holding her shoulders again, his expression grim with foreboding. "I'm dead serious, Molly."

"And maybe I put on that cape, after all these years, as a sign I need protection from you," she sniffed.

"You can't be serious."

"If you can be serious about your ridiculous interpretation, then I can be serious about my perfectly logical one."

"Time out!" He pulled her closer and smiled sheepishly. "This isn't getting us anywhere. Let's go to your place and start over. Fresh."

"I don't know." She was frustrated by her body's willing responses to the touch of this complete fanatic. "I want to work this out, Matthew, but you're driving me crazy. Can you promise not to talk about the dreams any more?"

"I promise. Except—"

"Matthew!"

"No, it's nothing. I just want you to remember,

next time you have your dream, to watch for the spool." When she groaned but nodded, he continued eagerly, "See if it's the same as the one in my dream. Mine is silver, with turquoise stones. Or beads, I guess you'd call them. It's a very ornate pattern. Very beautiful. There's a symbol—like a row of horseshoes divided into halves . . ."

Molly shook her head slowly, dazed by the description. Had she *heard* him correctly? Had he actually seen Great-Grandma's spool in his dream? "I think I'll have that drink you offered me earlier, Matthew."

"You mean brandy? I thought you said you don't drink."

"I thought I should stay sober around you. But," she bit her lip and admitted, "I've seen your spool, I think."

"What?"

"I've seen it, but not in my dream. It's at my grandmother's house, or at least, it was at her old house, for years. She keeps it in an old jewelry box. When I was a little girl, I used to pretend it was my Valmain treasure."

"You're saying you actually held the spool in your hand?" Patting her cheek, as though slightly disoriented, he moved toward a gun cabinet that had been converted to a liquor closet. "I think we both might need a drink." After finding two brandy snifters and pouring generous servings, he returned to her. "Until now, everything has been either legend or conjecture. This is proof!"

"Maybe it is," she murmured. *But proof of what?* she challenged herself nervously. *Proof that Matthew's going to fight someone, and you're going to help?*

"I've changed my mind again, Matthew. I don't

want any brandy. I want to go home—Alone." She raised her eyes to his, pleading for understanding. "I've got to think. Okay?"

"We should be together," he protested, setting the drinks on a low table, then stepping to within inches of her. "Especially tonight. With all that's happened, and your dream changing . . ."

"Don't push me. Please? Give me some space, or time, or both. I'm not into all this like you are. Legends, amulets, sorcerers . . . I don't *believe* in those things."

He nodded sympathetically. "Okay, Molly. I want you to be comfortable. We'll take it slow." As though to illustrate his intentions, he took a full step backward. "Will you call me if your dream changes again tonight? And call me first thing in the morning?"

"I promise." She started toward the door and then, on impulse, ran back to him and slipped her hands behind his neck, allowing her fingertips to play in his dark, wavy hair. "It doesn't make sense," she breathed, "but it *feels* right, doesn't it, Matthew?"

"Yeah." He rested his hands on her hips and smiled. "It feels right, Molly." Pulling her gently closer, he suggested, "Stay with me tonight. That'll feel right, too. I guarantee it."

It was true, and she knew it, but she wasn't ready for that, right or not. "I have to go home," she insisted, "but . . ." Pulling his head down, she brushed her lips across his, once and then again. "All these months . . ." she murmured, remembering the lectures, and his voice, and the loneliness of her starkly furnished apartment.

"All these years," he echoed in husky wonder. He duplicated her gentle, non-intrusive kisses until she pulled free, shaking her loose curls wistfully and backing away from temptation.

"Tomorrow night we'll have dinner at my place, Matthew. Okay?"

"Hold on, Molly. I'll walk you home."

She blushed and nodded, enchanted by his reverent tone. As they walked in silence, her hand resting in his, she thought about his warm lips, and about Lost Eagle, and about King Valmain, and about Matthew's bed, and the bola, and the spool . . . Would it ever make sense? Did it *have* to make sense, or was it enough that it made her heart yearn for more?

Then they reached her door, and he pulled her abruptly into his arms, kissing her, his mouth hot and his tongue desperate, until she pulled free.

"I have a question," she managed to gasp. "Before you go . . ."

"Ask me anything." The reverence had begun to resemble fanatical devotion. "Anything at all."

"Tell me what you think all this means. Please?"

He took a deep breath and nodded. "I used to think it meant I needed to find you, for guidance or advice, before I could get revenge for Lost Eagle."

"Revenge? Against some descendant of this sorcerer named Aaric? Do you think *his* descendant has been having dreams, too?"

"I don't know anymore. I've been training, and searching, and waiting—for you *and* for him—to show up."

"Now, here I am. And here you are . . ."

"That's right, Molly. I'm here. I'll protect you."

"I don't want him to come," she whispered, frightened without quite understanding why. "I don't want you to fight with him."

"It's my destiny." He urged her cheek against his

chest and smoothed her curls lovingly. "It's our destiny, Molly. Mine, because I'm descended from Lost Eagle, and yours because you're descended from Kerreya. The good sister. Somehow, you can protect me, and I can be your champion."

"My champion?"

"The Valmain champion that Kerreya's spell promised would always be there. Do you see?"

"But I don't need a champion. There's no Valmain kingdom to save, no threat of betrayal . . ." Then she smiled up at him shyly and added, "I don't need a champion, but I'm beginning to understand that I need *you*."

He smiled in return. "I'm your destiny."

"I don't believe in destiny, Matthew. I think you should refuse to fight Aaric's descendant if he ever shows up."

"I want to fight him."

She pulled free and locked eyes with him. "We'll sort this out. Together. Somehow," she blushed but held his gaze, "we were meant to be together. It's crazy, but it's true. You saw the spool in your dream . . ."

"That's right, Molly." He took her key and opened her door. "Remember that. Tonight, when you begin to think this all sounds impossible, remember the spool, and remember this . . ."

Again his mouth, hot and needy, descended to hers until she was almost swooning with desire. But she dared not give in to this. Not yet. She needed to understand, and she needed to rest, and she needed to be sure because she knew, in her heart, that once she made this commitment, it would alter the entire course of her simple life. "Goodnight, Matthew. I'll call you first thing in the morning."

She darted through the doorway before he could

change her mind and, once alone inside her tiny apartment, spun herself around in wonder, as though even at that moment she wore the luxurious silver and white dream cape.

What was happening to her? She was more alive, more frightened, more excited, than she had imagined possible! She had wanted to postpone this phase of her life but it had reached out and grabbed her! *Matthew Redtree* had reached out, pulling her into his bizarre world, and she was now alive with the implications.

His voice had soothed her for months, preparing her to trust and embrace him and, as melodramatic as it seemed, she now ached for that very embrace. Should she have stayed with him? "We should be together" he had said. Together?

Would he have made love to her? Would she have allowed it? Of course she would! She was mad with need for him!

And this spool business! What did it mean? She and Matthew Redtree? Linked from childhood? Destined to be together? "Incredible!" she announced to the empty room. "This whole thing is too incredible for words! That beautiful spool . . . I should call Grandma and make sure she still *has* it . . ."

It hit her all at once. Hard. Grandma? What if Elizabeth had mentioned the spool during Matthew's phone inquisition? What if . . . ? She remembered his face, sincere and handsome, as he calmly described the turquoise and the etching . . . As though he had seen the spool hundreds of times. But what if he hadn't? What if he had heard of it for the first time that very week, during a telephone call to Ireland . . . ?

Not bothering to consider the time, she dialed

frantically, praying all the while that she was wrong, and when Elizabeth answered, Molly almost wailed, "Grandma! It's me. No . . . I'm sorry . . . No, nothing's wrong. I just need to know . . ." Her grandmother's calm voice, telling her to slow down, helped her catch her own breath, and she offered, "Do you want me to call back at a more convenient time?"

"Of course not, darling. Tell me what's wrong."

"It's about my friend Matthew. The one you spoke with the other night . . ."

"He seemed quite nice."

"Yes, he is. He's very . . . interesting, but . . ."

"And good-looking?"

Molly grimaced. "Yes, Grandma. He's very nice-looking."

"And now," Elizabeth guessed, "you've had a little spat?"

"Huh? Oh, no. Nothing like that. It's just . . ." Taking a deep breath, she blurted, "Did you mention your silver spool when you spoke with him?"

"What on earth is this all about, Molly?" Elizabeth demanded. "You sound almost desperate."

"Please, Grandma. Did you say anything about it? About our having it?"

"Well, I believe I did," Elizabeth mused. "He was interested in Valmain, after all. I believe I even told him to come to Ireland and I'd show it to him. Is that it? You're upset that he's leaving? Oh, Molly, I'm so sorry."

She had clung to the slim possibility that his knowledge of the spool was genuine, original, and magically portentous. Now, disappointment washed over her, numbing her, so that her voice became a monotone. "It's fine, Grandma."

"Couldn't you come along with him? It would be so lovely! We could all visit."

"It's not that, Grandma. Matthew and I . . . well, I barely know him, and . . ." *And I wish I'd never met him,* she wanted to sob, but instead she fell silent.

"You sound like you need a hug," Elizabeth sighed. "Tell me what's wrong, darling. I'll help if I can."

"You already helped, Grandma. You told me just what I wanted—or rather, what I needed—to hear." Blinking back tears of anger and disappointment, she murmured, "I love you. Go back to sleep. I'll call again tomorrow. And don't worry."

"Don't call—come for a visit," Elizabeth countered firmly. "You sound like you need a vacation *and* a hug."

"I do," the granddaughter agreed sadly. "Maybe I will. My last final is on Thursday. I could get a flight . . ."

"Oh, Molly! This time, don't just say it—do it! I'll have a big party. Everyone's heard about you. You can meet my gentleman friend, Brian."

"That sounds nice."

"Promise you'll come? Do you need me to send the fare?"

"No. I've still got plenty of money from the accident settlement left." Summoning a more gracious tone, she promised, "I'll be there Friday, Grandma. And . . . I love you. More than you know. Now, go back to sleep."

She held onto the receiver long after the connection had been broken. *The Valmain connection,* she taunted herself, wondering what to do next. Should she call Matthew Redtree? Confront him? What could she say? *Matthew, I can't believe you'd lie like this about a damned spool. Why? To get me into bed?*

She thought of the fanatical gleam in his eye at the mention of Maya and shuddered. Sex hadn't been his motive. *Vengeance—that* was what drove him. He hated Maya, because she had killed Lost Eagle and *he* was Lost Eagle's descendant. But wasn't Molly *Maya's* descendant? Maybe he hated Molly! Maybe he wanted to humiliate her, in order to vindicate Lost Eagle . . . Or, maybe he was just plain crazy.

She pressed her fingertips to her eyes and forced herself to stop belaboring the events of the evening. What purpose could it serve? Whatever Matthew Redtree had hoped to gain from the deception, he had not succeeded. The whole episode had taken less than three days of her life. She should be grateful for that, at least. It wasn't as though she had fallen in love, although she had come disturbingly close . . .

She would put it behind herself, forever and humbly grateful that she hadn't slept with him. She wouldn't call him or demand explanations. She'd study, just as she'd planned, and chalk the whole fiasco up to inexperience.

Almost as a signal that it was over, the dream didn't visit her that night. Or the next. She managed to put Matthew off until after her finals, pleading academic desperation, and promising to go to Southern California with him the instant her last examination had ended. Instead, she had a cab waiting on the outskirts of campus to whisk her to the airport, leaving behind a note for Matthew that she had gone away to think. With friends. *To Mexico,* the note said. Just in case he was fanatical enough to try to pursue her.

Chapter Four

It was Molly's first visit to Ireland, but deep in her soul it was more a homecoming than a vacation. Her grandfather had always promised to bring her to Tralee as a high school graduation present, but Molly's car accident two months prior to graduation had postponed such an excursion. Six months later, when her grandfather died of a stroke, Molly's grandmother had reaffirmed the invitation but Molly had declined, moving instead from Boston to Berkeley and doggedly beginning a new life.

Now Matthew Redtree's machinations had finally made the promised visit a reality. For the first time in almost three years, Molly found herself in a true home—more humble, perhaps, than the stately Tudor Elizabeth had once inhabited in Boston, but filled with the very same cozy chintz furnishings, cinnamon scents, and prospering plants that had made Molly's grandparents' home so graciously inviting for so many years.

Although her dreams aboard the airplane on the long flight had been disturbingly vibrant, Molly had forced herself to draw comfort from the fact that she had still been alone in the dream meadow, just as she had always been. There was no fanatical warrior carrying bows and bolas . . . there wasn't even any mist! She wasn't anyone's "dream girl" after all, and that was something of a relief. Her dream was born of loneliness, not destiny, and if loneliness seemed suddenly unacceptable, she would simply finish her last few courses, graduate, and then find a normal man who met all of her criteria—from *both* lists. One day she might even thank Matthew Redtree for having opened her eyes to the world of physical pleasures she had so naively neglected for so long.

For now she was content to reindulge the pleasure of being the apple of Elizabeth Rose Scanlon's Irish eyes and, as she stood by the window, hoping to catch a glimpse of Brian Lafferty, who was due to arrive at any second to meet his fiancee's only grandchild, she basked in the glow of Elizabeth's concern. She had just finished regaling the older woman with the tale of Lost Eagle and his amulet, along with the details of Matthew's dream, and now she interrupted herself for a quick description of the "bola incident" and the fortress-like house in the Berkeley hills.

"You should see it, Grandma. It's on a huge lot, all planted with silver dollar eucalyptus trees, and it could be beautiful, but instead it's surrounded by a ten-foot high black iron fence—probably electrified. Like he's expecting invaders any minute."

"He's expecting the descendants of Maya and that Moonshaker creature," Elizabeth reminded her.

"Exactly! And he's got weapons everywhere."

"Even in the bedroom?"

Molly's eyes twinkled. "If you're asking how far things went—luckily, not *that* far. I'm just glad I was suspicious enough to call you, even in my fevered state."

"Until then you actually believed this man's dream was some kind of sign?"

"For a few moments I really did, Grandma! Can you believe it? I think I actually *wanted* to believe it was a sign."

"Perhaps it is."

"What do you mean?"

"What I mean, young lady, is that it's obvious from your letters that you spend all of your time studying. That you never go out and never see young men. It's not natural, Molly Elizabeth." The older woman's steady blue gaze left no room for argument. "You've left too much to your imagination. To fantasy. I think all of this is a sign that you'd better reexamine your priorities."

Molly winced slightly, unprepared for so stern a lecture. "I admit I've put my studies first, Grandma, but only temporarily. I lost a lot of time after the accident. I should have graduated by now . . ."

"Why? What's the hurry? You should take a long, long break. Stay with me until Christmas."

Molly shook her curls. "I have to be back in Berkeley by August first at the latest. One of my professors offered me a job as a lab assistant for a privately funded project."

"A job? Molly, if you need money, let me help."

"It's not the money, Grandma. I'd do this for free. It's a compliment Dr. Lewis selected me instead of a grad student." She grasped Elizabeth's hands. "My career comes first right now, but not forever. Once I finish my graduate work and find the right job, I'll take some time for a relationship. Okay?"

"It's just not natural," Elizabeth grumbled. "A

pretty girl like yourself, depriving herself of one of life's necessities."

"That's great coming from my own grand-mother! So?" she challenged playfully. "You think I'm not getting enough sex?"

"Molly Sheridan! You know what I meant! Companionship." Elizabeth seemed unable to maintain her stern demeanor, and it was obvious that spending time with Molly again, after the long separation, was no less than an exquisite delight.

Molly arched an eyebrow playfully. "Speaking of 'companionship,' what's keeping your Brian?"

"Be patient," Elizabeth blushed. "I know you'll approve of him, Molly."

"Of course I will!" She remembered Matthew's attempt to draw a parallel between this sweet romance and her father's treacherous remarriage and shook her curls emphatically. "Don't worry, Grandma. If you love him, that's good enough for me. Ooo! Is that him? Oh, Grandma, he's darling!"

Brian Lafferty had strolled into view, a walking stick in his hand and a jaunty spring in his step. He was nothing like Molly's grandfather, and she was glad of it. There had been only one Kevin Scanlon, after all—a straight-laced, iron-willed, distin-guished looking man with a quiet kind of passion—and any attempt to actually replace him would have led to dissatisfaction. Instead, Elizabeth had clearly opted for variety—in looks and demeanor—and Molly couldn't have been more pleased.

Elizabeth made the introductions and Molly ex-tended her hand, only to be drawn into a hearty bear hug. "We were beginning to think we'd have to come to America and kidnap you, Molly girl. Let me look at you!" He released her a bit, holding her at arms' length, and nodded. "You're even prettier than Betsy claimed!"

"Nice to meet you," Molly blushed, charmed by the fact that he could see her grandmother as a "Betsy." "I've heard a lot about you, too, Brian."

"You've got your grandmother's eyes," he observed solemnly.

"All of the women in our family have big, blue eyes," Elizabeth bragged. "And she has her mother's curly hair. But she also looks like her father's mother, who was considered quite a beauty in her time. Speaking of which," she added casually, "have you seen your father lately?"

"Give it up, Grandma," Molly laughed. "I want to concentrate on Brian." Taking his hand in hers she murmured, I'm so glad you and my grandmother have found each other."

"Speaking of finding a man," Elizabeth interrupted with a meaningful glance toward her fiancé, "Molly and I were just discussing the young man who telephoned last week."

"The storyteller," Brian nodded enthusiastically. "I've ordered a copy of his book. From what Betsy says, he's quite zealous."

"A little too zealous," Molly shrugged. "As I was just telling Grandma, Matthew Redtree's an interesting guy, but he's not for me. Not just because he's a liar," she paused to absorb the sting of her own accusation, "but because he's incredibly disruptive."

"Disruptive?" Brian exchanged glances with his fiancée. "Is that so very bad?"

"Molly's very organized," Elizabeth explained as she handed him a cup of tea. "She always has been."

"I like things to go smoothly," Molly confirmed,

adding, "He even disrupted my little sewing dream, Grandma. Do you remember it? It used to be so therapeutic. Now it makes me think of amulets and battles." Regretting the admission, she tried for a lighter tone. "I'm going to have lemonade instead of tea. Excuse me for a minute." Pausing in the doorway to the kitchen, she added with uncharacteristic vehemence, "I'm just so thankful I thought to call you about the spool, Grandma! Otherwise he'd really have me going by now. You should have heard him describing it, to the last little detail! Blue beads and horseshoes and all! Like he'd seen it all his life." Shaking her curls in disgust, she disappeared into the kitchen.

Elizabeth was frowning. "That's odd, Brian."

"Is it? In what way?"

"I didn't realize this young man actually *described* the spool to Molly in such minute detail. I may have been a bit flustered the morning of his phone call, but I'm sure I only casually mentioned it. I said we had a supposedly-Valmain piece of jewelry . . . I may not even have called it a spool, since I've always thought of it more as an ornament or pendant."

"And . . . ?"

"If he really knew about the turquoise and the etching . . . What does that mean?"

Brian shrugged. "It might not mean a thing, Betsy."

"Maybe not, but listen. He claims he's had a recurring dream since he was young. A girl holds a spool with a silver string. Young Matthew is dressed as a warrior and walks into the mist, holding the other end of the string. As though he's walking into a battle. He's an Indian, Brian. I mean, an

American Indian. His uncle tells him he's destined to avenge an age-old murder.''

"Fascinating. One of his ancestors?"

"Exactly. I had a feeling you'd like this," she accused fondly. "Matthew's ancestor supposedly had an amulet that protected him, but a witch seduced him, stole the amulet, and her sorcerer lover stepped in and killed the ancestor. Or some such nonsense," she added quickly.

Brian nodded. "And this frightens you? Because he's managed to tie his dream into the Valmain legend with the spool?"

"And with the witch's name—Maya. Just like in the story I told you. The one my mother used to tell me?" She crossed the room and retrieved an old jewel case from the buffet. "Look at this."

"So this is the famous Valmain spool." He examined the silver and turquoise admiringly. "It's lovely, Betsy."

"I always thought it was nonsense. But now the young man has described it. Seen it in his dream!"

"So he says."

"The more I think about it the more I'm sure I didn't mention the turquoise or markings on the phone!"

Brian smiled reassuringly. "Don't look so worried, Betsy. I'd say little Molly told him and then forgot, or someone else told him about such strangely decorated spools when he was researching his books. Makes sense, doesn't it?"

"But he lied to her . . ."

"Did he? I doubt it's sinister, in any case. You Valmain women can make a man do strange things."

"Flatterer. So, you don't think I should worry?"

"Worry more if she keeps running around alone.

It's not natural! You were married and having babies by the time you were her age. If he's got her charmed, go along with it. It has a ring of romance to it, don't you think?"

"I guess so. So, should I tell her—?" She broke off quickly as Molly re-entered the room.

"Should you tell me what?" the granddaughter prodded. "Let me guess. Wedding plans?"

Brian grinned. "I see I have an ally at last. It'd be grand to have the wedding while you were here, wouldn't it, now?"

"Absolutely."

"That's enough, you two," Elizabeth scolded. "We were talking about your Matthew, Molly. Brian has a theory about him."

"*My* Matthew?" Molly winced, her gaze falling on the spool in Elizabeth's hand.

"He wanted to charm you, Molly girl," Brian insisted. "He was so taken with you, his imagination got the better of him in trying to impress you."

"He lied to me," she corrected, "and it wasn't some sort of romantic line. He wanted to lure me into his own personal psychodrama, Brian. He believes he's going to have a fight with the descendant of a sorcerer, and somehow he believes I can help him win." Her eyes clouded as she added, "It almost worked. He had me believing that *our* spool was in *his* dream, like a link between us."

"And if he had been perfectly honest with you?"

"I've been asking myself that for the last forty-eight hours," she admitted. "I was pretty attracted to him. I think I would have kept dating him, even though he was a little frustrating." Squaring her shoulders, she added, "I'm glad he lied. If he hadn't, I wouldn't have realized how desperate he was, and I might have really gotten in over my head."

"He didn't lie, Molly." Elizabeth's voice was soft and hesitant. "I mean, if he lied, it wasn't because he repeated anything he'd heard from me. I never described this spool to him."

"Pardon?"

"At the very most, I might have said it was a jewel or trinket. But the beads, and the etching . . ." She spread her hands to indicate confusion. "I don't know what to say. I told him it existed, and I probably mentioned it was silver, but he didn't get the rest from me."

Molly's mind raced back to that night, in that strange, weapon-filled room, when he had described the horseshoes, and his eyes had been shining with sincerity and admiration, and he had taken her into his arms . . .

"Oh, no!" Her heart was beginning to pound with dismay. "If he wasn't lying about the spool, then he wasn't lying about the danger!"

"Danger? From the sorcerer's descendant?" Brian scowled. "Listen to yourself, Molly girl. He's charmed you for sure, and that may be for the best, but you can't go believing it all."

"I have to call him right away! Don't you see?"

"Molly Elizabeth!" The grandmother's concern was turning to complete disapproval. "Brian's right. Listen to yourself! As though people can be linked through dreams!"

"You don't understand. You weren't there . . ." She bit her lip, remembering Matthew's solemn words: *We should be together* . . .

It was true! They needed to be together, right away! Her dream had been changing, and the old uncle—what was his name? Augustus? August?— had told Matthew that change would signal the approach of the battle!

"Send for him," Brian suggested carefully. "Ireland's a fine place for romance."

"Romance?" she murmured. "This isn't about romance. Aren't you listening? I have to warn him."

"About danger? In a dream?"

"I know it sounds crazy, but I don't have a choice! I *have* to reach Matthew. Grandma, can I use the telephone? Please? I'll pay for the call."

Elizabeth seemed about to protest, but Brian took her arm and urged her gently toward the door. "Let's give Molly some privacy, Betsy. We'll go for a stroll."

Molly shot him a grateful glance, then dashed to the guest bedroom for her address book. As she dug through her suitcase, she encountered Matthew's legend book—she hadn't even remembered packing it!—and stared hungrily at the black-and-white photo on the back cover. He was so handsome . . . so incredibly handsome . . .

"And he needs me," she whispered, disbelieving and reveling all in one confused moment. "And I need him."

She dialed carefully, then groaned as Matthew's telephone answering machine played on, giving numbers where students could reach the appropriate assistance in his absence. Molly was about to hang up when she heard her name in the message. *"Molly, if you're calling, I've got to talk to you. Please give me a chance. Call my sister, Rita Camacho, in Los Angeles and give her your number and your address. It's important!"* She scribbled down the Los Angeles telephone number he recited, at once excited and embarrassed. How many other people had heard that tape? Exasperated, she dialed Rita Camacho, who answered with a cheery "Hello?"

"Hello. Is this . . . Am I speaking to Rita? Matthew Redtree's sister . . . ?"

"That's me. Who's this? Wait! Don't tell me. The famous Molly?" Before Molly could answer, she squealed in delight, "I can't believe you really called! My crazy brother said you would. He's frantic to see you."

Molly's head was spinning with relief. "Could I speak to him, please?"

"He isn't here. He left this morning for Mexico. Looking for *you*. I'm supposed to get your location and phone number. And to give you a message. Word for word. He's says you'll know what it means, but you sound too normal to get this crazy message."

"A message?"

"Right. Here goes. 'Molly, I put a dagger in the saddlebag. Don't be afraid to use it.' "

"What?"

"That's a relief!" Rita laughed. "You don't get it. Matt wouldn't explain it, so you'll just have to wait until you see him. And maybe someday you can explain it to me! What's your phone number there?" After a few minutes of polite, mindless conversation, Molly was alone in wistful silence, facing a myriad of strange thoughts.

A dagger in the saddlebag. For one thing, that must mean Matthew Redtree's dream was changing. He was seeing a horse. At least, that would be a logical assumption. Which meant he was no longer standing in the mist, but was moving and interacting with his dream environment. She remembered his raving that he had three weapons in his dream. A dagger, a bow, and, of course, the infamous bola. The dagger, then, was to be for her, assuming she could find the horse and retrieve the weapon.

"I must be going crazy! What am I thinking? Get the dagger? In *my* dream? And then what? Oh, Matthew, I wish you'd call!"

The call didn't come that night, but the dream was relentless. There Molly stood in her flowing cape, watching identical white stallions race by her again and again. How could they have gotten from Matthew's dream into her own? How could she be expected to catch one, much less get to the saddlebag? She'd had no experience with horses and had a feeling these two were not typical in any event. They were, however, magnificent, and she realized that, despite the strangeness, her fear had vanished. This meadow, surrounded by grassy mounds, was beginning to feel like a kingdom as well as a home, and she was—inexplicably but undeniably—a princess.

She belonged here. Something about it felt so right, just the way Matthew's arms had felt during their first, luscious embrace. Soon he would come to her, as her lover and as her champion, with his weapons and his finely-tuned body, and they would face their destiny together.

Two days passed—two days of restless waiting, two nights of restless dreaming. Elizabeth Scanlon could see that something was wrong, but hoped her granddaughter was merely preoccupied with amorous thoughts of "young Matthew." There had been no more talk of danger or warnings, yet it was clear that Molly was stressed almost to her limit. The doting grandmother wished she could distract the girl, not just because she seemed upset, but also because it seemed to be an appropriate time for Molly to deal, once and for all, with the chasm that had developed in her relationship with her father.

"Forget it, Grandma!" Molly insisted on one of their walks through the countryside. "We've been all over this a dozen times and your letters made every possible argument. But the bottom line is that my father betrayed my mother, while she was lying in a hospital dying! He cheated on her with that homewrecker Constance! And that was *un*forgivable. Period."

"If I can forgive and try to understand, why can't you? Your mother was my daughter, and yet I've managed to forgive him. At heart he's a good man, Molly. He made a mistake and, whether you want to admit it or not, all human beings make mistakes."

"A mistake?" Molly muttered. "Is that all it was to you? Fine. Let's drop it."

"His affair with Constance was a tragic mistake on his part, but you have to admit, once he discovered she was pregnant with his child, he had no real choice but to do the honorable thing . . ."

"Marrying that . . . that woman? That traitor? That's honorable?"

"She was carrying his child. And now their daughter is your sister."

"Half-sister."

"Fine. Half-sister. Still, the little girl is innocent in all of this. And," Elizabeth smiled hopefully, "she's undoubtedly adorable."

"I know," Molly groaned. "They send me pictures every Christmas. Her name's Nicole and she looks very sweet. Unfortunately, in order to get to know her, I'd have to tolerate her parents and *I won't!*"

"You're so bitter, Molly. I can't help wondering . . . If you only hadn't gotten such a huge insurance settlement after the accident—if you hadn't been able to just walk away, independent, at such an early age—if maybe you couldn't have worked it out with your dad. Maybe if I had stayed in the States, I could have engineered a reconciliation."

"No! Grandma, no. You had to come here. It was your lifelong dream. Remember how Grandpa used to show the slides and play his records for weeks after each of his buying trips?" She sighed wistfully. "He'd always bring me a doll. And he'd bring Mother her crystal from Waterford and he'd promise you that someday you'd move to Ireland for good."

"I remember," Elizabeth nodded. "Your grandfather loved us all so much."

"Yes. And he would have wanted you to come here. You inspired me! To go ahead with my plans. When I first moved to Berkeley I . . . well, I wasn't even sure what I was doing there, or why I had chosen it. I was just trying to get away from Dad and Constance at that point, I guess. But when you announced you were going to sell the house and move across an ocean . . . wow! I was impressed. And I decided I wanted to be like you. Committed. Determined."

"Well, you are that," Elizabeth laughed. "I just wonder what it is you're committed to."

"I guess, right now, I'm trying to be committed to Matthew."

"You hardly know him." Elizabeth studied the girl anxiously. "It's not this dream nonsense, is it? You don't feel responsible for his safety, do you?"

"No, no," Molly assured her. "He's just . . . very engaging. Fascinating, actually. You should read

his book. I enjoyed it from the start, but now that
I understand what motivates him, I really love it!
And," her voice grew dreamy, "you should have
heard him lecture. Like no lecturer I ever heard. He
was more like a storyteller. He made you believe
those legends, at least," she added hastily, "for the
moment. It was pure recreation for me, compared
to my other classes. Which is, I guess, why I never
saw the serious side back then."

Elizabeth watched her grandchild's face, wondering what to make of all this enchantment. Molly
was falling in love, obviously, but there was something else. The girl spoke of being committed and
determined, but the reality seemed to be that she
was being manipulated. Perhaps she should get
some sort of counseling, Elizabeth worried. When a
smart, capable, independent girl like Molly started
singing the praises of such a . . . legend-monger
. . .

"And you should see him." Molly was almost
breathless now. "He doesn't look like a professor,
he looks like an athlete. His hair is black and his
eyes are light brown, but there's gold sprinkled
through the brown, like glitter! I don't know what
group or tribe he's from, but his legends encompass
them all! The whole world! He's traveled everywhere, and he's gentle and strong, all at the same
time. And just when you think he's about to get
angry, he lets out this great laugh . . . Oh, you'll love
him. I promise."

We'll see, thought Elizabeth. *We'll just see about
that.* "What about the fact that he's so . . . what was
the word you used the other day? Disruptive?"

"And *you* thought I needed some disrupting, remember?"

Elizabeth shrugged. "When you talked about

your little sewing dream, it brought back such precious memories. I remember when you were tiny—not even in school yet—we'd ask you how you'd slept and you'd answer, 'I just sewed and sewed all night with the shiny thread.' "

"Didn't you think it was strange?"

"Actually, I think we were too busy appreciating it," Elizabeth admitted. "You have no idea how hard it is to get some children to go to sleep! With you, it was never a problem. And you never had nightmares or insomnia. You always slept like a lamb. Imagine." Her smile grew wistful. "Have you had the dream ever since then?"

"I had it for so many years, but then it stopped after the accident. I had awful nightmares during those months. I didn't have my dream for three or four years. I thought it was gone forever. Until Matthew came along."

"Yes," Elizabeth murmured. "Until him. I wonder why. Perhaps you're finally ready to face things. If that's so, why not start with your father?"

Molly's eyes narrowed. "No way! I know you mean well, Grandma, but you've got to drop that." She softened. "Please? I've got enough on my mind with worrying about Matthew. Can't we just drop it until I've seen him again?"

"Do I have a choice?"

Molly kissed the older woman's cheek. "No, but I love you for trying to fix my life. You have to trust me, Grandma. I know you worry about my being alone, but I think Matthew might be the answer to both our prayers."

"Maybe so," Elizabeth murmured. "Go on ahead to the house, Molly dear. I'll catch up in a few minutes." She smiled when her granddaughter's lovely brow creased with concern. *"Now* who's worrying needlessly? Run along, and put on the kettle. We'll have tea and look through some old photo albums . . ."

Molly studied her warily, then nodded. "Don't be long. And *don't* worry."

Seating herself on a low wall, Elizabeth watched her grandchild stride into the distance and sighed. The girl was a Sheridan in build and name, but those soft curls and softer blue eyes were a legacy from her mother's side of the family, and sometimes just looking at her was enough to make Elizabeth ache with love and memories and a few lingering regrets. She had failed Molly somehow, during those hideous months after the accident. She had failed the entire family by not healing the rift between Alexander Sheridan and his daughter before it was too late. She herself had been in mourning, but that was no excuse. If only she had been wiser, or firmer, or more intuitive, the family wouldn't be in shambles and Molly wouldn't be such easy prey for spiritual mumbo jumbo from a self-styled legend master.

Her own words concerning the "sewing dream" were echoing in her ears. *We were too busy appreciating . . . you.* Molly had indeed been a dream of a child—quiet, attentive, intelligent, calm and loving, and her parents and grandparents had indeed been too busy appreciating these qualities to notice the singlemindedness that was robbing the girl of her childhood. Only too late did they see that Molly wasn't really living. She was simply waiting. Waiting with infinite patience. But for what?

Then the accident had shattered all their lives and the calm, patient granddaughter had momentarily erupted, renouncing her father and desperately mourning her beloved mother. The doctors had feared Molly would never walk again, but within six months she had astonished them with her complete recovery. To the further amazement of all who knew her, she had then doggedly resumed her waiting stance. Of course, Molly had not perceived herself as waiting—was she not choosing to travel 3000 miles to Berkeley, California, to immerse herself in a challenging field?—but Elizabeth knew her granddaughter and grudgingly accepted the return of the quiet industry that masked Molly's lack of involvement in relationships or extracurricular pursuits.

Now Matthew Redtree had broken the spell. Or had he simply cast a new, less benevolent one? The ultimate irony, to Elizabeth, was Redtree's choice of the Valmain legend as his key to Molly's attentions. The legend had been Molly's favorite bedtime story as a young child. The spool had been the girl's favorite plaything. The line "strong and pure of heart" had been her childhood goal. "Am I strong and pure of heart, Grandma?" she had always murmured before she drifted to sleep, and Elizabeth had always assured her that, had there truly been an old sorcerer with two feuding daughters, he would have chosen a lamb like Molly to whom to entrust his magical legacy.

"Strong and pure of heart." A child's singsong guidepost. Hardly a sufficient preparation for dealing with scheming stepmothers and hypnotic legend-mongers, yet that had become Molly's fate.

"Do you see?" Elizabeth whispered sadly to her fiancé later that same day. "We were too busy appreciating my poor granddaughter, when we should have been preparing her. We should have seen how her sweet, trusting nature would one day leave her vulnerable. I've failed her, just as I failed both of my children, each in a different way."

Brian stroked Elizabeth's gray curls fondly. "Your Molly's all grown up, Betsy. That's the long and the short of it. It had to happen one day."

"One day," Elizabeth agreed. "The day she met *him*. A child should grow up gradually, not all in one day. It's as though . . ."

"As though she'd been waiting for him?"

Elizabeth nodded. "She's alive—exhilarated!— for the first time in her life. Over him! If he does anything to hurt her . . ."

"He claims he wants to protect her," Brian reminded her solemnly. "Could it be that young Matthew's been waiting, too?"

Chapter Five

By the time she placed her next call to Rita Camacho, Molly was frantic. "No," Rita reported cheerfully, as though Molly were a longtime acquaintance, "Matt hasn't checked in, or maybe he called when I was out. My answering machine keeps messing up."

"I really need to speak to him," Molly murmured. "I hate sounding so desperate, but . . . Can you think of anyone else I could call? Someone who might know how to reach him?"

"You're in luck. My uncle August is right outside, playing with my sons. He doesn't know where Matt is, unfortunately, but he thinks just like him. A little squirrelly." Rita paused to chuckle. "Just a second, Molly, I'll go and call him . . ."

Molly forced herself to breathe deeply as she waited for August—the old uncle who knew the Lost Eagle legend better than anyone. Certainly he would be able to help.

The old man's voice was reassuring, albeit mystical. "I saw Matthew just before he left. Many things have finally become clear. It is my sincere opinion that you two should be together now."

"I understand," Molly sighed. "I mean, I don't

understand, but I want to. I've been trying to reach him. His dream is changing, did you know? He's seeing horses now, and so am I."

"Yes, the time has come. It had to happen. Don't be so upset. Matthew is prepared."

"But *I'm* not! What am I supposed to do? Matthew and I never got past the basics. He said I can give him strength or guidance, and he told Rita he wants me to get a knife . . ."

"Yes. Your champion has left it for you. He was worried that you were unprotected, and hoped the dagger would give you protection until you learn to use your magic."

"My magic?"

"You are descended from a sorceress. You wear a cape in your dream, which is a mystical sign. It is our belief that you are a sorceress, at least in your dream."

"Wow."

"Be proud," August agreed firmly. "Be proud, but also be wary. Matthew and I believe his dream is being linked with yours by the silver thread. We believe it guides him into your dream."

"But why?"

"I cannot know. Perhaps we're wrong. But you're seeing horses, aren't you?"

"That's true. There must be a path between his dream and mine. I wish we could find it."

"Let's hope Matthew finds that path before the Moonshaker's descendant does. For now, you're safest in your own dream. You cannot be killed there."

"Killed?" Molly's head swam at the thought. "You're saying these dreams themselves are dangerous?" Her voice grew slightly shrill. "How do I know whose dream I'm in? This whole thing is crazy! And I can't get to the dagger in the saddle-bag—I'm *afraid* of horses—and even if I could catch one, I wouldn't know which one!"

"Relax," the old man counseled. "You're doing fine. Matthew will be with you soon, I'm sure."

"Yes, that's what I want. I'm even ready to leave now, to meet him back in Berkeley, if that would be faster."

"No! You must stay where you are. Stay with your family. Let him come to you, if you are strong in that land. Or come here to Los Angeles, where I can help you. Do you feel powerful in that place?"

"Ireland, you mean? I guess so. My grand-mother's here. She's my only family now." Collecting herself, Molly affirmed, "Yes, I feel confident here. But I'd feel better with Matthew."

"It is Matthew who draws strength from you, not the other way. Remember that! He will call soon. Rest. *Do not be afraid to sleep.* And when Matthew calls, tell him I have thought about his spool. I couldn't figure it out until I drew it. It's not a spool at all. It's a bead—an ornament, perhaps. To be strung on a thong, maybe. I don't know. But it could be important." The old man's voice grew hushed. "It could be the amulet Maya stole from Lost Eagle!"

"The amulet that protected Lost Eagle from Aaric?" Molly gasped.

"Yes. The Moonshaker would never have been able to defeat my ancestor if Maya had not taken away his protection. Now, if you give it to Matthew, it may offer great protection against Aaric's descendant, who we must assume will also be a sorcerer of great skill and cunning . . . *And* viciousness."

"I have the spool," she assured him quickly,

alarmed by the prediction. "Or at least, I can get it from my grandmother."

"Good! If I am correct, the spool is the key."

"But I played with it so many times as a child," Molly remembered. "If it were a magical amulet, wouldn't someone have guessed by now?"

"The amulet was created for Lost Eagle. Perhaps only his blood relatives would be able to use its magic. Or there may be a secret to using it. A certain manner of awakening the power. You could easily have played with it without discovering such a secret."

"I see." She moistened her lips nervously. "Let's hope Matthew can figure it out. He's determined to win the battle, you know. If he loses, he'll never forgive himself."

"If he loses, he dies." August's voice was ghoulishly matter-of-fact. "And if what he tells me of *your* legend is true, it will also be a catastrophe for your family. The Valmain."

"There isn't any Valmain anymore. I'm not worried about that, but I am scared for Matthew. I'll tell him all you've said, if he ever gets in touch with me. And If you see him first . . ."

"Yes, I will tell him you want him."

"What? No, don't say . . . wait . . . yes, say that. Say that I want him! And thank you, August."

Don't be afraid to sleep, the old man had said, but the advice rang hollow that night as Molly lay in her bed. She could hear the hushed voices of Brian and Elizabeth long past midnight, and she knew they were discussing her 'strange behavior.' She even thought she heard Elizabeth mention calling

Molly's father. Now *that* would be a catastrophe for the family! Did she really seem that far gone?

Then a loud, confident knock silenced the muffled conversation and Molly knew, beyond a doubt, that her waiting was over. Springing from her bed, she grabbed her white terry cloth robe and rushed out of her room, straight into Matthew Redtree's arms.

"I can't believe you're here!" Burying her face against his rock-hard chest, she stammered, "I'm sorry I ran away from you! Are you all right?"

"I'm fine." He brushed her curls back from her face and kissed both cheeks reverently. "Calm down, Molly. I heard about your conversation with Uncle August. "Have you been frightened?"

"I didn't know what to do! I shouldn't have left you!"

"Hey." He tilted her face toward his own and smiled reassuringly. "I scared the hell out of you that night at my house. You were right to leave. You had to think. You had to be sure. Right?"

She nodded in relief and relaxed her body against his. "I've never been more sure of anything."

"Do you have the amulet?"

"Shh!" Molly stole a wary glance at her grandmother, who was watching the reunion disapprovingly. With a sheepish smile she pulled free of Matthew and slipped into her robe as she announced, "Matthew Redtree, I'd like you to meet my two favorite people in the whole world. My grandmother, Elizabeth Scanlon. And Brian Lafferty, our close friend."

"So you're the young man who thinks our Molly needs your protection?" Brian's delivery made it sound like a challenge, and Molly blushed.

"Actually, I'm the one who needs her, sir. She's a remarkable girl."

It seemed to be a suitable answer, and Brian's guard went down. Then Elizabeth insisted that Matthew eat, which Molly considered a good sign. She knew he was anxious to talk, but he didn't embarrass her, except perhaps by the fire behind his eyes when he looked at her. She in turn felt almost panicked with physical need of him—his hands, his lips, and more. She wanted to sleep in his arms, to blurt out her hope and confusion, and to draw strength from his resonant voice and lean, powerful body. The thought that he might crave her with the same desperation was enough to make her tremble, and she dug her nails into her palms to maintain an expression that wouldn't send Elizabeth and Brian into a fit of overprotection.

It was decided, to Matthew's obvious dismay, that the young man would stay at Brian's home, several miles away. Still, neither of the young lovers protested. Before the two men departed, Molly and Matthew stole a few moments alone under the cloudy midnight sky.

He was different. More confident. Molly suspected he had even begun to enjoy his role as champion and avenger.

"It's true, Molly. Now that I've come to understand so much more—not all, of course, but enough—I feel really prepared. Almost anxious."

"To fight a battle with some awful sorcerer's descendant? Your Uncle August told me you could be killed!"

"That won't happen. Believe me, I'm ready for him."

"How will you know it's him? Do you think he'll come to Ireland?"

"Listen carefully." He held her face gently between his hands. "I think he'll come to the dream."

"Oh, no." He had confirmed her worst fear. *"My dream?"*

"You inherited some kind of magical dream ability from Kerreya."

"I wish I had the ability to keep him out," she countered ruefully. "Do you think he knows about you yet? Or about me?"

"If he doesn't, he'll find out soon," Matthew grinned. "Like I said, I'm ready for him. And," he pulled her toward him, molding her soft curves to his hard body, "I'm ready for you. Tonight. I've been thinking about you, Valmain."

"I know. Believe me." She blushed again but held his gaze. "I've been thinking about that, too, Matthew. But it would disappoint Grandma so. She's all the family I have, and I've already upset her with all this. I'm not going to talk to her about the dreaming anymore, that's for sure. Just go along for now, and we'll slip away together tomorrow. Please?"

"Yeah. Okay. I'll scout out a place for us to go during my morning run tomorrow. And then . . . ," he grinned and lowered his mouth to hers, probing with his tongue as he had done that torrid night in Berkeley.

Tomorrow suddenly seemed an eternity away, and Molly eagerly returned his kisses, her heart pounding as she sought to memorize his mouth with her own. When Brian's warning cough, somewhat less than subtle, startled them, they reluctantly separated, repeating, under their breath, "Tomorrow."

Returning to her bed, she curled up under a fluffy patchwork comforter, wondering what was to happen. She and Matthew would be dreaming at the same time now. Maybe they would see each other! The thought momentarily thrilled her. The reality, however, was as intimidating as ever. Would she actually witness mortal combat? And what was to be her role?

The dream that night was achingly beautiful. She never actually did see Matthew, but sensed that he was there, somewhere near that meadow, perhaps just beyond the smallest hill, looking for her. As she searched she encountered a myriad of treasures: fragrant, flaming wildflowers which she gathered into a sumptuous bouquet; a litter of pure white kittens romping innocently near a stream that Molly had never before noticed; even a long silver necklace, which she found dangling from the limb of a tree and which she fastened around her neck, allowing the cool links to swing sensuously between her bare breasts under her cape and lacy chemise. It was as though the meadow had become a land of magic and enchantment yet, while each new discovery temporarily delighted and distracted her, she stubbornly returned again and again to her fruitless quest for her champion.

The huge, fair-haired warrior was prepared. Restless. Pacing the meadow. Ready for battle. For life. Instead, he was trapped, helpless, in a Valmain dream! This had not been as he and Maya had planned! Aaric the Moonshaker—the world's most celebrated warrior!—helpless?

The spell that had sent him through the centuries had been powerful—"Powerful enough," he mourned, "to kill my beloved Maya"—but it had apparently been less than completely successful. Even with the combined magic of an extraordinary sorceress and the world's most powerful sorcerer, his path had been blocked by this modest little dream. Had circumstances been different, he might have found the situation intriguing, or at least amusing, but he owed Maya more than that. It was his duty to wreak havoc on the Valmain kingdom, so that she could rest, avenged, in peace.

He craved the upcoming battle—the excitement, the glory, the unleashing of his long-dormant powers—but instead he was being required to wait, impatient but effectively powerless. "But you are not totally powerless," he corrected himself with a grin. "Kerreya's protection is strong, but you can amuse yourself for a time with the curly-haired Valmain princess in the shimmering white cape."

She had admired the presents he had sent—the kittens, the wildflowers, the horses . . . especially the horses. Admired but feared them. That was good. Soon she would have the opportunity to experience the same feelings toward him. Aaric laughed heartily. It had been so long, and the princess's cool bearing was so like Maya's. The anticipation was almost worth the endless frustration.

The whole situation amazed him! Apparently, the long-awaited battle would take place in this dream, assuming the dreamer knew how to summon her champion, which Aaric was beginning to doubt. He had been watching her for an eternity—or was it simply an hour, or a day, or a second?—and had not yet seen her use any of her powers beyond simply coming to the dream. Still, she was Kerreya's descendant and undoubtedly a gifted sorceress.

She had not yet sensed his presence. Instead, she had spent her time searching and calling out to one named "Matthew." Aaric had attempted to find him as well but had ascertained that the dream was empty, save for himself and the pretty sorceress. Still, he felt something—a vague sensation, and one which he associated with his old nemesis Lost Eagle.

The huge sorcerer grinned. Now *that* had been a battle! He could only hope that the Valmain champion—this "Matthew"—was half the man Lost Eagle had been. With or without the amulet, Lost Eagle had been the most worthy of all opponents, and had died like a man, with a glint of strength still lighting his eyes and a curse against his slayer on his lips.

Again the odd mix of foreboding and excitement tremored through him and, at that instant Aaric understood. Kerreya's daughter had become paired with Lost Eagle's son! How could this be? Had this "Matthew" crossed the seas to make love to the princess, thereby becoming the champion of Valmain as well as the avenger of his hapless ancestor? If so, he would by now be in possession of the amulet, although that did not actually matter. The amulet would do the champion no good unless he knew how to use it and, if he had such knowledge, he would have taken control long before this time. Instead, control was still shifting between the sorceress-sisters. Maya and Kerreya had set this dream in motion. Or was their sorcerer-father still controlling the timing?

Or perhaps the curly-haired princess was in control! And *she* clearly did not want them to fight! But he could change her mind. Until then, the warriors would wait. Aaric, waiting for life . . . Son of Lost Eagle, for death.

Aaric did not intend to wait for the curly-haired one, however. He intended to have her at the very next opportunity.

* * *

The tension at the breakfast table was as thick as the jam Molly nervously spread over toasted home-made bread. Elizabeth was apparently convinced Matthew was a cult leader, or worse, and Matthew wasn't doing much to dispel the notion. In fact, from the way he looked at Molly—as though she might be somewhat divine, yet definitely attainable—he was rapidly making things worse.

Molly, whose curls were still damp from her morning bath, had chosen to wear a fleecy white warm-up suit in hopes that she would appear innocent, for her grandmother's sake, while appearing healthy and energetic for the sake of her upcoming bout with destiny. Matthew was dressed in his apparently standard fashion—white polo shirt, unfaded jeans, and black leather running shoes. The austere effect was complimented by his high cheekbones and bronzed skin, but subverted by the sumptuous quality of the thick, dark hair that he had apparently tried to tame, unsuccessfully, by shearing. His every move was powerful and graceful, with no wasted motion, and certainly no sign of hesitation or self-consciousness. He was clearly ready to take on the world; and Molly, who was as conscious as Elizabeth of his amorous stare, was more than ready to be taken. But when? Where? It seemed impossible.

Then Brian managed to coax 'Betsy' away, with stories of an ill friend in town, and the grateful granddaughter's pulse began to race. "You owe Brian a huge thanks," she informed Matthew breathlessly, as they stood in the doorway of the cottage and waved to the departing couple. "I would have bet a million Grandma would never leave you alone with me."

"Brian's a good man," Matthew agreed. "I told

him you and I needed to talk in private, and he understood."

"Okay," she slipped her arms around his neck and drew him back into the parlor, "talk." *Tell me you're crazy about me,* she wanted to prompt, but instead, she kissed him lightly.

His lips moved obligingly to her neck. "You shouldn't have run away from me, Valmain. Promise me you'll never do that again."

"I thought you were lying to me."

"I'd never do that. I swear that to you." Forcing her to acknowledge the solemnity in his eyes, he added, "I have to protect you. I have to be with you. Do you understand?"

The gold flecks were incredibly distracting, but she nodded as though completely lucid. "I want to be with you, Matthew. I was just upset."

"That's what we need to discuss." As Molly stared in dismay, he strode across the room and motioned toward the sofa. "Sit down."

"Am I in trouble?"

He grinned. "Let me guess. You're taking this affair Pass/Not Pass?"

Molly laughed and joined him on the sofa. "I want an 'A,' I'm afraid, so tell me what's wrong."

His serious mood returned. "I'm supposed to protect you, but you have a job, too. When you're calm and rational, I feel like I almost literally draw strength from you. It's an awesome sensation."

"If you want me to stay calm," she sighed, "you shouldn't be so handsome." Her fingers traced the line of his chin hopefully. "I think about you all the time, Matthew."

"I know. It's incredible, isn't it?"

It was clear to her they were on two different wavelengths, and so she tried a more direct approach. "Brian and Grandma won't be gone forever, Matthew. Shouldn't we kiss now and talk later?"

"This is important, Valmain," he chuckled. "I'm trying to tell you we have to be straight with each other. Always. If something's bothering you, you have to tell me immediately. Don't get angry, or run away, or freeze up on me. When that happens, this energy transfer thing I'm telling you about just doesn't work right."

"Don't *you* ever get upset?"

"Sure. But I control it. It's a matter of balance, Molly. Making your emotions work *for* you, not against you."

"I don't get upset easily, usually, but . . ." She cocked her head to the side and teased, "You can be very frustrating, Matthew."

"Yeah? Try searching for an Irish needle in a Mexican haystack someday," he laughed. "That was true frustration, Valmain."

"Good."

"Huh?"

"I think you're right, legend-spinner." She stood and urged him to his feet. "I think emotions and frustrations are very good things if you make them work *for* you, and right now, I'm very frustrated." She blushed slightly and added, "Are you going to make love to me?"

"Absolutely." His fingers began to work the zipper on her sweatshirt.

"And do I have to stay calm the whole time?"

"Quiet now, Valmain," he instructed softly, slipping his hand under the fleece and caressing her breasts through her lacy lightweight bra. "No more talking . . ."

Almost instantly she was mesmerized—by his

voice, and his touch, and his ability to focus. Her head dropped back, exposing her neck more completely to his warm, tantalizing kisses. There was no urgency and, inexplicably, no driving need. Instead, she was drifting, and as Matthew's concentration intensified, Molly's own consciousness dissipated and she melted against him, weak with delicious arousal. It was as though she were dissolving into a fog of love, with only a gentle throbbing to remind her of her former self.

He caught her, just as her body became limp, and carried her to her bed, murmuring reassurances that kept her within his power. Then he pulled off his jeans and stretched his lean body over her, his muscles working gently to memorize her supple curves. As he kissed her he undressed her slowly, without ever lifting his lips from her warm, responsive skin, then he knelt above her, shrugged out of his shirt, smiled encouragingly, and took her.

With her damp cheek pressed to his chest, she could feel as well as hear his strong, steady heartbeat and she allowed the rhythm to draw her back into some awareness of her surroundings. After all, this was not a tropical paradise or cozy little hideaway. It was her *grandmother's* house . . .

Stretching ruefully, she rolled free of his arms and sat up, pulling the sheet up to cover her nude form. Her eyes focused on his shoulders—so muscled and tanned—then down along to his tapered torso, then down to admire the rest of him.

"So?" Matthew smiled gently. "How was that?"

"Perfect." She arched an eyebrow accusingly. "I guess you always knew this would happen, right?"

"Not really." His tone was sincere—almost reverent. "The truth is I thought you'd be some fragile, otherworldly creature. This is better. It's almost like you're a real girl."

"I *am* a real girl."

Matthew chuckled. "I think I just verified that." Reaching for his jeans, he pulled them over his legs and explained, "I just meant you're not a dream. Not an idea. This aspect of our relationship was completely unexpected."

"Good. I'd hate to be predictable." Stretching again, she remembered with amusement how she had willingly avoided romantic entanglements in order to complete her studies, planning that she would then find a mate who would share her interests and commitments. At such time, she had suspected, her responses would be healthy. At worst, she had expected contentment. At best, she had anticipated perhaps a touch of the heat and steam promised by novels and movies.

Now Matthew Redtree had introduced her to love, and his approach had been so simple and thorough, his touch so reverent, and the effect so powerful—almost magical—that she was awed by both lover and love itself. She wanted him to take her over and over and forever, and wanted more desperately than ever for the dreams to go away.

"I'm glad I waited for you, Matthew."

"You had to wait for me."

"Well." Molly edged away primly. "You're welcome, Matthew."

"Hey! Don't do that, Valmain." He pulled her close again. "I love you."

"So you say. Of course, you *have* to love me, right?"

"I want to love you, need to love you, and," he nibbled her earlobe gently, "love to love you."

"Oh. Well, that's pretty, Matthew. You can be very persuasive." She surrendered easily, allowing him to caress her beneath the sheet.

"I was destined to love you," he murmured. "Since the day you were born. I just never understood your role until now."

"I think that's what bothers me the most about the dreams," she admitted, closing her eyes to more completely concentrate on his touch. "I mean, besides the fact that you think you may get killed. It bothers me that I'm so passive." She flushed slightly, remembering how yielding she had been during their lovemaking—passive definitely had its rewards, she admitted—but Matthew didn't seem to make the connection, and so she ignored her own interruption and continued, "My role is so . . . inert. I don't even seem to have control over myself! I look, I sew, I shiver. And in *your* dream I'm even less active! Holding a spool! Quite a responsibility."

"You're missing the point, Valmain." A touch of impatience had broken through the reverence. "The dreaming itself is what you do! At least in theory, you have the power to affect *my* destiny, by strengthening my performance in my fight with Aaric's descendant. Anyway, that reminds me—I brought you something. It's in the parlor, in my knapsack." He bounded from the room.

"A gift? That was so sweet . . ." Her eyes widened when he reappeared carrying a shiny, jagged gray blade. "You bought me a knife?"

"It's a dagger. Luckily, I had it made about four years ago by a guy in Canada so I could practice with it. It's not obsidian, like the dagger in the dream, but it's almost exactly the same size and weight. I want you to get used to the feel of it."

"Forget it! I'm back to being passive. This gives me the creeps."

"Be sensible!" Matthew thrust the weapon back toward her. "Handle it! Get used to it. There was a time when I didn't think there was any danger to you, but now I've changed my mind. I'm starting to realize that this isn't even *about* me. It's about you, as Valmain. And I'm supposed to protect you. This dagger is the best I can do until we're together in the dream."

"Somehow I associate you with danger, not protection. Hey, don't look so hurt. I'm just kidding." She kissed him gently. "You're my hero."

"It's good you can joke about it, Molly, as long as you understand what's going on."

"You're going to get revenge for Lost Eagle against Maya and Aaric by fighting Aaric's descendant. You're also going to fulfill Kerreya's promise that *my* family would have a champion. Right?"

"Because," Matthew nodded, "somehow, after Lost Eagle's amulet was stolen, it ended up in *your* family."

"So you agree with August that the spool is the amulet? Oh, wait, here . . ." she rummaged in the bedstand drawer, "this is for you. Grandma officially gave it to me this morning, and now I'm returning it to you." With a teasing smile she added, "Sorry about my Aunt Maya's thievery."

"Unbelievable," Matthew murmured, rolling the bullet-sized silver ornament between his thumb and finger. "It's exactly right. Look at this symbol."

"Like you said," Molly agreed, "a row of horseshoes divided into halves. I always thought it was a sign of good luck."

"Let's hope so. They're divided by an arrow.

See?" He traced along the etching. "An arrow with points at both tips."

"You're right. More weapons. Just what we needed, right? Maybe you'd better take it back to Brian's with you and put it under your pillow or something."

"Good idea. Although I'm not sure that's necessary. Last night, in my dream, you were holding the end of the thread instead of the spool and when I got to a meadow I had the spool in my hand and put it in my pouch."

"What about the thread itself?"

"It was gone."

"Oh no!"

"I don't think it's a problem," he reassured her fondly. "I felt we were still pretty connected. We'll always be connected."

"Oh, Matthew . . ." She snuggled against him happily.

"It's amazing," he agreed. "The outcome of the fight will affect both our legends. It's pretty heady stuff!"

"Like I said," she drew back far enough to shoot him a playful glare, "you seem to be enjoying all this."

"I am! I want to be your champion. I *want* to fight him!"

"I think I liked it better when you were worried. Now *I'm* worried."

"That's the idea! You do the worrying, I'll do the fighting."

"I'm not so sure about all this. For one thing," she complained, "we're not even dreaming the same thing, so we're probably not even in the same dream."

"Are the stallions in your dream?"

"Yes. Yes, I guess that's something." She fingered his earlobe and sighed, "I wish you'd never told me all this, Matthew. Now I'll probably dream a fight whether there is one or not. I'll be afraid to go to sleep."

"You have to go to sleep! I'm counting on you."

"Thanks for the pressure. Now I'm sure I won't sleep."

"I could tire you out," he suggested, pulling back the sheet to gaze at her nude, rested body.

She blushed as his eyes swept over her. Once again, there was no urgency . . . no lustful mood. His quiet confidence immobilized her, and, when he began to trail his lips along her shoulder and then over her left breast, pausing to savor a pink-tipped nipple, she felt herself melting into the mattress, dominated and adored all in one timeless moment. Her other breast ached for him and he immediately obliged it, as though he could read her thoughts and lived only to fulfill them. Then she willed him to kiss her mouth and once again he responded, courting her tongue gently with his own.

Her aroused nipples were thrilled by the press of his smooth muscles, but his jeans offended her naked legs and so she gingerly moved her hand to his zipper, only to be gently preempted. "Relax," Matthew whispered. "Just relax, Valmain."

He didn't seem to want her to *do* anything—he simply wanted her to lie back and allow him to please her and she might have protested had his slow-motion style been any less effective, but she was throbbing again, with an emptiness that she knew only he could fill and so she surrendered to him—to this art form he called lovemaking—and when he thrust himself reverently between her thighs she rotated her hips, but only ever so slightly, more to thank him than to assist him. Then his thrusts became more demanding, her hips responded in kind, and the rhythm intensified toward a mutual release of unbearably exquisite perfection.

She willingly drifted into sleep thereafter, warm with the hope that they would meet there, in her grassy meadow. More than anything, she wanted him to see her in her cape, in her tiny, perfect kingdom. More than anything, she wanted to be the woman of his dreams.

And then it happened! For the very first time, the figure of Matthew Redtree appeared in her dream, before her in the distance, and she moistened her lips in wonder and appreciation before raising her arms toward him in greeting.

Chapter Six

Bronzed and clad in skins and weapons, the warrior appeared in the distance astride one of the snow-white stallions. His magnificent hair was straight and thick, hanging to just above his shoulders and graced by a red-and-black beaded headband that sat low on his noble brow. His deerskin garment was fashioned like a tunic, laced across the bulging muscles of his chest, leaving his limbs bare, except for sandals laced up past his knees, and thick leather wristbands decorated in the same pattern that adorned his forehead.

It was the most powerfully masculine sight of Molly's life, and her heart pounded as he galloped toward her, yet when he scooped her up onto his horse and grinned triumphantly, she stiffened. It was not the reunion she had anticipated. This rough grasp of his was not a gesture of protection. The face did not reflect the emotions of a champion. The reverence was completely gone from the golden eyes and she knew, at that instant: *This was not Matthew Redtree!*

The pounding in her chest now proclaimed terror rather than adoration and, as she struggled with both the man and the panic, she remembered the dagger! Reaching down, she managed to locate the saddlebag despite the furious pace. The dagger felt exactly like the one Matthew had given her and, with her heart ready to burst with fear, she thrust the cold, jagged blade into the rider's leg, prepared for fury, for blood, for pain. Instead, the rider vanished and Molly awoke to find her champion beside her in the narrow bed, snoring gently, as though he had no cares and no fears. He was positively serene!

"Matthew Redtree!" She shook him angrily. "Wake up this minute! Are you crazy? I thought I might have stabbed you! Why is this happening? Did you see any of it?"

"Calm down," he groaned, lifting himself onto one elbow and studying her through sleepy eyes. "Tell me what happened. I was dreaming again, but it was beautiful. There were flowers and kittens and . . ."

"Forget all that! Someone who looked like you grabbed me! I thought I couldn't get hurt in my dream! But he had me!"

His sleepy mood vanished. "Who had you?" he demanded. "Did he hurt you? I'll *kill* him if he did!"

"I stabbed him in the leg with your damned knife!"

"Huh?" He blinked, then grinned. "You're kidding!"

"It was awful!"

"He made himself look like me?" Matthew nodded vigorously. "So he *is* a sorcerer. That makes sense. He's descended from one. It gives him a slight advantage . . ."

"Slight? You really *are* crazy," she groaned. "Are you saying he can make himself look like anyone he wants? Do you think he can be invisible? I *hate* that."

"The important thing is, it's finally starting to happen." Rubbing his hands together eagerly, he crowed, "Don't you see? He's here, but he didn't hurt you. Maybe he doesn't *dare* hurt you for some reason. Somehow he's just trying to make us angry."

"Us? Well, why aren't you, then? *I'm* angry!"

"Anger is too volatile, Molly. It's a nonproductive emotion. Hatred is steady and useful, but anger is undependable. He wants to make us angry so we'll be off balance."

"I'll tell you what *I* want. I want to find someone—some shaman or sorcerer or voodoo guy—someone powerful who can make this stop. And I'm not sleeping again until we do! You've studied all this. Who's the best? I want names and addresses. Now!"

"Calm down, Valmain. We can't go traveling now. Remember what my uncle said?"

"I need someone powerful! I'm scared!" she wailed.

"You are powerful. You did great! Don't you see? You took control. That's what you wanted, remember?"

"I won't sleep until you find me someone," she repeated sharply. "And if I don't sleep, the battle doesn't happen."

"No, if *I* don't sleep it doesn't happen. If you don't dream, then maybe I'm on my own. At least, I think that's how it is." He smiled ruefully. "I'm the one who'll fight, remember? And I need your help."

"Damn! I *hate* this. We don't know what the hell we're doing!"

"Watch your language, Valmain. What would Grandma say?"

"She already said it. She thinks you're having a strange influence on me. If she only knew." Molly buried her face in her pillow and groaned in frustration. "Damn!"

Matthew laughed and patted her shoulder. "You did fine. Just relax, now, and don't be afraid to sleep. You won't dream twice in one day. At least, I don't think you will."

"More guessing!" she glared. "Can't you see? We don't know the rules. Or there aren't any."

"There *are* rules. I'm sure of it. Your ancestors set this up to protect you. Kerreya and her sorcerer father care about you, Valmain. Don't you see?"

"All I see is, I'm in over my head, and you're crazy enough to actually depend on me for help!"

"Don't panic. You have to stay in control. I know a way to relax you . . ."

"Forget it!" she snapped, pulling the bedsheet higher on her chest. "That's almost insulting!"

"Get your mind out of the gutter, Valmain," Matthew chuckled. "I'm not talking about sex. I have Brian on tape. Last night he told me a bunch of incredible legends."

"Really?" She nodded in reluctant appreciation of the distraction. "That sounds nice, I guess. He must have felt flattered."

"Actually, I don't think he approved of my taping them. He said something about stories being supposed to change every time with the telling. According to him, these stories can't stay alive imprisoned in the pages of a book."

"Okay, I'll listen to your tape. Maybe it'll distract me." Molly glanced around herself, weary but wary. "They'll be home soon. If only we could relax and enjoy our time together without worrying about that awful man."

"The battle will be over soon. I'm sure of it. And then you can start enjoying your vacation."

"Have you been here before?"

"Not Tralee specifically, but I've been to Dublin and up to Drogheda. There are burial mounds in that area. Have you seen them yet?"

"Burial mounds?"

Oblivious to her lack of enthusiasm, he promised, "We can go over there if you want, although I was reading on the airplane about the area north of here. There are stone circles dating back thousands of years. And a reconstruction project . . ."

"Matthew!" Molly laughed. "Why do I feel that you're in a completely different Ireland than I am?"

"You said my world was a strange one. You were right. Now you're a part of it."

"Weapons on the walls? Vacationing in burial tunnels? You take a little getting used to."

"Take your time. I'm not going anywhere. Except," he pulled his jeans back over his legs, "for a run. I've got to stay in shape. Do you feel like coming with me?"

"That dream just gave me enough exercise for one day. Besides, I'm not the running type. Leisurely walking is more my style."

Matthew laughed. "I'll change your mind about that, too, someday. But for now I agree you should rest." He studied her proudly as she slipped into her soft bathrobe. "You always wear white, don't you?"

"Usually. It's simple, I guess. Like me. White blouses, white dresses . . ."

"Bare feet . . . Like a peasant girl. You don't look like a toxicologist."

"Are you kidding? The white lab coat is part of the allure," she giggled. "Anyway, you're in kind of a rut yourself. I never see the tweed jacket you used to wear to the lectures. Just blue jeans and a white shirt every single day . . ."

"Right. Tough and comfortable. But I do like shoes. We'll have to buy you some running shoes to replace your sandals."

"No, thanks. Like I told you, swimming is my only exercise. And walking. I don't pound my bones into the ground for anyone, not even you."

"After my run, I'll pound them for you," he promised.

"No way. We make love and then I fall asleep and then it's back to the war zone. I'm not falling for that again."

"The next time we make love," he predicted, "it'll be in tall, green grasses and it'll be perfect."

"I can't wait," she blushed. Reaching forward to run her hand under his shirt, loving the warm smooth mass of muscles that protected his heart, she sighed, "We'd better pull ourselves together. Grandma's probably on her way."

Matthew made no move to comply, choosing instead to be mesmerized by the sight of his dream girl primly cinching her belt and smoothing her curls. "You're so pretty. 'Prettier every time I see you,' like I told you that night at my house." He ran a fingertip lightly over her lips and eyelids. "So pretty. I love you, Valmain."

"I love you, too, Matthew," she whispered. "I can't believe it, but I do. I'm not sure I ever really believed I'd fall in love."

"Yeah. I know." He brushed his lips across hers. "We were destined for this. I don't know why I didn't realize it sooner."

"Did you kiss me? That first night in my apartment while I was sleeping on the couch?"

"I had to," he murmured.

"Well, maybe when all this is over, you'll kiss me because you *want* to, not because you have to."

"I 'want' to right now."

"Because you were destined to want to?" she suggested carefully, and was vaguely disappointed when he didn't contradict her. Still, destined or not, she craved his kiss, and so she relented, weak for the sensations he would now coax from the body that had fallen so completely under his spell.

It had been a confusing day and, even before she drifted into sleep that night, alone in her grandmother's guest room, Molly suspected she was 'destined' for further confusion before the night was over. She thought of Matthew Redtree—'her champion'—who, for all of his knowledge and training remained so reassuringly humble. She had spent hours with him, talking and teasing and sighing, and had been stunned by the vacuum his departure for Brian's house had created in her life. She could never again feel truly safe without him, and yet . . .

She smiled to herself, thinking of how she had joked about his humble manner of dress. Apparently the sportscoat from his Berkeley lectures had been atypical of the man. Jeans and running shoes seemed hardly the wardrobe of a warrior, let alone a champion, but she had no complaints about the lean hard body thereunder.

In the dream, that body had been showcased, and she remembered her initial reaction to the bronzed, bulging bare limbs and shoulder-length mane of blue-black hair. The wildly masculine sight had aroused her. Was that indeed the way Matthew would appear at their first dream meeting?

Both images had a purity to them—a simplicity that spoke more of character than of purpose. He was her hero because he was a man of principles and commitments, both in the dream and outside, but it was the warrior image that teased her as she drifted into sleep.

When the dream came, there were no horses . . . no flowers. The meadow was empty. Everything seemed different. Calm. As though something had happened. "So?" she whispered to herself, drawing her cape closely against herself. "It's true. Things can happen here without me. But what? It almost feels like . . . like it's all over."

There was something, in the distance. Near the second hill. A figure. Limping. A man limping. But who? She moved toward him slowly but, as the figure took shape, she found herself starting to run. Matthew! *Her* Matthew! She had yearned to see him in the dream but not like *this*. His face was twisted in pain and his tunic was saturated with blood. Broad scarlet gashes disfigured his limbs and chest.

"What happened?" She flung herself into his arms and sobbed, "Oh Matthew, what happened to you? I wasn't here! I'm so sorry! Forgive me!"

He grasped her to himself and groaned at the feel of her. "Do not cry," he murmured. "It is finished. I am glad you did not have to see it." Tilting her face toward his, he lowered his ravenous mouth to hers.

For a moment there was nothing in her world but his hot mouth and her hunger, then the full impact of his words forced her to pull back and stare into his amazing gold-dust eyes. "It's finished? You saw

Aaric's descendant? Fought him? Here? Oh, Matthew, . . ."

"I defeated him! He was a fine warrior but I destroyed him."

"How? I thought—"

"That I needed you? But I had the power of the amulet."

"I can't believe it! Oh, Matthew!" She resumed the kissing frantically.

"Believe it!" Taking her face in his hands again, he commanded, "I need you now!"

Molly's heart pounded as he took her cape and spread it on the ground. Never had she felt so aroused . . . so desperate! He pulled her down with him, groping under her petticoat feverishly, pushing his bloody hands and face between her thighs. She arched in total confusion, grasping wildly at his thick mane of hair. She was climaxing almost instantly and heard herself shriek with pleasure, then he mounted her, groaning that he needed her, and she stroked him as she guided him into the dripping folds he had so ravenously devoured.

He was mad with lust for her and she encouraged him with mindless writhing, digging her fingernails into his skin as though to ensure that he could never get away. When he finally exploded within her, she gasped with delight, and, when they were finally still, she whispered, hesitantly, that she loved him, but knew it wasn't love that had driven them. She knew only that she never wanted to wake up.

He rolled onto his back, smiling up at the sky as though seeing it for the first time. "That was perfect. You," he added dramatically, "are perfect!"

"You never touched me like that before," she marveled, belatedly shy.

He chuckled. "It was enjoyable? More so than before?"

"Matthew . . ." How could she explain? The steam heat that she had once expected, but never truly missed, had scorched her very soul. It had taken the place of the transcendental quality of their previous loving, and while she knew that she could not bear to lose that quality forever, for now . . . "It wasn't *more* enjoyable, but . . . incredible, Matthew. The other times, I was the dream girl. The girl with the spool. Now, I'm just a girl."

"A woman. *My* woman." As though to prove this, he now shifted himself so that his mouth was once again between her thighs, investigating gently, and Molly arched, disoriented yet ignited, in one long, hot moment, by the unfamiliar, decadent positioning of their hungry mouths—so far from one another, yet so able to taste of and to meet one another's most intimate needs. His every instinct seemed suddenly to be simultaneously crude and tender and she longed to satisfy him in ways that, until this moment, she had never truly imagined.

She could see that he was aroused—hard, throbbing, and insatiable—and as her tongue tasted him with tentative adoration her hands began to caress him gently. She wanted to please him but was unsure of herself . . .

Her hesitation seemed to amuse him and he quickly moved his own strong hand to grasp her wrist, gently forcing her to stroke him with longer, firmer, more satisfying movements. When he then groaned with unabashed appreciation of her newfound technique, she laughed—an unfamiliar, husky laugh—and he grinned in return. "Your innocence pleases me, and now," he shifted again, so that they were face to face, "I will please you in return."

"Matthew . . ." She melted into his arms, mesmerized by his unforgettably lyrical voice. "This is heaven."

His hand moved to caress her swollen breasts through the thin cotton of her chemise. "You belong to me now."

"Yes . . . yes, I do."

"I will teach you—slowly. Do you understand? We have forever to learn one another's ways."

"Matthew!" She blushed proudly. "I love this. I love being finished with spools and amulets and legends . . ." Embarrassed at her own enthusiasm, she pulled demurely away, smoothing her lacy undergarments and pretending to trace the silver patterns in the cape with her finger. To her amazement, the stitching that had always seemed painstakingly regular now appeared to form words, and sentences, and short chronicles of ancient exploits and happenings. "Matthew! Look here! It tells a story. *The* story!"

Lazily, as though it no longer mattered, he murmured, "It tells Kerreya's story?"

"No. Yes. I mean, it tells about all of it! About your ancestor, too! Lost Eagle! He was very strong, just like you said! And the bad guy, Aaric . . . Oh! I wish we could take this with us out of the dream! You could study it, sort it all out! And," she smiled mischievously, "I know the first person you'd show it to!"

"And who is that?"

"No, you tell me. I want to see how well I know you."

"No." He seemed confused. "You tell me."

She winced, slightly unnerved by his blank expression. "Matthew? Is something wrong?"

He hesitated, and then burst into laughter. "You truly are perfect! You try to be proper, like Kerreya. But," he traced his fingertip along her chin, then down her neck and between her breasts, "inside, you are much more like my Maya. So proud! So hungry. Kerreya never had your fire!"

"You're not Matthew?" Molly's head swam as the deception became clear. "You're the other one? Oh, no!" Jumping to her feet in horror, she snatched up her cape to obscure his view of her disheveled undergarments. *"You're the one I stabbed!"*

Chapter Seven

"Very good," the handsome Matthew lookalike grinned. "Yes, daughter of Kerreya, I am Aaric, who is called the Moonshaker."

Aaric? she shrieked silently. Not Aaric's descendant, but Aaric *himself?* "That's not possible . . ."

"Yet I am here."

"Is Matthew dead?"

"Not yet. He is at the designated place. I have provided a distraction for him. Are you not glad? He would not like to see *this!*" His grin was deadly. "Do not look so shocked. It is simple. Once I saw you, I had to have you."

"This is a dream!" She tugged her cape around herself indignantly. "So nothing happened. You had nothing. No one."

He laughed again. "I had you and you were exquisite. But I agree. The next time must be much more . . . elaborate. I give you my promise."

"You'll be dead and I'll be with Matthew!" she spat, edging further from his leering face. "He'll kill you for this!"

"No. You will be with *me.* But you will think it is he! Is that not convenient?"

"What?" A chill had reverberated down her spine. "What does *that* mean?"

"I will defeat him and take his form. Just as I have done in this illusion. It is arranged. You will see the form you say you love, and because you will want so desperately to believe that it is still he, you will. And so we will be together."

"If that happens, I'll know," she whispered. "You'll never fool me again. If you win . . . ," she bit back the words, wailing instead, "I hate you!"

"No," he corrected. "I have made love to you, and you have reveled in my touch. That will always be a bond between us. One day soon, you will love me completely. No woman has ever resisted me for long."

"One day soon, you'll be dead," she countered swiftly. *"I'll* see to that!" Forcing herself to stand her ground, she added proudly, "I have power, and Matthew has the spool."

"Spool? Do you mean the amulet?"

"Yes. The amulet. He'll kill you with it."

"So?" The confusing illusion of Matthew nodded resignedly. "He knows it is an amulet, after all. But he does not know how to use it, and so it cannot aid him. As for your power, I am afraid it is just not enough. Poor little princess. So much to learn. But I will be your teacher." He shrugged to his feet and moved to within inches of his trembling prey. "Ask anything."

Don't run, she commanded herself grimly. *Get the information Matthew needs to destroy this monster.* "How does the amulet work?"

"Clever!" he beamed. "But no. Ask anything else."

"Why aren't you dead? How can you be here? Why do you hate us?"

"I do not hate you. In fact," his leer had returned, "I am mindless with love for you, little princess. I have come to fight the Valmain champion, not to harm you."

"Why? Why are you fighting against Valmain?"

"It is simple. I fight because I loved Maya." His tone softened. "She came to me with an elaborate scheme of revenge. She had learned a dangerous and powerful spell that would send me here, but the spell required us to merge our powers. It is not done, as you must surely know. It is too dangerous. But Maya was bold. I even thought she might survive, but at the last moment she burned brightly in my arms and was gone. And I was sent here to wait."

"For what?"

"Maya had offered me something I had always wanted. Well," he spread his hands ruefully, "not exactly. I wanted immortality. But this—to live so many centuries into the future!—is so close to immortality! Maya saw this as a time when Valmain, if it still existed, would not expect her interference. I was to destroy Valmain by destroying the champion. But your dream has complicated matters."

"You weren't supposed to be in my dream?" She nodded, distracted from her fear by the knowledge that this enemy had been thwarted, at least temporarily. "You were supposed to reappear in our world, to fight Matthew?"

"To fight your champion. It never occurred to us that Lost Eagle's promise of revenge would also be awaiting me. It is remarkable. The Son of Lost Eagle, fighting for Valmain."

"You're stuck in my dream," she noted carefully. "What's the point of beating Matthew now?"

"When we battle, the victor will emerge from this

dream in the body of the champion. This body," he added impishly, gesturing toward himself. "It is smaller than my own, but acceptable. I will make love to you many times with it." His voice grew husky as he added, "I cannot wait to see your world, and to taste it. To share it with you!"

"But you'll kill me!"

"No. I will destroy Lost Eagle's son—your champion—but not you. My only regret, so long ago, in agreeing to Maya's scheme, was that I would have to live without her. I feared I would be lonely. But here you are! And so like her!"

"I'm *not* like her!" Molly gasped. "She was evil!"

"No, Princess. She was jealous, passionate, impulsive! She was wonderful. Her faults were the zest of my life. Even her infidelity."

"With Valmain!"

"For a time, yes. And with Lost Eagle. And others. But she always came back to me. I was *her* champion."

"And she brought you the amulet?"

"Yes. Without the amulet to protect him, Lost Eagle was no match for me. And so I killed him. And then I gave his amulet to Valmain and Kerreya, as a wedding gift, to take across the untraveled seas. I knew it would hold no power for Valmain and I thought that would be the end of it, and the end of Lost Eagle's hope for revenge." He grinned. "But Kerreya was smart. Or maybe it was my guardian. It was he who gave the amulet to Lost Eagle originally."

"Your guardian?"

"Maya's father," Aaric explained. "The most powerful sorcerer of all times. He was the cousin of my mother. Do you know none of this? How did you—a princess!—come to be so ignorant of your own heritage?"

Now that the leering had stopped, the warrior was again identical in appearance to Matthew. The resemblance reassured Molly, in a bizarre but effective way, and she found herself believing his claim that he did not intend to harm her—at least, not yet. He also seemed to have lost interest in her, sexually, for the moment. For some reason, he wanted her to understand what was happening and she needed to take full advantage of the opportunity, for Matthew's sake. Taking a deep breath, she pressed, "Was Maya so sure the curse itself wouldn't have destroyed Valmain by now?"

"She cursed your family with a curse of betrayal, which ordinarily is extremely effective, but Kerreya's provision for a champion prevented success unless the betrayal came from *within* the family, which seemed unlikely. Maya was not one to be thwarted, and so she devised this clever plan. Except that it was not quite clever enough. When I awoke, I found myself in your dreams. And the brothers of Lost Eagle had prepared his son well, and gentle Kerreya had given you silver thread to strengthen you. It is not the way Maya and I planned." He touched her arm gently. "Your champion cannot defeat me, my beautiful Princess. He will be killed. But I will be quick and merciful. For you."

"You'll kill me, too," she countered swiftly. "I'm Valmain."

"I cannot kill you. Not now." His eyes swept over Molly as though remembering every detail of their lovemaking, and then he continued. "I admit, that was Maya's plan. To send me here to destroy all of Valmain. Let me try to explain.

"When Maya realized that Kerreya's intervention—her spell guaranteeing Valmain a champion—was stronger than Maya had planned, she knew that only the greatest and most powerful warrior of all time could guarantee success. Only myself, the Moonshaker, could give her the assurances she needed. By sending me into the future, she hoped the champion would be caught unwary and unprepared. We also hoped that my guardian's legacy—that his power could not easily be inherited by his offspring—would render Valmain powerless and all the more vulnerable. But here you are! A dream witch."

"Don't call me that!" Molly flared.

Aaric grinned. "Have I insulted you? How strange your world must be. There is much I will teach you, pretty witch, but it seems you also must teach me."

"Why aren't you going to kill me?"

"Maya is gone. My allegiance is now to myself. And I want you. You are lovely and talented and you have this valuable dream power. It is that simple. As for the rest of your people," he shrugged, then smiled impishly, "I have not yet decided, but I will possibly kill them. Perhaps I will leave that to you, their princess. If you behave . . ."

"I'm not a princess," Molly protested. "There *is* no Valmain anymore. No kingdom, no kings and queens and curses and spells. It's all gone." She raised her chin defiantly. "Why don't you just go away, too?"

"No kingdom? So, it is just you then? And, of course, your champion. But soon he will be gone. And then we will build our own kingdom together." He reached for her and then hesitated. "Would you like to see me? As Aaric? For this one time at least before I take his form forever?"

Molly turned away in dread, then chastised herself, knowing that Matthew needed every scrap of information in order to defeat this trickster. When she shifted her eyes back to where he stood, an involuntary gasp sprang from her throat at the sight of him.

He was huge—perhaps the most incredibly built man Molly had ever seen, and certainly the most intimidating. A killer, she realized in complete horror. The contrast to Matthew could not have been more alarming. In place of a simple tunic, Aaric's chest was crossed by wide bands of leather, forming a grid that ended in a breechcloth. The strips of leather that were strapped to his wrists were highly tooled and studded, but not in an attempt at adornment—only defense. He was an intimidating fusion of muscle and scars, including a fresh wound on his thigh that made her momentarily proud.

Only his countenance remained unblemished. Pure, clean, almost noble. His skin was bronzed, his hair was long, burnished blond, and unruly, and his eyes were shining with the royal blue of a playful sea—all in all, more like a prince than anyone Molly had ever seen.

"So, I see you prefer this!" he boasted. "Just as did Maya! When we are together again, I will make your body soar with pleasure and you will forget that Lost Eagle's son ever existed. I will win you from him—first in battle, then in bed." He pulled her into his brawny arms and then frowned. "Your champion has awakened. This is not to be the night. Run to him, little witch. Tell him what has happened here. Make him burn with hatred for me! That is what has been missing until now."

The look of greedy anticipation in his eyes as he spoke of hatred and battle horrified her and, with a desperate burst of concentration, she wrenched herself free of him and, almost simultaneously, free of the dream.

She was drenched in sweat and the bedclothes were in complete disarray. With her heart pounding wildly, she pulled on a pair of white jeans and a blue and gold Cal sweatshirt. It would be three hours until morning—longer before Matthew would arrive for breakfast!—and she couldn't bear the wait. She would go to him, in the dark, Elizabeth and Brian notwithstanding, and beg him to kill the monster Aaric.

Then she heard the voices. Elizabeth and Matthew. Arguing. She hadn't heard his knock, but . . . Stifling a sob, she ran to the kitchen. *"Matthew!"*

Her champion embraced her tenderly. "You weren't in the meadow. There was a dragon there—an illusion of a dragon, I mean. I was fighting it, even though I knew it wasn't real, and all the time something in the air seemed horrifying and I was afraid for you. Are you all right?"

"Molly Sheridan!" Elizabeth snapped. "I won't have this nonsense. It's three o'clock in the morning! Tell your young man to come back at a decent hour."

"Grandma, please!" Molly couldn't stop the rush of tears as she clung to the front of Matthew's dark blue hooded sweatshirt. "Please let Matthew stay! I need him! I'm scared! *Please?"*

Elizabeth backed away in confusion. "This is intolerable," she whispered. "Brian wants me to be patient, but I can't stand this any longer."

"Grandma, I need Matthew."

"You don't need this . . . this . . . *legend-monger!* You need sleep!" She turned to Matthew. "I'm asking you to leave."

"If he goes, I go, too," Molly whispered.

The threat was effective. "Do your talking, then," Elizabeth nodded coolly. "I'll give you some privacy. But tomorrow, we'll settle this once and for all, or I'll be calling your father in Boston. Do you understand, young lady?"

Molly nodded and sank into a chair, accepting without hesitation the whiskey offered by Matthew. "It was him, Matthew."

"Aaric's descendant was in your dream again?"

"Not his descendant! It was Aaric *himself!*"

"Shhh, don't cry. Have another sip . . . My beautiful dream girl . . . I should have been there for you."

Her tears had stopped and she snuggled gratefully against his chest. "It was a nightmare, Matthew."

"Start at the beginning. Tell me everything that happened."

She buried her face against him, angry and humiliated, and unable to find the words. "He pretended to be you again," she began finally. "It was hateful."

"Did you try to stab him again?"

"No. I wish I had, but . . ." She forced herself to meet his concerned gaze. "This time, he was all bloody and injured . . . I thought it was you. This time, he was more convincing and he fooled me and then he . . . he raped me."

"What?"

"I thought it was you," she insisted weakly.

"You thought I would rape you?" Matthew shook his head. "That doesn't make sense."

"It wasn't rape exactly. He . . . he made love to me. I thought it was you."

"Oh." Matthew nodded, slightly dazed. "I get the picture." Wiping her damp cheek with his thumb he soothed, "It's over now. It was just a dream, Molly."

"He gloated. He made a fool of me. Of us. He said if he wins, he'll take over your body in real life. That's why he agreed to come here from the past. To live in our time. To be *you.*"

"And you're absolutely sure it was Aaric himself, not some impostor?"

"He told me . . ." She stopped, suddenly aware that Matthew's eyes had warmed with visions of revenge for his ancestor, and so she reminded him sharply, "He's a sorcerer! A very experienced sorcerer, not some twentieth century part-time warrior like we've been expecting."

"Like me?" Matthew smiled. "Don't worry, Valmain. I've trained as much as any man who's ever lived. I can handle him."

"You're underestimating him. He's tricky, and cruel, and—and—" To her dismay, she again burst into tears, this time of frustration and shame.

"Don't be so upset, Molly," Matthew whispered contritely. "It was only a dream."

"Not to him!"

"It wasn't sex to him. It was just a way to provoke *me* and to scare *you,* and we have to refuse to allow that kind of manipulation. We have to keep our heads."

"I can't believe this!" she wailed. "Aren't you angry? He expected you to react like my champion. My lover! Instead, you're . . . you're as calculating as he is! Why don't you hate him?" Her tears were replaced by righteous indignation. For that one moment, she wasn't sure who was the more hateful of the two men! "At least Aaric . . . at least *he* thinks I'm worth getting upset about. Or he has the decency to pretend to think I'm worth it."

"Decency?" Matthew murmured. "A minute ago you were hysterical because he treated you so villainously. Now he's the hero? Maybe I *should* be upset about this. Should I be jealous, Molly?"

"Better jealous than calm," she muttered. "Anyway, I *did* think it was you."

"He used you to get to me, and I guess he has gotten to me—to *us*—a little. He indulged himself with *my woman,* and that bothers me a lot, believe me, but we can't let him come between us. We need each other. And no matter what you think, I do love you, Molly." He kissed her cheek. "You shouldn't be sleeping alone. It doesn't make sense. Let's go to Limerick and get a room. I want us to be together tomorrow night, don't you?"

"Grandma will call my father," Molly protested uneasily. "You don't understand. I can't face him now, not with all this going on. I haven't told you very much about my family problems—"

"Brian explained it all to me last night."

"Oh?"

"You and your mother had the accident and you were both in the hospital. Your dad was home alone and some good-looking neighbor stopped in to offer her sympathy and they ended up having an affair. Right?"

"That's a gross oversimplification," she sighed, "but yes. That's how it went. Mother was dying in the hospital while Dad and Constance were being neighborly. Probably in *my* mother's house."

"And when your mother died, this Constance

turned up pregnant, so your dad had to marry her. It must have been tough."

"It was the worst day of my life," she corrected sadly. "I'll never forget how betrayed I felt."

"You were bereaved. Overwrought. It's understandable that you would overreact."

"Overreact?"

Matthew retreated hastily. "This isn't the time to deal with all that, Valmain. Let's figure out what to do about Aaric first. How about if we get married?"

"Married? You *are* a fanatic!" She could feel a smile tugging at the corners of her lips. "We hardly know each other!"

Matthew laughed. "How well do you have to know me?" He grabbed her with exaggerated passion and declared, "This is destiny, Valmain. You and me."

Molly shook her curls. "Destined for what? That's what I want to know. But I guess we could tell Grandma we're engaged or something. That might help her deal with all of this." The idea of being with him, twenty-four hours a day, was blessedly beginning to chase away the lingering image of Aaric. "We could say we want to see the rest of Ireland. Which is true, I guess. So I guess it's a good idea."

"There you go. You're thinking clearly again. Let's pack your things."

"It's not even four o'clock. You'd better go home and try to get some rest. Just don't dream again. And if you do . . ." She bit her lip.

"Go on."

"Matthew, please. Promise me you'll be careful! He's so intimidating! So huge!"

"Really? Describe him."

"His chest is massive. *Massive!* His arms are this

big around. I swear! His thighs are like pillars." She shook her head in confusion. She had, of course, been nearly frantic at the time, but the enemy *had* seemed huge!

Matthew was clearly amused. "Anything else bigger than mine that I should know about?"

"What?" She caught his meaning and jumped away. "Matthew Redtree! How dare you! Stop joking about that!"

"Come here," he grinned. "Don't be mad. I'm glad you're not frightened anymore."

"I'm disgusted! With you!"

"I noticed. And I prefer it to hysteria, but I'd rather you would just be calm. And strong. Cooperate with me, so we can defeat him. You want that, don't you?"

"Of course. I hate him."

"Control your hate, Molly. Try to focus. I need you."

"I need you too, Matthew." Wrapping her arms around his neck, she admitted, "I want you to fight him and I want you to kill him. You *have* to destroy that monster, now more than ever. You have to keep him away from me."

"I will. I promise."

"Okay." She remembered Elizabeth's threat and grimaced. "Now for my showdown with Grandma. Give me a little time alone with her, okay?"

"Sure. I'll just go for a run. But I'll be back at seven, so be ready."

Molly's head was throbbing as she watched him depart. This eruption of sex and violence in her life was proving to be too much for her. Not even one full day had passed since she'd parted with her virginity, and yet she was being asked to deal with a complex seduction and molestation by a demonic

stranger who had deceived and humiliated her. And
her actual lover was so preoccupied by his grand
view of the struggle that he couldn't seem to comprehend the enormity of her need for comfort and
reassurance.

She now hated Aaric as passionately as she loved
Matthew, but knew that much of her hatred
stemmed from the fact that Aaric had thrilled her.
Her own behavior and responses bothered her
deeply. Why hadn't she realized it wasn't Matthew?
The impostor had looked and sounded exactly like
Matthew, but his style—of speech and touch—
should have alerted her. Instead, she had actually
enjoyed the rougher, irreverent encounter. This was
the true humiliation. The true shame. She had enjoyed *not* being the curly-haired dream girl, and
Aaric had enjoyed *not* being noble and respectful.
They had enjoyed one another much too much
. . .

This is nonproductive, she scolded herself nervously. *You didn't know it was him. Aaric did a
reprehensible thing, and you were the victim. That's
what Matthew sees. That's why he isn't going wild
with jealousy. Follow his lead, Molly, or you're playing right into Aaric's hands.*

Aaric's hands . . . strong and rough and hungry
. . . and what about her *own* hand, boldly caressing
him as she had never yet caressed Matthew! Confused beyond the point of tears, she moved toward
the kitchen, intending to splash water on her face
before confronting her grandmother, when that
woman's tired voice murmured from behind her,
"Molly?"

She wanted to plead with Elizabeth to wait. To
back off. To offer comfort without judgment, before
the confusion became a true threat to her sanity.

Then she turned and flushed with concern at the elder woman's frail appearance. With her gray hair down around her shoulders, framing a face soft with lines and worry, she appeared vulnerable and helpless and, despite the fact that she was two full inches taller than her granddaughter, frail and tiny. A blaze of love brought with it renewed strength, enabling the beleaguered young woman to square her shoulders and summon a confident smile. Somehow she would find a way to reassure this tender-hearted woman, and then she would go to Matthew and plot the destruction of the monster Aaric.

Chapter Eight

Crossing quickly to her grandmother, Molly gathered her into an embrace. "Poor Grandma," she crooned. "I know I've worried you, but everything's fine. Please, please don't take my silly crying too seriously. I had an awful nightmare, but Matthew was so strong, and so sensible . . ."

"Sensible?" Elizabeth sobbed. "Him? He's . . . he's strange, Molly. He frightens me."

"Matthew?" Molly was honestly amazed. "If only you knew him better! He's the gentlest, kindest man."

"He should leave you alone. You came here for a rest. You needed a rest, and a chance to think, but instead he comes here, and pressures you, and frightens you, and now you're having nightmares." She pulled free of her granddaughter and stammered, "I meant what I said. I have to do what I think is right. I have to call your father. I'm going to insist he get on the next plane and come over. Even if you hate me forever, I have to do it."

"Hate you?" Molly sighed, guiding her toward the parlor sofa. "I could never hate you, Grandma. You're my family—my connection to Mom and all the happiness we knew when life was simple. I'll always love you."

Elizabeth was sobbing again. "I just can't deal with this alone!"

"Fine. Call Dad if you feel you need to talk to him, but before you do . . ." She took a deep breath, then blurted, "When Dad married Constance, with Mom's body still warm in the grave, he shattered my heart. I've been limping along—not really living at all. Now Matthew has somehow healed the hurt, and more than that, he's made me come to life again."

"Don't you see?" Elizabeth murmured, easing herself against a soft cushion. "That just isn't normal, Molly."

"My life hasn't been normal since the accident. It hasn't been *anything* since the accident." Kneeling before her, she took Elizabeth's worn hand in her own and whispered, "Don't call Dad. Even if he came on the next plane, I wouldn't talk to him. It would be a waste of time and money. Anyway," her chin jutted forward in gentle defiance, "he won't come. He never has, not in all these years."

Elizabeth's eyes widened. "Because you've made it clear you wanted him to stay away. But if he thought you were in danger . . ."

"Danger? From Matthew? Grandma, he's my protector. My lover. My world. *Try* to understand how much I need him."

"I'm trying." Pulling a lacy handkerchief from the pocket of her dressing gown, she dabbed at her eyes, then patted the cushion beside herself and tried to smile. "Sit with me a minute, Molly. I have something to tell you."

"Okay." Molly slipped onto the sofa and snuggled against her. "You can tell me anything, Grandma. Right?"

"This is something I never intended to share with you, or with anyone else, not even your mother, and she had a right to know, but . . . well, anyway . . ." She cleared her throat in nervous preparation. "When we were discussing your father the other day, I told you everyone makes mistakes, and you should forgive him."

"I remember."

"I almost told you then . . . Well, that I've made a few mistakes of my own, and one of those mistakes has haunted me for more years than you can imagine. If I was able to forgive your father for his unfaithfulness to my daughter, maybe it was because I had made a mistake that was eerily similar to your father's."

"Similar?" Molly stifled a groan, unprepared to hear about her grandmother's "mistake," which had apparently been some kind of love affair. And given the fact that Elizabeth had married when still quite young, the granddaughter suspected the affair had been extramarital and a betrayal of her beloved grandfather's trust. It seemed impossible! Her grandparents' marriage had been so perfect! But then, of course, so had her parents'.

"I met a man, and he was charming. Compelling. I made a mistake, and then I handled the aftermath badly, hurting innocent people in the process. You're young and inexperienced, Molly. You don't know how quickly an innocent mistake can spiral out of control. I hope you *never* have to learn it, but—" Her eyes turned a steely, determined shade of blue. "I don't want you to rush into anything with this Matthew. He's mesmerized you, and I know from experience how exciting that can be. I also know how dreadfully it can turn out."

"You're comparing Matthew and me to your . . . your mistake? That's not fair, Grandma. First of all," she tried for a teasing tone, "Matthew isn't charming at all. Or mesmerizing, for that matter. If he were, you'd like him more, right? He's actually pretty obnoxious and unromantic, and he's not sweeping me off my feet or turning my head with compliments, believe me."

Elizabeth smiled reluctantly. "I'm serious, Molly. If you rush into this—"

"Rush? I've known him for months, Grandma. I sat in his lectures, listening to the gentle love in his voice when he told his legends . . ."

"But he didn't know you existed," Elizabeth reminded her. "Except in some bizarre dream. That's what he sees in you, Molly. Not a flesh-and-blood woman, with needs and weaknesses and a tender heart, but a girl from a dream. If you didn't resemble that dream of his, would he still have fallen in love with you?"

Molly fidgeted, uncomfortable with this line of reasoning, which she had been resisting so carefully over the last two days. "What difference does it make what brought us together?" she responded finally. "The point is, we met—under bizarre circumstances, yes, but we met, and we fell in love."

"And? Has he asked you to marry him?" When Molly fidgeted again, Elizabeth sighed. "I was afraid of that. Just promise me you won't do anything rash. Don't elope, or go off with him to anywhere too . . . isolated. Stay in touch with me."

"I promise," Molly smiled through a haze of tears. "Do you think I could get married without you there? I'm going to throw you the bouquet, so you'll stop giving Brian such a hard time. It's all decided. Anyway," she added thoughtfully, "I'm engaged to Matthew, but we're in no rush to get married. There are a million things we need to discuss before we make that kind of a commitment." She blushed under her grandmother's probing gaze. "I love him, but I'm still me, Grandma—organized and cautious. Plus, I haven't finished my education yet, so marriage and children are definitely far in the future. Okay?"

"I feel a little better," Elizabeth admitted. "Would you like to ask Matthew to move in here for the rest of the visit? He could . . ." she was clearly struggling with the words, "share the guest room with you."

"That's so sweet," Molly hedged, "but I've been wanting to tour around a little, and so, as long as you're in such an understanding mood . . ." She sank into Elizabeth's arms. "I'm not nearly as confident as I've been pretending, but one thing is for sure. I trust Matthew with my life *and* my heart. You and Matthew are the only people in the whole world I can turn to. The only people I love, and who love me." Pulling herself together, she added softly, "Thanks for being here, Grandma. And thanks for telling me about your 'mistake.' Believe me, I understand better than you think. In my nightmare, I made a mistake that felt very real at the time, and very disturbing, and I wouldn't wish that feeling on anyone, even Dad and Constance. So," she hugged her staunchly, "I'll think about everything you said. I promise."

Matthew had tied his knapsack to a tree limb in a pasture outside of Limerick and was practicing his kicks while his barefooted dream girl paced anxiously. Blow after blow landed on the leather target as the warrior worked to perfect his almost flawless technique.

At any other time the outlandish situation would have amused Molly. Matthew had suggested this "picnic" as a means of soothing their frayed nerves in preparation for the battle, which he anticipated would take place that very evening. Taking the suggestion to heart, she had purchased an intricate green and white quilt, along with a willow basket filled with breads and cheeses, and then had turned her attentions to herself, cutting off her white jeans until they approximated a pair of sexy shorts, then pulling her hair into playful ponytail. She had never picnicked with a lover before and had been certain the experience would be unforgettable.

This was not quite what she had planned, and while Matthew worked out his frustrations, she found her own growing. Somewhere along the line she had completely lost control of her life, and her grandmother's warnings were echoing in her ears. She *could* make a mistake, and hurt innocent people, and carry regret with her for a lifetime, if she didn't somehow manage to extricate herself from this quagmire of conflicting demands and bizarre occurrences.

"What are you thinking about, Valmain?" Matthew demanded cheerfully, without taking his eyes from his target.

"I'm thinking about Grandma," she admitted, adding mournfully, "She looked so hurt when we left."

"Yeah, I noticed. We'll make it up to her, I promise." He aimed a final pulverizing kick at the branch itself and whooped loudly when it splintered on impact.

Molly tried to ignore his fanatical display. "Ever since the accident, she's been my only true family."

"But now I'm your family, too, right?" He paused in his workout to demand, "We're engaged, aren't we?"

"I guess so."

"Stop worrying about Aaric," he instructed briskly. "Talk to me. One good thing about us legend-mongers, we're great listeners."

She laughed in spite of her turmoil. "Okay, legend-monger. Give your poor feet a rest and come sit with me." She knelt on their picnic quilt and gathered up the wrappers that had accompanied their light supper. "What should we talk about?"

He stretched out beside her, his head supported by his bent elbow. "Tell me about the accident."

"No." Bowing to the determination in his eyes, she acknowledged, "It was awful. Mom and I were trapped . . . the car had gone completely out of control . . . My legs were numb, and Mom was delirious . . ."

"Take a deep breath," he ordered. "Better?"

"Yes." She took a second breath, struggling to control the image of pain. "Sorry. I always get so upset."

"You need to talk about it, so you can put it to rest. It's been four years, Molly."

"I know. I tell myself that all the time."

"But you loved your mother, right? I understand. Honestly. Just talk to me. Let me help."

"I loved my mother, and I loved my father. When I get upset, it's not just over losing Mom. It's him, Matthew." She raised her eyes to his. "You talk about betrayal. Maya betrayed Lost Eagle. Val-

main betrayed Maya. I *know* how they felt because
. . ."

"Because your father betrayed you?"

"He betrayed my mother. And me. You call me
your dream girl; well, . . . he was my dream father.
Loving and funny and strong and handsome and
talented. He spoiled me, I guess, and I adored him.
You can't imagine how I felt when I found out he'd
been having an affair. Grandma calls it a mistake,
but to me it was so much more. It was a violation
of trust so cruel and so unexpected . . ."

"Did you know the woman?"

"Constance?" She almost snarled the name, completely abandoning her reflective mood. "She lived
right next door! Isn't that disgusting? She used to
come over in the afternoon and have coffee with
Mom, and she used to flatter me—offered to take
me shopping or do my hair and told me how 'adorable' I was, and all the time—" Anger, so strong it
almost burned, welled up in her and she dug her
fingernails into her palms. "I *still* can't believe it."

"When did you find out about her and your father?"

"Dad acted strangely the whole time I was in the
hospital. I thought he was grieving for Mom like I
was, but he was actually just trying to get up the
nerve to tell me Constance was pregnant."

"But he was also grieving your mother," Matthew corrected firmly. "You can't honestly doubt
that, Molly. Give him a break. Just because he had
an affair doesn't negate years of marriage."

"I'll never forgive him. It was all so convenient
for him! A beautiful new wife . . . a new baby . . .
a new life."

"Which, according to Brian, he wanted you to
share."

"As though I could?" she glared. "I hated them. I hated Constance, for seducing him, and Dad for being weak."

"Is she really beautiful?"

"As though that might justify it?" she snapped.

"No. I didn't say that." He patted her cheek apologetically. "What about their baby? She's your half-sister, right?"

"Her name's Nicole. Nicole Sheridan. She's three and a half. I've seen pictures."

"I'd like to see one."

Molly grimaced. "She looks a little bit like I did as a kid. Only she's blonder."

"Cute, huh?"

"Cut it out, Matthew Redtree," she warned. "I don't blame Nicole, of course, but I won't be a member of their happy little family. I just won't. Case closed."

"How long were you trapped in the car after the accident?"

Molly flushed. "It felt like hours, but they told me later it was only forty-five minutes. Forty-five endless minutes. My legs were twisted, but I wasn't in pain. Mom was in agony. Delirious. Dying, I guess. I couldn't help her. I tried, but I couldn't."

"You did help her, Valmain. It helped her to hear your voice. To know she wasn't alone at the end. And to know—to hope—that you would survive." His eyes were shining with love. "Her strong, pure-hearted daughter. Brian says your recovery was almost miraculous, according to Elizabeth."

"They said I wouldn't walk, but I *had* to. I had to walk away—from Dad and Constance and Boston. I would have died of a broken heart if I'd stayed there."

"I'm glad you left. I'm glad you went to Berkeley, to find me."

"I went to Berkeley to study, but," she took his face between her hands and sighed, "I'm glad I found you, too. I've been a little lonely, I guess. I just didn't realize it."

"You needed me. I needed you, too, but I knew it, thanks to my dream."

"I guess I was lucky I didn't know. All those years, my dream seemed so benign. If I'd known I was preparing for a battle . . ."

"You could have trained, like I did," he suggested mischievously. "Judo and karate, right?"

"Please, spare me." She laughed lightly at the very thought. "If I had known judo or karate the day Dad and Constance came to my hospital room and made their little wedding announcement, I'd be serving time in a Massachusetts prison right now." She winced. "Listen to me! You're a violent influence, Son of Lost Eagle."

"Call me that again. It's inspiring."

"I'll call you it again when we're back in our room," she promised with a blush. "We really should be getting back there, Matthew. It's almost time . . ."

"Time to dream?" He pulled her close. "One last dream, Molly, and then we'll be free of it. I'll make it all up to you. I swear it."

"When I'm in your arms," she whispered, "I can handle anything."

"Do you mean that? Are you ready?"

"Yes, Matthew. I'm ready."

"Good girl." Brushing her hair back from her cheeks, he studied her wistfully. "For years I thought winning this battle with Aaric was my only purpose in life. Now I see that by protecting you,

I'm not just avenging the past—I'm protecting our future—our children and their destiny. Do you see?"

"Our children? Oh, Matthew . . ."

"I know. Don't worry." He stood and pulled her to her feet. "Kerreya wouldn't have made me your champion unless she thought I could pull it off."

Molly traced the line of a muscle along his lean, tanned forearm. "My champion. There isn't a doubt in my mind, Matthew. When Kerreya chose you, she knew what she was doing."

"And when Kerreya's father chose *you* to receive his power, after so many centuries of waiting, he made the right choice, too. I have the feeling that, together, we're unbeatable." He eyed the setting sun. "Go on back to the room without me. I'll just clean up this mess and take a quick jog down the road, then I'll join you."

"Training right up until the last moment? Aren't you afraid you'll get too tired?"

"The more tired I am, the more soundly I'll sleep."

Molly shrugged. "Don't be too long. I'll take a bath, I guess, and then I'll read."

"I'll be back by then, I promise. Just don't fall asleep without me," he added teasingly.

When she wrinkled her nose in exaggerated disdain, he laughed aloud, amazed as always by the playful side to this alliance and, as he watched her stroll away from him, heading toward the inn, his gaze settled on her bare, untanned legs and he almost sighed aloud, remembering how those legs—the loveliest he had ever seen—had distracted him more than once during his lectures at Berkeley.

Long legs, bare feet—his reaction in those days had been sexist and shallow, he knew, and Molly deserved better. She wasn't just a pretty woman, she was a sorceress, at least of sorts; a scientist in the making; a pacifist, strong and pure of heart; and, above all, she was the curly-haired, steady-eyed ally who would share in his triumph over Aaric the Moonshaker.

A lifetime of discipline and training had enabled Matthew to gain almost total control over his weaknesses and appetites, to the point where he could endure hours of activity in the blazing sun without faltering; hours in the freezing dark, asleep on bare ground under hostile conditions without shivering; and hours in the presence of female temptation without weakening unduly. Of course, like any healthy warrior, he was at his best, skill-wise, when he was well-rested, well-fed, and sexually satisfied. Nevertheless, a true champion knew that conditions were not always so ideal and prepared himself accordingly. That training had enabled him to offer Molly Sheridan comfort during this last, vital day, without making any demands, subtle or otherwise, that might resurrect memories of the Moonshaker's assault. Undoubtedly, Aaric had been rough with her—she had almost painstakingly avoided any details of his actual technique, but her anger and nervousness told Matthew all he needed to know, and so he had respected her need to heal, in mind and body, and had kept his hands to himself.

Her legs had all but disappeared from view and he sighed once again. Never in his wildest imaginings had he envisioned marriage to the dream girl as a possibility! In fact, he had intended to avoid serious romantic entanglements completely until after the battle of vengeance, but had occasionally pondered the attributes he might desire in a mate, always concocting for himself a warrior woman—tall and lean, with rock-hard thighs and small breasts, trained and cross-trained to perfection. Now he realized sheepishly that he had been blind to his true need—his *spiritual* need—for steady blue eyes to inspire and encourage him; a soft body to nestle gratefully against him; a soft voice to whisper to him in the night . . . in his arms . . .

The sex itself was superfluous to the relationship, although Molly had responded well to it and it seemed to be a healthy component of their evolving commitment. Was that still the case? he wondered. How badly had the Moonshaker's heavy-handed abuse of her trust tainted the gentle lovemaking that had calmed and balanced her so efficiently? Would she cringe now at the thought of physical intimacy?

If so, Matthew would understand, and comfort, and restrain his baser instincts for as long as required—even forever, if necessary. It would be a small, albeit frustrating, price to pay for a lifetime with the descendant of a sorceress and a king. He would be patient, turning his attentions instead to her other needs, giving priority to the rift with her father—*that* situation had festered for far too long, and had undoubtedly interfered with her natural balance. The family would be reunited, and the half-sisters would meet for the first time, and little Nicole could even be in their wedding!

And then they would travel the world together, and he would entertain his bride, and instruct her, and eventually begin to train her. Not physically, of course. Swimming had kept her trim and healthy, and her legs—well, they were clearly inherited from beautiful Kerreya herself! No amount or form of exercise could explain or create *them*. And they were doubly miraculous, given the fact that they had been mangled in an accident just four years earlier!

There was no need to physically train her, but her birthright had been neglected for too long. He would educate her, using myths and anecdotes, thereby enabling her to connect with her dormant magical powers. Or perhaps that moment would come sooner—perhaps even that very night!—for he suspected that, once they stood together in the dream meadow, he could coax true miracles from her, and perhaps he could also coax some magic for himself from the amulet!

A shiver of excitement ran through him as he gathered his shoes and knapsack. It was time—for the dream, and the battle, and the victory. He was the Valmain champion and this was the night for which he had waited all his life.

Molly had bathed and now, clad in her white robe, was fluffing her damp curls while bemoaning the fact that she hadn't seen Matthew glance, even once, at her legs during their entire picnic despite the clear opportunity afforded by her newly cropped shorts. Apparently, he wasn't a leg man, which was unfortunate, given the fact that they were the only feature of her anatomy that had attracted consistent comment over the years. She considered the rest of herself to be fairly standard-issue. Her waist was trim but hardly exceptional, her breasts full and firm but far from newsworthy, and her hips—well, her hips were just hips, and it seemed unlikely in any event that Matthew Redtree was a 'hip man,' and so they were irrelevant to this self-assessment.

He hadn't behaved like a lover during the picnic,

and she wondered if he was trying to focus on the upcoming battle, or whether it bothered him that Aaric had touched her, or whether he just hadn't been interested in her that way, given the myriad of distractions confronting them. Her grandmother's challenge came to mind. Was Matthew Redtree falling into love with Molly Sheridan—student, seamstress and future scientist—or was he drawn only to the dream girl . . . the sorceress . . . the princess in need of a champion . . . Did he see the woman at all?

It was both bizarre and unsettling that Aaric the Moonshaker had, at least momentarily, perceived her in a way that Matthew Redtree could not. Although she knew the fair-haired sorcerer's appreciation had been born primarily from deprivation—thousands of years of deprivation, in fact!—there had been something else, fleeting yet indisputable, in his interest. He had responded to *her,* rather than simply her role, and it had been both flattering and reassuring. And then, of course, it had been humiliating. So profoundly humiliating that even now she almost shuddered at the memory of it all. Love had turned so cruelly to fear . . . and then the sorcerer had revealed his true form, and the fear had become abject terror . . .

"Valmain?"

She spun toward the voice, grateful to be rescued from the images that were plaguing her. There he stood—her champion!——and in three long strides he crossed the room to her and gathered her into his arms.

Chapter Nine

"Cry if you want, Molly," Matthew whispered, waltzing her gently toward the bed. "I *hate* what he did to you, and I swear I'll kill him for you."

"I don't need to cry," she murmured, mesmerized by the odors and sensations overpowering her as she basked in his arms. Beneath his white shirt, still slightly damp with perspiration, the muscles of his chest provided a rock-solid resting place for both her cheek and her confused imagination. More than anything on earth she wanted this—to be in this man's arms . . . in his life . . . in his dreams and in his bed. "Just hold me, Matthew."

"Don't worry, I'm right here." Easing her carefully away from himself, just a bit, he urged her under the bed covers, then slipped off his running shoes and joined her, cuddling her against himself once more. "We'll talk, until you feel strong enough for the dream. Or, if you can't handle it tonight," his tone was wistful but committed, "we'll stay up all night, and try again tomorrow. How's that?"

"Matthew . . ." She slid her arms around his neck and smiled sheepishly. "You just caught me at a bad moment, but I'm fine, really. I love this," she added, brushing her lips across his. "I love you."

"You're amazing." His fingers played in the damp curls along her cheek. "Have I ever told you you have the most incredible eyes? They're so inspiring."

"My hair and my eyes," she nodded, euphoric at the nearness of him. "Is there anything from my neck down that interests you?"

"Your pure heart?" he teased. "Or are you flirting with me?" When she blushed, he shook his head and quickly disrobed. "I thought that incident with Aaric would have soured you on sex for a while." His hand moved to untie the belt at her waist. "Are you sure about this?"

"Are you?" she countered wearily. "How do you feel about the fact that . . . well, that another man touched me?"

"He never touched you," Matthew reminded her firmly. "That was a dream, and he was an illusion of me. He never touched you. Not here," his lips played along her neck, "or here," he was nibbling at an erect nipple, "or here . . ."

His mouth had returned to cover hers with a kiss reminiscent of an evening an eternity earlier, in a weapon-filled room in the Berkeley hills. Reverence and adoration mingled with anticipation so acute that Molly's entire body ached to be covered with similar tributes. Had she ever dared wished for more than this? Had she compared Aaric's feverish groping with this charismatic celebration?

His lips were traveling again, and the effect, both energizing and immobilizing, was exquisite torture. She thought of the exotic spiders that paralyze their victims with venom then take their time, lingering over them while they lay helpless under their spell. Those victims undoubtedly craved deliverance in much the same way Molly now craved her lover's entry and the monumental release that would result.

This was not the greedy lovemaking she had seen so often portrayed in films. Matthew had apparently seen other, more beautiful films, in which love itself became an art form, expressed in slow motion, drawing intensity from the sheer agony of the wait. Despite her fervent need to express herself in return, she dared not disturb the delicious balance he was so intricately maintaining. So close to the edge of ecstasy, poised at the gates of paradise, and yet dreading the moment when it would be over . . .

And then his mouth was kissing hers again, with a hunger that made her frantic with need, and as she wrapped her long legs around him and moaned his name, he whispered, "I'll kill that bastard for you tonight, Molly. I *swear* it." Then he entered her and brought her into ecstasy so electric and complete that any doubt she had had as to the depth of his love or the scope of this magical night vanished. This man was indeed a champion—*her* champion!—and with this consummate act of love and commitment, destiny's long-awaited drama had officially begun.

She stood alone in the dream, beyond the shadows of the grassy hills, and fluffed her shimmering cape with half-hearted confidence. This was no longer a fragrant wonderland; it was a battleground.

Still, this was *her* dream. It had been a source of comfort during her childhood, and even now, on the eve of battle, it was home in a way that Boston or Berkeley were not. This dream was her legacy from Kerreya and the old sorcerer, and she wanted to be worthy of their trust, for her champion's sake, if for no other reason.

Aaric the Moonshaker had called her a witch. Did she have powers that could aid Matthew Redtree? One thing was certain—as long as Aaric existed only in her dream, he dared not kill her. If he wanted his plan to succeed, he needed to keep Molly alive as desperately as he needed to kill the warrior-descendant of Lost Eagle. In the meantime, she was providing a venue for the battle, but could she do more? Could she affect the outcome of this conflict? Did she have magical powers? Shouldn't she at least try to find out?

Aaric had altered his own appearance twice, taking Matthew's form in order to humiliate Molly. Now she would attempt to do likewise. If she could appear as Matthew—if there were *two* Matthews, and Aaric didn't know which one was Molly—he would be temporarily thwarted, unwilling to guess wrong and kill the woman in whose mind he existed.

She concentrated, alert to any sensation of power. There was nothing. Then she raised her arms toward the sky and issued a silent shaky command that she be transformed. Again, there was nothing—no surge of power, no sense of oneness with the universe, no vision or enlightenment.

"Daughter of Kerreya," a soft voice teased. "Are you attempting to summon the Moonshaker?"

She pulled her cape close, remembering their intimacy, and glared. "I was trying to get *rid* of you."

"Ah." The fair-haired warrior stepped closer and surveyed her with cold blue eyes. "Where is your champion? I am restless for the kill."

It sent a chill throughout her, but her trembling was from rage rather than fear. "I hate you," she whispered. "I command you to *leave my dream.*"

For an instant his eyes warmed. "You are so like my beautiful Maya. She would have been proud of you, Princess. She would have wanted me to allow you to live, and so I shall."

"If you kill me, you're history. You can't afford to hurt me. And if you lay one finger on Matthew," her voice grew resonant, "I'll kill myself, and you'll die with me! I swear that!"

"No!" His command boomed and seemed to echo off the grassy mounds, and when his huge hands gripped her arms, she went numb with terror and despair. He was power incarnate—evil, focused power, intent upon victory. And he knew her shortcomings and fears—from their lovemaking or from her ancestry or perhaps from the inexperience in her every word and look.

He knew her, but she did not know him. She did not know Matthew Redtree. She did not even know herself. Years of study and quiet observation had come to naught and she was reborn in ignorance in a heroic world that had marked her as pawn rather than heroine.

"He is coming," Aaric hissed. "Tremble for him, Princess. Show him that even now I am victorious." His hand moved to her throat and he wrenched her around, pressing the back of her head against his leather-strapped chest, displaying her horror-filled eyes for her champion.

Matthew Redtree's ordinarily balanced countenance contorted with fury. "Take your hands off her, Moonshaker!"

"Throw your weapons aside," Aaric countered briskly. He watched with a satisfied smirk as first the bola, then the bow and quiver, were thrown a distance away. When Matthew seemed unable to part with the obsidian dagger, the fair-haired sorcerer clucked in feigned sympathy. "It is not to be, son of my old enemy. Lost Eagle shaped that weapon when he had seen only ten summers. It could prove a nuisance at most, but I will not allow it." He grabbed a handful of Molly's curls and wrenched her head back harder against his chest. "The blade for the beauty. Throw it aside."

"He won't hurt me, Matthew! If I die, *he* dies. Don't let him . . . aughhh!" The scarred fingers of their enemy had crushed the wind from her throat and she struggled and gasped in vain.

Matthew quickly threw the black-bladed dagger to the ground. "Now leave her alone, you bastard!"

Aaric laughed. "Amusing. You are an interesting opponent. I will enjoy killing you." He turned Molly toward himself and grinned. "Did you tell him everything, Princess? Did you tell him what you said to me?"

"Shut up!" Matthew ordered.

"She told me it was superior lovemaking. Superior to any you had shared with her. Ask her to deny that."

"You used magic on her," Matthew agreed stiffly. "That's the only way you can outdo me. It was your tactic with Maya, too, I'll bet. You're pathetic."

Aaric's face darkened. "Enough talking. Relinquish the amulet."

"No!" Molly wailed. "Matthew, no!"

It is useless to you," Aaric taunted. "You have not discovered its secret. Throw it aside before I use my teeth on your woman's face."

Matthew removed the amulet from his pouch and tossed it after the bola. "Now release Molly," he growled.

"*Molly?*" A broad grin spread across Aaric's face. "A preposterous name for such a temptress." Planting a rough kiss on her mouth, he then threw her unceremoniously to the side and the warriors stood eye to eye.

Matthew did not seem at all intimidated by Aaric's startling appearance. Instead, he seemed simply challenged. Yet for all of her champion's bravado, Molly had no doubt that, barring a miracle, he would be killed. It was not merely the contrast in body types that filled her with dread. She knew Matthew's leaner, more tapered form was both cause and effect of his prowess, and had watched him practice over the last several days, kicking and striking at imaginary enemies with startling power and grace.

All of this seemed for naught in the face of Aaric's masterful presence. He was perhaps only two inches taller than Matthew, yet appeared to tower over him as he taunted and circled with clear elation. *He's killed before,* Molly realized. *Many times.* Undoubtedly, Matthew had not. More important, Matthew seemed the personification of all that was honorable and civilized, while Aaric fairly reeked of infinite lust and hunger. An animal with the densely muscled body of a giant and the deadly tricks of an unprincipled sorcerer . . .

Matthew landed the first blow with a well-aimed kick, which seemed to impress rather than intimidate his foe. "Excellent!" Aaric boomed. "This was not the way of your fathers! You have surpassed them, *but not the Moonshaker!*" As though to prove this boast, he brought his huge forearm across Matthew's chest, knocking him to the ground. Matthew rolled, his eye on the dagger, but just as he might have reached it, the weapon vanished, appearing instead in Aaric's huge hand.

"No!" Molly shrieked. "It's an illusion! Matthew!" Her champion seemed oblivious to her as he

rushed at his foe, tackling him to the ground despite
the threat of the cold obsidian blade. Whether illusion or not, Matthew was quickly bloodied, while
Aaric seemed only invigorated by the struggle. Desperate to assist, Molly watched for an opportunity
to retrieve the weapons Matthew had abandoned,
despite the fact that she had no idea how to wield
them. In any event, her feet seemed rooted to the
ground with fear and uncertainly.

Never in her life had she seen a fight of any kind.
No boxing matches or wrestling events, not even
violent movie scenes, from which she had always
averted her eyes while covering her ears in intellec-
tual repulsion. Now she couldn't afford the luxury
of looking away. In fact, she needed to become an
active participant. "Don't panic!" she pleaded with
herself. "Aaric called your dream power valuable.
Prove it! Use it!"

She dived for the abandoned dagger and clutched
it to her heart. The blade, chipped and shaped in
Lost Eagle's youth . . . *He was ten years old,* she
panicked, *but he already knew how to fight! I'm almost twenty-two and I'm useless. Unless, of course,*
she added sarcastically, *I can sew my way out of this.*

Or had she done just that? For seventeen years,
hadn't she sewn information into the fabric of her
cape? She whirled it from her shoulders and sank to
the ground, spreading the folds as Aaric had done.
It was all there! Stories . . . clues . . . legends . . .

A loose piece of thread caught her eye and she
tried to break it off but it cut a deep gash in her
finger, and so she pulled it. Cautiously. Anxiously.
It was long and shining, and as keenly edged as a
sword, and she suddenly knew exactly what she
needed to do. She would wrap the ends around her

hands, tightly, and pull the taut line around Aaric's neck. She would *strangle* him!

When she tried to approach the warriors, a huge coiled serpent appeared from nowhere, hissing vehemently. She jumped back, trembling even after she had realized that it was simply one of the Moonshaker's damnable illusions.

"Stay back!" Matthew ordered.

Her champion's hoarse, almost exhausted voice shattered the last of her composure and she shrieked his name in despair. Their eyes met, for one instant, and in that instant she knew he had lost hope.

"It can't be so," she whispered suddenly. "All of this, for nothing? All of his training, all of my sewing, all of our dreams? It can't be that we never had a chance. And if we *had* a chance, we still *have* it." Her mind raced. "In the dream, I held the spool and he held the thread." Diving again for the discarded weapons, she retrieved the amulet and twisted several lengths of the thread around it. The other end was still attached to her cape, which she quickly draped around her shoulders. She would wear the cape, throw the amulet, and hope for a miracle.

"Matthew?"

He spun toward her and she almost shrieked again, this time in response to the grit-tinged blood that painted his face like the red ochre of his ancestors. Then she hurled the amulet and, when Matthew caught it and whooped, she felt an instant of respite from despair. He approved . . . he understood . . .

In fact, he seemed to read her mind, lunging for the confused sorcerer-enemy and viciously wrapping the razor-sharp metallic thread around his neck. Aaric gasped, and, as blood began to spurt from the gash in his throat, he vanished.

Molly sank to her knees, clutching the cape to her heart as relief—in the form of wrenching sobs—overcame her. Matthew stood and stared for one last moment at the spot where his ancient foe had stood, then ran to gather his dream girl into his bloodstained arms.

"You're hurt!" she wailed. "He was *killing* you!"

"I feel great! I swear it, Molly. We won!"

"He was so vicious. Oh, Matthew, look at this!" She traced the line of an ugly gash along his forearm, then moved her hand to his bruised cheek, exclaiming, "And this! Oh, Matthew."

"I've had worse," he assured her, then laughed at the skepticism in her teary eyes. "Okay, maybe I've never been this jacked up, but I *feel* great. I've won fights before, but this! This was a war!"

"It seemed so . . ."

"Hopeless?" He grappled her against his chest. "For a while, I think it was. But the image of you and me, connected again by the thread and the amulet, was too awesome for words! It was brilliant, Valmain. It intimidated him for a second, and a second was all we needed."

"You killed him," she whispered as the reality began to hit her. "I've never been so proud. Or grateful. Oh, Matthew, thank you."

"Don't cry," he soothed, kissing her eyelids tenderly. "It's over, Molly. All over."

"You killed him," she repeated softly. "You *had* to kill him."

"He was so incredibly strong," Matthew admitted. "And the amulet didn't help at all. I was hoping he had just been bluffing about that! But did you *see* him? I could have trained forever and not been ready for that body combined with those powers!"

"His power was from magic. But you! I was so proud! You fought so bravely."

"But he would have killed me, if it weren't for you." He stroked her hair gently. "It's over. *Really* over. Stop shaking. You were great. Again. You really kept your head. He wasn't expecting that!" His voice was filled with reverence. "We were quite a team. You came through for me, Valmain, like a true fighter."

"I've never felt so bloodthirsty," she admitted, fingering the hem of her cape unhappily. "It's unsettling."

"You lost your balance?" he teased gently. "Over me? I'm flattered." Pushing her back into the grass, he admitted, "I lost it once or twice myself. When he choked you . . ."

"And when he said I liked sex with him better than with you?" She tried to smile up at her lover as she explained, "I did tell him it was the best time, that time, and I've felt guilty about saying it ever since, but now I know why it was so wonderful. It was because I thought he was you, and you had just killed *him,* and *that* was such an inspiring aphrodisiac."

"In other words?"

The smile came easily now. "I'm afraid so. You just killed him, and now you've got your hands full. Make love to me, champion. Unless you're too injured, of course."

"Are you kidding? I want my reward now. But just so I don't bleed all over you and your cape, why don't we meet back in bed?"

"My cape?" For the first time she noticed its soiled condition, along with the flawed area from which she had pulled the silver thread. "My poor, beautiful cape!" Fresh tears streamed down her cheeks. "It's ruined! All those years of hard work!"

"It's not ruined at all," Matthew soothed. "Look here. This part's in perfect shape. It tells about Lost Eagle."

His enthusiasm was contagious. "No! Read this part. About my great-great-et-cetera-grandfather. He was so powerful! Much more than Aaric or the daughters. Matthew! Pay attention!"

"You read about your ancestors and I'll read about mine. This record of Lost Eagle's exploits is unbelievable." Matthew scanned the cape for a few more seconds then smiled mischievously. "Or . . . ? Maybe it's time to forget about ancestors and start working on descendants?"

"Shouldn't we *date* first? Then get engaged? Then married? Before we have descendants?"

"I've been ready, remember? I'll marry you as soon as we wake up."

She gave the cape a final hug. "I wonder if we'll miss all this."

"We'll be able to come back here, I'm sure of that. I've studied dreams for years, Molly. You'll see this whenever you want, but for now," his eyes flashed with inspiration, "wake up!"

Molly eagerly complied and found the first rays of Irish dawn subtly lighting their cozy room. She stretched, wiped the sleep from her eyes, and smiled at Matthew's quiet slumber. He had been in such a hurry, and now he was sound asleep! She would fix that! Kissing him with teasing thoroughness, she whispered his name and an amorous invitation while running her fingernails provocatively down his torso.

But something was wrong. He was too still. Almost lifeless. Unreachable. "Matthew!" Aaric's prediction was suddenly more than a memory. Aaric would win. He would kill Matthew. He would take his form. And Molly would never know for sure!

They were fighting again. It was suddenly a fact, not a guess. Aaric had tricked them! He had waited for Molly and her dream power to depart, knowing Matthew couldn't win without it!

Burying her face in the pillow, she desperately willed herself to sleep, but her head was pounding while her imagination ran wild. She had no idea how much time she had. Panic soon turned to terror, making sleep more impossible than ever. He would be killed. It was almost a certainty. He would be killed, and it would be left to Molly to mete out the long-overdue vengeance against the Moonshaker. And for that, she needed her dagger . . .

"You impress me, Son of Lost Eagle. You have trained your body well. I am grateful for that."

Still clutching Molly's cape in his hands, Matthew had leapt to his feet and was staring, speechless at the sight of the Moonshaker, alive and apparently refreshed.

"That body will be mine before this night is through," Aaric continued cheerfully. "I will use it to fight in your world, and I will use it to make love to your woman."

"Just shut up and fight," Matthew suggested, drawing upon his hatred and his years of training to achieve renewed balance and confidence. "I killed you once. I'll kill you again."

Aaric chuckled. "When I join your princess, I will make her forget you. Shall I tell you how?"

"Shut *up!*"

"I will rub the amulet between her legs. The sensation of magic is strong there. I would often please Maya with similar toys, and she would lose her mind and will to me."

"You'll never touch Molly again!" Matthew glared.

"It is inevitable," the brawny sorcerer corrected. "I am the world's most powerful magician." As though to prove the boast, he raised his scarred arms toward the skies, which darkened ominously, while the air became thick with stifling humidity and the odor of death and decay.

Shit, Matthew thought, as his ordinarily well-trained pulse began to race. He needed Molly *now.* Lightning flashed, distant voices shrieked, and the earth beneath his feet began to buckle and rumble. From the corner of his eye he could make out slithering, threatening forms—forms of loathsome, lecherous demons—and while he knew they were simply Aaric's illusions, they made his flesh crawl. Forcing himself to turn and confront the images, he took comfort in the silky feel of the lustrous white fabric in his hands. Perhaps Molly herself was gone, but at least he had her cape, with the silver embroidery and the amulet, hanging by a thread . . .

Noting the source of Matthew's renewed confidence, Aaric chuckled again and whistled softly. Almost immediately, an image of Molly—a nude image with exaggerated curves—stepped from behind a tree and smiled seductively—toward the Moonshaker. "Aaric," she moaned, moving to the fair-haired warrior and rubbing herself wantonly against his hip. "Take me again. *You* are my champion now."

"You asshole!" Matthew growled. "That's not Molly! That's *your* kind of woman. A whore!" He chose his next words carefully, knowing they could be his last. "You call yourself a champion? The only way you could have Maya was to murder Lost Eagle, the man she loved. Molly's tougher. You'll never touch her again. She won't just hate you. She'll fucking kill you, you coward."

The Moonshaker's face darkened and he waved the female illusion away. "Make your peace with your universe, Son of a Coward. You are a dead man."

Chapter Ten

Dawn had brightened into morning and the room was bathed in sunlight when the warrior's eyes opened. Molly knelt above him, fully dressed, straddling his torso while positioning the dagger so that the point rested against his throat. If it was Aaric, she would kill him. And she was sure she'd be able to tell.

Then he moistened his lips, glanced down at the weapon, and smiled a shaky smile. "Did you figure it out? That Aaric wasn't really dead? Just waiting to get me alone?"

"Don't move a muscle," Molly warned softly. "Don't underestimate me. I can do this." Her grip on the dagger's hilt tightened and she edged it forward, one quarter of an inch.

"Put the dagger down, Valmain." His eyes were filled with compassion as he reached for her wrists and forced them back gently. "It's okay. I killed him."

It was Matthew's voice and Matthew's manner, with no trace of Aaric's bluster or arrogance. Of course, he had predicted she would see and hear what she desperately longed to see and hear . . .

"Put the dagger down," he repeated firmly.

She climbed away slowly, aiming the blade toward his heart until her feet were planted on the floor. "Start talking," she ordered, her voice hoarse and low. "And don't touch me again, or you'll be sorry."

"Just relax. I'm not going to touch you. We'll take this nice and slow." He sat up and reached for his jeans, pulling them over his tanned legs with one eye always on the blade. "As soon as you left the dream, Aaric was back—totally confident. With you gone, he figured he could kill me easily, then impersonate me until he won you over."

"You . . . Matthew couldn't have won," Molly protested, desperate to resist the familiar strains of his calm-inducing voice. "You're too powerful. With your ugly magic! You're not a real man at all. Your strength was just illusion." Grief poured from her heart, causing her chest to ache and her eyes to sting with tears. "Matthew was stronger—braver!— but no match for your cruel tricks!" She waved her weapon wildly. "He was my champion!"

"Molly, listen! I killed him! I used the amulet."

"You . . . he didn't know the secret!" she spat. "He didn't stand a chance! All his training, and sacrifice, and all his commitment . . ."

In one quick move, the bare-chested warrior toppled her to the bed, restraining her forcibly while prying the dagger from her grasp and tossing it to the floor. "Listen! When we were reading the cape. Remember? I saw the story. Of the amulet."

Dazed but hopeful, she repeated, "The cape?"

"Yeah! Your dream power to the rescue again. It said my ancestor wore it tied to his right wrist. When you disappeared and I couldn't wake up, I suddenly knew! And then, there he was!" His eyes were dark with remembered tension. "I was holding

your cape, and I used the loose thread to tie the
amulet to my right wrist. It cut me, but the moment
I had it secured . . . well, Aaric started taunting me
with tales of what he had in store for you and him
and . . . well, I beat the shit out of him, basically.
And this time he's dead!" His pride burst through
and he grinned broadly. "I wish you could have
seen it!"

"Dead?"

"Yeah. This time I checked. I swear, Molly, the
man was incredible! When he realized the amulet
was helping me he went crazy! Calling me Son of
Lost Eagle and changing his appearance—bigger
and more musclebound, and he even made his eyes
glow red!—to intimidate me. But none of his tricks
worked, thanks to the amulet, and we fought—I
wish I had been able to get my hands on the dagger,
but it was yards away. Anyway, it didn't matter. I
was covered with blood and it felt like my shoulder
was dislocated, but," he paused for a recuperative
breath, *"I won!"*

Molly squirmed a bit under his eager weight and
searched his golden eyes for further confirmation.
"If you really are Matthew, then tell me the title of
your book."

"A test? Good idea. Nice to know you wouldn't
have just fallen into his arms. According to *him,* he
really knows how to push your buttons." With a
teasing grin he reached down to the floor, grabbed
one of his running shoes, and pulled the lace free.
Then he strung it through the amulet, which he tied
carefully to his wrist. "Look at this, Molly. Just like
Lost Eagle."

"Matthew!"

"Oh, yeah." With a sly wink, he pronounced,

"The title to my masterpiece was . . . *Symbolism in Legend and Myth.* Okay?"

"Oh, Matthew! I was so frightened!" She covered his face with kisses, then pulled back in alarm when his hand slipped between her legs. "What are you *doing?*" She caught his wrist and glared at the amulet, which had scratched her right through her jeans. "That hurts!"

"Sorry," he grinned wryly. "Aaric claimed you want a little more rough stuff in bed."

"What!"

"I'm kidding. Lighten up, Valmain." His voice grew husky. "I think if I told you how much I want to make love to you right now, it would actually scare you."

"I see it in your eyes," she whispered. "Like you . . ."

"Like I've been reborn," he nodded. "That's exactly how I feel. Like I've been given a second chance at life. I don't intend to waste it, Molly."

"Oh, Matthew . . . when I thought I'd lost you . . ."

"You were going to kill him for me?" His lips trailed along her cheek. "You're incredible. When I woke up and saw you with that dagger . . ."

"I hated him so much! I love you so much!" Wrapping her arms around his neck, she kissed him frantically. "It was the longest hour of my life! I couldn't get back to sleep . . ."

"Luckily, I had the amulet. It gave me such an incredible rush." His tone turned mournful as he added, "I don't feel anything from it here."

Remembering her similar reaction to the loss of her beautiful cape, Molly soothed, "It's just a symbol now. We don't need it. Aaric's dead and we're together again, forever."

"A symbol?" the warrior repeated slowly. "It was more than that for Lost Eagle. It worked for him, outside the dream, so why not for me? Uncle August used to tell me such incredible stories about Lost Eagle's exploits."

"You should give the amulet to your uncle," Molly urged. "After all, he trained you and prepared you. Where would we have been without him?" She was completely taken with the thought. "We'll go and see him, together, and give it to him as our gift."

"No. It stays with us. We might need it."

"For what? Lost Eagle is avenged. The battle's over, right?"

"I'll feel safer if I have this with me," he countered stubbornly.

"But Aaric's dead and you're you. You proved it." She snuggled against him. "What a relief, Matthew."

"Although technically, if Aaric had won, he probably would have been able to answer your test question correctly," her companion smiled.

"How do you figure that?"

"In the dream, he was just an illusion of me. But if he actually took over my body, you'd think he'd also get my brain, filled with my memories. Right?"

Molly felt as though a gentle electric shock had been sent through her heart. "What?"

The warrior winced. "Sorry. I didn't mean to scare you. I'm me, I promise. Don't look like that."

"It's true! He'd know the title of your book, and he'd call me Valmain, because he'd know . . ." She couldn't finish the thought.

It made a perverse kind of sense. Matthew's memories were stored in his brain. *That* was the reason Aaric had so confidently predicted Molly would be deceived into believing Matthew had won. *". . . you will want so desperately to believe . . ."*

But she wasn't desperate. Instead, she was simply exhausted—too exhausted, both mentally and physically, even to be frightened. In her heart, she was sure that this was Matthew, but hadn't Aaric predicted just that? With a weary sigh, she slipped from the bed and moved beyond his reach. "I have to think about this."

"Cut it out," he frowned. "Come back here."

"No, Matthew." She was backing toward the door. "I need to think. About this. And about why you're afraid to let August have the amulet."

"I'm not 'afraid'! I just want to keep it."

"August could use its power," she reasoned aloud. "He's descended from Lost Eagle. He's a threat."

"I'm not Aaric. I'm Matthew Redtree and . . . oh, fine!" He seemed both amused and frustrated by the fact that she had bent to retrieve her dagger. "Now you're going to kill me again? Come on, Molly. You know it's me."

"I have to think."

"There's nothing to think about! You've got to decide to trust me."

As much as she longed to agree, she simply couldn't afford to be wrong, and so she kept her face expressionless. "I'm going to my room. Just until I can sort this out. If you're Matthew, I think you'll understand. If you're Aaric," the pause was chilling, "I'll be back to kill you. I owe Matthew that, at least."

As she was closing the door she caught a glimpse of his face. He looked completely amused and, for just a moment, she surrendered to her fear, envisioning her champion lying in a crumpled, bloodied heap at the Moonshaker's feet. Then she remembered the cape, with its myriad of stories and secrets, and nodded vigorously. "I'm not helpless. It's time I learned to use my *own* weapons."

Hurrying to the small second room they had taken for her for appearance's sake, she slipped between the bedcovers, invoking whatever "dream power" she might possess. "I need to read that cape," she commanded herself. "I need to find out, once and for all, *who that man is!*" She searched for the dream—for the silver stitches that held the answers—but neither could be found.

Without the dream to rescue her, sleep was a tortured state. By ten A.M., she was on her feet and pacing. There had to be an answer to this dilemma. There had to be a way to prove to her brain what her heart instinctively knew—that the man in the next room was Matthew Redtree, and that it was a day for celebration, not panic and dread.

But what if that man was a sorcerer? An arrogant bully with strange powers to back up his fantasies of domination and seduction? Had she and Matthew unwittingly unleashed a monster on a naive world in which magic was considered nothing more than illusion combined with gullibility? What havoc could Aaric the Moonshaker wreak under such conditions?

"He's your responsibility," she decided grimly. "You're the only one who knows who he is. You have to stop him. You have to avenge Matthew. You have to stop pacing! Every minute you hide in here just confirms the fact that you're scared of him, and monsters like him thrive on stuff like that." Securing the steely dagger in the waistband of her white jeans, she obscured any view of it by means of an oversized Cal sweatshirt, then moved to the door.

Just as her hand touched the knob, there was a gentle tapping from the hall. "Valmain?" his familiar voice called out. "Are you awake?"

Molly grimaced. He had somehow known the exact moment to knock! Did that mean he could read her mind? What *else* could he do? Walk through walls? Turn straw into gold?

"Molly? Open up. We have to talk."

Taking a deep breath, she flung open the door and marched into the hall. "I didn't get much sleep," she informed him briskly, "so don't push me. I don't know who you are yet, and I don't want to discuss it."

He grinned reluctantly. "Never?"

"We're going downstairs to find something to eat."

He was clearly fascinated. "If you think I'm Aaric, aren't you a little bit scared?"

"If you're Aaric, then you killed my champion, and if you killed my champion," she glared, "I hate you too much to be afraid of you."

"That's an interesting piece of illogic," he chuckled. "Anyway, your troubles are over. I thought of a way to prove I'm Matthew Redtree."

Brushing his hand from her arm, she repeated, "I don't want to discuss it until we've had something to eat."

"You're not curious?"

"I'm tired, and I'm hungry, and . . ." she pulled the dagger from her waistband, "I'm armed. I don't feel like playing games."

He burst into laughter. "You're too much, Molly. Do you really think you could kill Aaric when *I* couldn't? I don't know whether to be impressed or insulted!"

She resisted an impulse to smile. "Okay, you have sixty seconds. How can you prove you're Matthew?"

"Let me make love to you. I guarantee you'll know after that."

Molly flushed. "You're obnoxious. I'd rather kill Matthew by mistake than make love to a creep like you again."

"That's my point! Aaric *was* a creep. A brute. A cretin who wouldn't know real love if his life depended on it." He reached again for her arm and smiled when she didn't rebuff him. "He was an animal, Molly. Even with my memories, he couldn't *feel* the things I feel for you. He wasn't capable of that kind of emotion."

"I thought about that myself," she murmured, allowing herself to enjoy his touch for a long moment before stepping back and glaring, "Nice try."

"Fine." He scowled and started down the hall toward the staircase, adding over his shoulder, "Don't stab me in the back with my own dagger until you're sure, okay?"

Once he had disappeared down the stairs, her face softened into a reluctant smile. This was so obviously Matthew Redtree that she could barely restrain herself from tackling him and smothering his frustrated face with kisses. She had seen this side of him so many times! Every time his 'balance' was threatened, those gold flecks in his eyes would begin to spark, and he would struggle, always tenderly, for a solution. He never succumbed to anger or physical violence unless threatened with immediate peril. He used the energy behind his emotions, including pride, without allowing them to manipulate him. A man with a nickname like 'the Moonshaker' would hardly be able to accomplish so sophisticated and controlled a task.

"Or he's pretending to have balance," she muttered under her breath, "just because he remembers Matthew used to do that. This is *hopeless!*" She stared at the dagger in her hand, knowing she would never be able to plunge it between Matthew Redtree's magnificent shoulders.

She needed help and she needed it soon, before her bluff became so transparent that she could no longer temper Aaric's lusts and habits. For the first time, she understood the need for a champion, but her champion could not help her now, and so she would turn to the man who had trained the young hero for twenty-eight loving years. She would turn to August Redtree.

"You're brilliant, Valmain. Going to see my uncle is the perfect solution. Of course," he eyed her mischievously as he slipped his arm around her shoulders, "my idea would have been more fun."

"We've discussed this," she reminded him coolly. "Please take your hand away from me. Read a book, *if* you know how to read. This is going to be a long flight, and I intend to spend most of it catching up on my sleep."

He unhanded her immediately. "Try to get to the dream, Molly. I'll bet your cape tells the whole story. It's the most incredible living document I've ever heard of. It saved my life," he added solemnly.

"I keep trying, but I think the dream is gone."

"It can't be. I've studied these things, and dream powers are always lifelong gifts. Maybe my uncle will be able to help with that, too."

Molly closed her eyes and tried to relax. "Tell me more about him, Matthew. He sounded so gentle on the phone. Almost mystical."

"You'll love him. He's really my great-uncle—my grandfather's brother—and he raised my dad completely on his own. Then, when my parents were killed, he finished raising me and Rita."

"Killed? How were your parents killed?"

"It was a burglary that went wrong. Real wrong. I was only eleven, and Rita was fourteen. We were at August's ranch, visiting. We always did that during the summer."

"And your parents' house was robbed?"

"Right. Dad had some valuable Incan pottery—he's the one who got me started on collecting. He never even finished high school, but he was self-educated and just about the most scholarly guy you could ever imagine. After all these years, I still miss him so much."

Molly resisted an urge to offer sympathy, reminding herself that this might be Aaric's despicable manipulation of Matthew's tragic orphanhood. "What was your father's name?"

"Jason. He always said he was named after the Jason who went looking for the Golden Fleece."

"Jason of the Argonauts? I remember your lecture about that. It was so compelling." To her dismay, a lump was forming in her throat. *Don't think about all that,* she chided herself, then turned her displeasure to her companion. "Don't keep changing the subject. Let's get back to August. He lives on a ranch, you said. Is it cattle? Horses?"

"Two mules, two horses, assorted goats . . . too many chickens, and sometimes a pig."

His tone was teasing, and she smiled despite her better judgment. "So? How does he earn a living?"

"Good question," the warrior chuckled. "Ask him, and if you get a straight answer, let me know, okay?"

"What does he do all day?"

"He gathers plants, from the desert. Sometimes he heals a neighbor's livestock, or gentles a nervous colt. It's always very low-key, very natural." Matthew stretched and closed his eyes. "My best memories are the times I spent out at his place. It's all desert, with bleak hills and no buildings in sight for miles. My uncle watches so intently, for signs—like a hawk or an odd-shaped cloud—and after a while, you realize it's not a barren place at all. It's teeming with activity and information. And at night, with a fire blazing, and the old guys telling stories, it's the most lively place on earth. Anyway, the day I told him about my dream was the day he started coaching me, to prepare me for the fight."

"How old is he?"

"Probably around eighty-two or eighty-three."

"Wow! And he lives all alone in the desert?"

"Yeah. Rita says she goes out there at least once a week, to check on him. She's a nurse, you know, and she really wants to take care of him, but he doesn't believe in doctors and hospitals, and he won't move into Los Angeles to live with her and the boys, so . . ."

"Rita Camacho," Molly murmured. "You've mentioned her two sons. What about her husband? Are they divorced?"

"He's history," Matthew growled, "and good riddance. He was a jerk, Molly, believe me. AJ and Robert are better off without a father at all. They have August, after all, and they have me."

"AJ's the one you told me about during our picnic? The one who's so good at martial arts?"

"Right. He's the older of the two—he just turned ten. So Robert must be eight. Robert reminds me of my father—real studious and serious. According to the tests they give the kids in school, he's some kind of genius or something. They keep pressuring Rita to send him to special classes, or skip him ahead."

His voice was especially charming when he was bragging about his family, and Molly responded easily. "I'm surprised you moved to Berkeley. Couldn't you have found a teaching job closer to them? It sounds like you're all pretty close."

"You were at Berkeley," he reminded her. "I had to go there to find you. Destiny sent me there."

Pure Matthew Redtree, Molly thought, suppressing a smile. *Everything is preordained and global.* Then it occurred to her that destiny might have betrayed the young champion, pitting him against an impossible foe, and anger surged through her. "That's enough," she informed him briskly. "Get some sleep."

"I answered your questions, now I want to ask you a few." When she opened one eye and sent him a disdainful frown, he insisted, "I've been cooperating, haven't I? And let's face it, if I didn't want to, you couldn't make me. I sat in the car outside your grandmother's house while you said goodbye, and I'm taking this trip to LA without arguing, but now I want to talk about something important."

"You're cooperating with me because you need me," she shrugged. "And because you know I'll kill you if you step out of line."

"Tell me how *you* could possibly kill *me*. I'm fascinated."

She summoned her haughtiest stare. "You've heard the expression, 'If looks could kill . . . '? Well, I'm a sorceress. It's not just an expression with me."

"Why did you choose that?" he demanded. "Do you have some instinctive, gut-level feeling it might be within your powers?"

It annoyed her that he was parlaying her bluff into a full-blown conversation. "That's right," she sniffed. "I could destroy you with a glance."

"Try it."

"Pardon?"

"Zap me with a look. Don't kill me, just give me a little jolt. If you're right about this, it's incredible!"

"If you're Aaric, you already know I can do it easily, and if you're Matthew," her tone became a drawl, "you're getting on my nerves."

He laughed and patted her arm. "You're in a tough spot, Valmain. I guess we should have discussed this before the battle, although . . ." his grin widened, "maybe it's better we didn't discuss it, after all."

"Why?"

"I think I would have told you to kill my body if you had any doubts at all. I wouldn't have wanted you to risk associating with that jerk."

Molly sighed. Would Aaric the Moonshaker ever say such a thing? Of course he would. It was *precisely* what he would say. "You said you had a question for me? Make it quick."

"When I was reading about Lost Eagle on your cape, you were reading about Maya's father, the sorcerer. Tell me as much of it as you can remember. I want to start piecing things together. Now that I've come face to face with Aaric, and I've seen how he operated, I think maybe I can come up with some strategies for training you."

"Training me?"

"You're a sorceress. We just need to find out

what kind of sorceress—in other words, what types of magic you can control. Certain gifts are almost universal, like summoning fire and easy stuff like that, but seeing Aaric has shown me your people were extremely sophisticated. His illusion power, for example, was phenomenal. If you've got *that,* don't you want to know about it?"

She turned in her seat until she was directly confronting him, then growled, "You honestly think I'm going to sit here and have *that* conversation, right now, knowing you might be Aaric, who already *knows* every tiny detail of my heritage and limits?"

"Good point. So, just tell me what you read on the cape."

"None of your business." She frowned when a slender, accommodating flight attendant leaned across her to furnish her companion with a magazine.

"Thanks, miss," he smiled. "I hope it wasn't too much trouble."

"No trouble at all," the pretty woman gushed. "Is there anything else I can do for you?"

"No, thanks. Molly? Do you want anything?"

Molly gave the stewardess a withering glare. "We don't want to be disturbed for the rest of the flight."

The woman drew back sharply and disappeared down the aisle.

"Nice move, Valmain. I didn't know you were the jealous type."

"Jealous? I probably just saved her life." Fluffing her pillow, she reclined her seat and murmured, "I thought I made this clear at the airport, Aaric. Don't talk to anyone, or touch anyone, or try anything tricky."

"Whatever you say," he sighed. "Get some sleep.

Find the dream." His lips brushed her cheek. "I love you, Molly. More than ever, now that I've seen you like this. You really are an amazing woman."

It was all she could do to keep from melting. There was such love in his voice. And she *had* been jealous of the stewardess, although Matthew hadn't given her a second glance. In fact, he hadn't given any woman a second glance, even in the bustling airport where several well-dressed, well-built female tourists had given him a flirtatious smile. And why not? He was so handsome! So virile! And he was dedicated to his dream girl, to the exclusion of all other women.

Or, he was Aaric.

Chapter Eleven

"Tell her who I am, Uncle," the handsome warrior was insisting as he paced the floor of August Redtree's modest four-room ranch house. "I'm trying to have a sense of humor about all this, but it's been almost twenty-four hours and it's getting a little annoying. I *won,* but I get no credit at all. And Molly treats me like a leper. Tell her I'm me, okay?"

The old uncle, who had been staring at the familiar form of his nephew, now tore his gaze away and focused on Molly. She was clearly not what he had expected and, for the tenth time that night, he reached out one dark, gnarled hand and touched the soft, sun-streaked curls that framed her face.

Molly had been staring herself, enchanted by August's snow-white shoulder-length hair and soft brown eyes, which made him appear part shaman, part saint. An aura—so intense it seemed not only visible but actually tangible—surrounded him, bringing comfort to his exhausted visitor. "Take your time, August," she urged quietly. "We have to be absolutely certain."

"Ask me anything, Uncle," the younger man challenged. "Test me."

"It's as the dream girl has said," August sighed.

"Even if you *are* the Moonshaker, you would have my nephew's memories, and more."

"I thought you'd be able to tell for sure," the warrior grumbled. "You've known me since I was a baby. You trained me. Practically raised me. I thought once you saw this . . ." He untied the lace that bound the amulet to his wrist and handed it to August, who accepted it reverently. "If I was your enemy, would I turn it over to you like this? You're Lost Eagle's descendant, too, and so it can make you powerful."

"In the dream, at least, it could make me powerful," August agreed. "I'll admit, it's bold of you to relinquish the amulet. It's either a sign of trust or a sign that the Moonshaker's powers are so great he has no fear of an old man wearing an amulet."

"In Lost Eagle's time the amulet worked outside the dream," Matthew grumbled. "Now it's powerless! It doesn't make sense. Molly can't get back to the dream. The amulet is useless . . ." He straightened and challenged quietly, "We can't solve these riddles until you agree to trust me, Uncle. There must be a way I can prove myself to you."

"Or persuade me?" August mused. "If you are a sorcerer, you may well have the power to persuade me, and perhaps to persuade the dream girl as well."

"There's your answer, then!" Matthew crowed. "I must not have that power, or I would have used it by now, so I must be me. Right?"

"If you are the Moonshaker," the old man continued coolly, "you are very clever—clever enough to know that winning our trust is more efficient than constant use of magic, despite the temptation. You are clever. And patient."

"*If* I'm the Moonshaker," Matthew finished.

"But I'm not. That would have been incredible." His eyes sparkled with poorly disguised curiosity. "What do you know about possession, Uncle? I've studied it, of course, but never this form. If Aaric had defeated me and taken my body, I would have been dead. How much of me would have remained?"

"Honestly, Matthew," Molly glared. "What a time for research!"

"Sorry. Bad habit. *My* habit, not that bastard Aaric's."

"What about *that?*" Molly turned to August with a hopeful smile. "He can't say anything nice about Aaric. Not a thing."

"Clever," August repeated, then he turned to the warrior and suggested, "Bring the bags from the car and put them in the guest room. You are both exhausted. Once you've rested, we'll sift through all of these facts until a clue to your true identity presents itself."

"Sure, Uncle. Whatever you say. Molly can have the guest room and I'll sleep on the couch."

"You're sleeping with me," Molly corrected, then flushed at the obvious double entendre. She wanted him where she could keep watch, to ensure he didn't escape and invade an unwary world, but . . .

He was grinning broadly. "She's wild, isn't she, Uncle?"

"She is vigilant," August shrugged. "If you wish, Molly, I can guard him while you sleep."

And what would you do if he tried to overpower you? she wanted to sigh. "Thanks anyway, August, but he's my responsibility," she insisted instead.

From the doorway, the figure of Matthew murmured, "Just figure it out, okay, Uncle? I've waited for years to enjoy my victory over the Moonshaker.

To enjoy it with you and," he smiled wistfully, "with you, Valmain."

"Go away," she advised without emotion but, when the warrior had departed, her calm evaporated. "Say anything, August. Anything at all. Help me with this, please? It's driving me crazy!"

"I'm confused," he admitted sadly. "Matthew has always been more a son to me than a nephew, and yet," his eyes narrowed, "the Moonshaker is our ancient enemy. I have lived with hate in my heart over his cowardly treatment of my ancestor, and I have lived for the moment when Matthew would crush him. If Matthew did not succeed, and if Aaric the Moonshaker now walks my land, then it falls to me to avenge the murders of both Lost Eagle and my beloved nephew."

Molly shuddered. "Tell me about Aaric's so-called powers. You mentioned 'persuasion'?"

"Yes. A powerful tool, especially against one such as I. You could possibly resist, since you are something of a witch. If you could only discover the method."

"Okay. What else?" She paused and resumed her haughtiest stare as Matthew reentered the room, burdened with their luggage. His wink annoyed her and, as soon as he was safely out of earshot, she hissed, "He's so obnoxious!"

"He is exhilarated," August chuckled. "As he said, he has prepared for his whole life to win this battle, and now he is deservedly bursting with pride. Or . . ."

"Or he's Aaric, and it's a rush just to be out of my dream and here where he can wreak havoc," Molly nodded. "Anyway, back to his powers. In the dream, he could make himself look like Matthew."

"According to legend, 'illusion' was the Moonshaker's finest skill. He undoubtedly used it to defeat Lost Eagle."

"Can he do it out here? Out of the dream?"

"Certainly. I don't know the details . . ." August smiled reluctantly. "Your companion asked about possession. It would be Matthew's way, as you said, to do research even in a time of conflict, but the truth is, we could use a little research ourselves. I know that, when one being or spirit possesses another *living* being, the two spirits are at war until the end. One may dominate, but each struggles to manifest itself.

"This situation is unusual if, as the Moonshaker claimed, he intended to kill our Matthew before he took his form. I believe that under such conditions, our Matthew would no longer exist. His memories and, to a lesser degree, his instincts would be mere tools to be manipulated by the Moonshaker. When we see our Matthew in this man, we are being duped. Do you see?"

"If Aaric won."

"I feel as you do. Our only safe course is to proceed as though we are confronted by the Moonshaker. If this man is actually Matthew, he will understand. In fact," the old man's eyes twinkled, "I believe he might chastise us should we be too easily convinced."

"Okay. So we proceed as though it's Aaric. But in your heart . . . ?"

August nodded. "I feel great love for him. I ask myself, is it persuasion at work? And the answer is: I cannot know."

"I feel love for him, too—love and hate. It's eerie, isn't it? He draws incredible rushes of emotion from me."

"Gratitude, love, hate, lust, curiosity?" August

chuckled. "These next weeks will be difficult for you, dream girl. He will wish to be your lover."

"Don't worry," she blushed. "I've set some pretty strict ground rules and so far, he's behaved. He's tricky, but basically he does what I say."

"I have noticed, and I am impressed."

"It's been awkward." She smiled ruefully. "I need your help, August. Can we stay here for a while?"

"Certainly. As I said, if he is the Moonshaker, it falls to me to kill him."

"No! Please, promise me you won't even try! You've never seen him in action, August. It's frightening." She shuddered visibly. "He's a sorcerer. If we discover absolute proof that he's Aaric, I'll kill him myself. I can do it with my dagger." She pulled the weapon from her purse and confided, "He thinks I left it in Ireland with my grandmother, but I packed it in my suitcase and I guess Customs thought it was some cheap replica, because they passed it through."

"It *is* only a replica," August reminded her gently. "The real dagger is in the dream. If you could lure him back into the dream, that would be different."

"Oh?" She tucked the dagger back into her purse. "Would he appear as Aaric or as Matthew?"

"I cannot say. I know very little of the dream power. I've heard references to it, but only bits and pieces. I always assumed that you were in Matthew's dream, and that the combat would be in the real world. It never occurred to me, during all those years I trained Matthew, that the battle would be fought in a someone else's dream. It's fascinating but bewildering."

"That's an understatement. And I can't lure him back to the dream. I can't even get back there myself! It's never been a conscious choice with me, August," she explained. "I just end up there from time to time. When I tried to stay away from it last week, I couldn't, but now that I'd dearly love to go there, I can't. I'm beginning to think it doesn't exist anymore."

"It will exist until you die," August assured her. "And you should be able to go there whenever you wish. You must concentrate, child." His eyes were bright with curiosity. "Tell me what you would do if you could return to the dream."

"I'd read my cape. It's possible there's a clue that could help us decide whether that man is Matthew Redtree. There's a lot of information stitched into that beautiful fabric."

"It must be amazing. Still," he reminded her, "the information came from you. The cape cannot know anything you do not know. You're the one who stitched the words, after all."

"I don't know anything about Maya and Lost Eagle, but it's all there," Molly objected.

"Perhaps you do not know it personally," August smiled, "but we have more than our personal memories to guide us. We have an ancestral accumulation of knowledge—part instinct, part culture. Deep within you, there is the history of your people, as stitched into the cape."

"Really?" Molly felt strangely comforted, if not convinced, by the bizarre notion. "Matthew and I have so much history in common. If only I knew . . ." Tears stung her eyes. "I miss him, August."

"Your destinies were intertwined," August sympathized. "It is very unfair for you to have been allowed to love him for so short a time, but is that not better than having never known him?"

No, she thought sadly. *We had no time to be lovers*

. . . To go to dinner and movies and dances . . . To learn one another's favorite foods or colors or seasons . . .

August seemed to read her mind. "You shared more with him than many lovers share in a lifetime, child. One day you'll understand."

"I'll never understand," she countered softly. "My life was so orderly. So perfectly mapped out. Then Matthew came and I was swept away."

The old man nodded. "The world became a frightening place."

"Frightening, but also beautiful and magical. And I felt safe because I had Matthew, and he thought he was invincible because he had me. The dream girl," she added in self-mocking frustration. "If only I had spent those years training, like Matthew did, I suppose it would have been different."

"You spent those years sewing, as was intended. Do not question your destiny, child. Embrace it, as Matthew did." He leaned closer and stared into the deep blue eyes. "Did you mean what you said? Will you kill the Moonshaker?"

"I'll try."

"You're a witch. You may have powers beyond dreaming. It will be necessary for you to study."

"Study witchcraft?" Molly winced. "You mean, like spells and potions? I'm not that kind of a witch, August. I dream, I sew, I hold the spool." Her shoulders slumped in defeat. "I'm essentially useless."

"You're exhausted," he soothed. "In the morning, your life will seem more balanced. Try to sleep." He squeezed her hand and added, predictably, "Try to dream."

Molly nodded. Her sleep on the airplane had been light and unproductive. Would it be any different here, in this strange man's house, with another stranger—a potentially dangerous one—sharing the same room? She needed to be alone, to think, but didn't dare leave Aaric unguarded, and so she headed toward the tiny guest bedroom.

And there he was, waiting for her, his head propped up against several pillows as he sprawled, fully dressed, on the single narrow bed in the sparsely furnished room. "You look tired, Molly. Close the door and come here for a minute."

Without replying, she crossed to him, yanked one of the pillows free, then crossed back to sit with her back against the closed door. "My nerves are shot, Aaric. Just go to sleep."

"You're going to sleep there?"

"That's right."

"You can have the bed, you know."

She frowned. "I don't want you wandering around."

"Or away?" he chuckled. "Here, then." Leaping to his feet, he pushed the small bed across the floor so that it blocked access to the door. Molly scooted aside, silently amused by his typically physical solution.

"Thanks, Matthew." She had kicked off her shoes earlier, and now climbed into the bed without undressing. "What are you doing *now?*" she murmured when he moved toward the window.

"We need some air in here," he explained, opening it wide as he spoke.

"Close that and stop fooling around!" she snapped. He was telling her she couldn't guard both the window and the door. In other words, he was telling her he could leave at any time and that she and an eighty-year-old man couldn't stop him. "Don't push me, Aaric."

"Or else?" His smile was sympathetic. "My uncle was right, we both need some decent rest. Together, in that bed. I won't force my attentions on you, Molly, and you won't be able to sleep unless you know I'm right beside you, so . . ."

"Okay. Open the window, but just a crack, and then you can sleep here." When he turned away to follow her instruction, she slipped the dagger out of her purse and under her pillow. Then she snuggled under the covers, her back to the center of the narrow bed, and tried to ignore the fact that he had joined her.

"Molly?"

"Go to sleep."

He moved closer, until his mouth was within inches of her ear. "In your heart, you know it's me, don't you? I know you have to be careful but, deep down inside . . . ?"

It brought an unexpected lump to her throat and she remembered August's remark. Matthew had waited a lifetime for this victory, only to be put into emotional limbo when he should have been being praised and petted and generally adored. Would it be so wrong to give him this one, brief moment? This crumb?

"Back off," she whispered, but her tone was devoid of the distance and disdain that had marked their earlier exchanges. He was immediately encouraged and, to her dismay, began to knead her weary shoulders with strong, capable hands.

It was paradise—tender and effective, all in one blur of pleasure, and she hadn't the strength to pull away. The dagger was within reach, and this man, whoever he was—and she *knew* it was Matthew— seemed content just to serve her. What harm could it possibly do?

"You're stressed out," he murmured in her ear. "That's why you can't get to the dream. You're out of balance, and that's affecting your powers. Try to remember those nights, long ago, when your great grandma would tell you about Kerreya, and Valmain, and you'd drift into the dream as though it were second nature . . ."

"Mmm," she agreed dutifully. It was true. When she was relaxed, the dream came to her easily. Why else would it have stopped so abruptly after the car accident? Because she was stressed, as she was now; and out of balance, as she was now; and missing the person she loved most in the world, as she was now . . .

"You're tense and confused," he repeated, as one hand moved to her neck, rubbing gently, while the other circled her waist, drawing her back against himself. "Remember how you felt after you stabbed Aaric with the dagger? You wanted to stay awake and never dream again. But you had to sleep, and you had to dream, because it was your destiny. *Our* destiny."

"Mmm . . ." She was barely listening to his words. Instead, she was floating gratefully toward the first real sleep she had had in more than twenty-four hours.

"You need to be calm and balanced, Valmain. Let me make love to you. That always works. That's how you've prepared for every major dream event, and it's always worked. First you're tense and scared, then we make love, then you're centered and ready." He turned her gently to face him, then scowled at the flash of the dagger in her hand.

She almost smiled, so tangible was his frustration. "You're right, Moonshaker. When I'm relaxed I'm much more effective. Now, back off and go to sleep."

"No problem," he growled, turning away from her and muttering, "I wish I'd never given you that stupid dagger. I should just take it away from you and throw it down the well."

"Pardon?"

"I said goodnight. Try to find the cape soon, will you? You're not the only one who's tense around here."

She wanted to snuggle against his back and nibble at the base of his neck. If they made love, she could confirm what she already knew, and they could live happily ever after—the Valmain dreamer and her champion. It was so tempting . . .

Forget about all that. Just find the dream, she instructed herself. *That's the only way you can learn the truth without making a mistake that'll haunt you the rest of your life. If you're wrong, and this is Aaric, and you allow him to make love to you, you'll never forgive yourself, and you'll be dishonoring Matthew's memory. He died to protect you from Aaric. You can never forget that. Never!*

But 'never,' like 'forever,' was a very long time. For how long could she be expected to endure this situation? And, if he really was Aaric, how much time could *he* be expected to wait? He could walk away, and she was essentially powerless to stop him. Being sorcerer, he might even have ways of overpowering her, both physically and emotionally. For now, he was trying to win her trust and love naturally, but his patience undoubtedly had its limits.

And for now, he was staying with her because of what he hoped she could do for him. He wanted her magic and her heritage. Or perhaps he was concerned with what she could do *to* him. As the only

magician in the world who knew his origins and
identity, she could unmask him. And there was always the possibility that she could destroy him, although that seemed laughably improbable.

In the dream he had said he would teach her, and
then they would pool their talents and rebuild the
Valmain kingdom together. He had been amazed at
her ignorance, implying that she had untapped talents that were quite extensive and useful. He had
plans for those talents—of that she was certain.

She was also certain he didn't intend to lead the
modest life of Matthew Redtree for long. He
wanted to be a ruler—a flamboyant and ruthless
power broker. If he was Aaric, this Matthewesque
gentleness was a charade, and he was bursting with
need to abandon these simple accommodations and
celibate ways in favor of lust and luxury.

His boast rang in her ears: *When we are together
again, I will make your body soar with pleasure and
you will forget that Lost Eagle's son ever existed. I
will win you from him—first in battle, then in bed.*

"Never," she whispered into the night, clutching
the hilt of the dagger as she tried to ignore the
steady, even sounds of her bedmate's breathing. At
this point, she had three choices. She could plunge
the weapon into his back right then, while he slept;
or she could wrap her arms around him and give
him the adulation he deserved; or she could sleep,
and search for the dream, and hope that August
Redtree would have good news for her when she
awakened.

Chapter Twelve

She hadn't expected to sleep soundly or to awaken refreshed, and might have attributed both to the fact that she had spent the night nestled at the side of the man she loved, with a dagger under her pillow for good measure. Unfortunately, when she finally opened both eyes and stretched, the man she loved was nowhere in sight and the dagger had vanished into thin air.

The bed was still flush against the closed door and she was about to panic, wondering if perhaps he *could* walk through walls after all, when she noticed that the window had been opened wide. Racing to it in a futile attempt to stop his apparent escape, she flushed to see him sitting right outside, on a low bench, tying his running shoes. As though sensing her presence, he glanced up and grinned impishly. "Hi, Valmain."

"Where's my dagger?" she demanded, hoping her eyes were faithfully exhibiting her anger.

"Don't worry, I didn't throw it down the well. You waved it in my face once too often, and so I've put it away in a safe place." He shrugged to his feet and stretched out his arms. "It's a beautiful morning, Molly. Come on out and enjoy it with me. I'm willing to postpone my run."

She spun on her heels and strode to the bed, which she pushed away from the door with one frustrated shove. When she found August in the kitchen, frying eggs over a propane burner as though he hadn't a care in the world, she had to force herself to take a deep breath and to keep her tone even as she demanded, "Did I miss something? Did you know Matthew was outside?"

"Good morning," August smiled. "Our enigma has been awake for hours. He and I had a long, long talk, and then we had breakfast. How did you sleep?"

"Our enigma?" She slumped onto a bench seat at the kitchen table. "I guess that means you still don't know who he is?"

"He is clever, and entertaining, and confident. His version of the battle in your dream was the most amazing story I have ever heard. I pray that it is true."

"He went on and on about it on the airplane," she nodded. "All about how Aaric was strong and well-coordinated, but not cross-trained, right? He even said . . ." she paused, remembering how difficult it had been not to laugh when Matthew had proclaimed that the Moonshaker's technique had been "all upper-body" and that the sorcerer was "essentially ineffective from the waist down." "Well, let's just say he insulted Aaric's virility."

August was chuckling as though he, too, had heard this particular insult. "If he is the Moonshaker, he must be tiring rapidly of this impersonation. His rivalry, first with Lost Eagle and then with your champion, would make it difficult for him to sing his opponent's praises." Setting a plate of eggs before her, he sat beside her on the bench and smiled encouragingly. "We will know soon."

"This smells so good, August. I didn't realize how hungry I was. Thanks." After a few hearty mouthfuls she insisted, "We have to plan our strategy. I can't take another night like last night. Did you know he stole my dagger from me?"

"It is in the trunk of your rental car. He was concerned you might injure yourself while you slept, or so he said."

"He was afraid I might kill him, assuming," she added thoughtfully, "he can be killed at all. Wouldn't it be awful if he was immortal or something like that? I'd finally work up the nerve to kill him, and he wouldn't even die."

"We must assume he is mortal. Deal him a fatal injury and he will die, but you must not miscalculate. A sorcerer can heal any nonfatal injuries very rapidly and his anger would be great. And because of his special gifts, it will be difficult to catch him off his guard."

"What if I stab him in the heart when he's asleep?"

"That sounds sufficiently fatal," August chuckled.

She liked the sound of the old man's laughter, so rich with understanding and wisdom. With life. And, unexpectedly, with love. Apparently Matthew Redtree wasn't the only member of the family who had developed an attachment to the idea of the dream girl over the last twenty years.

His obvious affection gave her the confidence to risk some small embarrassment in exchange for needed advice on the sexual aspects to her quandary. "He's not going to keep pretending forever to be Matthew, you know, August. He has big plans for himself in our world. He told me he wanted to rebuild the Valmain kingdom with me. Of course, I'm sure he now knows that's absurd, but I'll bet he still wants to build a power base, and I doubt if he'd choose a university as his headquarters."

"I agree. He pretends, for now, because he needs you. And he needs to study our world, and make his plans."

"Right. He made two predictions to me in my dream. The first was that I'd want to see and hear Matthew so much, I'd be easily fooled if he took over Matthew's body. And he was right about that."

"And the second prediction?"

"Like I told you when we first got here yesterday, Aaric pretended to be Matthew a couple of times in my dream. The second time, he tricked me into making love with him." She paused to appreciate the old man's nonjudgmental expression, then continued, "His approach was very different from Matthew's. More aggressive. More demanding."

"Did he harm you?"

"No. I liked it, and he knows it." She could feel the heat in her cheeks, but continued briskly. "Which leads us to the second prediction. He said, when he came into our world, he'd pretend to be Matthew until we made love. He said it would be so 'elaborate' and effective that after that, I wouldn't be in love with Matthew Redtree anymore; I'd belong to him. It was such arrogance. Such conceit. But," she stared into August's warm eyes, "he was serious. He sees himself as such a great lover—because he can use magic on women, I guess—that he thinks he can make me forget Matthew."

"Interesting."

"I know." Her cheeks were now burning. "Do you see what I'm getting at?"

August nodded. "You do not wish to make love with my nephew's murderer, but it may be the only true test—the only time he relaxes his guard and reveals his true identity."

"Exactly. I've been hoping it wouldn't come to that, but . . ."

"But you may have no choice? Matthew would understand, child."

"I know, but . . ." She took a deep breath and voiced the fear that had been gnawing at her. "When you talk about Aaric's powers, I can't help but wonder. Can he . . . put me under some sort of love spell? You talked about his power to 'persuade' people. Can he persuade me to fall in love with him?"

August chuckled. "If he could, I believe he would have done so by now."

"I think maybe he already tried," she confessed. "When he first came out of the dream, he did something weird. He touched me, in an intimate way, with the amulet, and . . ." Her eyes had settled on the old man's bare right wrist and now widened with alarm. "Where *is* the amulet?"

"It is with Matthew," August explained quickly. "I could see in his eyes how he longed to wear it."

"But, August! He knows its secrets!"

"And I do not, and so it's worthless to me. I am not the Valmain champion, nor the one chosen as Lost Eagle's avenger. He didn't force it from me, child. He didn't even ask."

"Somehow he made you give it back," she grumbled. "Now I'm worried."

"Why?" The old man studied her curiously.

"When he touched you 'in an intimate way' with the amulet, were you seduced?"

"No. Actually, it annoyed me." When August laughed aloud, she joined him ruefully. "Either Aaric overestimated his skill as a lover, or it's really Matthew, right?" Sobering quickly, she murmured, "Every time I find some humor in this, I suddenly remember Matthew could be dead."

"And still we must welcome the occasion to smile through our tears," August soothed. "You must laugh, and eat, and take good care of yourself during the next days. You must keep your strength up, so that he cannot trick or confuse you."

"I guess you're right."

"You must be cautious and resourceful. You are safe because he sees you as his woman. His ally. But never forget," he added carefully, "he is a warrior and a sorcerer. He could destroy you with one blow. Perhaps with even a single glance."

The notion disturbed her. "Are *you* safe, August?"

August shook his head. "If he is the Moonshaker, it would be wise for him to kill me. He came here with you willingly, hoping I would be somehow convinced. Once he sees that I'm suspicious, he will worry that I'll turn you against him."

"And he'll kill you? Then I should never have brought him here! I'm so sorry, August. I just didn't think."

"You had no choice. And at least I've heard the amazing story of your dream power and my nephew's bravery. I only wish I could have witnessed it."

"You would have been so incredibly proud." Her eyes filled with tears at the memory. "Matthew was so brave and strong. So confident . . . Oh, August!

I'm sorry! If only I hadn't left him alone in the dream! We said we'd meet back in bed, and then I woke up, and he was still asleep, and that's when Aaric ambushed him, and if only I had stayed, until he was safely out of the dream . . ."

The old man grappled her against his chest and whispered, "You cannot blame yourself, dream girl, any more than I can blame myself for not having trained him well enough."

"I just can't stand it," she moaned, burying her face in his shoulder. "I feel so helpless."

"You're trembling. Tell me why. Are you frightened?"

"No. I'm angry! I can't go through this again."

"You have lost someone?"

"In a car accident. She was bleeding—crushed! I was two feet away, but I couldn't do anything, and now it's happening again. If Matthew was murdered right in *my* dream, and I could have done something, but I just slept and—and—"

August held her at arms' length and murmured, "I did not understand until now. I see now why you are so strong."

"Strong?" she gasped. "I'm falling apart!"

"With me, you are sad, but with him . . ." The old man's eyes were shining with admiration. "When you speak with him, your voice is commanding, as though you are fearless. And your posture and your movements . . ." A proud smile spread across his face. "I asked myself, how can so mild a woman be so formidable? Now I know. You grieved once in helplessness—never again. This time, you will strike back."

"I grieved in helplessness." Her tears disappeared as she savored the telling phrase. "That's exactly right. She was dying, and I was helpless."

"But you are no longer helpless. You are a princess, and a sorceress, and a woman in love, willing to fight for her man." August touched her cheek. "He will return at any moment. Go and prepare yourself for him. Wear your prettiest dress, and brush your curls, and let him see that he has not crushed Valmain. Study him carefully, and when the time is right, make your decision. I will try to help, if I can."

"You've already helped." She kissed his leathery cheek. "Stay away from him while I change, okay?"

"He will behave," August assured her. "He enjoys telling me his stories, and I enjoy listening. That voice has always been the sweetest of music to my soul."

"Tell him I'm just changing my clothes, and then we're leaving." When the old man seemed about to protest, she silenced him with a hug. "No arguing with the dream girl, right?"

He was chuckling reluctantly when his gaze wandered to the window and was captured by the figure of his nephew in the distance. Without another word, he moved to join the younger man, and as he did, Molly's chest tightened with concern. She had had no choice but to bring Matthew to August—the man who knew him better than anyone on Earth—but saw clearly that she now had no choice but to take the Moonshaker far away from this place lest harm befall an innocent old mystic.

But first, she had to prepare, and August was correct—she couldn't let Aaric the Moonshaker see how effectively he had frazzled her. She didn't need a mirror to know that she was indeed a mess. The only clean outfit in her hastily packed suitcase was a waltz-length white eyelet skirt and a gauzy peasant blouse, and while she might have chosen a colder, less seductive outfit, she had to admit August's instincts were sound. The fact that Aaric saw her as an attractive mate was probably keeping her alive and in a position to monitor him, and she would be foolish to sabotage that image unduly. With a sigh, she returned to the guest room and began to groom herself.

"Hey, Valmain, you look great."

Positioning herself between uncle and nephew, she smiled coolly. "Are you ready to go? I'm all packed."

"There's been a change of plans," the handsome warrior smiled. "Look over there." He was gesturing toward a powder-blue station wagon that was creating a cloud of dust as it negotiated the dirt road leading to August's ranch. "You're about to meet my sister and her kids."

"Rita?" Molly gasped. "How did she know we were here?"

"I called her from the rest room in the airport. Hi, guys!" He ambled toward the driver's door and pulled his sister from the seat. "Hi, beautiful. What took you so long?"

"What took *me* so long?" The tall, raven-haired female laughed lightly. "You're the one who disappeared for weeks without a word! And look at you!" She held him at arm's length and nodded. "You're looking pretty good, Matt." Glancing beyond him, she ordered, "Now, introduce me to poor Molly."

" 'Poor' Molly?" Matthew chuckled. "So much for sisterly loyalty. You're already on *her* side."

Molly locked eyes frantically with August, who

assured her, "There is no reason to panic. We'll monitor him carefully."

"But those children!" She watched uneasily as the two boys, both dark-haired and adorable, assaulted their uncle with greetings and handslapping. "If he dares to hurt them . . ."

"To what purpose?" August sighed. "It is more likely that he will try to win their support. Come and meet them."

"Molly?" Rita demanded, striding to greet her. "I can't believe it! You managed the impossible—you got Matt to come for another visit! And look at you! So pretty!" She hugged her impulsively. "He doesn't deserve you."

"Yeah? Well, she's mine anyway." The brother's eyes twinkled. "Take a good look at her, Rita. She's the girl from my dream. The one dressed all in white."

"Give me a break," Rita groaned. "You're crazy, Matt. Boys! Come here and meet your uncle's girl-friend."

"Yeah." The warrior grasped the older boy by the shoulders and pushed him forward. "AJ Camacho, meet your Aunt Molly."

The boy's eyes widened. "She's my *aunt?*"

"That's right, so behave. Molly, this is AJ. Ten years old, and already a great fighter. And this," he tousled the younger nephew's luxurious black hair, "is the genius I told you about. Robert Camacho."

"Hi, Aunt Molly," Robert grinned. "It's nice to meet you."

"Are you telling us you're married?" Rita wailed. "I wanted to *be* there!"

"We're not married," Molly blushed. "But it's a pleasure to meet you all. Matthew? Could I speak to you alone for just one second?"

"She's mad at me," the warrior confided to his nephews with mock sincerity.

AJ was clearly fascinated. "What'd you do?"

"Beats me. Have you been practicing?"

"Sure! Will you practice with me today, Uncle Matt? Please?"

"Sure. How about right now?"

Molly's expression hardened. "Practice? You mean fight? Don't you dare. Someone could get hurt."

"Please, Aunt Molly?" AJ wheedled. "We won't get hurt. We promise. We do this all the time! *Please?*"

She squarely faced her honorary nephew and found herself staring into eyes so reminiscent of Matthew's in color, sincerity, and impish energy that she was unable to resist. *If only he hadn't called me Aunt,* she thought, frustrated by her own vulnerability, and sighed aloud, "No rough stuff? And you promise to be careful?" Stepping between the boy and his uncle, she informed the latter stiffly, "I'll be watching carefully. Don't provoke me."

He whistled softly and brushed a curl from her scarlet cheek. "You're incredibly brave. If I were really Aaric . . ." Then he turned to AJ and demanded, "Are you going to hide behind this woman's white skirts all day?"

The boy grinned and moved into the open yard, assuming a relaxed position that again evoked memories of his uncle. Rita Camacho took Molly's arm and urged, "Come on, 'Dream Girl.' Let's go inside and have a cup of tea. They'll be fine. They do this all the time."

Molly shook her head. "Go on in with August, Rita. I'll be in soon. I need to watch this." Turning to the younger of the boys she added, "Robert? Would you like to sit and watch with me?"

"Sure." The eight-year-old settled next to her on a rough log bench and began an interrogation that belied his young age. "Uncle Matt told Mom you're a chemist. Do you go to Cal? Are you going to be a doctor? Do you understand about lightning?"

"I'm at Cal studying *bio*chemistry."

"Is that like biology and chemistry combined?"

"In a way." She tore her eyes away from the fluid, nonconfrontational exercises that had totally absorbed the two fighters. "You're eight? Is that second grade?"

"I'm starting third grade in September."

"Your Uncle Matthew told me what a fine student you are. Do you like school?"

"It's pretty good."

Remembering his barrage of questions, she offered, "When I was your age I lived in Boston. I used to look over the bay and watch the lightning and try to understand what caused it." Taking a deep breath she explained, "Lightning is a kind of giant, atmospheric electrical discharge. Almost as though so much energy has built up in a cloud that the cloud acts like a giant battery."

Far from being confused by this, Robert seemed inspired. "And thunder is the shock wave all that energy causes when it heats up the air and makes it expand. Right?"

"Either that, or it's angels bowling."

He laughed appreciatively. "*Are* you going to be a doctor?"

"Not exactly. More like a chemist than a doctor. My father's a doctor, though."

"My father's a bum," Robert replied quietly, then added, "We never see him."

"I never see my father, either. It's been almost four years."

"Really?" The boy seemed depressed by the news. "I guess even doctors can be bums."

"And I guess we have something in common."

He brightened immediately. "We have lots in common, Aunt Molly. I want to be a doctor. I study real hard. Uncle Matt told Mom you study real hard, too."

"That's true." She winced as AJ flew through the air, landing unhurt but disgusted with himself.

Robert laughed gleefully. "I'm glad Uncle Matt's back. I'm usually the one who ends up getting thrown, when AJ makes me practice with him."

"Do you study kung fu, too?"

"That's judo," Robert smiled. "Mom and Uncle Matt won't let AJ take anything rougher." He noticed her wince again. "Don't worry, Aunt Molly. Uncle Matt would never hurt AJ or me."

"I know that." She touched his sleeve lightly. "Your uncle has been through a lot these last few weeks. I guess I'm just a little overly-cautious."

"He does seem different," the boy acknowledged casually.

"Oh?"

"He doesn't usually smile so much."

Tension was slowly building in her neck and shoulders. Could this child see something she and August could not? "Is that so?"

"I guess he's in love with you. That's what Mom hopes. So you'll 'civilize' him. But AJ hopes you won't."

She smiled reluctantly. "And what do you hope?"

"I just hope he visits more often."

"I'll see what I can do." She noticed that August

had emerged from the house and was beckoning to her. "August?"

"Go inside and get acquainted with my niece," he urged. "I'll watch over the boys."

"'Watch over us'?" Robert seemed perplexed. "Uncle Matt's out here with us, Uncle August. We're safe."

"Danger comes in many forms," August suggested with a weary smile. "Perhaps it is your Uncle Matthew who needs *our* help."

"Him? He's invincible." The young boy's eyes burned with pride and he turned back to watch his uncle spar effectively, effortlessly, and with infinite gentleness toward his opponent.

It was a reassuring sight and Molly welcomed the slight reprieve from her anxieties, accepting August's offer to change places for a while. She found Rita parked at August's pine table, pouring fragrant herbal tea from a simple unglazed pot.

"Finally! Come and sit with me. Let me look at you." Her appraisal was frank and unapologetic. "I never pictured Matt ending up with a girl like you, and I have to admit, I'm relieved."

Molly flushed at the ambiguity inherent in the compliment and accepted a steaming mug. "Relieved?"

"He usually goes for Amazons. Real self-sufficient women of the world. Scary ones."

"I'm self-sufficient," Molly protested. "I have been for years, and I intend to stay that way."

"You're self-sufficient in the social sense, like me. I'm talking self-sufficient in the jungle sense," Rita laughed. "It's just as well you don't know what I mean. You're so sweet!"

Molly wondered what Rita would think if she knew she was addressing a witch who slept with a dagger under her pillow. Assuming, of course, that Molly *was* a witch, as Aaric and August had claimed. Any further discussion was cut short by the arrival of a dusty, grinning AJ.

"So?" Rita demanded. "Are you still alive?"

"Barely." He glanced shyly at Molly and added, "I'm fine. Uncle Matt was real careful."

"And what was Robert's opinion of his new aunt?" Rita pressed.

"He said she's nice. And smart." He slid onto the bench beside Molly and accepted a tumbler of cool water from his mother. "Uncle Matt says you're descended from the same tribe as us, Aunt Molly."

"Uncle Matt has a vivid imagination," Rita hooted, fingering Molly's light curls expressively. "Molly's Irish, AJ. That's a whole ocean away. Can you imagine what your kids will look like, Molly? I want a niece first, okay?"

She nodded quietly, wondering what this loving family would do without Matthew Redtree. Her heart went out to AJ and she confided, "You remind me a lot of your Uncle Matthew."

"Really?"

"Yes. Your eyes and your smile . . . and you stand like him, when you're preparing to fight. I noticed that right away."

AJ beamed with pride. "I *practice* standing like him. And like my Dad. He and Uncle Matt met in judo class, did you know?"

"No, I didn't."

"And I really look like Dad, more than like Uncle Matt. He's bigger than Uncle Matt, so someday, I'll be bigger than him, too. But," his young eyes twinkled as he delivered what was clearly a well-worn family joke, "I won't hurt him then, Aunt Molly."

"That's a relief."

Rita laughed. "Humble as always, AJ. Molly, are you and Matt staying in LA for a while?"

"We're leaving today, unfortunately. Matthew has some research . . ."

"Some things never change, I guess. Matt and his research."

"Uncle Matt said it's like a honeymoon trip they're taking," AJ contributed.

"Honeymoon?" Rita's eyebrow arched. "What about that, Molly?"

The Valmain dreamer grimaced. "We're definitely not at that stage yet."

"Don't go getting married in Timbuktu, Molly. Please? Matt's not much, but he's the only brother I've got and I want to go to his wedding. Promise?"

"Yes. If Matthew and I decide to get married, you'll all be there. I wouldn't have it any other way."

"Your kids will be my cousins," AJ supplied with growing enthusiasm. "Our family will get really big. It's too small right now. Maybe . . ." He glanced toward Rita. "Maybe you and Dad will have another baby, too, Mom, to play with Uncle Matt's kids."

"Anything's possible," Rita shrugged, adding for Molly's benefit, "My husband's a wanderer, like my brother. We don't see very much of either of them."

"Families should all live in one house together," AJ pronounced solemnly. "You and Uncle Matt should move to LA with us. We should all be together."

"I agree." August's slight form looked almost holy, framed by the sunlight in the doorway. "You *are* a part of our family now, Molly, no matter what else happens. Never forget that."

"Thanks, August." She stood and stretched. "I'd

better not get too comfortable. Matthew and I have to leave right away."

"But you just got here," AJ grumbled. "Please, Aunt Molly? Just stay one week?"

"They will return, for a long visit," August soothed. "In the meantime, you and Robert may stay with me, if your mother consents."

While Rita and her boys negotiated the terms of the impromptu vacation, Molly edged away and onto the porch where her warrior-companion awaited her.

"Did you miss me, Valmain?" he teased, slipping his arm around her waist. "Has Rita been turning you against me?"

"She clearly adores you. And the boys are wonderful."

"Do you really have to leave today, Matt?" Rita sighed from the doorway.

"Yeah. Molly wants me all to herself. Right, Valmain?"

"That's right. I want to get to know the real you a little better."

"The real me?" he chuckled. "What about the real you? Did you tell Rita you're a witch?"

"Wow!" AJ's eyes sparkled as he wriggled past his mother and into the sunlight. "Are you really a witch, Aunt Molly?"

"Believe it or not, they mean it as a compliment, Molly," Rita giggled. "Tell them they're insulting you."

Molly's eyes locked with her would-be lover's, although her words were directed to his nephew. "I'm not a witch like in a fairy tale, AJ. That's not what your uncle meant. He just meant I have the power to . . . keep him in line, and I'm not afraid to use it."

"Well, you've definitely bewitched him," Rita smiled. "He seems like an entirely different person."

The warrior winced. "Bad choice of words, Sis."

"Don't worry." Rita bestowed a sisterly peck on his cheek. "I like the new you better than the old one, believe me. Stop frowning."

"I'm the same me I always was."

There was a tinge of frustration in his voice and Molly felt her throat tighten. If this man was Aaric the Moonshaker, then these trusting descendants of Lost Eagle were flirting with incredible animosity. Forcing herself to smile, she patted each boy's shoulder in turn and promised, "Our next visit will be much longer. I promise. But right now we have to run. Rita? We'll keep in touch. Matthew? Could you get the bags?"

"Sure, Valmain. Whatever you say. Sis? I love you. AJ? Practice! Robert? Study."

"Or vice versa?" Rita suggested. "Anyway, you two have fun, and don't get married without giving me a chance to be there to give my bonehead brother away."

August drew Molly aside and added softly, "Try to return to the dream. Find the answer there."

"I'll try. In the meantime . . ." Her proud shoulders drooped.

"In the meantime," August insisted, "you must protect yourself from him. Try not to antagonize him or challenge him. Observe. Trust your instincts. If he is the Moonshaker, he is a murderer. His selfish lack of respect for the sanctity of life will eventually show itself."

"And then?"

"You can contact me through my niece. Don't try to make the final decision on your own."

"Thanks, August. I'll do my best," she added half-heartedly.

"Your best has proved to be quite remarkable," he reminded her. "Matthew told me of your steady eyes and pure heart. Now I have seen for myself and I am confident they will prevail."

She wondered whether to embrace him but settled for firmly grasping his gnarled hand. With Rita, however, she was given no option but to return an enormous bear hug and, as she slipped into the seat of their rental car, she concentrated upon drawing strength from the boisterous family that had so generously welcomed her. After years of solitude in Berkeley—isolation from a fair-haired half-sister and a distant father—she was almost achingly vulnerable to this warmth and solace.

Aunt Molly. It meant so much—much more, in many ways, than "princess" or "dream girl." She would prove herself worthy of the title. She would protect Lost Eagle's clan with her life.

"Where to, Valmain?" her companion demanded cheerfully, as he started the engine and shifted into gear.

"I guess we should just head back to Berkeley. I have to touch base with Ken Lewis about my job." She savored the slight connection to normalcy. "And your house is sitting empty. Shouldn't you check on your gruesome collection, or have you lost interest in weapons?"

"You're on vacation, Valmain. Let's do some traveling. Between the burglar alarms and the fence, I've got my stuff in Berkeley covered completely."

Molly considered her next move soberly. Returning to Ireland seemed completely unacceptable. There was no way on earth she was going to endanger Elizabeth or Brian by exposing them to a possible evil magician. "We're not going back to Ireland."

"I agree. I'm in no great hurry to be insulted by Elizabeth. She'd probably jump for joy if you told her I wasn't myself anymore," he added playfully

"Leave my grandmother out of this."

"Your job doesn't start for weeks. Come traveling with me. Let me show you the world. You've spent too much of your life in an ivory tower."

"In other words," Molly frowned, *"Aaric the Moonshaker* wants to see the world. For the first time yourself. Through my Matthew's eyes."

"Humor me, Valmain," he laughed. "How about a compromise? Fifty percent of the time you can treat me like I'm Aaric, and the other fifty percent you'll treat me like your champion. Agreed?"

"No."

"How about just one hour a day? Preferably at night," he added mischievously. "Come on, Molly. You know in your heart it's me!"

"I do not! Stop that!" She removed his hand from her neck and replaced it on the steering wheel. "No more touching until we get this resolved. I'll *never* forget," she added hotly, "the way you taunted me that afternoon in the dream. Telling me you'd make love to me with Matthew's body. You disgust me."

"I thought my uncle would help you gain some perspective," Matthew growled. "Instead, he's made it worse."

"No!" she protested quickly. "When we were alone, August told me he's convinced you're Matthew Redtree. He's your ally. I'm the only one with doubts."

"Nice try, Valmain." He patted her hand. "You're protecting him? I love that."

"Your family's very devoted to you," she sighed,

then added hotly, "Don't you *ever* touch one of those sweet little boys again!"

"I don't think even a bastard like Aaric the Moonshaker would hurt a little kid, Molly. Don't be so suspicious. I *need* to train AJ."

"For what? Don't tell me he's destined for battle, too!"

"Who knows? It's best to prepare him. He's been wanting to learn karate, and I've been insisting he stick with judo, but now . . ." His hands tightened visibly on the steering wheel. "I learned the hard way with Aaric that judo's not enough. It was my karate that bought me time." He seemed saddened by the thought. "I love judo—like a way of life. Like an art form. But it relies on balance and using your opponent's momentum against him. Aaric's illusions made it impossible for me to throw him."

"But AJ won't ever fight Aaric," Molly protested, then she glared, "At least, you'd better *not.*"

"I have to teach him karate," he repeated stubbornly. "That's the kind of cross-training that saved my life until the amulet could kick in."

"Speaking of which," her gaze was fixed on the silver spool that adorned his wrist, "why did you make August give that back?"

"It was his idea."

"Right," she drawled. "With a little 'persuasion' from you?"

"Give it a rest." He flashed a charming smile. "I love you, Molly Sheridan. Come traveling with me. I'll show you a Europe that most people don't even know exists."

Chapter Thirteen

Two weeks later, Molly was willing to admit that his boast had proved accurate. His Europe, like his Ireland, was a land of myth and legend, and he was a consummate guide. His England was based in Sarum rather than London; the catacombs of Rome were the scene of two full days' exploration, with the Sistine Chapel being relegated to "Next time, I promise" status; and the roots of Celtic legends were traced to France and Germany and beyond. And through it all her companion proved to be the most charming and seductive of escorts.

His soft, sincere voice mesmerized her as he recounted ancient tales of love, loss, and heroism. His touch—unwelcomed yet unavoidable—unnerved her, and his need, so strong it was almost tangible, disarmed her. There were times when the mere awareness of him—his thick, unruly hair, tightly-muscled torso and warm, sweet breath—could turn her insides to molten fire. Again and again she had to remind both herself *and* her love-starved body that this dark, impassioned man could be the cold-blooded slayer of the Valmain champion. After all, he *did* seem intent upon dragging her to isolated, desolate spots. He could dispose of her body so easily at any one of them! Of course, from the way he rested his hand protectively on her elbow or waist while guiding her along the rocky paths of his Europe, she knew, deep down inside, that his plans for her body had nothing to do with murder and everything to do with pleasure.

"You promised we'd tour someplace civilized today, Aaric," she grumbled, as he led her to yet another in a seemingly endless parade of stone circles.

"This is civilization at its finest. Its purest," he assured her proudly. "Put your prejudices aside and just look at this place, Molly. Isn't it incredible?"

"They put so much work into dragging these rocks here and arranging them just so," she agreed lightly. "You'd think they would have finished the job and carved them into beautiful shapes."

"The Celts believed that each tree and rock had its spiritual counterpart and they weren't about to carve it without a good reason," he explained patiently. "You've seen how elaborate and decorative their bronze and silver work was. They were artists second, mystics first. It's awesome."

"You would have made a great Druid, Aaric. Maybe you *were* from around here! That would explain your light-colored hair."

"Give it a rest, Valmain," he groaned. "You've called me Aaric all week. Call me Matthew, just for the rest of today, and pay attention. This is your heritage I'm about to share."

"You're going to lecture me?"

"Right."

She steeled herself, remembering how seductive his lecture-hall voice could be. "Go ahead. Until recently, the most I heard about Irish mythology had to do with leprechauns and stew."

"Right. Just like most people's idea of Indian culture is a rain dance. That's the American melting pot for you—melt away all that's threatening, individualistic, and distinct. Leave nothing but the innocuous and bland. But the truth is, the Celts were far from bland." His tone grew smoother. "Picture the Celts, Molly. Big guys, for their time. Fierce and mystical. Along come the Romans, in their neat little legions, with their neat little myths about predictable gods—ripped off from the Greeks, of course—and they're suddenly assaulted by hoards of wild men. *Naked* wild men."

"I beg your pardon?" Molly glared.

"I'm not kidding, Valmain. Your guys used to charge into battle naked. No beards, just long, wild moustaches, and helmets and metal battle collars. Awesome."

"Did they have shields, at least?"

"Sure. Remember the one at my house—*our* house—in Berkeley?"

"Oh, right. Helmets and shields, but naked. I think I've got the picture. Now can we go to Paris?"

"Sometimes they painted their bodies blue." He shook his head in frank admiration. "Really wild."

"They could have had a colorful battle with *your* relatives," she quipped irreverently. "Didn't you say in one of your lectures that your 'guys' used to paint their bodies red?"

He burst into laughter. "I'm glad to hear someone was listening to me during those lectures. Yeah. My 'guys' rubbed red ochre onto their bodies, which is reputedly the original source of the term 'red man.' You get an A, Miss Sheridan."

"I miss those lectures," she sighed. "Don't you?"

"Not even a little. This is real life, Valmain. It's ironic, though. I did a little digging into Celtic and

Norse legends for my book, but I concentrated on North American Indian mythology because I naturally assumed it was the only place to find mention of Maya or the Moonshaker."

"I like the Native American legends better than the Celtic ones, anyway," Molly confessed. "At least the ones I've heard. The Irish ones are so violent and absurd."

"Are you kidding? They're the best!"

"They leave me cold. For one thing, the men are always cutting off someone's head."

"Yeah. The Celts knew instinctively that the head, not the heart, was the source of a man's identity. That's why they cut the head off and brandished it around. Some of those guys actually preserved the heads of their enemies and displayed the collection on request."

"So you've mentioned," she groaned.

"It makes sense. They were a very individualistic culture, battlewise. They liked to fight one-on-one. Sometimes two big armies would face one another just to watch two guys duke it out. When you think about it, it's pretty civilized. Reduces the bloodshed considerably."

"It's almost noble," she agreed blithely.

"There are stories of some confrontations where no battle at all took place. The top guy from one side would recite his exploits, then the top guy from the other side would recite *his,* and then, if they were clearly mismatched, the loser would just concede and everyone would go get drunk."

"I'm bursting with pride."

"Of course, at their feasts, more fights would usually break out. They were a boastful group."

"They had a lot to boast about. Right?"

"Show a little respect, Valmain."

"I can't get past the decapitation issue," she confessed. "It disgusts me."

"There's a hilarious story about an Ulster warrior who used to carry his latest victim's head around under his arm," he laughed. "It seems that one time, at a feast in Connaught, they were trying to decide who should get the prime cut of meat, which traditionally went to the toughest guy in the room. And so the host was trading stories with the others, trying to top everyone.

"Anyway, this Ulster warrior comes in carrying a head under his arm and starts to recite his conquests, and yeah, it seems he's the top guy. But the host is really riled and complains that if only his brother were there, *he'd* show up the Ulster guy by a mile. And so the Ulster guy says," a smile danced behind his eyes, " 'Your brother *is* here!' and he turns the head around and it's the host's brother's head!"

Grimacing at her escort's appreciative laughter, Molly sniffed, "Like I said, these little jewels leave me cold. The men are always brutes, and the women are always overly sturdy."

"Yeah," Matthew teased. "Did you hear about the Celtic woman who stabbed a huge warrior in the leg with an obsidian dagger and then ate a huge dinner two hours later?"

"Don't forget it," Molly shrugged. "Sturdy *and* deadly."

"You're amazing," he agreed easily. "Now climb up on that rock. I want to take your picture."

"Climb up there and antagonize some rock spirit?" she mocked. "I told you before, I don't want mementos of this trip. Anyway," she glanced around impatiently, "I don't like it here. I want to go to Paris. It's less than six hours' drive from here, right?"

"We're headed there soon. Climb up now." He grasped her by her elbow and urged her to the top of the eight-foot obelisk. "This place is incredibly powerful. I'll bet there were thousands of ceremonies held here. Maybe even human sacrifice."

"Ugh." She wrenched her arm free, losing her footing in the process. Only the warrior's quick reflexes prevented her from toppling over.

"Watch it, Valmain," he warned, then smiled when she momentarily clung to him. "What's this, a show of gratitude? Finally?" His lips brushed hers. "Nice."

She jerked her face away. "Did you engineer that little rescue, Moonshaker?"

"Huh?"

She slid to the ground and smoothed her skirt angrily. "You made me fall, so you could save me. Very convenient. I'm going back to our hotel, with or without you."

"I'd never endanger you and, frankly, I don't think old Aaric would have, either. He was pretty hot for you, remember?" Catching up with her in two long strides, he spun her toward himself and demanded, "If you think I'd hurt you, why do you stay with me?"

"You're my responsibility! I'm the one who let you loose on an unsuspecting world."

"Even if that were so," he shrugged, "it wouldn't be your place to stop Aaric. You're the dreamer, not the champion."

"I'm the witch," she countered coolly. "Maybe that's what's protected me from you so far. You're just a little bit afraid of me."

He burst into laughter. "Yeah, I'm quaking in my boots. Come here."

"We've discussed this," she glared, pulling away once more. "Keep your hands to yourself and let's get out of here. I hate this spot."

"You feel the power here, and it scares you," he speculated. "I guess I should have taken you someplace more beautiful."

"I had enough beauty yesterday when you showed me that gold-lined skull," she shuddered. "We don't define beauty the same way, whoever you are. The thought that anyone ever drank out of another person's skull . . . Yuck."

"I explained that," he laughed. "You've got to embrace your heritage, Valmain. The severed head of a worthy opponent was the most valuable trophy a Celtic warrior could imagine."

"It's gruesome."

"I've heard the Irish Celts used to play a game like field hockey, with sticks called hurling sticks, and guess what they used for a ball?"

"I want to go back to the hotel," she repeated in disgust. "And I don't want talk about heads on the way."

"Let's go," he agreed. "I haven't practiced today yet, and you should take a nap. You're getting cranky."

Practice, practice, practice . . . Molly grumbled to herself. The man—*whoever* he was—was indefatigable. He trained every day, refining his fluid moves and sharp kicks, and running for miles on end without becoming winded. For variety there was climbing and shadow boxing, and lunging with the infamous dagger or experimenting with the various new weapons he had acquired for his collection.

With the amulet tied proudly to his wrist with a

leather thong, he was a magnificent sight, Molly often admitted as she watched. She could remember him, sparsely clad in skins, his bow draped over his bronzed shoulder . . . She would then remember Aaric, fierce and deadly . . .

There were times when she was sure—absolutely sure!—this man was truly Matthew Redtree and the love that would well within her would threaten to erupt, yet Molly would remember the other times—times when she would catch an unfamiliar expression on his face or perceive a moment's hesitation in his usual single-mindedness—and so she waited in vain for a foolproof sign.

He had ushered her into their silver-gray touring sedan and now urged, "Go to sleep. I'll wake you when we get there."

"It's only a ten-minute ride. I'll wait."

"Actually," he eased their vehicle onto a dirt road, "we checked out of that place, and into another one."

"Again? You never consult me . . ." She moistened her lips and tried to sound casual. "Don't tell me we really are going to Paris. Finally!"

"It's on the list," he assured her, "but first, I have a surprise for you. A place much more romantic than Paris. Just close your eyes and, when you wake up, we'll be there."

She resisted an urge to smile. This debate over Paris had become a running gag with Matthew—or Aaric—and she could only imagine what hellhole he was daring to propose now as a "romantic" substitute. It could be anything, from absurd to gruesome to simply bizarre and dusty. The only certainty would be that it wasn't a charming bistro or a restful spa. That wasn't this man's style, whoever he was.

Despite her doubts, she was able to rest easily by his side as they drove along the heavily wooded back road. Over the last two weeks the hatred she felt for Aaric the Moonshaker had been lessening, as though being tempered by her growing need to spend the rest of her life with this intense, confident man, whoever he might prove to be. She now found herself reexamining the entire Lost Eagle legend from Aaric's point of view. Hadn't it been a particularly complex love triangle? A sorceress, a sorcerer, and a warrior. The sorcerer and the warrior had each wanted to eliminate the other, so that the victor could have Maya for himself. Maya, renowned for her temper, had obviously driven these men wild with passion and jealousy and then *she* had stolen Lost Eagle's amulet, leaving him defenseless.

And then what, Molly? she taunted herself, as she shifted in her seat. *Then "poor Aaric" couldn't help but kill Lost Eagle? Then Lost Eagle vowed that his descendant would kill "poor Aaric" and so he again had no choice but to manhandle you and slaughter Matthew? He was despicable! Remember how he bragged about how he would deceive you? Remember how he admitted he had always wanted to be immortal? Hardly "poor Aaric."*

Still she vacillated, acknowledging that Aaric could have molested her in a much crueler and more violent manner. As a huge warrior-sorcerer, he could have thrown her to the ground and terrified her. Instead, he had seemed genuinely interested in reassuring her—in explaining the story to her—and the experience had been less traumatic than it might have been . . .

In fact, it had been intensely flattering. He had praised *her*—her body, her sound, her very *smell*—

in contrast to Matthew's praise of her "goodness" and "strength" and balance . . .

That's what this is all about! she accused herself mercilessly, not daring to glance at her companion lest he read her mind and see her weakness. *He was a good lover and so you're ready to forgive his other minor faults, like murder and deceit. And Aaric would have praised any female—after all, it had been hundreds—no! thousands—of years since he'd made love to a woman!*

If only Aaric hadn't used Matthew's body, she realized finally. While she resisted this man with apparent coolness, she was far from cool, knowing that, whether it was Matthew or Aaric who used that body, the result would be magic in bed.

"Molly?"

She scowled without bothering to open her eyes. "Forget it, Moonshaker."

"I was just trying to tell you we're here," he teased. "What's on your mind, Valmain? You're blushing!"

"I'm not blushing and . . ." She stared out the window in amazement. "We're here? Where is here?"

He was pulling the car onto a circular drive in front of a stately, if slightly run-down and eerily secluded, mansion. "I leased this for us. For a week. Like it?"

She straightened, determined to fathom this strategy. They were literally in the middle of nowhere, and for the first time in more than a week, she questioned her own safety. Had Aaric tired of her resistance? Did he intend to kill her? Seduce her? Strand her while he made his escape?

"Why are we here?" she murmured. "This place is huge, and it looks abandoned. Are there servants?

Is there a phone? I promised August I'd call again this week."

"It's not as remote as it looks," he assured her. "Get out, Valmain. Let's explore it a little. I think you'll love it."

"It looks deserted."

"I told the owner to give the servants the week off. We can fend for ourselves, and we need our privacy."

"We do?"

"For one thing," he grinned mischievously, "I'm tired of sleeping on the floor."

She gave him a practiced glare. After all, if he had kept his massages to himself, she would have let him sleep with her, but his wandering hands had been too much for her and she had been forced to institute a new ritual—they always stayed in a room at least three stories off the ground, to prevent window escapes, and they always pushed the bed against the door, for Molly, leaving generous albeit hardwood accommodations for her roommate.

"Here," he swept his arm to encompass the view of the surrounding impenetrable forest, "I can't sneak away. You can sleep in one bed, and I can sleep in another. There are seven bedrooms, all completely furnished. My imagination has been working overtime all day on the possibilities." He unlocked the heavy oak door and swung it open. "After you, dream girl."

Seven beds. Molly's own imagination was beginning to grind out scenarios, none of them acceptable. As she stepped onto the gleaming marble of the huge entry hall, she trembled with the realization that this was someone's dream house, and that someone just might be Molly Sheridan. "It's cavernous," she insisted half-heartedly. "And I'll bet it's freezing in the winter."

"But this is summer," he reminded her cheerfully. "It's six centuries old and permeated with history."

"Is that what that is? I thought it was mold." She feigned a shudder. "I wonder how many dead bodies are hidden here."

"We'll start counting tomorrow," he grinned. "For now, let's explore. It may be old, but supposedly it has all the modern conveniences, including an Olympic-sized swimming pool for you to do your laps."

"Oh!" She had honestly missed her daily swimming and was touched that he had remembered. If only she'd thought to bring a bathing suit.

"I picked up a swimsuit for you. It's in the trunk."

"I wish you wouldn't do that!" she snapped.

"What? Shop for you?"

"No. You read my mind again." They had reached an endless row of French doors opening onto a sweeping terrace. The sun was just beginning to set in the distance and a string of photosensitive hanging lanterns were beginning to flicker, creating a magical effect. "Oh, Matthew!"

"It's pretty, isn't it? The pool should be just beyond the pines there. We could go for a dip tonight, if you'd like, although . . ."

She liked the hesitation, bordering on shyness, in his voice. He hadn't brought her here to kill or abandon her. It was time for the seduction and she had to admit she was relieved. No longer did she believe he could "persuade" her by use of love spells or potions—if that were possible, he would have done it by now, on one of those long, lonely nights he had spent on the floor, banished and uncomfortable. Instead, he had been forced to use this more traditional and wildly romantic approach.

Someone had set a tray of tiny spinach quiches on a white wrought-iron table in the shadow of a grape arbor. Next to the food, a bottle of champagne was chilling. Her wily escort had arranged all this and, when she turned to him, she knew her eyes were shining with consent.

"You agree?" he whispered. "We can't go on pretending we aren't in love, Valmain. I'm going crazy, sleeping without you, and hearing you call me Aaric instead of champion. I can't take one more night of it." He stepped to within inches of her. "I love you, Molly Sheridan."

"And I love Matthew Redtree," she affirmed in return. "I want you to be him more than I've ever wanted anything—*any*thing!—in my life. I'll love him until the day I die and . . ." her eyes searched his for strength, "no other man can ever take his place." Swaying forward, she allowed him to take her into his arms and as he did, the heat between them flamed into passion. His mouth was over hers, tasting with the hunger of a starving man, while his hands found her hips and pulled her hard against his torso.

She had dreamed of this moment . . . craved it . . . *lusted* for it! All doubts exploded into hot, sensuous certainty. He was her lover, and he had planned all this, with spellbinding precision, because he craved and lusted for her as well! Her grandmother had been wrong, after all—Matthew Redtree was so clearly and utterly in love! So desperate was his need that, despite his "balanced" style, he had conspired to sweep her off her feet in this gloriously romantic hideaway, complete with champagne and a hundred other possibilities for excess and indulgence.

"You're trembling, Valmain. Are you frightened?"

"No," she breathed. "I . . . I . . ." She was literally speechless with arousal. "Matthew, please . . ."

Then, to her abject dismay, he relaxed his hold on her until it was less than a gentle caress. "We don't have to do this," he was assuring her solemnly. "I know I've been pushing you, and I'm sorry."

"Matthew, no . . ."

He was clearly furious with himself. "We *never* have to do this if you're uncomfortable with it, Molly. I can live without it, believe me. This part never really mattered to me."

She stared, certain she had misheard him.

"All I want," he insisted desperately, "and all I've ever wanted, was to fulfill my destiny as Lost Eagle's avenger and as your champion. I can live without the rest."

And he meant it! There was no doubt, although she now craved doubt more than she had craved certainty only moments before. *All I've ever wanted* . . . It was true. All he had ever wanted from her was the role, the strength, and the purity. He could live without the rest!

Or he's Aaric, up to his old tricks, she tried to remind herself under her breath but the old refrain didn't ring true. She almost wished it would! She wished this man could be Aaric, for just this one excruciatingly painful moment. Then it would all be a lie. Aaric, for all his flaws, needed more than destiny's approval. He needed a woman—a mistress, a playmate, a challenge. He had said he would own her, but wasn't the reverse also true? Wouldn't she own Aaric the Moonshaker, in a way, if she satisfied him sexually?

She could never own Matthew Redtree.

"Molly? Are you upset?"

She had almost forgotten he was standing there, so acute was her loneliness. "I'm fine," she whispered.

"You still think I'm Aaric?"

There's only one way to find out, she answered silently. Slipping her arms around his neck, she directed softly, "I want you to make love to me. I want you to pour your whole heart and soul into it. I want it to be . . . magic."

An amazed grin spread across his handsome face. "Yeah? I'll see what I can do."

Closing her eyes, she dropped her head back, allowing his lips full access to her neck. This would be paradise, she knew. It wouldn't be love, of course. If this man was Matthew, it would be worship at the dream altar, and if it was Aaric, it would be unbridled lust. Either way, it would be paradise of a sort. For all their faults, each of the two warriors knew how to make love to a woman.

And, if it was Aaric, it would be the last thing he ever did, because she could and would kill him in his smug, self-satisfied, love-soaked sleep that very night. And if it was Matthew Redtree . . .

If it was Matthew, she would leave him in the morning.

Jealousy. It was not a new sensation to the warrior-sorcerer, and yet it was different this time, somehow. The Valmain princess was different, too. Different from any woman he had ever known. She could be fragile—almost helpless—one minute, and a lioness the next. She cried piteously when her heart ached, but responded to threats with the hiss of a cat and the courage of a dozen warriors. She had a beauty that was unselfconscious and, curiously, more pleasing to him than that of the voluptuous, flashing-eyed females who ordinarily won his attentions.

The thought of her in the arms of Lost Eagle's son was enough to send him hourly into a rage. Where *was* she? Why didn't she revisit the dream? What was the cause of her ignorance, and why did she struggle so desperately against her heritage and against the flame that had been kindled between them during their lovemaking? Was she frightened? Lonely? Injured? Could her champion have dared mistreat her?

"No," Aaric taunted himself grimly. "It is much simpler than that, Moonshaker. They endlessly celebrate their victory over you, and that is understandable. To have defeated the Moonshaker—Lost Eagle's son must be reeling with prideful memories. He regales his princess with retellings of his prowess, but does he tell her how truly beautiful she is? How inspiring and seductive is her manner? Does he praise those shapely legs, or the soft curve of her waist, or the tremble in her voice when she is overcome by arousal? No. Lost Eagle's son is not one to speak of such things, and the Princess is a woman who longs to be spoken to just so." His smile became one of confidence and anticipation as he assured himself, "She will return to this dream eventually. She will not be able to deny her needs and her nature forever. She will return, and when she does, I will be ready."

* * *

Molly snuggled against her champion and sighed. Any thoughts she had had of leaving this man had vanished in a blaze of passion during their torrid reconciliation. The facts were now crystal clear. Even if Matthew Redtree could accept the prospect of life without lovemaking, Molly Sheridan could not. As strange as it seemed, Aaric had been right. A man *could* own a woman after lovemaking, and Matthew Redtree owned Molly Sheridan, body and soul. She wondered if he knew it.

She wanted to tell him how close he had come to losing her. She wanted to plead with him to take back his insultingly sweet offer of permanent celibacy. She even wanted to coach him—to provide him with the lies she longed to hear—lies that would make her enslavement seem less one-sided. Instead, she found herself murmuring, "I love you so much, Matthew Redtree. Don't ever let me leave you."

"Huh?"

Her smile was wistful. "Never mind. You're my hero. I'm just sorry I've been so rough on you these last two weeks. And I'm sorry I didn't stay in the dream long enough to see you beat Aaric. And," she rolled onto him and stared into his eyes, "I'm truly, truly sorry I wasn't there to help."

"It was for the best," he assured her, stroking her love-dampened curls lightly. "The more desperate he got, the more bizarre his illusions got. He probably would have found a way to use you against me." With a rueful chuckle he added, "I guess he *did* find a way to use you against me, right? All that stuff he told you that day in your dream worked against me these last few weeks. He got a little revenge, in a roundabout way."

"He psyched me out completely," she admitted. "Every time I was *sure* it was you, I remembered him saying," she adopted a deep, resonant tone, " 'You will want so desperately to believe it is he . . .' " She made a sour face. "It was like some kind of weird curse."

Matthew rolled her to the side, then sat up and gathered her nude body into his lap. "What if I *had* been Aaric?" he scolded gently. "You should have put as much distance between yourself and me as possible, Valmain."

Molly laughed lightly. "Don't lecture me, Professor. I think I handled the whole thing really well."

"If I *had* been Aaric, I would have done something to you to make you trust me and you would have been sunk."

"I wasn't afraid of you."

"That's my point. You *should* have been afraid. Without your champion, you were vulnerable. You were right to contact my uncle, of course, but you should have gotten clear of Aaric first."

"I needed August's advice. And it all worked out. Maybe," she sighed, running her tongue along his smooth, muscled chest, "I always knew it was you."

"No way. You should have seen how you looked at me." His tone softened and he tipped her chin until she was gazing into his shining eyes. "You hated him for killing me, and you couldn't stand to see him taking my form again. It was nice, Valmain."

"It was unbearable to think I could lose you when we'd had so little time together," she confessed. "I'd be lost without you, Matthew. Don't ever let me go."

"That's the second time you've said that. Don't you know how I feel about you?"

"You explained it eloquently earlier," she murmured.

"Well then, what's the problem?" His smile was angelic. "It's funny, isn't it? Fighting Aaric was always my purpose in life. My goal. Then suddenly . . ."

"Yes, Matthew?"

"I was free. Free to hunt and explore and have kids—with you, of course. I wanted to be everything to you, but instead you hated me. And so I had to prove myself to you . . ." He cocked his head to the side and studied her. "How exactly did I do that? Was it like I said? An animal like Aaric couldn't be tender or loving, like I can, so you could tell by letting me make love to you that I was me?"

It brought another wistful smile to her lips. "Not quite. It wasn't so much what you said or did, it was what you thought." She brushed her lips across his. "Aaric could look like you, and sound like you, and he could spout statements that were stored in your thoughts, be he couldn't actually think like you."

"True. And?"

"And I don't think he understood the destiny angle completely. I think he would have tried harder to actually romance me. He would have taken me to Paris, for example."

"But you saw the cave paintings at Lascaux! How many people can say that? It was a real honor that they gave us that private showing, Molly. *Anyone* can see Paris. That doesn't require any imagination and I don't see how it proved I was me."

She grinned darkly. "Here's a better example. Aaric would know how to charm a girl. How to sweet-talk her. And he would have known instinctively that a girl doesn't want to hear that a guy would have loved her even if she'd been boring and ugly and dimwitted."

"I don't remember saying that."

"You said you were 'destined' to love me," she sighed. "You might as well have added that it was nothing personal."

"You were destined to love me, too," he reminded her weakly. "It doesn't offend me. I like it *better* this way."

"There!" she gloated. "You just proved it again! You're definitely Matthew Redtree. My champion," she added dutifully.

"Don't ever forget it. I'd do anything for you, Valmain." His eyes twinkled as he added, "I'll even take you to Paris tomorrow, if you want."

"Next week," she corrected. "We leased this place for a week, right? And it has seven beds, one for each night, and I think we should try them all, your offer of platonic love notwithstanding."

"My what?"

"You said you didn't need to sleep with me. Remember? All you care about is the dream girl stuff." She flushed slightly, surprised by the raw hurt in her voice. "But you're not getting off the hook that easily. I want to spend this whole week making up for lost time."

"No problem. My goal for the week is to keep you happy."

"Why don't you just try one week without any goal at all? Don't you think you earned it? You got revenge for Lost Eagle, and avenged my honor in the process. Why don't you just make love to me all week because you *want* to?"

"I do want to," he chuckled. "And if I get the amulet working again, you really *will* want to stay in bed with me forever."

"That's a pretty obnoxious statement," she scolded. "And anyway, you don't need an amulet. If I told you how great a lover you are, you'd blush." Just the thought of his lovemaking made her warm, and she wriggled out of his lap and stretched her nude body hopefully.

Matthew's eyes sparkled. "I'm glad I can satisfy you, Valmain. I think that's the key to getting back to the dream."

"The dream?" With a frustrated glare she bounded from the bed and pulled a plush red velour robe from a nearby hook. A matching, larger robe had also been provided, and she realized that this huge room with its heavy oak furnishings was intended as the master suite, after all. Matthew had chosen it simply because of its proximity to the terrace and she winced as she remembered how mindless and amorous he had seemed, as though he would explode with suppressed passion if he didn't find a bed following a particularly earthshattering kiss under the flickering lamps of the grape arbor. When would she ever learn? This was not, and never had been, and never would be, about *that* kind of love to Matthew.

"What are you doing?" he demanded. "I thought we were going to make love."

"Put this on," she directed, tossing him the larger robe. "We have to talk."

Chapter Fourteen

Matthew was clearly intimidated by the change in Molly's mood. "Don't tell me you think I'm Aaric again!"

"Worse," she assured him. "Sit up and pay attention. We have a problem and frankly, if we don't settle it tonight, I don't think we ever will."

He pulled the robe over his tanned arms and cinched it quickly, then moved to confront her. "I know what's bothering you. The dream, right? I mentioned it, and you got upset. I understand perfectly."

"The dream is gone, Matthew. Do you understand *that?* I'm not going to build my life, or this relationship, around the dream. If you can't get past it, then we can't be together."

He gripped her arms tightly. "Are you listening to yourself? Five minutes ago you were begging me not to let you leave me, and now I know why. You're still intimidated by all this, and you don't need to be. The bad part is over."

"It's *all* over!" she wailed. "Are you going to live in the past forever?" She caught herself, ashamed of the harsh tone. "I know you trained for this and waited for it for more than twenty years, and I can't even begin to imagine how that must have been. And now that you've won, you deserve to be proud, and to revel in the whole damned experience for weeks and weeks, and you'll always remember it. But you're young, and talented, and you have your whole life ahead of you. And," she flushed slightly, "you have me. I'm so crazy about you, Matthew, it's embarrassing. I want to marry you, and have your babies, and go to Paris with you, and sew for you, and . . ." She wiped away a tear born of frustration. "I want to dance with you, and go to movies and plays, and build a life. You'll research legends, and I'll research cures . . ."

He was staring as though fascinated rather than intimidated by the diatribe. "You should see your eyes," he murmured. "They just radiate energy and inspiration. Do you realize what an incredible team we make?"

"Matthew!"

He caught her by the waist as she tried to spin away from him, then he pulled her hard against himself and forced her chin up so that their eyes were locked together. "We can have it all—everything you just described. I swear it to you. You believe me, don't you?"

"I don't know. I want to . . ."

"We can have it all. The kids, and the research, and the sewing, and Paris . . . everything except," he smiled sheepishly, "maybe not the dancing. But the rest is yours."

"Matthew—"

"Do you think you're the only one who's been thinking about all that? I want to marry you, Valmain. I want to be with you until the day I die, and I want to spend every day making you happy. I swear it. And as far as the dream goes . . ." His grip tightened, as though anticipating an escape attempt. "The dream is a part of our life together. We can't deny it, even if we want to."

"And of course, you don't want to."

"I won't lie to you, Molly. The dream and the amulet are a challenge. They're also an opportunity. I won't turn my back on them, and I won't let you, either."

His grip had relaxed and she pulled free slowly, then moved to sit on the edge of the four-poster bed. As always with Matthew, she felt overwhelmed and confused by the intensity of his commitment, both to her and to his destiny. Of course, she reminded herself swiftly, they were ultimately the same thing—the dream girl *was* his destiny.

They would never have a normal life. At best, he would find new legends and riddles to explore. At worst, he would become frustrated and bitter over having peaked too soon in his young life. Could she honestly be expected to stand by and watch that?

"Talk to me, Valmain," he urged, dropping onto one knee before her. "Tell me what's really bothering you and I'll fix it."

He had called *her* eyes inspiring, but *his* were positively spellbinding. The golden flames promised passion and adventure, while the warm brown background spoke of sincerity and unselfishness. It would be so easy to place her heart, and her life, in his hands, knowing that he would never abandon or hurt her. His dedication was fierce and unshakable. His lovemaking was hypnotic and thrilling. She loved him with a passion that could never be extinguished, and yet she feared for him, and for herself, if they failed to resolve the past before embracing the future.

Her voice was small and unfamiliar when she

finally responded. "I have a theory about the dream, Matthew. I want you to listen, and then I want you to be honest with yourself before you try to answer me. Please?"

His smile was triumphant. "I knew it. It's been bothering you too, right?"

"That's right. It's been bothering me, but not because I miss it. It's bothering me because I'm afraid we'll waste the rest of our lives looking for it, when there's so much else in store for us."

He sat beside her and took her hand in his own. "Go on."

She had spent endless hours, alone in bed, thinking about this over the preceding two weeks. "I think the amulet worked for Lost Eagle, hundreds of years ago, during the same century Maya and Aaric and Kerreya and all the others were fooling around with magic. The power of the amulet was somehow tied to *their* practice of magic."

"That makes sense."

"It does?" She smiled wryly. "I thought you'd think it was crazy."

"You paid more attention during my lectures than you thought," he smiled. "Amulets and lucky charms and all other mystical artifacts like that are channels. They allow the user to draw magic from a primary source, but they're never primary sources all on their own. So the amulet must have a source, and Maya's family could easily have been the key to that source."

"Okay." She took a deep breath. "That was a long time ago, right? And now they're gone, just like the Valmain kingdom and the Celtic headhunters and all the other phenomena of that time."

"Celts weren't headhunters, Molly."

"Whatever. My point is, the source of the amulet's power disappeared with Maya and all the others."

"Except the amulet worked less than a month ago."

"True. The amulet worked in a dream. The Valmain dream. An ancient dream that made some kind of temporary reappearance in the twentieth century so you and Aaric could fulfill all the old curses and prophecies. The amulet worked in my dream because my dream was a part of that ancient time, not this time."

Matthew nodded. "That's intriguing. You came up with this all by yourself?"

She ignored the possible insult. "My dream was a kind of portal, giving us access to Maya and Aaric's world. It's like we time-traveled, in a sense. Now the need for that access is gone, and so is the dream. And the amulet is just a trinket again because its source no longer exists."

His long silence concerned her, but she reminded herself it was better to shatter his illusions now than to watch him throw his life away on a dream that could never be repeated. Finally he suggested, half-heartedly, "According to the legend, the power could be inherited again one day."

"By me? Let's face it, Matthew, except for the dream, which was hardly a conscious ability, I'm just a run-of-the-mill college student with a rich heritage." With a shy smile she added hopefully, "Do you love me anyway?"

"You always wear white," he reminded her. "And you had the nerve to stand up to me when you thought I was Aaric the Moonshaker. You're not a very typical college student, Molly. You're incredibly strong."

"My strength comes from my love for you, not

from magic or Valmain bloodlines. I thought he had murdered you, Matthew, and I couldn't bear it. *Not* because you're my champion, but because you're my lover." She scooted into his lap and demanded, "Is good old-fashioned love enough for you? Answer yes or no."

A sly grin spread over his face. "You're forgetting something." When she just stared, he continued confidently, "Aaric the Moonshaker knew more about all this than we do, and he believed your magic still existed, even centuries later. And he never would have agreed to 'time-travel' to the future if there'd been any risk that *his* magic wouldn't work when he got here. Which means," the grin widened, "the source is still here somewhere, and all we have to do is find it and tap into it." He tumbled backward, taking her with him, then rolled until he was poised above her. "You had me worried, Valmain," he scolded, "but I forgive you because . . ." he spread her robe open, revealing her breasts to his admiring eyes, "you're the most incredible woman on earth and I can't live without you."

Because you're the dream girl! her brain screamed to her body, but it was too late. She was back under his spell, all too willing to be the dream girl if that's what it took to be in his arms. Even before his lips touched her, she was throbbing with remembered desire and gratefully moaning his name.

He began as always, with the gentlest of kisses rained over her face and neck. His mouth was warm and skilled and thoroughly Matthew Redtree as he worked his way down to her nipples, which he treated as fonts of erotic nourishment. Spasms of need engulfed Molly, whose fingernails were anchored in his neck. Then his mouth moved lower, trailing over her stomach and down to her hips. By the time his mouth arrived at its destination she was writhing with anticipation.

As always, the climax was mind-shattering in intensity and then he was in her and the power of his movements seemed stronger and more effective than ever before. On his face was the expression of a victor and she knew, without caring, that he was reliving his glorious battle even as he brought her again and again to cataclysmic ecstasy.

Then the final magnificent thrust was made and he collapsed onto her, dazed but clearly impressed with himself. As Molly waited for her heart to cease its frantic pounding, she stubbornly attempted to remember why this wasn't the most perfect love match the world had ever known. If something was missing, she was at a loss, at that moment, to recall what it was.

And then he reminded her. "You'll dream tonight, Valmain. I guarantee it. And if you don't," he grinned mischievously, "we'll just have to keep trying until you do."

"Is that all you care about?" she murmured under her breath.

"Pardon?" He rolled, taking her with himself so that she could stretch out over him. "If you have a complaint about *that,* I'd like to hear it."

Molly giggled reluctantly. "It was adequate, believe me."

"Yeah? In that case, it's time you retracted your remarks about Aaric." When she frowned, he added helpfully, "About how he'd know how to romance a girl, and I don't. I think we just proved that wrong."

She laughed again. "You're too competitive, Matthew. Don't tell me you're jealous. What about your famous balance?"

238 Kate Donovan

"You keep trying to sabotage it. First you treat
me like a leper for two weeks straight, then you tell
me the Moonshaker was more charming than I am,
then you threaten to leave me, then you try to prove
the amulet will never work. I think I've been a
pretty good sport."

"You're right," she mused, half to herself. "I
don't know why I keep looking for trouble when I
should just be enjoying falling in love." Sifting his
blue-black hair through admiring fingers, she promised, "From now on, I'm just going to relax and let
you entertain me. We'll swim together, and make
love in all seven bedrooms every day for a week, and
then we'll go to Paris, and then . . ." her eyes were
shining with love, "we'll get married."

"You read my mind," Matthew enthused. "See?
We have the same goals after all."

"I'm so happy." She closed her eyes and rested
her cheek on his chest. "I never thought I'd ever be
happy again, Matthew. Not like this."

"This is just the beginning, Valmain. After Paris,
we'll head for Boston and clear things up with your
dad. And we'll meet little Nicole."

"Matthew," she groaned. "Sometimes, you're so
hopeless. I don't want to visit Dad. I want to visit
your family. I didn't get to enjoy them last time, and
those nephews are so cute. Oh!" She sat up, straddling him while she tugged her robe back into place.
"We haven't called August yet! I promised I'd call
tonight, and now it's more important than ever."

"We'll call right away. Here," he reached for the
cordless telephone on the nightstand, "don't get up,
and definitely don't get dressed. I may not be done
with you yet."

Molly laughed proudly. This was more like it! Six
more nights of this and she was fairly certain she

could get him to retract his celibacy insult. While he dialed his uncle, who was staying with Rita awaiting news, she nibbled on his earlobe, but when the number began to ring, she temporarily abandoned the play and grabbed the receiver. "He won't believe it coming from you," she reminded Matthew, then beamed when the old man's voice came over the line. "August? It's me! Guess what!"

The old man chuckled. "So? Can I assume my nephew is nearby?"

"He's right here. The one and only Matthew Jason Redtree. I'll let you talk to him, but . . . August? I want to thank you first. I couldn't have survived this without your help."

"You would have survived," August assured her. "You are the dream girl, after all."

Molly shook her curls. No wonder Matthew couldn't have a straight conversation! "I'll put him on, August. And we'll see you in a couple of weeks, okay?"

"Or sooner," August replied. "We have much to tell each other."

"Right. Bye." She handed the phone to Matthew. "I think he wants details."

Matthew covered the mouthpiece with his hand and teased, "Should I tell him I proved myself in bed?"

"I think he already knows that," she laughed. "I told him sex would be the ultimate test."

"Huh?" His shock faded into amusement. "Like I said, you're not a typical college student, Valmain. You're definitely one of a kind." Then he boomed into the phone, "Uncle? I've waited almost three weeks to hear you tell me I did a good job."

Molly smiled fondly as her champion's face lit up. Apparently, August was praising him beyond his wildest expectations. His eyes were flashing with excitement and he was concentrating completely on the conversation, despite her attempts at teasingly distracting him with gentle kisses.

"Are you serious, Uncle?" he was demanding. "What makes you so sure?" He listened for another moment then almost crowed, "I forgot all about that! I'm so dense! Why didn't I realize . . . ?"

"Matthew?" Molly waved her hand in front of his eyes. "What's going on?"

"You won't believe this," he assured her, then turned his attentions back to his uncle.

Molly watched with growing interest. Apparently, August's news, whatever it was, had eclipsed their own bombshell. What could be more fascinating than the fact that Matthew was Matthew and Aaric was dead?

"We'll catch the first plane out tomorrow, Uncle. Should we come to the ranch, or will you still be at Rita's?"

Molly waved her hand again, this time frantically. Had he lost his mind? "Six more beds," she hissed hopefully. "Tell him we'll see him next week. Matthew?"

"Molly's anxious to hear the news, Uncle, so I'll say goodbye. I'll call Rita from the airport with our flight information. Take care . . ." He listened for a moment, then said "goodbye" and turned his full attention to Molly. "You won't believe this, Valmain," he began, then winced at her stern expression.

"For your sake," she glared, "you'd better be about to tell me you're Aaric the sorcerer and you have the power to be in two places at once."

"Huh?"

"Huh?" she mocked. "Did you or did you not tell

your uncle we'd be back in California tomorrow?"

"Sure, but—"

"What about Paris?" she wailed, jumping to the floor and waving her arms wildly. "And the seven bedrooms, and the pool? What's going on?"

He chuckled nervously. "Calm down, Valmain. I can explain everything."

She paused to glare, "Are we going to Paris?"

"Eventually, yes. But it's postponed because we're going somewhere else first. Somewhere a thousand times more beautiful and romantic, I guarantee you." Leaping from the bed, he grasped her hands and announced, "We're going to your dream meadow."

She stared, still angry but now baffled for good measure.

"Uncle August knows how we can find it. Can you *believe* that?"

"No."

"It's true! And it's so simple! I can't believe I didn't think of it myself weeks ago." He scooped her into his arms and carried her back to the bed. "Just when you were ready to give up on it, Valmain. *Think* of it." He studied her eagerly. "Say something."

"I'm counting to ten."

Matthew winced. "Why?"

"The dream meadow? Are you crazy? Since when is there such a place as the dream meadow? That's a figment of *my* imagination!"

"I thought it was a portal," he teased, his euphoria returning. "Pay attention, Molly. My uncle has it all figured out."

"Well, that's a relief. The man who taught you everything you know about obsession and fantasy . . ." She caught herself and added, "I adore him,

Matthew, but he's as crazy as you are. And he's never been to the dream—*my* dream, I might add—and so how on earth would he possibly be able to find it?"

"He wouldn't. He just knows where to look. You and I are going to do the legwork."

"I don't think so." She was on her feet again. "My job with Dr. Lewis starts in one week."

"Quit. I have plenty of money, Valmain."

She was struggling to hold on to the last vestiges of her temper. "That job is important to me. *Me!* Not the dream girl. I'm renouncing that status as of this minute."

"Hey!" He caught her by the arm and, for a moment, his expression revealed an unfamiliar anger. "You shouldn't even joke about stuff like that. Don't tempt fate, Molly. It's not safe." Softening immediately, he assured her, "You'll always be the dream girl, and once you actually step into that meadow, I think you'll finally understand what an honor that really is. I think," he added solemnly, "this may be just what you need. To embrace your destiny. I think this came just in time."

"So do I," she murmured. "I almost married you."

"Molly!"

"There are seven beds here," she reminded him sadly. "Pick one for yourself. I'm tired and I want to be alone."

"Wait!" He caught her arm again. "I'm willing to compromise. Isn't that how we always do it?" His smile was desperately charming. "We're both tired, so let's not decide anything tonight. We'll get some sleep—together—and tomorrow I'll give you all the details of my conversation with August. If you still don't agree that it's a possibility, we'll just put it on the back burner and head straight for Paris."

She was too heartsick to argue. "Either way, we'll go home tomorrow. For now . . ." She twined her arms around his neck and murmured, "Let's just get some sleep. I can't bear to argue with you, Matthew."

"I know," he whispered, leading her tenderly toward the bed. "When we're out of balance with each other, the world is a pretty scary, lonely place, isn't it? But when we're connected . . ."

"When we're connected, it's paradise," she admitted, snuggling against his chest. "I'm glad we had this time together, Matthew. I'll never regret it."

"That's what I've been trying to tell you," he agreed, stroking her hair tenderly. "Sleep now, Molly. It'll all make sense in the morning."

"It still doesn't make any sense," Molly grumbled late the next evening as she languished on August Redtree's overstuffed sofa and listened to the two fanatics exchange excited nonsense. "You're saying the hills in my dream are burial mounds? And you've actually been there in real life and it's a place called Seven Hills."

"Right," Matthew nodded. "What's the problem?"

"Seven?" she glared. "There are *three* hills in my dream. No more, no less."

"The other four were possibly built much later than the original three," August explained gently.

Resisting an impulse to scream, she settled for burying her face in a cushion and moaning in unintelligible frustration. After all, little AJ was asleep on the porch—he had graciously given up the guest room for "Aunt" Molly—and the last thing she wanted to do was disturb that adorable child's sleep.

Because he reminds you so much of Matthew, she accused herself silently. *You're hopelessly weak for gold-dust eyes and judo stances. And you call yourself a scientist? What on earth are you doing in this lunatic asylum they call a ranch house?*

Then she reminded herself, quite sharply, that her presence was a tribute to Matthew Redtree's love-making style combined with her own feeblemindedness when it came to his touch. If she hadn't been so completely seducible that morning, and if he hadn't been so handsome and entertaining . . .

Seven hills. It reminded her of the seven beds they had left behind themselves in Europe. Now Matthew and August were adding insult to injury by insisting that her dream meadow was in central North America, and she knew it couldn't be so. Her dream meadow, if anywhere, was much more likely in Ireland, or some other Celtic stronghold. They were searching on the wrong side of the "untraveled sea" and she didn't seem to be able to get through to them at all.

"Whose dream is the meadow in?" she challenged finally.

The uncle and nephew exchanged knowing grins. "Yours," Matthew admitted.

"Right. And I say, if there were people buried in my dream, I'd know it."

August chuckled. "Perhaps it is the reason you were never lonely there as a child."

"Ick. If I'd known, as a child, that I was sewing in a graveyard, I think I would have passed."

"You were sewing in a graveyard?" a tentative voice whispered. "Really, Aunt Molly?"

"Now look what you've done," she accused the two men. "You woke up poor AJ with this nonsense." She crossed the room to the doorway and ushered the boy over to the sofa. "I didn't sew in a cemetery, AJ. Don't let all this gruesome talk give you nightmares, okay?"

He snuggled at her side. "I thought I was dreaming, but then I heard Uncle Matt say something about the Moonshaker. He's the guy who killed Lost Eagle . . ." His sleepy smile was identical to Matthew's in charm and effect. "I didn't want to miss the story."

"There's no story," Molly assured him. "Right, Matthew?"

The warrior grinned. "There's a story, AJ, but you have to be older to hear it."

"Aww . . ."

"Sleep," August counseled. "You will sleep and train and the time will pass quickly and soon you will be old enough to hear the story."

Molly stroked the boy's tousled hair. "You already know most of it, right? If you know about the Moonshaker, and Lost Eagle . . ."

"And Maya," AJ nodded. "She was real bad. She stole Lost Eagle's amulet."

Molly sent a quick warning glance toward Matthew, knowing he was tempted to show off the spool to his nephew. "Try to get back to sleep, AJ. Is it too uncomfortable for you on the porch?"

"It's great. Uncle Matt and I always sleep out there when we're here."

"Oh?" She smiled toward Matthew. "That's a wonderful tradition."

"Cute, Valmain," he laughed. "You can't get rid

of me that easily." Then he caught his uncle's frown and added quickly, "It really is nice out there on the porch, though."

"It is settled," August nodded. "AJ, you will return to your sleeping bag. You will be tempted to listen, but you will not. Uncle Matthew will join you in a short while."

"Right." The boy shrugged to his feet. "Good night, Aunt Molly."

She kissed his cheek. "See you in the morning, AJ. I'm glad you're here."

"Yeah. Robert will be bummed, and so will Mom. You better stay for a long time this time, so they can meet you a lot more too."

"I have to go to Berkeley in a few days, to start a new job, but I'll be back for a visit soon, I'm sure."

Matthew waited until the boy was out of sight, then grumbled, "I thought we settled that Berkeley business this morning. We have to go look for the mounds, Molly. Aren't you even a little curious?"

"Dr. Lewis will probably close the lab for a few days over Thanksgiving, and definitely for Christmas. We can go wild-goose hunting then," she suggested.

"Uncle? Can't you convince her?"

"She is frightened," August explained. "She knows that, if you find the meadow, she can no longer deny her destiny."

"Deny? I'm not the one in denial here," she countered. "You and Matthew are the ones who won't let go of the past." Remembering AJ, she lowered her voice to a whisper. "Lost Eagle is avenged. The circle is closed, or whatever. Let's all try to adjust."

"Why do you think she's frightened, Uncle?"

Matthew demanded. "If she has magical powers, that should give her confidence, not fears."

"To use them, she must change the course she has set for herself. The safe path she has chosen. She has hidden from her destiny, but it has found her."

"Wait!"

"No," August corrected firmly. "The waiting is over, child. You have placed the cape over your shoulders, and you have returned the amulet to its owners. You can no longer hide."

His tone, soft as always, was remarkably intimidating. He was chastising her, as he had chastised AJ for eavesdropping—as he had chastised Matthew for suggesting that AJ be exposed to their premarital sexual status. Molly had to struggle to remind herself that he wasn't *her* uncle and didn't really know her very well at all! "You're entitled to your opinion," she sniffed. "I don't want to argue about it anymore. I'm going to Berkeley. If Matthew needs to go looking for burial mounds, I understand, but I'm officially washing my hands of the whole dream girl thing."

Matthew cleared his throat and shook his head slightly, as though warning her against any further outburst, but it was too late. August Redtree's soft brown eyes were filled with displeasure aimed directly at Molly. "It is wrong to waste a gift," the old man chided. "You are a dreamer, and you must dream. You are a sorceress, and you must train. Matthew is a warrior, and he must be forever vigilant."

"Okay," she nodded. "I'm not disagreeing—at least, not exactly. On the other hand," she took a deep breath, "dreaming isn't my only gift. I have a talent for science and math. I don't want to waste that, either."

August nodded. "I agree."

"So, I'll go to Berkeley, but . . ." she raised her hand to discourage any further scolding, "as soon as Matthew locates the dream meadow, I'll drop my test tube and go have a look. How's that?"

"That's how Molly and I work things out, Uncle," Matthew interjected. "We compromise. I'm okay with that plan if you are."

Molly cast him a grateful smile. Her champion, defending her against the family patriarch! She was even willing to ignore the fact that their so-called compromises were really capitulations in disguise and *she* was always the one to capitulate. "So?" She moved to the old uncle and touched his arm. "Shouldn't we all get some rest?"

He embraced her gently. "Try to dream, child."

She knew better than to suggest that the dream was gone, and so she smiled sweetly, then hurried toward the guest room, with Matthew one step behind her.

"You're hilarious, Valmain," he whispered, when he caught her at the doorway. "For two straight weeks you stood right up to Aaric the Moonshaker—a sorcerer and a murderer!—but you back down from my uncle."

"I have a weakness for the sons of Lost Eagle, I guess. AJ affects me the same way." She twined her arms around his neck. "Oh, Matthew, I'll miss you so much. Even though you drive me crazy, I've never been happier than I've been since I met you."

"Thanks for admitting it, Valmain. I was beginning to get worried. Is it safe to leave you alone in Berkeley?"

"I'll miss you, but I'll be busy. I have to check in with Dr. Lewis, and get my trunk out of storage, and find a place—"

"Whoa! You already have a place. My house, remember?"

"The armory? I don't think so, but thanks for the offer. It's too far from campus to be practical."

Because you don't have a car? I'll buy you one. They make some now that are really environmentally sound, and safe at the same time."

"When I finally get a car, it's going to be a white Mustang convertible," she corrected firmly. "We're talking destiny here, champion, so don't interfere. In the meantime, I can walk or ride the bus." She studied him fondly. "I'm surprised you don't have a car of your own."

"I have a motorcycle. When I need more, I rent a truck or car. Our society is much too spoiled and dependant on the automobile . . ." He stopped and smiled. "End of lecture. Will you stay at my house?"

"Have I ever successfully said no to you?" she sighed. "You aren't going to search forever, are you, Matthew? I mean, eventually, you'll give up and come home to me, right?"

"I'm hoping I'll luck out on the first try. There are dozens of burial mounds scattered across the continent, of course, but the ones my uncle was referring to were special to me, once. It's the last place I went camping with my dad before he died. He's the one who called it Seven Hills. It's not really called that on any official map."

She patted his arm. "That's sweet, Matthew, but if that were the dream meadow, wouldn't you have recognized it? It didn't seem familiar to you, right?"

"I think the extra mounds must have confused me. But if my uncle's right, and the hills in your dream are actually burial mounds, then Seven Hills is a good place to start. It's remote, and the area around it is thinly populated. My dad and I only ended up there by accident. Our car broke down, on our way to Ohio, and while we were waiting for it to be repaired, we backpacked around and sort of stumbled onto the site, and then, we had the best time ever. I remember Dad saying the spot had a kind of magic to it."

"For a champion," she sighed, brushing a thick lock of hair back from his forehead, "you're quite a dreamer, did you know that, Son of Lost Eagle?"

"And for a dreamer, you're pretty practical," he smiled. "Like I said, we make a perfect team." He kissed her lightly. "I'd better get outside before you get me into trouble, too."

She slipped into the guest room, undressed hastily, and was soon tucked into bed. There would be no dream meadow, she knew. Not that night, and not at some campground in the middle of nowhere. Reality was waiting to clash with destiny, and she wasn't sure anymore which side she hoped would triumph.

Chapter Fifteen

To Molly's amused distress, her fanatical champion was so intently focused on his new quest—the *dream meadow*—that all else seemed to fade in its wake. Not that he didn't diligently provide for her needs, of course. Taking leave of AJ and August in the early hours of the morning, he delivered his dream girl straight to the "armory," where he proceeded to instruct her on all do's and don't's in relation to the complex security system that protected his weapons. It became clear that he was less concerned with his own self-interest than with keeping these dangerous and valuable artifacts from falling into the wrong hands, and so she memorized codes and added keys to her key ring with a minimum of protest.

She also tried to seduce him one last time before his departure, but his mind was so clearly elsewhere that she eventually contented herself with exploring his citadel, questioning him carefully on the string of idiosyncracies that presented themselves with each new room or closet. "There must be three dozen shirts in here," she accused cheerfully. "All exactly the same. And ten pairs of jeans?"

"Once I found the right thing in a catalogue, it made sense to stock up," he shrugged.

Then she found the sexy tweed sport coat from their lecture days and wanted to insist that he wear it for the remainder of his stay except, at that moment, he was kissing her forehead and hoisting his knapsack over one shoulder in preparation for a hasty departure. "Change your mind and come with me," he urged one last time, but she was strong, and he left and, after only several lonely hours, she was inconsolable with missing him.

"Take a lesson from Matthew and do a little focusing yourself," she chastised herself and, with that in mind, hiked down to Dr. Ken Lewis's office to report several days early for her new assignment.

As she walked, she reminisced. The first time she had visited this particular office had been three years earlier, when she had mustered the courage to ask Lewis's permission to enroll in his toughest course. It had been an unheard-of request from a freshman and the professor had interrogated her relentlessly, only to announce finally that she had learned more on her own, during her months of self-study in her hospital bed in Boston, than most students learned in four years in his department. He had adopted her, intellectually, on the spot. Thereafter both he and his charming wife had attempted to adopt her socially as well, but she had resisted.

When her silver-haired mentor caught sight of her, standing in his doorway once again, he grinned from ear to ear, as though her arrival had transformed his day. "Welcome home! Ireland definitely agreed with you. I don't think I've ever seen you looking so radiant."

Molly smiled in return. "Hi, Ken."

"Hi, Ken?" he chuckled. "That's it? That's the whole report?"

"It's been a remarkable summer," she admitted, "but I'm ready now for something a little more down-to-earth. I thought you might have time to give me more details about my new job."

"Not so fast," he laughed, motioning for her to join him at a paper-strewn conference table. "I want to hear all about this 'remarkable' summer of yours. Are you implying you actually made time for a social life?" When Molly flushed, he teased, "Don't tell me you've fallen in love! And I had such big plans for you. Do I need to find another protégée?"

"That's enough." Despite her habitual desire to keep her emotional distance from her colleagues, she felt a rush of affection, noting that her friend's hair had gone from salt-and-pepper to gray in just a matter of weeks—or had it been happening gradually, without her noticing?

In any case, he was clearly enjoying her fall from aloofness. "Who's the lucky guy? Caroline will insist on having all the details, so there's no sense in trying to be private. You're the daughter she never had, and she's been living for the day you fall in love."

"I'm engaged," Molly admitted. "His name is Matthew Redtree. Have you heard of him?"

"The guy from the Anthro department?"

"Sociology, although for now, he's taken a leave of absence."

"He's the last man on earth I would have imagined you with," Ken stated flatly. "On the other hand, I admire him. He came in here a mini-celebrity because of that book of his, and I was sure he'd just clean up on lecture bookings and press interviews and all, but he turned out to be very dedicated, at least from what I heard. In other words," he grinned, "I approve. Bring him to dinner tomorrow night so Caroline can make it official."

"He's out of town. And," she tried for a brisk tone, "you and I have work to do. Right?"

"Work, work, work," he grumbled. "We'll give you a rain check on dinner, then. When do you expect him back?"

Molly shrugged. "It could be a week, a month, or more. In the meantime, I'm dying to know about this project. You didn't give me any details in June."

"The good news is, it's privately funded. The bad news is, I'm already a month behind and it hasn't even officially started yet, so for a few weeks, at least, you're going to be running yourself ragged . . ." He caught himself and glanced uneasily toward her legs. "Any trouble with those? I mean, they look as gorgeous as usual, but . . ."

"They're fine," she blushed. "That was years ago, Ken."

"I'll never forget it," he declared. "You came limping in here, so determined to alleviate suffering when you were so obviously suffering yourself."

"That was almost four years ago. My legs are better and," she studied him carefully, "I like to think I'm more mature. Maybe even more realistic about my goals."

"Meaning what? You're still the best student I've ever had. Keep on the right track and you'll be able to name your salary when you get your doctorate. Although," he resurrected his timeless entreaty, "I'm hoping you'll follow in my footsteps and choose the underpaid world of university research."

"My goals haven't changed completely," she

hedged, "and you know money isn't my standard of success. Still, the drug problem . . ." She bit her lip. "I'm wrestling with the ethics, Ken. I'm still committed to drug research but I guess, because of some of the talks I've had with Matthew, I'm reexamining my role."

"Good girl," he grinned. "More and better drugs cannot possibly be the answer, at least not until we can increase public awareness of the price they're paying in terms of dependence. After all, we're toxicologists, not pharmacists. *Our* job," his eyes twinkled, "is to *de*toxify."

"What?"

"I was going to spring this on you after graduation, but since you got there on your own, Molly, why wait? It'll make your work a lot more interesting for you, I guarantee."

"And what exactly is my work?"

"It's a variation on the wind-chill factor," he smiled. "You're familiar with that?"

"Sure. The thermometer registers a certain temperature, but when the effect of the wind is taken into account, it's really much colder."

"Right. In the same way, a breathalyzer, or more accurately, a blood test, gives a reading on the level of alcohol in someone's blood. But when certain over-the-counter cold preparations are thrown into the equation . . ."

"The level of impairment of reflexes is higher than the reading indicates?"

"Exactly. Of course, I used the term 'equation' loosely. There isn't one yet."

"But by the time we're finished," Molly smiled, "there will be?"

Ken Lewis took a deep breath. "I'm not going to kid you, Molly. For the most part, you'll be entering data and running errands. You're not going to be first team, but if you stick with me on this, you'll learn more by Christmas than I could teach you in years of lectures."

*De*toxify. Molly shook her head in amazement. She had expected an explosion—from Ken, if she changed her career course, and from Matthew, if she pursued it. Was it possible to please everyone? Not that it was her job to please everyone, of course . . .

"Things will start slowly, while we set up. I'll need you to help bring some equipment over from the lab in San Francisco," Ken was explaining cheerfully. "You can use my car, or . . ." his smile widened, "did you finally break down and get that Mustang you're always talking about?"

"I'm still waiting until I graduate. It's my incentive, remember?"

"As though you needed it? You're the most motivated student I ever had. Too bad," he added kindly, "it had to be such a tragic event that motivated you."

"I'm over that," she lied. "Would I be buying a white convertible for myself if I wasn't? After all, that's the kind of car we crashed in, so . . ." She pushed her chair back and reached for her purse. "I can start today, Ken. Just give me a list of errands you need run."

"Back off," he laughed. "It's not August yet, you know. Your position doesn't officially start until next week. Have you found an apartment?"

"I'm staying at Matthew's. It's in the hills."

He cocked an eyebrow playfully. "You really are engaged? He's a fast worker. So, go home and enjoy his house. Unpack and get settled, and we'll get started bright and early Monday morning. And in the meantime," he took her hand and dropped the bantering tone, "Caroline would love to see you. With Redtree out of town, you'll be eating alone, so why not come for dinner? At least this time she won't be trying to set you up with one of the neighbors."

Molly sighed. The Lewises were always trying so hard to take care of her, and she was always turning them down. Now, she had the additional incentive of needing to be next to the phone when Matthew called, and so she'd continue to resist. "Let's wait for Matthew," she hedged. "I really do need to unpack and settle in."

His eyes were warm with concern. "Just remember, we're here and we're available. You aren't alone, Molly. Of course," he pretended to grumble as he walked her to the door, "now that you're in love, no one will be able to get a minute with you, I suppose. Matthew Redtree?" He chuckled ruefully. "I never would have believed *that.*"

She now had six full days on her hands, with nothing to do except to yearn for her lover. Pining away hardly appealed to her and so, with predictable industriousness, she made a brief stop at the fabric store for material and embroidery supplies. Then she trudged back up the hill and checked the answering machine, just in case. Of course, it was too soon and so she turned to the stacks of mail that had arrived over the early weeks of summer. As Matthew had predicted, the fan mail was consistently bizarre—either critical of his open belief in magic, or worshipful in the sense of claiming to have found hidden meanings in certain passages of his book.

When a phone call finally came, it wasn't Matthew, but instead a dealer in ancient weapons who expressed relief at having found someone home "at last." He had to leave the country soon, for an indefinite period of time, and had several pieces he *knew* "Redtree" would definitely want to view. Promising to convey the message, Molly placed the phone back into its cradle in weary disappointment. Was this business-as-usual in an armory? Mail from crazies and calls from weapons dealers?

"But that was before *you* moved in," she reminded herself. "The spare bedroom gets plenty of light, and you can set up your sewing machine in there. And you can use this time to catch up on your reading, and write to Grandma, and . . ." And wait for the phone to ring.

Matthew Redtree stood atop the largest of seven burial mounds and inhaled sharply, invigorated by the astonishing freshness of the air as it rushed into his chest. His backpack remained where he had dropped it, at the base of the hill. He no longer needed it, or any other earthly possession. He had found something more valuable and in the finding had become a conqueror, a hero, a champion!

The longing to share this newfound glory with the dream girl was strong, yet he was unable to tear himself away from this remote paradise for the time it might take to place the simple telephone call. Not that any call to Molly could be simple, of course. She would debate, and doubt, and tease, and the prospect of arguing with her now, of all times, when destiny's design had become so wonderfully clear, was more than he could stand. Better to go to her, in person, and convince her.

But the spot was a magnet, holding him benevolently within its power. At first he had thought it was his imagination, and had attributed the effect to the beauty and purity of his ancient homeland, but it was so much more! From the moment he had guided his rental car off of the highway and began to hike the wooded stretch that shielded the mounds from the world, he had been assaulted by a heady wave of strength and confidence. By the time he had actually come into viewing distance of the meadow, all doubt had fled. The amulet was working . . . the son of Lost Eagle had come home . . . the Valmain champion had become invincible.

"Your eyes shine as brightly as the charm on your wrist," a soft voice informed him, and he spun around to stare at the woman who had managed to approach so noiselessly. She was old—in fact, the word "ancient" sprang to his mind again, although in only the most respectful of senses. There was a serene smile on her wizened face and a curious kind of empathy in her small, dark eyes.

"I didn't hear you," Matthew murmured, glancing about for a vehicle. "I didn't expect to see anyone out here in the middle of nowhere." Her smile intrigued him and he found himself smiling sheepishly in return. "Did you walk all the way here?"

"I walk here every day. Every day I grow more weary and more frail, yet I cannot stay away. There is a magic to this spot." The old woman extended a pale hand. "I am Deborah Clay."

"I'm Matthew Redtree." He accepted her handshake gently. "This spot *is* incredible. Have you lived around here for long?"

"All my life. Ninety years, more or less. I have come to this place each and every day since my childhood, and I have never seen you here before."

"I came here once with my father, over fifteen years ago." *And less than a month ago, in a dream,* he added to himself in silent wonder.

"And were you wearing that bracelet fifteen years ago?"

Matthew glanced proudly at his amulet. "Why do you ask?"

"It bears the markings of this place. If you had been wearing it when you visited, as a child," Deborah added, "you would not have waited fifteen years to return."

"The markings?" Matthew's pulse began to race. "The horseshoes?"

"The mounds," she corrected firmly.

For the first time, his eyes saw the truth and it humbled him. "I never made the connection . . . There are four of them on the amulet," he added, more to himself than the old woman.

"Four," she agreed. "This one on which we stand. That small one to our left, and the one directly behind us. The fourth was never constructed, which is the reason this place was eventually abandoned."

"But there are seven . . ."

"And yet, only three." The woman's eyes left no room for doubt. "How did you come to possess this treasure?"

"It's been in my fiancée's family for years, but of course, she never suspected what it was. I didn't fully appreciate it myself until just this morning."

"Your fiancée? Is she a witch?"

Matthew stared. "Why do you ask *that?*"

"Never mind," Deborah laughed. "If she were a witch, she would never part with her amulet. And if you were a sorcerer, you would have guessed at its true nature before today. And so . . . what are you?"

"I'm a warrior," he announced solemnly. "The son of Lost Eagle."

"Forgive me for not recognizing the name," she shrugged. "Tell me how you feel at this moment, Matthew Redtree. You say you appreciate the amulet. Tell me what it does for you."

Matthew responded easily to the inquisitive glow in her eyes. Wasn't he feeling the same degree of curiosity? And her candor was refreshing, inviting the same from him. "I'm a warrior," he repeated, "and with this amulet, I'm unbeatable."

"That's very true. If it channels the power of these mounds to you, you are a formidable man." She gathered her worn brown shawl closer about herself. "If you'd like to learn more, you may visit me tonight. I can provide a simple meal, and I have some old, old pottery that also bears the markings of this spot."

"I'd love to see that," he enthused. "Do you want me to walk you home?"

"It's kind of you to offer, but I'm fine, and I prefer to stay here for a while. To think. It's my habit, Matthew. Unlike you, I cannot draw magic from these mounds, but they have always given me comfort."

"You asked if my fiancée was a witch," he reminded her. "Do you know any witches?"

"Do you mean, am I a witch? No, Matthew. Sadly, I am not." Her eyes twinkled. "All of your questions will wait until tonight. We will have a meal together, and win one another's trust."

He nodded, accepting the dismissal easily. "If you're okay here alone, maybe I'll go for a run. I'm anxious to see what the amulet can do." It pleased him to be able to speak of it to one who so clearly understood and appreciated. "Then I'll hike back to my car and head into town to get a room. Any suggestions?"

"There is only one motel. Or, you could stay with me. My home is tiny, but clean and warm."

He could imagine Molly's reaction and grinned reluctantly. "I wouldn't want to impose. I'll get a room and call my fiancée, then I'll head for your place. Can I bring anything?"

"Some Chianti?" she suggested impishly. "It is my only weakness."

Matthew chuckled. "Great. How do I find you?"

"Follow the Hill Road into the woods, then take the dirt road that forks into the sunset. My cottage is the only one for miles, and in the evening the lights from my window are the only lights, other than the stars and the moon. You cannot miss it."

"Seven o'clock?" Matthew reached for her hand and squeezed it respectfully. "I'm grateful to you for this offer, Deborah. I want to learn everything I can about this place. It's difficult to explain why it's so important to me, but . . ." He took a deep breath. "I've spent a lifetime studying legends, and amulets and sacred spots, but this is different. This time, it's completely different."

She stopped him with her knowing smile. "This time," she finished for him, "you have come home. Welcome home, son of Lost Eagle."

Matthew's house, with its heavy maroon drapery and dark-stained wooden floors, was the perfect house for a warrior—or a witch. *A witch like you?* Molly would chide herself nervously, remembering Aaric's words. Occasionally, on a whim, she would wiggle her nose or wave a hand, commanding a needle or textbook to fly across the room to her, and then would giggle sheepishly—and gratefully—at the lack of success.

Her main function in the house seemed to be to race to the phone each time it rang, only to be disappointed when it was never Matthew. First it was Ken Lewis, then later his wife Caroline, persisting in their dinner invitation. Thereafter, and more annoyingly, the weapons dealer called to say he was "leaving the country on Friday morning, for an extended tour" and was "dead certain Redtree will kick himself for missing a chance to at least view these artifacts." Molly did her best to explain that Matthew was simply unreachable at this point, with the image of him kicking himself growing perversely more intriguing by the moment.

As the afternoon faded into evening, she found herself prowling the halls, feeling like a prisoner. *And why not,* she muttered to herself. *There are bars on every window and a twenty-thousand-dollar security system on top of that! This isn't an armory, it's a dungeon.*

In fairness to Matthew she acknowledged that he was as concerned with keeping curious neighborhood children away from the dangerous weapons as he was with keeping thieves at bay. Still, when she gazed through the iron bars, staring down at the city, she felt isolated and disoriented. In desperation she fumbled in the closet, retrieving Matthew's tweed sport coat, which she donned in lieu of her bathrobe while she returned to her latest project, which seemed almost painfully romantic and futile at the moment. Still she persisted, embroidering the hems of each of his ubiquitous white polo shirts with a strong geometric pattern in red and black, reminiscent of the trim on his dream headband and wristbands. He had been so brave and strong for

her, and now he was so, so far away. If she had
doubted whether she truly loved him, those doubts
were now resolved. *I miss you,* she thought sadly.
*It's as though you're a million miles away. As though
we're not—what was that word?—connected.*

"Call," she found herself whispering aloud. "If
you call me, I'll come. I promise." She waited, and
sewed, but in vain. The silence seemed to prove once
and for all time that she was neither a witch nor a
sorceress. Wouldn't a witch—even one of pitiful
talent, such as herself—be able to summon a loved
one in an emergency, even if only an emergency of
the heart?

Chapter Sixteen

"Matthew!" Deborah Clay grasped his free hand and pulled him through the doorway. "I was beginning to worry you might have changed your mind."

"No way," Matthew grinned, presenting the requisite bottle of Chianti with a flourish. "I wouldn't miss this for the world . . . Oh! I didn't realize . . ." He stared past Deborah, completely silenced by the sight of a dark-eyed young woman who stood, smiling tentatively, in the shadows of the living room.

She presented an unlikely blend of exotic, almost mesmerizing beauty and angelic innocence. Blue-black hair hung in two thick braids down over her breasts, which were full and enticing, despite the modesty of her high-necked blue corduroy dress. Her skin was freshly scrubbed and radiant, with no makeup at all, save for the kohl shadows around her huge, almond-shaped eyes. It was clear to Matthew that she had no conception of how astonishingly beautiful she was, and this fact more than any drew him to her.

Matthew knew, without asking, that the young woman's name was Angela. Just one hour earlier, the manager of the motel had responded to Matthew's simple request for directions by launching into a diatribe concerning "that old witch" Deborah Clay and her "tramp" of a granddaughter, Angela. At that time, Matthew had shown his displeasure by a simple scowl and curt "Good evening." Now he wished he had broken the disrespectful lout's jaw!

And Deborah herself was just as he remembered—frail yet lively, and completely lacking in pretense. How predictable that certain elements in town would find the Clay family threatening. Innocence, individuality, and wisdom were valued by society only as ideals. When actually encountered, they were often feared, misunderstood, and derided. It was an old story, and Matthew had heard it a thousand times.

Deborah was leading him into the center of the room. "Matthew, I'd like to present my granddaughter. Angela Clay, this is the young man I was telling you about—Matthew Redtree."

To Matthew's delight, the young woman's voice was as sweet as her smile. "It's so wonderful of you to come all the way out here to visit my grandmother," she breathed. "I worry about her so."

"Angela visits every day," Deborah explained. "She fusses over me as though I were a queen."

"To me, you are," Angela insisted, planting an impish kiss on the old woman's cheek. Then she extended a hand shyly toward Matthew. "You're just as Grandmother described you. I waited, just in case . . ." She blushed to a deep crimson. "Not that I suspected you, of course, but . . ."

"But she's precious to you," Matthew nodded. "I understand completely. Are you joining us for dinner?"

"I need to get home before dark, or," she giggled,

"the shoe will be on the other foot and it will be Grandmother who is worried about *me.*"

"I can take you home," Matthew protested.

"I have my horse, out in back."

"She must leave right away," Deborah interrupted firmly. "I don't like her riding in the dark. She and her horse know the trail so well, but still it worries me."

"I understand." Matthew's eyes swept admiringly over Angela's calf-lengthed split skirt and soft white cowgirl boots. "I think it's great you ride instead of using a car."

Angela beamed at the praise. "Are you a rider, Mr. Redtree?"

"Call me Matthew, and yes, my uncle has a ranch. I spent all my summers around horses."

"Then you must borrow one of mine to use during your visit. It's much easier to travel over the mounds on horseback than on foot."

Matthew's imagination was instantly engaged. "I'd be happy to pay you—"

"Nonsense! Just go to the stable at the end of Center Street and tell them I sent you. Are you staying at the motel?" When Matthew nodded, she gushed, "That's so close to my house! If you need anything during your stay, please let me know. And now," she glanced toward her grandmother, "I'd better go."

"It's about time," the old woman scolded, but the stern expression lasted only a second. It charmed Matthew to see how close these two were—reminiscent, in fact, of Elizabeth and Molly. Good people, generous and loving . . .

"I'll leave you two to trade your stories, then." Angela's smile was gently teasing as the three moved to the doorway. "Enjoy yourselves, and,

Matthew?" She extended her hand again, this time
with more confidence. "Please accept my offer to
use my horses while you're here. And," a faint blush
colored her high cheekbones, "perhaps we'll meet
again." Her fingertips had come into contact with
the amulet and she stroked it as though mesmerized.
"This is so lovely, Matthew. So very lovely . . ."

She dashed away then, before he could respond
properly, and he stared after her in open admiration
of the flawless combination of energy and naïveté.
For a few moments he lost sight of her, then she
reappeared in a blaze of glory on a prancing Appaloosa stallion. All traces of shyness had vanished
and Matthew reacted almost viscerally to the imag-
ery of so stunning a female mounted upon so powerful a beast. Then she was gone and he turned back
to the grandmother, hoping the old woman had not
sensed the uncharacteristically dark fantasy that
had momentarily engaged his imagination.

"When I told Angela you were interested in the
mounds, she was pleased. She is patient, but tires of
listening to my stories, which she can not bring
herself to believe. She's too modern, I suppose, although," Deborah's voice rang with pride, "in all
the ways that count, she is old-fashioned, despite
what you may have heard in town."

Matthew flushed. "Pardon?"

Deborah shrugged. "I don't care for myself—let
them talk!—but they've ruined Angela's life with
their jealous prattle. Her only error was to resist the
advances of a powerful man, who then spread ugly
rumors . . ." She shook her head. "Forgive me,
Matthew. I'm sure you aren't interested in all this."

"I don't listen to gossip, Deborah. I listen to
stories, and legends, but I've learned to distinguish
folklore from malicious prattle, and," he patted her

shoulder in reassurance, "I think I'm a pretty good judge of character. I could see Angela was a fine person the moment I laid eyes on her."

"Well, then . . ." There were tears in the old woman's eyes. "You must think I'm a terrible hostess. Come in, and I'll serve you some of my favorite dish—lamb stew. Do you like it?"

"It smells good, and I'm starved." He followed her into the kitchen. "I don't know how many miles I ran today, but I really built up an appetite."

"The amulet can fuel you," Deborah nodded, "but eventually, even the finest of warriors must rest and eat. Sit down." She set a basket of fresh rolls before him. "Were you able to reach your fiancée?"

"Unfortunately, I didn't have a chance to try. Like I said, I ran further and longer than I had expected. Suddenly it was getting late, and I had to race into town to get my room and the wine . . ." He grinned sheepishly. "It doesn't matter. Telling Molly about the mounds over the phone won't work. I'm going to have to go to California and convince her in person to come back with me."

"If you don't call," Deborah scolded, "she will worry."

"True." He was munching contently on a warm roll. "I'll call her as soon as I get back to my room. No problem."

Deborah placed a juice glass filled with Chianti before him. "Shall we drink a toast to her? She is a lucky woman, to have a warrior like you for her man."

"I'm the one who's lucky, believe me." He raised his glass. "Let's drink to the mounds, shall we?"

"To the mounds," she echoed reverently, and then, to Matthew's amusement, she drained her

own glass dry in one long gulp. Wiping her mouth
with the corner of her apron, she gave him one of
her impish smiles. "You've been so patient. Now,
would you like to see my artifacts?" Before he could
answer, she had crossed to an old sideboard and
flung open a door. "My prize possessions."

Matthew almost groaned aloud. Even at a distance of eight feet, he could see that the two pots
were hardly ancient. In fact, the trendy pink and
apricot glazing put them at less than twenty years
old. He only hoped the old woman hadn't paid
much for them.

She presented a pot and a vase for inspection.
"For so many years, I wanted something with the
markings of this place. Then, six years ago, these
practically fell into my lap. Aren't they beautiful?"

"I like them," Matthew hedged, studying the pattern carefully. "It really is amazing that they're so
much like the amulet, but . . ."

Deborah licked her lips. "You don't think they're
authentic? Neither does Angela. She thinks I was a
fool to pay what I paid for them, but . . ." She
seemed almost broken-hearted. "How do you explain the markings?"

"I don't know. Maybe someone saw something
ancient, and patterned these after it. Actually," he
added soothingly, "these really are pretty. It doesn't
really matter if they're quote-unquote authentic, as
long as you take pleasure in them, right?"

Deborah sighed. "My grandmother taught me
the symbols of the mounds. She says they were
carved on many rocks, in the old days, before the
town was built. Everything was cleared away then,
you know, and so much was lost."

Matthew silently mourned the loss. He would
have given his entire weapons collection to have

seen those rocks! Still, there was no point in making Deborah feel any worse than she already did. "These symbols on your pots are exactly right. It's nice to know your granddaughter got to see the markings, even if only as a copy."

"And she has seen your amulet, which is definitely authentic," Deborah agreed. "I believe you impressed her, Matthew. Maybe now she'll take my stories more seriously." She filled her glass again with Chianti, then drained it as quickly as before. It seemed to energize her and she bustled to the stove to ladle stew into two bowls. "Tell me more about your fiancée. You said her name is Molly? And she is in California?"

For an old woman, she was an excellent listener, Matthew noted. Anxious to distract her from his discouraging assessment of her "artifacts," he explained, "Molly's a student at the University of California. I was teaching there when we met."

"And the amulet had been in her family for many years?"

He hesitated, suddenly annoyed with himself for having discussed Molly in such easy detail. "She didn't know what it was until I told her and, even then, she didn't believe me. She's like your granddaughter that way, I guess. Skeptical."

"If she's like my Angela, she must be a wonderful girl."

"She's the best. Anyway, back to the amulet. I know you recognized the markings, but how did you know it was . . . magical?"

Deborah smiled. "From the expression on your face, I suppose. I've studied magic for so long, I've learned the signs."

"Tell me about that."

"Very well." She joined him, motioning for him

to eat while she talked. "I wanted to be a witch, Matthew, from the day I first heard such women existed. The thought of drawing power from nature, and bending it to my will . . ." Her smile was rueful. "My parents thought I was crazy, and maybe I was, but I'd still give anything to experience that kind of power. Of course, I have learned through bitter experience that one cannot become a witch."

Matthew nodded. "I've always heard it's something you have to be born with. I guess it's hereditary, right?"

"The daughter of a witch will not surely be a witch," Deborah shrugged. "It can be inherited, as you say, but that is not foolproof. The only foolproof insurance is a charmed womb."

"Pardon?"

"A charmed womb." She eyed him playfully. "You said you've studied this all your life?"

He laughed. "I guess I missed this. Every witch I've ever heard of had a mother or father who was a magician."

"The womb became charmed through some action, conscious or unconscious, of one of those parents," Deborah explained. "But any witch can charm any womb, if she uses the right spell. And even a layperson can charm a womb if they have the right charm."

Matthew touched his amulet. "Like this?"

"No. That is a channel, designed to bring the physical power to you. It was fashioned for your ancestor, and all of his blood descendants. It will not enable you to work magic. It simply enhances the abilities you already possess."

"That's true." He studied her admiringly. "You really know your stuff."

"If only my mother had known," Deborah

laughed, "she could have found some way to have her womb charmed, and I could have had the one thing in life that mattered to me."

"How did you learn all of this?"

"When I was fourteen, I became an apprentice for an old woman who claimed she was a witch. She promised to teach me the secrets of witchcraft if I served her faithfully." Deborah's eyes clouded. "For so many years I slaved for that woman. On her deathbed, she told me the secrets. Of course, the biggest secret of all was the fact that I had slaved in vain. I could never become a witch."

"She tricked you," Matthew murmured. "You must have been furious."

"She was dying," Deborah nodded, "or I might have strangled her with my bare hands! I had given her twenty-seven years of my life."

"What?" He stared in horror. "Twenty-seven years?"

"I had never married. Never had children. All I cared about was witchcraft. The fabulous things I would see her do, there in her workshop, or under a full moon . . ." The old woman shook her head. "Some things were never meant to be, Matthew. After the old witch died, I met my husband, who was a cruel man in his own right, and used me much the same as she had . . . Even then, I hadn't learned my lesson. I wanted to have a daughter, so that she could be a witch. And even though I was almost past my childbearing years, I was able to become pregnant."

"Let me guess," Matthew sighed. "You tried to find some way to charm your womb?"

"Exactly. Once my old teacher died, her friends began to come to her house, to collect her treasures—witch treasures, of course, not earthly

wealth. And I asked each of those women to help
me, and one agreed. And so, when I was certain I
was pregnant, I stole from my new husband to pay
the witch's fee. She pretended to charm the womb,
but it was a deception."

Matthew almost hoped Deborah was lying to
him, although the expression on her face told him
otherwise. "Did you have a daughter?"

"I had a son. A dolt. Handsome, but not very
bright, and," her smile was filled with bitterness,
"definitely not a magician. But I loved him anyway,
and when his father took him away from me, it
broke my heart."

"He took him away?"

"Can you blame him? By then, everyone in town
was calling me a witch. The boy was raised in Balti-
more, and I didn't see him for many years. His
father tried to turn him against me, but as soon as
he was fully grown, he came to see me. He had a
new bride, and she was pregnant with Angela, and,"
she raised tear-filled eyes to Matthew's, "I was given
a second chance. I put all thoughts of witchcraft
behind me and found out that a baby can be a
magical, miraculous person, even without charms
or spells."

"And now, Angela looks after you," Matthew
smiled. "It's really an amazing story, Deborah."

"Angela humors me, and pampers me, and she's
been the only good, pure thing that's ever happened
in my life. My only true regret is that she has been
so poorly treated in this town, because of my repu-
tation for eccentricity."

"But you seem happy. And Angela is practically
radiant."

Deborah nodded, then stood to remove his empty
bowl from the table. "You're very observant, Mat-

thew. Angela and I share a love for life, and for this place, that makes us strong against all the rest. I think you have that kind of strength also."

"I feel strong here for so many reasons," he agreed quietly. "It's incredible to imagine my ancestors hunting and fishing and building their lives on this very ground."

"You mentioned Lost Eagle." Deborah refilled both their glasses then sat opposite him again, her eyes burning with curiosity. "Tell me about him."

"He was a great warrior, but made the mistake of getting into a love triangle with a sorcerer. The amulet protected him from his rival's jealousy but, when the woman they both loved stole the amulet, the two men fought and Lost Eagle was killed."

"The sorcerer was a mounds magician? Do you know his name?"

"Aaric."

Deborah's withered hand flew to her mouth. "The Moonshaker?" she gasped.

Matthew's pulse quickened. "Tell me what you've heard of him."

"All legends agree," she whispered. "He was the most flamboyant and effective of all sorcerers. And his woman . . ." Her eyes widened with astonishment. "The woman who stole the amulet! Was it Maya?"

"You've heard of her, too? And of her sister Kerreya?"

"I knew there was a sister," Deborah nodded, slightly dazed, "but she ran off with a stranger and little more is known. And who can blame her? To have lived in Maya's shadow . . . Maya, the most beautiful and talented of all . . ." She grasped Matthew's hands. "Your ancestor must have been a remarkable man. To have taken Maya, even temporarily, from the Moonshaker. And then to have fought him . . ." She was shaking her head in wonder. "He never stood a chance, you know. Maya was the most scheming and unprincipled of women, and the Moonshaker was invincible."

"Not quite invincible," Matthew smiled. "In fact, I killed him." He enjoyed her blank expression, then repeated, "I killed him. It was my destiny to avenge Lost Eagle."

"How can that be?" she whispered finally. "Tell me everything."

Not everything, he reminded himself firmly. It wasn't his place to reveal the nature or scope of Molly's incredible heritage. That would come in time, but from Molly herself, and only after they had been convinced that Deborah could be trusted to keep the secret. This old woman clearly loved her role as expert, and would long to share the news with others, and so for now he would divulge only what he *wanted* the entire world to know. "When Lost Eagle was dying, he swore one of his descendants would avenge him. And so Aaric came here— or rather, to Ireland—last month. He claimed Maya sent him through the centuries. He said they combined their magic, so that he could come and face me in battle."

"Combined their magic?" Deborah shook her head. "For the magicians of the mounds, that was a dangerous practice. On the other hand," her tone turned wistful, "the legends have always said Aaric and Maya never really died. They disappeared in a blaze of glory. That must have been an explosive spell." She leaned forward and added, "A lake spell, wouldn't you say? Not a mounds spell."

"Lake?"

Deborah laughed. "You have not heard of the

lakes? Remind me to tell you about them later. For now, I want to hear about the battle! How could you defeat Aaric's magic? Did the journey from the past weaken him?"

"I had the amulet," he reminded her.

"But it could not work in Ireland."

Matthew cursed himself for the blunder. If he wasn't careful, Molly would pay a price, in terms of privacy, for his boasting and bragging. Had one glass of wine loosened his tongue? Rarely had he allowed his defenses to drop so easily with a stranger, even one as lacking in guile as this Deborah. And *was* she actually "lacking in guile"? Hadn't she candidly admitted she lusted after magical powers?

Then Deborah's fertile imagination came to his rescue. "I think I understand," she murmured. "If Maya considered the battle to be important enough to die for, she would have ensured that the amulet was on your wrist and fully powered on the day Aaric arrived. That must have been a part of the spell from the start."

"Yeah, I guess so."

"Which means," she added mischievously, "Maya played matchmaker for you and your fiancée."

"Huh?"

"The amulet was in your fiancée's family," she reminded him cheerfully. "Maya must have arranged for you to find the current owner." She was nodding, clearly proud at having pieced together the facts. "Maya was a powerful and devious sorceress. She could have arranged all this just so the battle would be a magnificent one—worthy of a rivalry over *her*." She leaned forward again. "Did the Moonshaker use his illusion power when he fought you?"

"He tried. They were earthquakes and dragons."

"But the amulet helped you to see through them? Oh, Matthew!" She seemed almost lightheaded with excitement. "You're the most fortunate man on earth! And," her tone grew more resonant, "you killed the most powerful warrior of all time, which makes *you* the most powerful. When you defeated a legend, you *became* a legend."

"I had help," he replied, hoping to sound more modest, at that moment, than he felt in the face of her praise. "I had the amulet."

"And Aaric had his sorcery! And so much more experience! It was a fair battle, and you won."

"Yeah. It was a great moment. Probably the greatest moment of my life."

"You have many great moments to come. I saw that in your eyes when you stood on the mounds and surveyed your homeland."

"You're right," he whispered. "That moment was awesome, too. Standing there, seeing the mounds, feeling the amulet . . ." *And missing Molly,* he reminded himself sharply. *Go to Berkeley right away—tonight!—and get her.* Shrugging to his feet, he extended his hand to his hostess. "It's getting late, Deborah. If I don't leave now, it'll be too late to call my fiancée. And if I can get a flight, I might just go and talk to her in person."

"You must go right away," she agreed briskly. "We will have many more chances to talk. You'll tell me more details of the battle, and I'll share my scraps of knowledge of the lake wizards who destroyed your ancestors."

Matthew sank back into his chair. "Lake wizards?"

"I know so little of them," the old woman hedged. "You have heard nothing at all?"

"Not a word. You say they destroyed my ancestors?"

"The mounds were always vulnerable," Deborah shrugged. "There were supposed to be four, but only three were completed and so the power was strong but erratic. And once Maya and Aaric disappeared, the backbone of the tribe was easily broken."

"By lake wizards?"

"And witches. Dozens of witches. All of them weak—the wizards controlled their power. Those are the only facts I have about them, although rumors abound."

"Do these witches and wizards still exist?"

"I don't know. It's been centuries since the last incident, although that one was horrendous. They say . . ." She caught herself sheepishly. "I'll talk all night if you don't stop me, Matthew."

"Are you kidding? This stuff's great! If you're not tired . . ."

"At my age, sleep is a stranger that comes only fleetingly, and only after midnight. Put a log on the fire, Matthew, and we'll trade stories of the lakes and the mounds."

"Where is she?" The Moonshaker's tormented cry reverberated over the mounds and beyond, to the edges of the woodlands that marked the outskirts of the dream. The helplessness that had thwarted him during the early days following his arrival had been tempered by the knowledge that she would come, from time to time, to sew, and he would be allowed to gaze upon her, and admire her, and covet her. But it had been an eternity since the battle, and more than an eternity since he had held

her, and made love to her, and caused her to tremble with fear and admiration and womanly need.

His sea-blue eyes softened at the memory of her and his voice became a whisper. "Where are you, Daughter of Kerreya? Why do you stay away? Are you ill? Injured? No. I would *feel* that, just as I now feel your loneliness and confusion."

It was true. For endless hours he had felt a new kind of ache, not for himself or his own exile, but for hers. It was torturing his soul and winning his heart, and he would have gladly given anything, short of his very existence, to soothe her. Never before had he felt so strong a bond, so strong a need to comfort another. Never before had a woman touched him with such gentle, thorough intensity.

Why was she lonely? Where was her champion? Had their love affair waned? If so, the Son of Lost Eagle was a monumental fool. Did he hope to find a woman with more strength? More beauty? More magic? Impossible! The Valmain princess was a dreamer, with the steadiest of eyes and the softest of skin and the most delicious innocence he had ever encountered. Her loyalty and bravery had stunned the sorcerer, most particularly at the moment she had threatened to kill herself in order to destroy her champion's foe. And she had kept her head despite the fierce confusion of battle, using her cape and the amulet to buy her champion time. *She* had won that battle as surely as had Lost Eagle's son.

"NO!" he rebuked himself sharply. "The one called Matthew was the victor, and you must accept that from this moment until forever. He won the battle and he avenged Lost Eagle. But," a ray of hope warmed the sorcerer's heart, "has the fool somehow managed to lose the prize?"

It was a dangerously seductive thought, yet it

explained the unexplainable. Why was she lonely? Why did her heart ache? Why did she fear the dream?

"Come to me," he insisted into the breeze. "You fear me without reason. Have you not guessed at the truth, not even once? With your dream power, you command my destiny. And with your beauty and soft smile," he smiled in rueful acknowledgment of his vulnerability, "you command my heart."

Chapter Seventeen

If someone had told Matthew Redtree it was possible to feel this way—this alive!—he would have thought they were exaggerating wildly, yet here he was, galloping across his homeland on a powerful Appaloosa, his head ringing from the dozens of stories of heroism and magic with which Deborah Clay had regaled him long into the night. Each story—each priceless piece of history—had inspired and amazed him, but the stories themselves paled in comparison with the story he was living at that very moment! The Son of Lost Eagle . . . the Valmain champion . . . the bearer of the amulet that fueled his finely tuned muscles and offered him boundless opportunities for adventure and victory.

When he finally slowed his steed and dismounted, it wasn't from fatigue. Fatigue no longer burdened him, thanks to the amulet. He was invincible—the man who vanquished the Moonshaker himself!—and if he stopped now, it was simply to study the mounds of his ancestors. He saw only the three now, the others fading into nothingness. Sometimes, he could almost see the fourth mound that had never come into existence. The mound that would have ensured the continued existence of his people. They were all gone now, except the Red-trees.

"And Molly," he reminded himself quickly. "She's Kerreya's descendant, after all." He had had to bite his tongue more than once the night before, knowing that if he shared Molly's secret, Deborah would be impressed and helpful beyond belief! She would honor Molly as a powerful sorceress, and would share the secrets of witchcraft she had learned so long ago and at such an unfair price. It had been so tempting, yet each time he had almost revealed the truth, he had imagined the dream girl, or more precisely, the dream girl's eyes, scolding him. Warning him. Loving him and strengthening him, just as the amulet strengthened him. He needed to go to her right away, yet even as he vowed to do so, he felt a vague discomfort at the thought of being away from the mounds for even so brief a time.

"Matthew!"

Turning toward the voice, he smiled at the sight of Angela approaching, leading her stallion by a simple rope. She had ridden bareback, as had Matthew, and she presented a charming picture in her faded jeans, shiny boots, and frilly red blouse.

"I knew I'd find you here," she pretended to scold. "Shouldn't you be sleeping? Grandmother said she kept you up until four o'clock with her stories."

"Did she tell you she covered me with a hand-made afghan, and when I woke up, she had my breakfast all prepared?" he grinned. "I'm getting spoiled."

"She loved the company. No one but you has ever let her drone on and on about these mounds." She flushed slightly and added, "I don't mean to sound disrespectful, but she really takes it all too seriously. I've tried to convince her to move into town with me, so I can take care of her, but she loves it out here."

"She's amazing."

"She told me a story about your amulet." Angela reached for his wrist tentatively. "May I see it again?"

"Sure."

While she admired the design, he found himself admiring her long, delicate fingers. No nail polish, no rings, just simple, fresh-scrubbed beauty, like their owner. Memories of the motel owner's slanderous comments haunted him and, on an impulse, he squeezed her hand. "You're a good granddaughter, Angela. I admire you."

Her cheeks reddened and she pulled her hand quickly away. "Grandmother sent me, to invite you to dinner again tonight. Will you come?"

"Tonight?" He shook his head. "I'll stop by her place and explain myself. I want to talk to her some more, but I have to leave for a day, to get Molly." He cleared his throat and smiled tentatively. "That's my fiancée."

"Grandmother told me all about her. She sounds like a wonderful person," Angela assured him. "Grandmother says she's the one who gave you the amulet."

"Right. You'll like her, Angela. And you'll have plenty of time to get to know her. With any luck, she and I will be moving here permanently when I return."

"Oh, Matthew! It will be so nice to have friends here in town!" Angela eyed him playfully. "I hope you're planning on having dozens of children."

"At least," he chuckled.

"Well then, you'd better go and get her," Angela laughed in return. "What time does your plane leave?"

"I haven't made a reservation yet."

"Well, let's go for a quick ride, then you can head back into town, and I'll go and make your excuses to Grandmother. The truth is," she added with a wink, "if I were you, I'd avoid Grandmother completely for a while. I know what's coming next."

"What's that?"

"Now that she's filled your head with silliness about the mounds, she'll start telling you all about the lake wizard she met when she was a girl. Or should I say, the wizard she *thinks* she met when she was a girl."

Matthew was staring in wonder. "She told me a little about the lakes, but she said she didn't know whether they still existed."

"Of course, silly. She doesn't want you to think she's crazy, and believe me, when she tells you *that* story, you really will start to wonder." She took his hand back into her own and soothed, "For heaven's sake, Matthew, you don't really think it's possible, do you? Grandmother just sees what she wants to see and hears what she wants to hear."

"You don't believe any of it?" he countered. "The mounds, the amulet, Maya?"

"I never believed one word of it until I met you." Angela flushed again. "I mean, until I saw your amulet."

"And?" he prodded.

"And it's so intriguing, and you're so confident. If I only had half your confidence . . ." She sighed aloud. "I don't believe any of it, Matthew. I want to believe, but I can't."

"You remind me of Molly," he began, but almost

instantly regretted the comparison. Molly was special. One of a kind. He was standing here, talking to this virtual stranger, when he needed to be talking to his dream girl.

But first he needed to make a brief stop at Deborah's house. He *had* to hear about the lake wizard! He didn't blame the old woman for holding this story back from him, the first night. Hadn't he done the same? He hadn't told her about the dream power, or the Valmain connection, and of course, he still wouldn't tell. Not until Molly arrived and consented.

And Molly would never arrive unless he went to Berkeley to get her. And so he'd go, but first he would talk to Deborah.

"Are you coming with me, Matthew?"

"What? Oh, yeah." He helped her onto the stallion's back. "Let's go to your grandmother's house right away, okay? I want to hear about the lake wizard."

"Oh, no," Angela warned. "You shouldn't tell Grandmother I mentioned that to you. You'd better wait for her to bring it up. It's a secret, Matthew." She hung her head and murmured, "I shouldn't have said anything. I just know how Grandmother is. I know she's planning on telling you, but . . ."

"But it has to come from her? I understand," he soothed. "I won't say a word."

"She told you about the witch she worked for, didn't she?"

"Yes."

"Well, then, . . ." Angela's smile was playfully conspiratorial. "Accept her dinner invitation. Bring a nice big bottle of Chianti. Then just ask her if she's met any other witches or sorcerers. She won't be able to resist."

"Brilliant," he chuckled. "You should have been a spy."

Angela giggled. "If you'd like, I'll come to dinner with you. Maybe I can help prompt her a little. But," her dark eyes teased him, "no Chianti for me. I'm strictly the champagne type, and I never drink it alone."

"The guy at the liquor store's going to start wondering about me," Matthew laughed, "but it's a small price to pay for such charming company and such great information. So? Should I pick you up tonight?"

"I'll be ready by six-thirty. In the meantime," the playful eyes flashed with challenge, "does the Son of Lost Eagle dare race against the granddaughter of a wannabe witch?" Without waiting for his answer she leaned forward and whispered to her stallion, who bolted, leaving Matthew momentarily in their dust. Then flooded with adrenaline and energy from the amulet, he whooped his favorite war cry and vaulted onto his borrowed horse's back, urging him toward certain victory.

Hi, Valmain. Sorry I missed you. I've got so much to tell you, but I'll make this short and sweet. I love you, I want to marry you, and I want you to come with me, no questions asked, and see this place! I'll be home tomorrow, so be all packed and ready. And, Valmain? If my uncle calls, tell him he was right, and tell him we'll send for him soon. I love you, Molly
. . .

Molly replayed the message, willing it to reveal Matthew's location, or at least a telephone number at which he could be reached, but there was nothing. After forty-eight lonely hours of silence! *What time tomorrow?* she wanted to scream. *Where is "this place"?* But of course, he had specifically requested "no questions asked," and, by failing to leave a number, he would have it his way, for the time being.

"But when you walk through the door tomorrow, Matthew Redtree," she seethed, brushing a mass of curls from her forehead, "don't expect me to be all packed and smiling and ready to melt in your arms just because you *say* you love me. If you really loved me, you'd want to hear my voice *and* my questions."

On the other hand, it was Thursday, and so, if she flew with Matthew to points unknown on Friday, she could be back in time for the first day of work. If she argued with him and resisted, she'd end up going anyway, so why fight it when, technically, it worked for her schedule?

She could tell, from the tone of his voice, that he had found the meadow or, at least, a reasonable facsimile thereof, and once she calmed down, she had to admit that she, too, longed to see it one last time. It would be a fitting end to a bizarre episode, and maybe, paradoxically, Matthew would be able to let go of it now that he had found it.

In any case, there was no real doubt in her mind over whether or not she was going. Just hearing his voice on the machine made her yearn to see him and touch him, and she played the message again and again as she made her plans.

He wanted her to be packed and ready to go. Fine. She'd be ready. In fact, she'd be lying in wait! A dress that had caught her eye in a store window the day before might be just the weapon she needed to snare this wandering lover and, as added insurance, she'd buy a real weapon as well. Grabbing the phone, she contacted the weapons dealer who had hounded her for two days straight, informing him that "Redtree" would not be back in time to see his assorted wares, but that she could come, as Matthew's representative, early the next morning. The dealer's flight was leaving at ten A.M., and so Molly promised to be at his hotel by seven-thirty sharp. She'd buy Matthew something suitably gruesome and pleasing, and she'd buy the hot pink, curve-hugging, champion-taming halter dress on the way back home. And when Matthew Redtree walked through that door, she'd be ready.

Swords, sabers, cutlasses, daggers . . . There was something disorienting about a modern-day hotel room strewn with such weaponry, especially at seven-thirty on a summer's morning. The dealer himself was hardly what Molly had expected. From the diamonds on his fingers to his perfectly tailored silk suit, he seemed an unlikely purveyor of implements of destruction, yet he was clearly knowledgeable. He had dealt with Matthew several times, apparently, and seemed to know his tastes *and* price range intimately.

"If you only want to buy one piece," he was advising her smoothly, "it would have to be this. Redtree can't resist a good, solid, hand-rubbed antique bow."

"Who can?" Molly quipped, but her eye had been drawn to a rough chunk of obsidian on the man's bedstand. "This is interesting. Did you find it yourself?"

"It's from Oregon. But Redtree wouldn't be interested."

"I'm interested. Is this the type of rock a person would carve a dagger from?"

He eyed her impatiently. "Those skills take a lifetime to master, and even if 'a person' managed to carve a dagger, it wouldn't be a substitute for these authentic pieces I'm showing you."

"If it's hand-carved, it's authentic," she countered cheerfully. "How much do you want for it?"

His smile was thin and wary. "You mentioned you were only going to purchase one item . . ."

"One for Matthew and one for myself," she glared. "Is it for sale or not?"

"It will be my gift to you, to take along with your purchase."

"Great." She examined the black glass rock carefully. "Do you sell any tools?"

"No, Miss Sheridan, I don't. Did you want to buy the bow? I don't mean to rush you, but I need to get to the airport." As though to illustrate his predicament, he pulled a heavy trunk from the closet and began to rearrange the contents.

"I'm in a hurry, too," Molly sighed. "Matthew didn't tell me what time he'd be arriving today. In fact," she frowned, "you might run into him at the airport, and if you do . . ."

"I won't spoil your surprise," the man chuckled, setting a rustic ax onto the floor beside him. "Take my advice and buy him the bow. He'll be delighted."

"What's that?" Molly knelt beside him, charmed by the rough-hewn simplicity of the weapon. "How old is *this?*"

"It's quite old, but hardly appropriate for Redtree's collection."

She stroked the copper ax head with her fingers. "This thing is incredible! It looks like people really used it. These other things," she gestured impatiently to encompass the room, "look too polished. Like decorations, not weapons. I think Matthew would like this."

"He'll polish this, and it will also seem like a decoration. And it's simply not his type of weapon, miss. For one thing, it's completely undocumented."

"You think it might not be old?"

The man shook his head. "My opinion doesn't matter. But Redtree would want to know more about it than I can tell him."

"He'll love it." She pulled her wallet into view, fanning through the stack of hundred-dollar bills with which she had armed herself for this shopping spree. "Didn't you say you were in a hurry?"

He'll love it, she repeated to herself as she lugged the purchase up the hill. *It's got that mystical quality those Celtic ruins had, and remember how nuts he went over them? It's got energy . . . charisma . . . magic! He'll love the ax, and he'll love the dress, and he'll love you in the dress or the ax will definitely fall!*

She was almost giddy at the prospect of seeing him. His message had said he would arrive with intent to leave right away, which told her she probably didn't have much more time to get ready. In fact, it was possible, although unlikely, that he'd be in the armory when she arrived. She had left him a note promising that the wait would be worthwhile, and almost hoped he would be there, despite the fact she'd have to face the reunion in her jeans and sweatshirt. She liked the idea of Matthew waiting alone for her for a change, even if it meant postponing the silk dress seduction for a time.

The simple act of trying that dress on in the store had been an intoxicating one. The color was hot and sexy, and the silken fabric almost too sensuous for words. It hugged Molly's curves and set off her long legs perfectly, and in the matching pair of four-inch heels, she had felt like another, more daring and irresistible woman. Even a stoic like Matthew Redtree would have to be impressed by the sight of his dream girl in something so much scantier than her cape. Perhaps it would motivate him to call more often when he traveled in the future—assuming she ever let him go without her again.

After impatiently dealing with the three burglar alarms that separated her from the entryway to his home, she hauled her purchases through the door, then bristled at the emptiness that confronted her. Now the waiting would begin again, but at least she could use the time to slip into the sexy outfit and brush her curls to a seductive sheen. Passing the living room she glanced, as was her habit, toward the answering machine and felt a gentle warning cramp in the pit of her stomach at the sight of the flashing message light.

Ken or Caroline Lewis? Or Grandma? Or some legend-struck fan? "It can't be Matthew," she assured herself aloud. "Why would he call when he's due to walk through that door any minute? And," she consoled herself, "at least you know it's not that obnoxious weapon dealer."

Hi, Valmain. I can't believe I missed you again! I guess this means your job started early, so you won't get this message until this evening, so . . . well, plans have changed a little. I was hoping to reach you, to get you onto the noon flight out of Oakland . . . I made you a reservation, but I'll call and change it until tomorrow at the same time. I'll pick you up in Chicago tomorrow afternoon—I know I said I'd be there today, but so much is happening. I need to be here, and I need to have you here with me. Get some time off, okay? Be on that plane tomorrow. Do it for me, Valmain. There's no way you can reach me—I'm staying at a little motel in Colhaven, but I'm knee-deep in research and I'm never there, so just come. I'll see you tomorrow . . .

A glance at the grandfather clock in the corner told her that, with a little luck and a lot of hustling, she could make that noon plane. Ken Lewis had been clamoring to assist her, and now she'd take him up on it. She couldn't wait one more day for this reunion and wouldn't waste time now wondering why Matthew was finding it so easy to postpone it. She'd have a chance to mull that over on the plane, and on the ride from Chicago to Colhaven, wherever *that* was.

"Wherever it is, it's where you need to be," she admitted, slipping out of her fleecy sweat suit while simultaneously dialing Ken's office number. "Meadow or no meadow, Matthew's there, and that's all that matters for now."

There was only one motel in Colhaven, and its name alone—the Hillside Motel—was enough to make Molly smile. Seven hills—it was almost romantic, and as she stepped out of the cab that had brought her from the bus station, she straightened the slightly rumpled but still provocative pink silk dress hopefully, imagining the expression that would light her champion's face. Assuming she could locate him, of course.

"Matthew Redtree?" The motel clerk was a robust man with an easy smile. "He's in room eight, but he's hardly ever here. That's his car . . ." He gestured toward a green sedan. "He goes running around on horseback, mostly. Are you his girlfriend?"

"His fiancée," she corrected, wondering if this kind-faced man would be expecting her to take a separate room. The parking lot was empty except for Matthew's rental car, and she imagined that this man was the owner and that this was a family operation. She didn't want to offend anyone, but suspected they wouldn't be fooled for long by pseudo-separate accommodations.

"I can set your bags in his room," the man offered, "and if you're hungry, there's a coffee shop about a block from here. We can leave a note for Mr. Redtree."

"Thanks. Can you give me directions to the burial mounds? Maybe I can call another cab." A momentary image of Matthew on horseback distracted her, awakening thoughts of the dream, and the dream meadow, and the lovemaking . . .

"Burial mounds?" the man frowned.

"The hills?"

"Oh, sure." He hefted her suitcase and motioned for her to follow. "They're about four miles outside town. Nothing much to see this time of year. Wait 'til the leaves start turning, then you can stand on those hills and have a real pretty view of the woods."

She smiled, remembering the woods at the very edges of her dream. She had never had a chance to explore or appreciate them. And the leaves had always been deep green—perpetual spring, perpetual daytime, perpetual peace—except, of course, for the brief intrusion by Aaric . . .

"Kind of a daydreamer, aren't you?"

"Pardon?" She flushed under the man's scrutiny. "Not usually, but . . . I'm on vacation, I guess, so . . ."

"It's good you came, miss." He set her bag on the ground in front of room 8, then fumbled for the key while he gave one quick knock as a formality. To their surprise, the door was pulled open by a bare-footed, bare-chested, sleepy-eyed Matthew.

"Oh!" Molly's heart began to pound with unbridled love at the sight of her champion, looking so handsome and tousled and strong.

"Your girl's here," the clerk announced with a sly grin. "I didn't know you were in, but . . ." He stepped aside and folded his arms across his chest as though waiting for the show to begin.

"Hi," she managed to whisper, then lunged forward and flung her arms around Matthew's neck. "Oh, Matthew . . . You're here."

"You came today?" he murmured into her curls, dazed but clearly grateful. "Damn, Valmain, you feel so good."

And so did he. Matthew through silk—it was a gloriously decadent feeling. His chest muscles were hard and smooth and tensed with the need to hold her close. Soon he would take her back to his bed, which was undoubtedly still toasty warm from his aborted nap.

"You were sleeping?" she sighed, lifting her head to stare into the gold-flecked eyes she adored.

"You're here," he repeated, more coherently, and a wide grin spread across his face. Then he glanced toward the clerk and his grin became a scowl. "Thanks for your help," he informed the man curtly, grabbing Molly's suitcase with one hand while tugging her into the room with his free arm.

" 'Bye . . . ," Molly called out one instant before the door had slammed shut. Under other circumstances she might have scolded Matthew for treating the man so rudely, but the thought that her champion couldn't bear to share her for even one more second with the outside world pleased her, and so she melted against him in complete submission.

"Valmain," he chuckled. "I can't believe you came all this way, so quickly, to see me. I'm flattered. And," he nipped at her earlobe, "I can't wait to show you the mounds. They're worth the trip, believe me."

"I didn't make this trip to see the mounds, I made it to see you and," she dragged his face down in preparation for a steamy kiss, "you're definitely worth the trip."

"Yeah, but you've got to see them right away. It'll be dark soon." He pulled free of her embrace and reached for the wrinkled polo shirt at the foot of the bed.

She had forgotten how fanatical he could be and now chided herself as she moved to sit on the unmade bed, stroking the warm sheet hopefully. "The sun will come back up tomorrow morning, Matthew. I can almost guarantee it. Shouldn't my first view of the mounds be by dawn's early light?"

He grinned as he tucked his shirttails into his jeans. "Cute, Valmain. Don't tell me you're not just a little curious."

She remembered her plan to seduce him and stretched out on the bed, hoping the dress was earning its price tag. "I'm a little tired from my trip,

Matthew, and you must be tired or you wouldn't have been taking a nap."

"I was up until four this morning, talking to Deborah."

"Oh?" Her eyes narrowed. "Is that your horse's name?"

"Huh? Oh." His grin returned. "Cute, Molly. Let's go. I'll tell you all about Deborah on the way."

"Mmm . . ." She closed her eyes and snuggled into the pillow. "Go on without me, Matthew. Lucky for you, I'm not the jealous type, so you can tell me all about Deborah later."

"Molly?" He sat on the edge of the bed and patted her curls. "Are you really tired? I thought your energy level would be way up here, like mine is."

"Mmm." Without opening an eye, she reached out and found his hand, which she pulled to her lips and kissed gently. "Sleep with me, champion. Don't make me beg." When he stretched out beside her and gathered her against his chest, she sighed with relief. "I don't think I've ever wanted to make love more than I do at this moment, Matthew," she confessed.

"I know," he whispered, fumbling with her skirt until it was high on her thighs. "Because of the amulet. It enhances everything here, Valmain, and this . . ." his breath was hot and mesmerizing on her neck, "this is going to be incredible."

"The amulet? Hey!" She caught his wrist as he moved it into an all-too-familiar position. "Not that again!" Pulling free, she sat up and glared. "That *hurt* last time, Matthew! I told you that."

He laughed sheepishly. "It won't hurt this time, Valmain. I promise. The amulet works here. It's got something to do with the burial mounds being close by."

"I don't want the amulet working against *my* tender skin." His grin, boyish and stubborn, made her laugh in spite of her frustration. "You're obsessed."

"With you."

"With power." Her eyes softened. "I've missed you. Please be gentle, Matthew?" The hurt resurfaced and she couldn't resist accusing carefully, "You should have kept in touch with me, Matthew. I felt like our relationship was a little one-sided."

"One-sided?" His eyes and voice grew soft. "In a way it is. I'm your champion. Your slave. I'm bound by honor and destiny to defend you—"

"And bound by love to call me when you're out of town?"

"Were you really concerned? Sorry, Valmain. It'll never happen again. We'll never be apart again. Now that we've found the mounds . . ."

"Now that we've found each other," she corrected seductively. "Isn't that what you meant to say? Mmmmm . . . I thought so." Her hands caressed his shoulders. "I had some pretty wild thoughts about you on the airplane, Matthew. I hope you're ready to be ravaged."

"Just lean back and relax," he laughed. "I'll take over from here."

"But I want to make love to you." She was wriggling out of her dress as she spoke. "I'm not inexperienced anymore, thanks to you, so why not let me help?"

"Your job is to inspire me," he reminded her, his voice hoarse with devotion, as though he had just fully realized she was there. "My dreamer. My destiny . . ."

She wanted to dispute this, but he had moved his mouth to soothe the skin so recently assaulted by the amulet and she almost swooned at the sensation. He made love to her, with his lips and with his tongue, until she was pulsing with pleasure, and the fanatical attention to detail that had annoyed her earlier now brought her exquisite delight. He was everywhere at once, yet there was an unhurried tempo to his assault that made it seem as though some elusive time barrier had been broken and this lovemaking would last for an eternity. Then the smoldering pleasure surged into a burst of white hot ecstasy, causing her to call out his name in a voice rich with gratitude and amazement. When the erotic wave had fully crested, he mounted her and flashed a victorious smile before taking her with an intensity and thoroughness that thrilled her beyond belief, then satisfied her just as completely.

Well, you got your way as usual, Valmain," Matthew teased, sliding out of the bed and reaching for his discarded jeans. "Now it's too late for you to see the mounds."

"They've been there a thousand years," she reminded him, her eyes locked on his muscular form. "They can wait. This couldn't."

"Yeah." He sat back on the edge of the bed and prodded, "Tell me the truth. You did notice it, didn't you? The amulet?"

"Matthew! Enough. If I noticed it, it's because it kept jabbing me. You should have taken it off."

"It enhances everything I do," he corrected stubbornly. "You have to admit how perfect this was."

"Because of the amulet? Or because we've been separated? Or," she smiled impishly, "because of my new dress? You didn't say what you thought of it."

"Huh?" He shrugged. "You always look fine, Valmain. Your beauty comes from your pure heart. That's why all dresses look fine on you."

She bristled in disappointment. "In other words, you didn't like it?"

"It's not your style," he explained patiently, "but it looked fine." He stroked her cheek with his thumb. "You look prettier every time I see you, remember? But you look best in white."

"I guess you didn't get the whole effect without the matching shoes," she grumbled, wishing she hadn't opted for comfort in deference to the fast pace of her trip.

"I like you in bare feet."

"Bare everything?"

Matthew chuckled. "Absolutely. But for now," his tone became brisk, "you need to get dressed in something comfortable. I want you to meet Deborah. She's an old woman who lives out beyond the mounds, and she's a little senile and odd, but she's also amazing. When it comes to the mounds, she's like an encyclopedia of knowledge."

"That's nice, Matthew. But tonight?" Her eyes left no room for argument. "I don't think so."

"I *have* to go out there, at least for a while. I accepted a dinner invitation, when I thought you wouldn't be here until tomorrow."

"She'll understand. Call her."

"She doesn't have a phone."

Molly grimaced and drew the covers over her head. "You go. I've been running since early this morning. And now this amulet loving! Let me catch up on my sleep. You can wake me up in time for dinner and I'll be fresh."

"You're always fresh, that's your problem," he laughed, then his golden eyes began to sparkle. "You'll have the dream here, Valmain. I'm almost sure of it."

"Oh, Matthew." She wished he would simply let it go, but knew better than to argue. "My dream's gone. Please don't get your hopes up."

Matthew shrugged. "The amulet's powerful here, and I'll bet the dream is, too. I'd join you, to test the theory, but there's no way I could get to sleep. I get so pumped when I do anything active with the amulet." His smile was teasing. "Making love was definitely a rush."

It was as close to a compliment as she could hope to receive, and so she accepted it eagerly. "You're welcome. Bring me back some yummy takeout food as my reward."

"You'll be okay alone?" An ominous frown creased his handsome face. "Stay away from that jerk of a manager."

"That sweet guy?"

"He's not so sweet, believe me. Just stay in here and put the dead bolt on the door. And put some clothes on." He began to rummage in her suitcase. "Did you bring a nightgown? Oh, good, you brought me some fresh shirts. Hey . . ." His eyes were positively glowing with appreciation as he studied the design she had so lovingly stitched into the hem of each shirt. Then he sat on the foot of the bed and whispered hoarsely, "Just when I start to think you don't get this destiny thing at all, you do something so incredible . . ."

"You like it?"

"Like it? It's just like my dream headband. Come here, Valmain."

She knelt before him, eager for her erotic reward,

then smiled with frustrated amusement when he pulled the shirt over her head and down over her naked breasts. "There," he pronounced reverently. "You look more beautiful than ever."

"That's it," she sighed, "you're officially hopeless."

"Huh?"

"What did I expect?" She sank back into the pillows and pretended to glare. "I should have known, the day you offered to have a celibate love affair with me."

"I wish I'd never said that," he groaned. "I was just trying to reassure you, Valmain. Aren't you ever going to drop it?"

"Make me," she suggested impishly. "Prove to me you never could have kept your hands off me for that long."

"If that's all it'll take," he smiled, "no problem. I'll start as soon as I get back from Deborah's." After kissing her forehead, he moved to the closet, where he commandeered an oversized bottle of Chianti. "I'll see you in an hour."

"Wait! What's that?"

"The key to Deborah's heart," he grinned. "It'll make things easier, believe me. Now," his eyes grew warm with love, "stay inside, lock the door behind me, and try to dream."

"I'll dream of you," Molly murmured sincerely. "My hero."

Flushed with pride, he turned and was gone.

Molly shook her head, amused but confused. She wasn't sure if it was the amulet or just his buoyant mood, but he really did seem sexier than ever, and she could hardly wait for him to get back and prove his boast to her.

On the other hand, she was completely exhausted, not only from the trip, but from the apprehension she had harbored over this reunion. If it hadn't gone as perfectly as it had, she might have found it necessary to reexamine the whole affair, and that fear had apparently weighed more heavily on her than she had realized. When she had stepped off the bus and into the taxicab that took her to the motel, innumerable scenarios of disaster had tried to sabotage her, but she had trusted Matthew Redtree and his love, and now she could relax and congratulate herself for having had faith in him.

And she could sleep, so that she was rested for his return. Drifting easily, she discovered, with wary delight, that August and Matthew had been right after all. The dream wasn't gone. If anything, the meadow was more vibrant and beautiful than ever. And there were the wildflowers, and the doves, and the stallions, all of them glorious. And then . . .

"You!"

"Daughter of Kerreya!" The Moonshaker bowed mischievously. "You have returned to me at last."

Chapter Eighteen

"It can't be!" Molly backed away in confusion, pulling her cape close. "You're dead."

"Am I? I feel amazingly well in spite of it. I have been waiting for you."

Molly shook her head, wary of his affectionate tone. *"Waiting* for me? Like a vulture?"

"No. Like a lonely admirer, hoping to catch a glimpse of the woman of his dreams."

Her confusion faded into frustration. "I thought you were gone forever."

"I am *here* forever. Unless of course I win a battle and take another's form. Please do not be frightened. I cannot do anything to you that you do not wish."

"Frightened?" she sniffed. "There was a time I was frightened of you, but not now. I've had some practice dealing with you . . ." A cool smile tugged at the corners of her mouth as she remembered the many times she had chewed him out during the weeks of doubt over Matthew's identity. Standing up to Aaric the Moonshaker was hardly a novel or terrifying experience. "You don't scare me a bit."

"I see that." A disarming grin lit his handsome face. "You are more beautiful than ever, Princess. A man could go mad with the need to hold you in his arms."

"So? I was right," she murmured, half to herself. "You *would* have taken me to Paris."

"Paris?"

"Never mind." She studied him carefully. In place of his battle gear he now wore a soft, high-necked white tunic with a crimson belt. This philosophical garb, along with his wavy golden hair and sea-blue eyes, brought to mind Apollo rather than Ares. Still, his bare arms rippled with well-trained muscles and Molly had to admit again that he was a powerful, blood-stirring sight. "You're in *my* dream," she reminded him finally. "You can't hurt me without jeopardizing your own existence."

"That is very true."

"You lost the battle with Matthew."

"That is also true."

"But you didn't die?"

"I was defeated," he explained patiently. "I am suspended here—without life or death—for as long as *you* allow it. You are the only one who can kill me, either by killing yourself, as you so boldly threatened once, or by using your power to banish me."

"Banish?" She savored the word, which reinforced the image of the dream as a kingdom under *her* rule.

"If you banish me, you lose the rare opportunity to learn from the finest of teachers."

"And if I let you stay," she shrugged, "you'll use your magic to trick me. And eventually you'll fight Matthew again, hoping to take over his form."

"No. Sadly, that can never be. *That* is the nature of his victory over me. If another warrior came, I would have another chance at freedom, but my chance to win your champion's body has been lost forever."

"For the moment I'll accept that as true." She stepped closer. "Are we expecting any other warriors?"

Aaric chuckled. "Unfortunately, that is unlikely, unless I can convince you to summon òne here from your world. Of course," his tone grew more serious, "if other magicians in your world learn your secret and invade this dream, I would have no choice but to fight them. However," the smile returned, "you need not fear that. I can teach you to block them." He reached out one hand and touched her cheek. "I have yearned to see you again, Princess. Why did you wait so long?"

"I don't know," she sighed, lulled by his amorous tone. Then she straightened and glared, "I never know *when* I'm coming here. And I definitely didn't come to see *you*. I thought you were dead."

"Have you quarreled with your champion? Has he mistreated you?"

"Of course not."

"I have asked myself why you are lonely. It cannot be that he has found another woman. He would be a fool to look at anyone else," the warrior declared heartily. "And it cannot be that you have found another man. If that were to be, I would be he."

"Lonely? I'm not lonely."

"Have you forgiven me for my transgression?"

"Which one?" she glared.

"There was only one. When I took his shape to seduce you." Taking both of her hands into his, he insisted, "I did not know you then. The conflict was all that concerned me. I apologize for taking you the way I did. I wanted to provoke him and . . ." he grinned sheepishly, "it had been a very long time."

Molly frowned and pulled her hands free. "I don't want to discuss it. It never happened."

"I did not know you then," he continued sincerely. "I did not know you were so innocent. So easily wounded. Did I injure you? Was I too rough?"

Gathering her cape around herself, she reminded him nervously, "I thought you were Matthew."

"But I was not." He shrugged. "It is best forgotten. I regret it."

"You do?"

"Of course. I see that it has placed an obstacle between us. Had I waited, perhaps in time . . ."

"Are you serious?" Molly was fascinated by the man's confidence. "I love Matthew Redtree, Aaric. Haven't you learned that by now?"

"Love?" He waved one arm as though frustrated. "One word to describe many feelings. Your language can be very confusing."

"How *do* you know English, anyway? It didn't even exist in your day, did it?"

"Not in my world, at least. It is the language of your dream, but it troubles me. You must promise not to judge me by my use of it. I may err occasionally."

"So?" she prodded. "In your language, there are different words for different kinds of love?"

"The feeling that your champion has for you. The reverence . . ." Aaric shrugged and then grinned. "I have a love for you too, but it is much less lofty."

"Never mind." Her cheeks had grown hot. "Let's talk about something else. You clearly don't know the first thing about love." Weakening, she suggested, "You had reverence for Maya?"

"Hardly," he laughed. "That was much, *much*

less lofty. Still, I would have done almost anything to please her. To protect her. It seems that perhaps *you* are the one who knows little of love. I will teach you." He took her hand once again and kissed it respectfully. "I am your humble servant."

"Humble? Never." A wave of boldness swept over her. "Your bravado is part of your charm."

"So you find me charming. At last. But you still prefer the other one?"

Molly winced. "I have to go. I want to see Matthew."

"Or perhaps you *need* to see him?"

"Meaning what?"

He shrugged. "I believe the bond between you is weak. And growing weaker. Destiny threw you together. The strongest bonds," he insisted quietly, "are forged when destiny tries to tear you from one another and you must fight to stay together."

"Like you and Maya?"

"Yes, that was strong. Forever. She was tempted away many times but she came back because I loved her. Truly loved her. I was the only man who ever saw that she was the more astonishing of the two sisters."

"Someday I'd like to hear about it. But now I have to go." She hesitated and then admitted, "Maybe it's best that you're still here, Aaric. There's a lot Matthew and I want to know."

"Until next time," he bowed dramatically, "I shall remain your not-so-humble servant."

"Just so there's no mistake," she added weakly, "I still hate you."

"Do you?" he chuckled.

Unnerved, she escaped to the safety of Matthew's motel bed, only to find that her champion had returned and was towering above her, studying her as though she were an artifact rather than a person. "Well?" he demanded.

"Huh?" Still groggy, she recoiled from the intensity of his gaze and murmured, "Is something wrong?"

"Were you dreaming?"

"Dreaming?"

"Damn! I was so sure! You should have seen your face." He collapsed heavily at the foot of the bed. "I was *sure* you were in the dream. I almost tried to join you—"

"Join me?" She blanched at the realization that another brutal confrontation had been so narrowly avoided.

"Yeah. You know, fall asleep and join you. I've tried a bunch of times to get there, but . . ." He smiled reluctantly. "Why does that frighten you?"

"There could be more warriors, coming from the past, to fight you!"

"Yeah, I know."

"And you'd love that? To fight again?"

"To fight and win again," he nodded, raising his wrist before her eyes. "With this."

She touched the amulet and nodded, grateful to him for being so completely honest. Now it was her turn. She would gather her thoughts and tell him all about Aaric over dinner. "What time is it, Matthew?"

"It's after eight o'clock. You slept forever."

"How was your visit with Deborah?"

"She wasn't there."

"Oh?"

"I guess she forgot. She's as senile as they come, Molly. But Angela showed me some old arrowheads they found by the river, so it wasn't a totally wasted trip."

"Angela?"

"Deborah's granddaughter. She's the one that lends me her horses. We've gone riding together a couple of times."

"Well, I'm glad you haven't been lonely."

In his enthusiasm Matthew missed the touch of sarcasm. "I don't think I *could* be lonely here! Even when I'm alone, I feel the presence of the ones who went before."

"Wait! Isn't this where I came in? You, off in a strange world, trying to lure me out of mine?"

"Yeah, and wasn't it worth it?" he challenged confidently.

"I guess so." Confusion was threatening to overwhelm her. "When did you get back, Matthew?"

"About five minutes ago." He shook his head. "I was sure you'd have better luck with the dream, being here so close to the mounds. Did you even try?"

"Yes, I tried." She struggled to find the words to tell him about Aaric, but an image of the two warriors battling anew held her prisoner. "Matthew?"

"Yeah?"

"Promise me you won't try to get into the dream without me." Grasping him by the shoulders, she locked eyes with him and insisted, "Please? Give me your word?"

"You're still worried I might run into another ancient enemy?" he chuckled. "I appreciate the concern, Valmain, but it's pretty unlikely, don't you think?" His eyes softened. "Is that why you've been resisting going back? Are you afraid?"

"Exactly. I won't be able to concentrate on dreaming if I think you're trying it."

The benevolent threat clearly hit its mark. "I

promise," Matthew agreed quickly. "On one condition."

"Anything."

"You promise to try to get back. Every night. And," he adopted a pseudo-stern tone, "to report to me the moment you're successful."

"That makes sense, I guess." Her heart almost broke at the facile deception. She had always been scrupulously honest—strong and pure of heart. What was Aaric doing to her?

Or could she blame Aaric? She dreaded another battle—although Matthew could no longer be killed by Aaric in the dream. In fact, he would order her to banish the Moonshaker, and then . . .

And then you'll never have the answers, she reminded herself. *To your past or your "destiny." If Matthew were capable of being rational on the subject of Aaric, he'd agree you should pump him for information.*

But Matthew couldn't be rational—only blinded by an ancient feud—and so Molly would be rational for him, until a calm, balanced opportunity for full disclosure presented itself.

"Tell me more about Deborah and Angela," she pressed, anxious to change the subject.

"Deborah knows all about witchcraft, and amulets and channels and the mounds. She's an encyclopedia of information."

"So you mentioned. And Angela?"

Matthew smiled fondly. "Angela's special. She has an incredible way with horses."

Molly's jealousy flared. "How exactly did you find them?"

"I didn't. Deborah found me. She saw this," again he held the amulet up, "and she recognized the symbols and began talking a mile a minute."

"Oh?"

"She grew up in this area, and she's studied this stuff for years. She gave up her life for it, in a sense. She's real poor, Molly."

"Oh? That's too bad."

"Yeah. And she's too proud to accept help. I offered to pay her for her time, and Angela's tried to convince her to move to her house here in town, but . . ."

"Angela isn't poor?"

"She's an artist's model, which I guess pays pretty well."

And which answers my next question, Molly fumed silently. *She's beautiful!*

"I can't wait for you to meet them, Valmain. And wait until we tell them you're a witch!"

"What?" She stared in complete horror. "You'd tell them that?"

"I haven't told them yet," he insisted quickly. "And believe me, they'll be impressed. Jealous, even."

Biting back an urge to call him an idiot—or beast—or worse—she congratulated herself for having had the sense *not* to tell this naive fanatic about the Moonshaker's return. He'd share it with beautiful Angela and senile Deborah and soon every tabloid in the world would run witch-hunt headlines.

"Are you upset, Valmain? I hardly told them anything, and nothing about you, except that you're the one who gave me the amulet."

"And?"

"And," he tried for a charming smile, "I told them about the battle, but not about the dream."

Molly felt almost nauseous. "The battle? With Aaric?"

"Right. Deborah knew all about him. She says, since I killed a legend, I *am* a legend." He flushed and added quickly, "She's melodramatic sometimes." When Molly simply stared, he pulled her into his arms and soothed, "I shouldn't be talking so much. You're tired from your trip. Let's eat, and we'll discuss all this in the morning."

"I'm not hungry," Molly whispered. "I'm confused, Matthew. I have to think."

"Are you angry?"

"No, but maybe," she admitted, "I'm a little jealous. You were spending time with Deborah and Angela while I was pining away alone in Berkeley for all that time."

"It seemed like a long time to you," he sympathized, "but it only seemed like hours to me. The time flew by. Otherwise, I swear I would have called more."

He really is an idiot, she decided wearily, unable to fully resist his anti-romantic charm. His sincerity and loyalty were beyond question—could she say the same for her own?

She decided again to tell him about Aaric over dinner. The sooner the better. "Let's go eat, Matthew."

"I brought food with me," he smiled. "Chinese takeout. Between you and Angela, I'm too worn out to go to a restaurant."

The dream girl's eyes darkened. "I know how *I* wore you out. What was Angela's technique?"

Scooping chow mein onto a paper plate, he grinned, "A horserace. Past the mounds—all the way to the river and back. She's wild, Molly."

And so it went. Just as Molly would begin to divulge her astonishing secret, Matthew would make a reference to Angela, or moving to the mounds, or Molly's "pure heart" or caffeine intake, and she would lose the moment. Finally, all moments were lost and she slipped between the sheets, made blissful love with her champion, then listened to the sounds of his contented slumber long into the night until sleep and dreams—and Aaric—overtook her.

"Did you tell your champion of our meeting?" the sorcerer demanded playfully as soon as she arrived.

Molly smoothed her cape haughtily. "If I had, you'd be too busy fighting—and losing, I might add—to talk."

"I knew you would not tell him, but still it pleases me."

"I didn't do it for you, I did it for Matthew. I've decided to take you up on your offer to teach me a little about my heritage."

Aaric beamed. "Become comfortable, and I will entertain you." Waving one arm, he caused a huge oak tree to appear, then motioned for Molly to sit beneath its leafy branches.

She bit back a smile of delight. "Tell me about the first Valmain," she urged instead. "The stuff I read on my cape doesn't make any sense. It says he came to the "lakes," but Maya brought him to the mounds. What's that all about?"

Aaric took a deep breath, then intoned, "There was a land of many lakes. Many days journey from our mounds. When Valmain's ship landed, he sought a cure for a plague, and was advised by those he met to go to the lakes, to ask for lake magic."

"The cape talks about lake witches and lake wizards."

"An ancient group," the sorcerer nodded, beginning to pace. "Much older than the mounds. Very distinct. They were like us in some ways, but they practiced their magic more frequently and intensely than we did. We considered them cruel and unnatural. But I suspect that they considered us fools."

"Why?"

"We rarely used our magic, except for amusement or defense. We hunted our food, built our dwellings, raised our young, conducted our lives basically without magic. The lake dwellers relied on magic for everything! They were more practiced than us, but not more powerful. Perhaps more successful, I suppose."

"And Valmain went to them?"

"Yes, and luckily Maya was there visiting. They would otherwise have made sport of him and perhaps killed him. But Maya was angry with me, and she saw Valmain as a chance to make me jealous."

"Why was she so angry?"

"It is a long story." He paused, and when Molly nodded for him to continue, his smile became gently nostalgic. "Maya had convinced me to take her to the lakes for her own purposes—to learn new spells. To study. She had contempt for the lake dwellers but she envied them their hours of practicing. Her father would never allow her such idle pleasure."

"She wanted to become more skillful?"

"Always. She wanted to be the most skillful sorceress on Earth. There were things she could do that the lake ones could not, but Maya noticed only that which they could do that she could not."

"Such as?"

"They allowed their women to be warriors. And, they had the power to hear thoughts. Not ours, usually, because we could prevent it. But common men's thoughts . . ."

"They were mind readers!"

"Strange expression, but yes. Their power was limited but fascinating to Maya. Of course, Maya would have despised the life of a lake witch. They were closely controlled and relatively powerless. They could hear thoughts and disguise themselves with their illusion power, but their spells were weak and they were ineffective against the truly powerful."

"So the mounds were more powerful than the lakes?"

"As individuals, yes. Unfortunately, we were unable to easily combine our powers. The lakes could pool all of their magic, through their assembly, making their leader almost invincible. He is called the First Wizard, and he is a channel."

"I thought channels were objects."

"The amulet is a channel," Aaric agreed. "For the mounds, a person is never a channel, but for the lakes, the First Wizard is always the conduit through which the power is controlled. He disburses the power to his wizards and witches, always jealously guarding it. Occasionally, he may send another wizard or witch on an important errand and temporarily channel the assembled power to that messenger. Otherwise, as individuals, they were no match for us." He frowned. "You know *none* of this?"

"Of course not. How could I?"

"And your champion is also ignorant of these things?"

"Yes. Aaric. It's been hundreds of years."

He shook his head. "We are—or perhaps were—a young culture, but a powerful one. You are a part of that culture. The culture of the mounds." His arms swept to encompass the dreamscape. "We draw our power from these mounds, Princess.

When we are near to them, we are fortified. When we are absent long from them, we weaken. Because you have the power of the dream, you are near to the mounds wherever you travel. It is an awesome gift."

"Who built the mounds?"

"Our people built them, at the direction of a pair of powerful sorcerers from the south. Twins, who left their own corrupt world and roamed until they found a people who displayed sufficient fearlessness and loyalty. They intermarried with us, giving us access to their magic. Unfortunately, they fought over a woman and died before they could complete the fourth mound. The one that would have guaranteed our survival."

"There are only three mounds here in the dream," Molly agreed, "but Matthew says there are seven in the outside world."

"Burial mounds. We continued to build them, but without the knowledge and direction of the twins, we were unable to complete the pattern of power. Still, the first three mounds provided protection for many decades. Can it have come to an end?"

It almost broke her heart to see the realization dawn on the mighty sorcerer, and she hastened to remind him, "I don't know if it ended or not. I only know I'm not a part of it, except by accident."

"Accident?" Aaric bent to stroke her cheek. "Your pure heart garnered for you this amazing gift, Princess, and you have used it well. Your ignorance saddens me only because I wish for you to have the magical life your grandfather intended."

"My grandfather?"

"Maya's father. He bequeathed great power to you. I wonder if he knew . . ." Aaric's eyes narrowed. "Perhaps he did! If he suspected our culture would be destroyed, he may also have intended for you to be its rebirth! And if so," he knelt to take her hands, "he could not have chosen a more worthy woman. You have the demeanor of a princess, and the heart of an angel. And your skin is so soft, and your legs . . ." His gaze swept over her admiringly.

"That's enough." She blushed and tucked her legs more securely under herself. "You're such a flirt."

"A man has needs," he explained with a grin. "A great man has great needs."

"Matthew says a truly great warrior overcomes his needs in favor of balance," she sniffed.

"He is mistaken." Aaric's blue eyes twinkled. "Even Lost Eagle—I assume your champion considers *him* great?—had three wives and yet hungered for Maya."

"Three wives?" Molly laughed reluctantly. "How many wives did you have?"

"I never married. I loved many women, in my own way, and I loved Maya above all others. And now I love you."

"Stop changing the subject. And *stop flirting!*"

Try as she might to keep her gaze fixed on his noble face, it kept roving to the broad, broad shoulders and massive chest. She had once viewed him as a human weapon, and had dreaded the moment he would descend upon Matthew. Now he seemed more lover than fighter, and she was dreading the moment when he would descend upon *her*. She wouldn't allow it, of course, but the awareness that he wanted her was combining slyly with her latent fantasy of being a seductress. Jumping to her feet, she assured him primly, "We'll talk again. If you behave, I won't banish you for a while, at least."

"And do you intend to discuss my presence with your champion?"

"That isn't your business." She could feel her grip on the dream loosen and knew she would be with Matthew in a moment or two. Extending her hand for the obligatory kiss, she allowed the sorcerer one playful smile before departing.

"And do you intend to share the pleasure with your champagne?"

"That," said the smuggler, "is—" she had her whole dream lover and knew she would be his. Matthew knew at once, as their bbrstdine her had for the ostensibly was and would the smoke cut on you gently before their steps

Chapter Nineteen

"So?" Matthew's expression was filled with pride as he watched his dream girl's steady eyes take in the sight of three large mounds and four smaller ones arranged in random patterns.

"I don't know what to say," Molly gushed. "It's my meadow!"

"I know."

Out of habit, she reached to gather her cape about herself then sighed when her hand encountered only the fleece of her sweatshirt. "I miss my cape. I feel naked here without it." Her gaze was wandering over the mounds. "Do you realize Maya and Aaric could have stood on this very spot?"

"I knew you'd be blown away, just like I was."

When he pulled her against his chest and kissed her deeply, she melted, savoring the reverence. "You found the mounds, just as you said you would. You're amazing, Matthew Redtree, and I love you. I missed you *so* much."

"We'll never be separated again, Valmain. We're home at last."

Forcing herself to shake off the erotic fog of his kiss she repeated, "Home? Here?"

"Yeah. We can live at the motel for a while—I

don't want to rush into selecting a parcel—it has to be exactly right. The closer to these mounds the better, but I don't want to have to do a lot of clearing—"

"Wait! Parcel? Clearing?"

"I want a big enough place to raise some horses. You need them around here, believe me."

"Matthew!" She caught his face between her hands. "We're home? And we're going to raise horses? Even though I go to school a thousand miles from here and I'm *afraid* of horses? Did I miss something?"

"You said it yourself," he explained patiently. "Maya and Aaric stood on this very spot once."

"And we don't like them, remember?"

Matthew chuckled. "Okay, let's talk about Kerreya and Lost Eagle."

"Let's talk about reality," she suggested quickly. "I need to finish college. And then to get a job! I can't work here in the middle of nowhere."

"You can write my books with me! I'm learning so much from Deborah, I definitely need the help. And you'd find it fascinating! It'll help when you meet her."

"I'm sure I'll be fascinated," Molly sighed. "But my life, not to mention yours, is somewhere else."

"Maybe not. Just give it a chance, Molly."

"Matthew, . . ." She struggled to find the words that would communicate her disappointment. "Can't we put some of this behind us? We need to build a real relationship. I need some normalcy."

"Such as?"

"I don't know. Maybe going to the movies? Going out to dinner. Graduating!"

"At least you didn't suggest dancing this time," he smiled sympathetically. "And I agree that you should graduate. And it would be silly to transfer closer . . ."

"For two classes? I'd say so! And there's your job to think about. This leave of absence—"

"I quit yesterday."

The silence was too long for comfort. "Pardon?"

He cleared his throat before repeating, "I quit yesterday. I thought I mentioned it in my message."

"Was this before or after you went riding with Angela?"

"What?"

"Never mind," she sniffed. "We aren't married or anything. I guess you can quit your job without consulting me."

"We're not married because you don't want to! And I really didn't think you'd mind."

"I don't. Let's forget it. Let's just get something to eat."

"I've got a better idea." The gold in his eyes ignited. "Let's make love, right here."

"Forget it! The only thing that ever excited me was that I was doing it with a college professor." She was finding it impossible to stay angry in the face of his exuberance. "Now that you've quit . . ."

"I've got something that will excite you more!" His grin was now deadly. "The amulet, remember?" Pulling her closer, he cajoled, "Remember this morning?"

She molded herself easily to him, seduced by his arousal. "We can't make love out here in the open."

"Why not? Spiritually speaking, we *own* these mounds. Aren't they the most incredible things you've ever seen?"

"The most incredible things I've ever seen are

your eyes," Molly whispered seductively. "And the most incredible sound is your voice."

"Yeah?"

She smiled shyly. "I've missed it. Last spring, in your lectures, you used to hold the entire room spellbound. Talk to me, Matthew."

"Okay." He pulled her down to the grass. "I'll tell you some of the things Deborah has taught me. Especially about the amulet."

Molly nestled against his shoulder. "Such as?"

"She confirmed the fact that it can only be used by Lost Eagle and his blood relatives. It channels power directly from these mounds, so I *need* to live here. And I need to wear it all the time. Angela's cousin is a jeweler, and he's going to design a silver cuff that'll hold it in place permanently on my wrist."

"They sure have adopted you," Molly mused. "It makes me uncomfortable to know you've told them so much."

"I've only told them about the battle, and the amulet. And in exchange, Deborah's shared much, much more." His eyes twinkled. "Did I mention she apprenticed under a witch?"

"Don't remind me. Doesn't that give you the creeps?"

"You're a witch yourself," he laughed. Rolling her onto her back, he began to nuzzle her neck. "My dream witch . . . You should be dreaming here, of all places. I wonder why you're not."

"I should be dreaming in Berkeley," she countered half-heartedly. "My job starts in a couple of days."

"Quit. Let someone else have it. If you really want to find cures and save lives, find a way to do it *through* magic. There are herbs, and spells . . ." He had felt her stiffen and now laughed nervously. "Bad idea?"

She shoved him away in disgust. "Herbs and spells?"

"I know it sounds overwhelming, but Deborah could teach you."

"You don't have any respect for my goals," she whispered unhappily. "I want to be a scientist, not a witch doctor. It's arrogant for you to suggest I give up everything I've worked for."

"Arrogant?"

She had offended him and she knew it, but knew also they needed to resolve this and so she persisted, "What happened to balance, Matthew?"

"I guess we define balance differently," he muttered. "Or maybe you don't appreciate this place yet. Just give it time, Valmain, and you'll understand."

"I admit, it's an amazing place," Molly conceded.

"Okay, so maybe I was coming on too strong." He touched her shoulder in apology. "Spend a little time here, then we'll talk about it again."

"Okay." She glanced about herself, suddenly curious. "I wonder why the archaeologists have left this place untouched for so long. There must be fascinating artifacts in these mounds."

"Molly!"

"I'm not saying they should dig it up," she assured him hastily. "I'm just wondering. Anyway, what's the big crime? How else can we learn about the history of past civilizations? I would think you'd understand that more than anyone! Where do you think all those weapons of *yours* came from?"

Matthew's eyes flashed. "I know the history of each and every weapon in my collection! Not *one* was acquired by exploitation or desecration. I have respect for the past, not just idle curiosity."

Her face flushed, Molly made a mental note to dispose of the copper ax as soon as she returned to Berkeley. Too bad, she thought ruefully. It had a special, almost otherworldly quality. But with her luck, it was probably acquired by both desecration *and* exploitation. "I'm sorry, Matthew," she murmured, "I didn't mean to sound disrespectful. I just wondered why this spot has been ignored for so long."

"Who knows? Maybe there's a spell protecting it. I'll ask Deborah. Or you could ask her yourself. We could go over there right now. Or," his tone grew softer, "we could go back to the motel and make love. I love you, Valmain."

"Well, there are many kinds of love." Immediately, Molly winced. Did she dare quote Aaric the Moonshaker to the son of Lost Eagle?

"What does that mean?"

"It means reverence isn't very romantic," she shrugged.

"Romantic? I ask you to stay. To sleep under the stars with me! To make love to me here, where the amulet fuels me. But you choose to bury yourself in books and then call *me* unromantic?"

They stood in midst of the ancient burial mounds of their ancestors and stared at one another—a slight, curly-haired young woman in a simple white denim jumper and sandals, facing a deeply tanned, dark-haired warrior in faded jeans. Matthew's stance was uncompromising—almost unapproachable—even in the face of Molly's clear vulnerability.

She reached over to his tightened jaw, smoothing the muscle gently with both her fingertips and her tone. "I love you, Matthew, and I know you love me, but I need to know there's more to us than legends and amulets."

"This is our world," he insisted stubbornly. "I'm powerful here. I can be your champion here, if you'll just let me."

"You can be my champion anywhere. When we're together, we're complete. Remember Ireland? Lascaux? Stonehenge? You were my champion in each of those places."

"But now we've found the mounds. This is our homeland."

She turned toward the smaller mounds, unwilling to allow him to see her confusion. *Did* he love her? Was she so completely the dream girl in his eyes that he could relate to her only in fantasy terms? How did he relate to Angela Clay?

"Hey, Valmain," he teased, clearly unnerved by her withdrawal. "Are you mad at me?"

"I love you," she repeated quietly. "I want to be with you. You know I have to get back to Berkeley. We should be together, and," she attempted a lighter tone, "it gives me the creeps to be all alone in that armory. Maybe it's time for another one of our famous compromises. You come back to Berkeley now and, when I graduate, we'll come back here—to the mounds—for a long, romantic visit."

He seemed momentarily tempted, but it was as though the mounds were pulling him away from her. The mounds . . . the amulet . . . the dinners with an encyclopedic old woman named Deborah Clay . . . the wild rides with Angela . . . All of these seemed to have reinforced his desire to stay, whatever the cost.

* * *

"Are you sad, Princess?"

"No." She blushed and pulled her cape closer. "Tell me more about the twins, Aaric."

"Loneliness haunts you again," the sorcerer insisted quietly. "Even in your absence I sensed it. Have you quarreled with your champion?"

"No," she lied. "Everything's fine. Just tell the story, Moonshaker, and stop trying to cause trouble."

"I am not the cause of this. There is something lacking in his love for you. I noticed it from the first. It angers me to see him mistreat you."

"He doesn't mistreat me!" She felt tears sting her eyes and turned away quickly. The last thing she needed was to discuss her love life with an unprincipled bully. And the fact was, in terms of lovemaking, Matthew had been treating her royally. Between his natural reverence for his dream girl and the added zest of the amulet, Molly was certain no woman had ever been treated quite as effectively as she had been treated that very night, the argument at the mounds notwithstanding.

"He is gentle with you?" Aaric persisted doggedly. "Attentive?"

"Yes." When she turned back to him, the kindness in his eyes overwhelmed her and she confessed, "It's not a lack of anything. It's almost as though he loves me too much! Me, and the mounds, and the amulet . . . He's totally obsessed. It's not normal."

"He is obsessed with your beauty?" Aaric suggested.

"It's not physical with Matthew, it's mystical. Physically, I guess he usually falls for a different type." She blushed, wondering if she was losing her mind, discussing this with so inappropriate a listener. But something in his eyes told her he understood. And who else was there to listen to her?

The Moonshaker touched her cheek. "Is he *your* 'type,' as you call it?"

"Matthew?" She thought of his thick hair, so black it seemed almost midnight-blue . . . his lean, tapered torso, and vibrant eyes, and soothing voice . . . his hands and his mouth, making love to her for hours on end . . . "Yes," she whispered unhappily. "He's my type."

"Then he is a fool." Aaric gathered her against his massive chest and stroked her curls lovingly. "A blind and soulless fool. Has he never drowned in the deep blue pools that are your eyes? Has he never trembled with need when your warm, sweet breath mingled with his own? Is the man so perversely spiritual that he cannot crave the taste of your—"

"Aaric!" Flushed with arousal and shame, she jerked herself free of the hoarse, sexy voice. "This is crazy . . . I'm sorry." She took a deep breath. "That was my fault, and I'm sorry. The truth is," she managed a half-smile, "Matthew and I did have a little argument. It happens sometimes, but we always make up, so let's drop it, okay?" When the sorcerer nodded, she smiled gratefully. "Thanks. So? You were telling me about the twins? My cape mentions them, but it's all in riddles. One power shared by two hearts, and something about a guide . . ."

He motioned for her to be seated, then settled down before her. "As I said, they were killed prematurely. Many legends and prophesies were created to soothe the grief of their descendants. The legend of the sorceress-guide was the most moving. But perhaps our fates were sealed at the moment of the twins' demise, as many wise men feared."

"I'm sorry, Aaric."

"I cannot believe it is all gone. All?" He shook his head. "We of the mounds were a new people. I can almost believe that we somehow managed to destroy ourselves. Even in my day, we could sense that our power was lessening. But the lakes? They had been so entrenched in their land. So organized. They had learned over many centuries to manage their powers. They could even wrap their witches—put them into a deep, empty sleep—when they perceived that the drain on their power was too great."

"Wrapped in a deep, empty sleep?" Molly shuddered. "Did they do that often?"

"No. Wrapping a witch was a drain on a wizard's power, although in a different sense. It was an extreme measure. It was sometimes used as punishment, but generally reserved for managing the flow of power."

"Where does the power come from?"

Aaric shrugged. "My guardian—your grandfather—would say ours comes from the earth itself. Whereas the lake power came from water. Which is probably the reason our people—your ancestors—were terrified of deep water."

"They were?"

"There were legends of a race of immortal water masters, who supposedly inhabit the seas, rivers and lakes, and enslaved our people for years before our escape. Of course, since I was raised at sea, I had no such superstitions. I would often swim in the river," he remembered, "and Maya and the other females would be wide-eyed with admiration for my fearlessness."

"You were born at sea?"

"That," he grinned, "is another story. A very long story. I will tell you soon, but for now . . ." His eyes twinkled. "Perhaps I should swim in our river. Would you be impressed? Seduced?"

"Hardly. I love to swim myself and I learned in the ocean."

"You have no fear?"

"Of course not. It's superstition, like you've said."

"So, how shall I impress you?" He kissed her hand mischievously. "Shall I make an illusion of a dragon and slay him for you?"

To her delight, he proceeded to do just that, clothing himself in a gleaming golden glow, brandishing a three-foot-long jewel-studded bronze blade, and ceremoniously vanquishing a twenty-foot-long fire-breathing—yet nonthreatening—green-scaled creature, which conveniently disappeared upon contact with the sword.

She clapped her hands in glee, then spread her cape and nestled contentedly beneath the towering oak. "I love it here, Aaric," she sighed.

The sorcerer pretended to scowl. "You are endlessly frustrating, Princess. In that sense you remind me of Maya."

Molly was grateful for the change in subject. "I want to hear more about her. She wanted to be skillful. And you argued about it?"

"No. We argued because I wished for her to bear my child. She refused."

"Why?"

"She believed it would weaken her, as it had her mother. She asked me to wait. And to wait. I became impatient. Then, at the lakes, a wizard taught me the way in which his barren wife became the bearer of another woman's child."

"What!"

"Yes. It was complicated. They called it a carrying spell. But I thought perhaps Maya would allow another woman to bear *our* child. So that Maya would not be required to endure the physical effects. I thought perhaps she could then remain strong."

"And Maya hated the idea?" Molly guessed.

"Exactly. Her fury became boundless. Valmain was my punishment."

"What was he like?"

"Valmain?" Aaric shrugged. "I had to admire him. He had no magic, and yet he was fearless."

"What did he look like?"

"Maya claimed he was handsome," the sorcerer recalled, "but I thought his appearance strange. His hair and his beard were red."

"Did he have blue eyes like mine?"

"Nothing about him was like you."

"Okay. So Maya gave Valmain the cure and took him to the mounds. And then he met Kerreya."

"That was a moment to be remembered. Kerreya, the dutiful daughter, laid eyes on Valmain and the glow in her heart lit the northern skies! And Valmain, who feared nothing, was on his knees. And Maya . . ." Aaric smiled fondly. "Maya was undone."

"Wow. That really *was* a moment to remember, I guess. You always say I look like Kerreya."

"No. I say you resemble her. In size, perhaps, and in your countenance. Her hair was curly, like yours, but very dark."

"And Maya?"

"You are like her also—in bearing and spirit. But Maya was tall. Much taller than you. She had hair that was black and straight, and eyes that could pierce through any deception, all the while practicing deception themselves. I was the most powerful warrior the world knew, but before those eyes I became a slave."

"Wow!"

Aaric laughed. "You could have learned much from her. She would gladly have taught one such as you. She was complicated," he added fondly. "She wanted to love her family, but could not compete with Kerreya's vulnerability. Everyone, especially the old man and Valmain, preferred Kerreya's meekness to Maya's willfulness."

"Except you."

"It was their loss! Maya could have shown them such excitement, and that," he took Molly's hand urgently, "is why you must not allow your champion to overshadow you. Allow him to try, but not to succeed. You are a blend of the two sisters: Kerreya's innocence, with Maya's need for independence."

"You always say that!" she protested. "I still don't see how I'm like Maya. I'm not promiscuous or deceitful."

"Have you told Lost Eagle's son of our meetings?"

"Not yet. But that's different! I'm protecting everybody. And I'm not doing anything wrong."

"So you say."

"Okay. You're right, I guess." She plucked nervously at a stray silver thread. "You say I shouldn't let Matthew dominate me. I'm having a lot of trouble with that concept lately. I don't want to deceive him, but I know if I tell him about this dream, he'll use the amulet to come here to fight you again and he'll *definitely* object to *my* coming here. If that happened . . ."

"You would take the amulet to keep him from being able to come here? Or you would block him.

And by defying him, it would be finished between you."

"Maybe not. Maybe I'd agree not to come back here."

"No! Not you. That is what I mean. Kerreya would obey her lover's command. Maya would spit in his face. But you are a blend. You disobey, but you are filled with remorse."

"What about you? You let Maya dominate you! You called yourself her slave."

Aaric laughed. "Words of passion. Of love. Of lust." He spoke this last lasciviously. "No, Valmain Princess. We were equals, Maya and I. That is rare, I see, in any time. Our powers differed, and she defied me, but she needed me. Came back to me. And I needed her. As I now need you."

"I feel like any step I take now is bound to be wrong," Molly sighed. "I wonder what Maya would have done."

"She would have taken what she wanted—what she needed—from both the world outside and this dream. She would have enjoyed reverence from the son of Lost Eagle and passion from the Moonshaker. Her nights would have blazed with pleasure. Instead," his smile was wistful, "your nights are filled with frustration and loneliness, because you will not allow yourself to be weak."

Molly stared into his steadfast blue eyes. "And your nights are lonely, too? I'm sorry, Aaric."

"Night and day," he shrugged. "They are all the same for me. Do not worry for me, Princess. Worry for yourself."

"Night and day," she mused. "It's true. I never thought of that, but it's always daylight here, isn't it? Doesn't that bother you?"

"I am a sorcerer," he reminded her gently. "If I

wish it to be evening . . ." His eyes locked with hers
and slowly, dramatically, the bright sun of the
dream began to move across the sky, setting in a
burst of reds and oranges that preceded a coal-black
darkness, dotted with pinpoint lights from thousands of silvery stars. A new kind of beauty filled
the dream—soft, romantic, seductive—and new
sounds, of crickets and rushing waters, filled the air
with their music. Then the sorcerer stepped closer,
until the heat from his muscled chest warmed her,
preparing her for his caress.

He was seducing her, and she was responding
completely, and only one word could break the
spell. With a voice soft with confusion, she managed
to murmur, "Matthew." Only then did the sorcerer's gaze flicker—with understanding and disappointment—and only then did he restore the
daylight to her dream.

"I'm so sorry, Aaric," she blushed. "That was
beautiful."

"It was an illusion," he reminded her, his tone
oddly sad. "If you had concentrated, you would
have seen past it. Instead," his rebuke was tender,
"you allowed yourself to be fooled by it." He moistened his lips before adding solemnly, "For a moment, I almost fooled myself."

"I should go."

"Yes. For now, you should go."

Reaching for her cape, she repeated, "It was a
beautiful illusion, Moonshaker. I'll never forget it."
She needed to make a dramatic exit, but the dream
was holding her prisoner and so her companion
raised his arms above his head, managed a rueful
smile, and vanished.

He was still there, of course. She knew it was
simply another illusion. A kind and sensitive one,

allowing her to regain her poise and perspective. Glancing around, she realized how important a part he now played in her affection for this dream. It seemed empty without him—a stage without an actor. If she called his name, he would reappear, but what would it mean?

She needed to be with Matthew, not Aaric. She needed to confront her champion, and argue with him, and bring him to his senses. But first, she needed some rest and so she spread her cape on the cool grass of the meadow and curled into a cozy ball, allowing thoughts of the mounds by moonlight to lull her into sleep.

She spent the next day reading on a brightly colored blanket at the foot of the largest of the mounds. Twenty feet away Matthew practiced, kicking his well-worn knapsack and everything else in sight. With the amulet as supplement, his strength, stamina and accuracy had gone from finely-tuned to flawless, and he radiated pure self-satisfaction. Without need for rest, he still occasionally joined his dream girl, for a kiss, or some judicious praise, or to share some tidbit of magic he had learned from the infamous Deborah.

Molly had always adored his confidence, and even now, watching him practice was a source of great pride to her. Why, then, did she also feel uneasy? "Because it's no longer balanced," she answered herself, her voice hushed but audible.

Matthew was at her side in an instant. "Did you say something, Valmain?" His eyes danced with mischief. "Did you miss me?"

"Don't you ever get tired?" she countered half-heartedly. "You never relax anymore, Matthew. You're almost hyper."

"It's a whole new world here for me," he agreed, closing her book firmly. "For us. You and me and our children. Marry me."

"And live happily ever after in the middle of nowhere?" she sighed. "What about *my* dreams?"

"Look around, Valmain." He gestured toward the mounds. "See anything familiar? Your dream come true."

"In *my* dream," she corrected softly, *"I* matter. As a person. Not a prop."

"In your dream, you were a seamstress, not a toxicologist," he reminded her. "Maybe it's a sign we should get back to basics. I can hunt and fish and protect us. You can cook and sew and have babies . . ." He broke off and grinned apologetically. "Sorry. I got a little carried away."

Molly jumped to her feet and smoothed her white skirt. "I'm a princess and a sorceress, *not* your servant girl!"

"Huh?"

"Oh, go kick a tree! I'm going back to the motel." Leaving her books for her champion to carry, she stormed toward the car, more confused than angry. *A princess and a sorceress?* What was *that* all about? What had happened to the student and scientist?

She no longer knew what she wanted from life. She only knew that the sun was setting and, after a quiet dinner, her powerful champion would make love to her and then she would see Aaric . . .

The prior night's attempted seduction was preying on her mind, not so much because it had been so tempting, but because Aaric had retreated so graciously, so lovingly, as though he truly could not bear to contribute to her confusion. Did he honestly sense her loneliness, as he so often claimed? Because it was true. There was great loneliness in her relationship with Matthew. Great loneliness and great waste, when there was so much she wanted to share with him.

Hadn't her grandmother summed it all up when she asked if Matthew Redtree would have fallen in love with Molly Sheridan under ordinary circumstances? The answer was a resounding no. He was the Son of Lost Eagle—the Valmain champion. He needed the dream girl, not the actual woman.

And what about Aaric? she challenged herself, as she edged away from her lover later that night and prepared to fall asleep. *Isn't his interest based on your status as a dream sorceress?*

Then Aaric was there, in the dream, standing before her, and her pulse began to race. There was something in his eyes that told her his interest went far beyond her status or heritage. For whatever reason, this man had come to care for her—for *her!*—and the effect was a dangerously magnetic.

"I was concerned you might stay away," he smiled, kissing her hand gently. "I am glad you are here."

"I never control whether I come or go," she reminded him with a shy smile, "but tonight, I wanted to come."

"After tonight, that will no longer be a concern," he promised. "Tonight, your lessons will officially begin."

"Really?" Her chest tightened at the thought. "You're going to teach me to control my dream power?"

"Your powers are not confined to this dream, Princess. You will learn to control fire and wind.

You will learn persuasion, and infliction, and confusion, so that you can defeat any enemy."

"And illusion?"

Aaric chuckled. "A mounds sorceress does not
have the power of illusion. That is the province of
the male." When she pretended to pout, he added,
"I would gladly trade my illusion power for your
ability to inflict pain from a distance. With that, my
battles would have been much more interesting."

"Infliction," she repeated dutifully. "I think I'll
like persuasion better."

"Persuasion is gentle, like yourself," he agreed.
"And it is easier, and so you will learn it more
quickly. But first, you will learn to control fire and
wind."

"Why?"

"Because, fire is first. Fire is always first."

"In other words, you're the teacher, and you get
to call the shots," she translated. "Okay, proceed."

"Before we proceed, I have something to say."
He took a deep breath. "I have tried to compete
with the Son of Lost Eagle for your affections, and
I now regret that."

"Oh?"

"If your Matthew feels as strongly for you as I
do, then you are wise to choose him over me. He is
the one who can be with you, protecting you." He
reached forward and tilted her face toward his, adding solemnly, "You must remember something else,
Princess. If, as you say, Matthew's obsession with
the amulet is growing, this may someday pose a
threat to you. You may be forced to turn to me for
guidance and protection."

"Matthew would never harm me. Or betray me.
He loves me!"

The Moonshaker frowned. "Then convince him to break with the amulet. As Lost Eagle did."

"Look what happened to him!"

"Yes. Because of Maya's carelessness."

"Carelessness?"

"Yes. I know you think she betrayed Lost Eagle, but it was not so. She did not steal the amulet."

"What?" Molly's eyes widened. "Tell me what really happened, Aaric."

"Lost Eagle realized the amulet was controlling him—making him less in his own right—and so he resolved to move to the western sea, without the amulet."

"Away from you?"

"Correct. He gave the amulet to Maya. As a gift. And when she thought he had departed, she gave it to me. She knew I could not use its power, but thought it would give me pleasure to know Lost Eagle would never dare come back to our land. But she was mistaken. He did come back, and when he did I knew he was unprotected. And so I fought him."

"And killed him easily with your magical powers."

Aaric shook his head. "No. That was not necessary. I defeated him with only my skill. Just as, with your Matthew, I would not have needed to use my powers if he had not had the amulet or your help."

"But he does have the amulet and if he comes here again, he'll beat you with it again. Is that why you want me to convince him to get rid of it?"

"You misjudge me, Princess. I merely suggest that he not wear it so often in your world. In the dream, he will be wearing it in any case, if it is still under his dominion." He chuckled reluctantly. "I can still remember the first time he arrived, with the

amulet. *In his pouch!* Without wearing it on his
wrist, he was powerless to enter, but you called to
him, as you searched for him, and in that way you
summoned him here."

Molly nodded. "Until then, he dreamed we were
standing in a mist. Not talking. Just waiting, I
guess."

"Waiting where your dream and his meet?" Aaric
sighed. "No one can come here without power or
summons, Princess. That is the essence of this
dream."

"And now he has the amulet on his wrist."

"During those lonely nights when you denied the
dream, you blocked his path, just as you blocked
yourself. But now you must learn to block him, or
he may one day interrupt our lessons."

"He promised me he wouldn't try to come here,"
she confessed.

"That is good." He moved toward her boldly. "I
enjoy having you to myself."

"I think that's my cue to leave."

"No! I shall behave," he promised, grabbing her
hands and smiling desperately. "Forgive me, Princess. It is just that I have come to adore you . . ." He
broke off, his eyes widening as though he had been
physically shocked. "Princess!"

In that instant, the Valmain champion appeared,
his face contorted into an expression that made his
dream girl shudder.

Chapter Twenty

Without hesitation, Molly moved between the two warriors. "Matthew! Listen."

"To what? To his declarations of love?" her champion demanded harshly. "No wonder it's so easy for you to plan to go back to Berkeley. He's always with you, isn't he?"

"You're making a mistake. He and I are friends. You can't really think—"

"That he's your lover?" Matthew's eyes were bright with hurt pride. "Maybe not. But he's using you, can't you see? Why didn't you tell me you were dreaming again? That he was still here? Damn! I'm your champion, Molly, but I can't protect you if you aren't honest with me."

"She no longer needs protection from me, warrior," Aaric interrupted coolly. "It is you who poses the danger now."

Matthew's scowl deepened. "What does *that* mean?"

"The amulet has clouded your judgment. Look at you now. You behave as though you think you are some kind of god or sorcerer. But you are just a man, Son of Lost Eagle."

"Aaric, please be quiet! Go away and let me talk

to Matthew." Molly slipped loving arms around her champion's neck and pleaded, "We need to talk. And you don't need to fight. There's no reason to fight Aaric again."

"I don't need a reason to fight him. And," Matthew's eyes flashed again, "I'll win, and he knows it! I have the amulet."

"Ah, but will our princess let you use it? It is her dream, after all. She can disarm it easily."

The silence was terrifying. As Matthew waited for her to declare her allegiance, Molly searched for the words that would restore the "balance" that he had proclaimed to be a warrior's most useful weapon. "Don't let him unbalance you, Matthew," she murmured. "You've always said that leads to mistakes."

Coolly, as though she no longer existed, her champion pulled away from her and motioned for the battle to begin. Aaric, however, was distracted and had turned toward the largest mound, where a stormcloud was taking shape, and where, with a clap of thunder and lightning, a new form was appearing.

"Incredible," the Moonshaker murmured, his eyes aglow with recognition. "I would not have believed this possible. Now we will have a fair match. My guardian will see to that."

"That's Maya's father?" Molly gasped, her eyes fixed on an imposing gray-haired figure who was descending to meet them.

"Yes, Princess. Your grandfather has come to your rescue."

Clad in silvery white robes and smiling gently, the newcomer glided slowly past the warriors and embraced the dream girl. "I am proud of you, Granddaughter. You truly are strong and pure of heart. I have waited many lifetimes for one such as you."

Molly sighed, enchanted by his regal manner. "Can you really help me?"

He stroked her cheek. "How lovely you are. Different, and yet familiar. I must ask you to trust me, Granddaughter." Then he turned to Matthew. "Can you restrain your hatred for just a few moments, so that I may confer with the Moonshaker and my granddaughter?"

"Five minutes," Matthew agreed, amazed but uncowed. "And no tricks."

The old man laughed. "You are very like your father, Son of Lost Eagle. He also showed no respect for either my age or my powers, which, I might add, are impressive, even under these unusual circumstances."

Aaric grinned. "This Matthew is Lost Eagle reborn, sir. He fights like a man possessed. Now, tell me, how is it that you are able to be here, in the Princess's dream?"

"I heard, only too late, of Maya's folly, and of your agreement to participate in her scheme of revenge. It was unwise, Moonshaker. I am disappointed in you."

"It was our decision," Aaric shrugged, "and I have not regretted it. Whatever happened, I have met this woman, and I am a better man for it."

"I admit," the old man sighed, "when I saw how it had ended—this pure-hearted granddaughter with the son of Lost Eagle in one world and with you as her tutor in this dream world—I almost believed that catastrophe had been avoided. Now, sadly, that is not to be."

"And you somehow followed me? Destroyed

yourself? Such a loss to our people," Aaric
mourned.

"It was necessary. You and my daughter planned
revenge, but there were things you did not know.
This dream was not placed here for your amusement, Aaric. My granddaughter here, and the Valmain champion, are here for finer reasons." He
sighed. "Foolish pride is an enemy the mounds cannot afford. Have you never heard me say that?"

"Tell us the purpose of my dream," Molly
pressed anxiously. "We've always assumed it was to
allow Aaric to fight my champion. Tell me the rest."

"The rest?" The old man shook his head. "Perhaps it is too late, Granddaughter. And if not . . ."
He shook his head again. "No interference with the
outside world, however benevolent, can be justified.
My own hopes may be foolish."

"Hopes for what?"

"I always knew we could not survive," he explained sadly. "Our power was strong but incom-
plete. Our numbers grew . . . our enemies waited
. . ." His smile was wistful. "Kerreya was our only
hope. So strong. So pure. She lived far from our
enemies, in a land where magic was not allowed. I
hoped she would survive to give me a grandchild
such as yourself. I wanted you to flourish in har-
mony with your power. Instead, disruption has tormented you, due to Maya and her jealousies."

"Why didn't you interfere sooner? If you could
have stopped the battle . . ."

"It was proceeding well. One champion to
emerge. That could be tolerated, whether Aaric or
this ambitious suitor prevailed. Even, as I said,
when each world contained only one champion, the
danger was slight, as long as you were safe, Granddaughter."

"There's no danger to the princess," Aaric insisted. "At least, not from me."

"As I said, she is safe. For now. But two champions constantly at war? I cannot reconcile this with my hopes for a rebirth of our people. It will tear her poor heart to shreds." He took her hand and touched it to his lips. "It must be dealt with by you, Granddaughter, with my help. After that, I will be gone from this dream for eternity. It is the bargain I have made with destiny. Do you understand?"

"You'll help me to deal with this?" Molly smiled, amazed by the intensity of pure love that flowed toward her from this stranger. "Thank you, Grandfather. Will you use your powers to convince them not to fight?"

"I think your five minutes are up, old man," Matthew interrupted. "Why don't you save everyone a lot of time and leave the dream for eternity, like you said, and take your moonshaking friend with you."

"Matthew!" Molly gasped. "Don't be rude! He's my grandfather!"

"Pay attention, Molly. He's thousands of years old. Hardly a close relative."

"Time is important to you, Son of Lost Eagle," the old man chuckled. "Five minutes. Thousands of years. Eternity. They are all the same to me. Can you not see that?"

"All I see is that I'm Molly's champion. I'll fight anyone who tries to use her. Including you."

The old man ignored this, turning his kind eyes to Molly. "You are pure and strong, Granddaughter, and so now I give two choices to you. You can keep your magic and your dream. The Moonshaker will be trapped in here, forever. Your champion will be trapped outside. He will no longer have access to your dreams, even with his amulet. But he will still have the amulet, and the power and folly that attend it."

"And my second choice?"

"I will strip them both of their power. They will fight as two men were meant to fight—to the death. The winner will go with you to your world in the body of this Valmain champion. The dreams, the powers, the amulet—all will be gone."

Matthew was impatient. "Why do you hesitate? Take the second choice!"

"But you'll never have the amulet again!" Molly protested.

"I don't care. The only reason I ever needed it was to protect you! From him! And he'll be dead. Not just defeated this time!"

She looked to Aaric, who agreed quickly. "Yes. Take the second choice. I, too, wish only to protect you. To do that, I must go into your world. I want to be with you, Princess." He touched her face tenderly and leaned forward as if to kiss her, but the old man raised an arm to block him.

Molly was trembling. Had she dared to doubt Matthew Redtree's love? It was *she* who had betrayed *Matthew* by allowing Aaric to fall in love with her. Were both warriors honestly willing to give up their power—magic and amulet—and to risk their lives, in order to be with her? Her heart broke at the thought of such loyalty and she acknowledged her responsibility to them both. They were noble and brave—each in his own way—and each deserved to be loved and appreciated. With that understanding came the realization of just how she could be true to their trust.

"Please, Grandfather? Couldn't we try another way?"

"What is it that you wish?"

She put her arms around the old man's neck and whispered, hesitantly, the one word that might solve the dilemma: *"Maya."*

The old man's eyes glistened with tears. "So, you do not hate her, granddaughter, even after all this?"

"I understand her now. I was wrong to ever call her evil."

"Yes. She was imperfect, but not evil. She made mistakes, but so did I." He embraced Molly gratefully. "You are truly pure of heart. My legacy to you is well deserved." He studied her shining eyes. "You are certain that you want this? You do not fear her? Here, always, lurking in your dreams?"

Molly smiled fondly. "No, Grandfather. Aaric will keep her busy. And Matthew and I will get on with our lives, outside of here. The way it should be."

The old man pursed his lips in thought. "You understand that you will still have your powers? Including the power to banish her and Aaric whenever they become a burden? And the amulet's power will be preserved." His eyes were shining with relief. "Yes. This is the way it will be. The end of Valmain, do you see?"

"Yes," Molly nodded. "I will gladly 'betray' Valmain if it will end all this fighting."

Matthew grabbed her shoulders. "What are you *saying?* What are you *doing?* Stop! Talk to *me,* not to him!"

"Try to understand, Matthew," she pleaded. "Valmain isn't a kingdom with citizens anymore. It's a wedge, a feud. It divided Grandfather's family. He's given me the power to end it. The first Valmain started all this trouble by betraying Maya, and maybe only betrayal can end it."

"Are you *listening* to yourself?" her champion roared. "I *forbid* this!"

The vehemence of his objection stunned her, and, while she balked at his wording, she panicked to realize perhaps she *should* have considered his advice. She turned back to the old man, but it was too late. He was dissolving into a silver cloud before their eyes and beyond the cloud a blue haze was forming—forming and taking shape—and the shape was that of a stately young woman of uncommon beauty.

"What have you done?!"

For a moment, Molly thought the enraged Matthew was going to strike her and she turned to Aaric for help, but he had left, running toward his Maya, and so she turned back to her champion.

"Please listen to me," she insisted desperately. "Maya's not what you think. I know the whole story now—"

"She betrayed my ancestor!" he spat. "So Aaric could murder him! And now you reunite them? And betray not only *your* family, but mine as well? You talk about a wedge . . ." He stopped, choking on the words, and was gone.

Molly sank to the ground, weak with confusion. Why hadn't he listened? It all made sense! She could explain it. But he was gone from her dream and she knew that, when she awoke, he would be gone from their bed and from their motel room.

She couldn't face that empty bed. In the distance, Maya and Aaric were locked in a steamy embrace, and so she spread her cape forlornly on the damp grass and sobbed, pleading with sleep to rescue her from her dream.

* * *

Matthew knew better than to try to run himself into exhaustion, despite the attractiveness of such a prospect. Exhaustion might have wiped the images of Aaric and Molly from his brain, but thanks to the amulet, his stamina was too great, and so the images remained vibrant, even as the miles flew under his feet.

He had no destination. While Deborah Clay would undoubtedly have welcomed him, despite the lateness of the hour, he suspected she would see his pain, and ask questions he was unwilling or unprepared to answer.

Molly's words were ringing in his ears—*I will gladly betray Valmain . . .* Was she honestly that insane? He could still see her, with her amazing blue eyes, staring up at the Moonshaker as though he were her closest friend in the world! And the Moonshaker's expression had been that of a man in love! Was Molly naive enough to believe that? Did she honestly trust Aaric and Maya more than her own champion?

When she renounced Valmain, she renounced me! he railed inwardly. *How did it come to this? Why couldn't she have listened to me? I thought I was invincible . . .* With an almost vicious gesture, he tore the amulet from his wrist and threw it to the ground.

Without his channel to fuel him, he became instant prey to both exhaustion and confusion. Sinking to his knees, he whispered into the darkness, "Molly, what's happened to us? Are you in love with Aaric now?"

Then his heart began to pound with a new kind of fuel, from the memory of the love in her eyes as she had tried to explain her actions to him. She had proved herself to him at that moment, but his anger had blinded him to it! She had brought back Aaric's mistress so that the sorcerer's interest would be distracted. It had been an incredibly stupid move, but motivated as always by Molly's amazing desire to please everyone. Her strong pure heart, her desire to cure the ills of the world.

If ever a person needed a champion to advise and protect her, it was Molly Sheridan. Instead, he had ignored her needs and left her defenseless. *He* had forced her to turn to strangers and manipulators for comfort and advice, by arrogantly suggesting she abandon her career, and by leaving her alone with her growing doubts in Berkeley.

And now she needed him again—perhaps more than ever. He had to go to her and try, one last time, to reason with her. He was still the Valmain champion, and there was no way on earth he'd leave his dream girl in Maya's clutches without a fight!

A gentle voice spoke his name, interrupting his thoughts. "Matthew?"

"Angela?" He jumped to his feet. "What are *you* doing out here?"

"When I can't sleep, I ride. The moonlight is beautiful, and my horse knows his way . . ." She reached out and touched his cheek. "Where's Molly?" When he didn't answer immediately, she cooed, "You've had a fight? Poor Matthew. Tell me everything."

"I can't talk about it."

"I'll bet Molly feels as miserable as you do." Angela shook her head and, as she did, her lustrous waist-length hair caught the moonlight. "You shouldn't be running around in the dark, Matthew Redtree. Go back to the motel and apologize."

"Apologize?" He almost laughed. "Are you so sure it was my fault?"

"Of course." She slipped her arms around his waist. "I adore you, Matthew, but you get *so* carried away! You probably told her one too many stories about witches, or bragged too much about your precious amulet . . ." Her fingers had strayed to his wrist and she frowned. "Where *is* the amulet?"

Matthew glanced sheepishly toward the ground. "I took it off."

"Why?" Angela gasped. "What were you thinking?" Bending hastily to retrieve the channel, she tied it to his right wrist, then caught his face between her hands and repeated, forcefully, *"Why did you do that?"*

"Angela, . . ." A renewed rush of power from the amulet mingled with curiosity over the nature of this young woman's distress and, despite his need to be alone, or with Molly, he found himself resting his hands on her hips.

"Listen to me," she was instructing sharply. "The amulet is a part of you. As much as your hand, or your mouth, or your heart. Lost Eagle took it off once, and it led to his death. *Promise* me you won't remove it ever again."

"Lost Eagle? You suddenly believe all that?"

"I always thought Grandmother was crazy, but then," her voice began to tremble, "I met *you* and I understood. The mounds and the amulet—they're your destiny. It's all true."

"You really do understand," he murmured, dazed at the thought. "I tried to make Molly understand, but she couldn't, or wouldn't . . ."

"She did this to you!" Angela hissed. "She drove you to it. She doesn't deserve you!"

"Angela . . ."

"To think I was going to try to bring you two

back together!" Her tone was choked with commitment. "She doesn't appreciate you, Matthew Redtree, and I . . . I adore you! I worship you. I have since the first moment you touched me."

"No!"

"Make love to me, Matthew." With a fevered gesture she tore open her cotton blouse, allowing her breasts to spill into view. "Make love to me with your amulet." Dropping to her knees, she began to claw at the zipper to his jeans.

"Angela, don't." He knelt also, hoping to restrain her, but to his astonishment she now straddled his right wrist, then moaned with delight at the resulting contact with the amulet. Her nipples became fiery coals, igniting him even through his clothing, and when he moved his mouth to taste them, for just the briefest of moments, his last coherent thought disappeared.

Returning to Matthew's house in Berkeley, Molly packed her possessions in a daze, remembering another time, not that long before, when she had left her father's house with the same throbbing knot in her stomach, the same stinging tears in her eyes, and the same numbing dread in her heart. What was she to do now? How could she have come so close to happiness—to security—twice in one short lifetime, only to have it wrenched away by . . . *betrayal.* To so many persons it was only a word. It seemed instead to be the story of Molly's life. Only this time, it was she who was cast in the role of traitor.

Ken Lewis helped her find a room in a boardinghouse, moving her few belongings in one trip in a borrowed pickup truck. He groaned under the weight of her old steamer trunk, trying in vain to prompt a smile, then he hugged her gently, swearing that everything would be fine, and telling her that maybe this was for the best—"You two were each so driven, but in totally opposite directions . . ." And it was true. And while Molly had dutifully sent Matthew a letter explaining how she had come to trust Aaric and to understand Maya, she remembered her champion's righteous fury and knew he would be unmoved.

He would contact her eventually, she was sure, if only to say goodbye. Opening the trunk, she gazed wistfully at the silly childhood mementos and masses of term papers and reports. The copper ax was there, too, tucked in the folds of the handmade baby quilt. The ax would be the only souvenir she would take from this catastrophe, she decided sadly. The ax, and her now-worn copy of Matthew Redtree's *Symbolism in Legend and Myth*.

Chapter Twenty-One

"You are just going to allow him to leave you? To be with this Angela creature?" Maya was beside herself with indignation and Molly was regretting her decision to allow this passionate, strong-willed woman access to her life. For three full nights the raven-haired sorceress had reveled in her newly-awakened status, seducing her old lover while fussing proudly over the pretty witch-niece who had so conveniently resurrected her and whose dream power was as impressive in its scope as it was amusing in its limits.

"The manager at the motel says Matthew moved to Angela's house, but I don't know for sure they're . . . romantically involved. And if they are," she chewed her lip at the thought, "it's because she's what he wants."

"She is a beautiful woman, and you left him alone with her," Maya scolded. "He does not want her. His pride is wounded, that is all. Tell her, Aaric. Tell my niece how you felt each time I wounded your pride."

Aaric grinned, still clearly enjoying the reunion. "You never wounded me, my love. Unless of course

you are referring to your affair with Valmain. Or
Lost Eagle. Or—"

"Enough!" Maya's dark eyes flashed and she
drew her blue and gold cape closer in a threatening
manner.

"Yes," groaned Molly. "Enough. Don't *mention*
Lost Eagle. If only I had asked Grandfather to
bring *him* back, too."

"Him?" Aaric boomed. "Never! Your dreams
would have become nightmares."

"Aaric is right, little niece. That would not have
succeeded. Not only would it have been beyond
Father's powers, but also, Aaric and Lost Eagle
would have fought until the day you died, just as
they did from the time they were youths. That is
why Father had to give Lost Eagle the amulet."

"I despised him," Aaric admitted, "but still I am
sorry all this has cost you your Matthew, Princess.
Lost Eagle would not have wanted that. But," he
smiled encouragingly, "your champion will come
back when his anger has cooled."

Maya was growing impatient. "Why wait? She
has the power. If she wants him, let her bring him
here, and I will place a love spell on him."

"She does not need to win him that way, Maya,
my love. You never did with me."

"No." Her laughter echoed through the hills. "It
was never necessary with you, my love. But this
Matthew is not you. He is confused, and hurt, and
he has the amulet. Lost Eagle so often said it made
things twisted. Out of balance."

"Balance?" Molly sighed. "Matthew's favorite
word." She stared into the distance, fighting the
tears that had plagued her every night since Matthew's outburst.

"Do not cry, little niece," Maya soothed. "Talk

of something else. Tell me about your life outside this dream. I wish to hear every detail."

Aaric nodded. "Tell us, Princess. What do you do in your world, now that you are without a mate?"

"Well," she sighed, "I work, although I'm doing a poor job. I just can't concentrate. Maybe when my classes start again, I'll do better."

Maya and Aaric shrugged toward one another, and Maya prodded, "Have you returned to your father's lodge, now that you have no mate?"

Molly frowned ominously. "I didn't consider Matthew a mate. I lived alone when I met him and I was perfectly safe and busy. Now I live alone again."

"And your father allows this?"

"My father has a new wife, and she and I don't get along. I don't want to talk about it." She almost smiled at the expression this refusal brought to Maya's chiseled features. "Okay, okay. I'll tell you. My mother was killed, in an accident, and my father married our next door neighbor, whose name was Constance, and they had a baby girl. End of story."

There was a long silence, and Molly almost thought the subject closed, when a small, constricted, unfamiliar whisper came from her sorceress-aunt. "You must tell me about this accident that robbed you of your mother. When did it occur? What was its nature? How . . . how did you feel . . . ?"

"You're crying?" Molly whispered in return. "What is it, Maya? Why are you so upset?"

The dark-haired beauty burst into tears. "I feel your pain, and your rage, and I mourn with you. You are my niece. My future!"

"Aaric?" Molly's eyes shifted to the sorcerer. "I didn't mean to upset her."

He shrugged to his feet. "I will leave Maya to grieve with you, Princess. A man cannot always choose the right words . . ." Looking completely confused, he grabbed his shield and disappeared over the smallest mound.

"My heart aches," Maya moaned.

"But it was years ago! Please don't cry."

"I must have every detail. Tell me now!"

By the time Molly had finished the story, the women were sobbing in one another's arms as though the body of Molly's mother were yet warm in its grave. "So cruel a choice . . ." Maya wailed. "To heal a dying woman, beyond the reach even of the strongest magic, or to heal yourself . . ."

"Heal myself?" Molly gasped. "You think I did that?"

"I am certain of it," Maya nodded, dabbing at Molly's tears with her soft blue cape. "You say your injuries were crippling, my poor, sweet niece. Such healing would have occurred naturally in a mounds witch, with or without her awareness or training."

"But with training," she murmured, "I might have saved my mother? Is that what you're saying? Oh, Maya!"

"Shh . . . no more tears, now. Your mother was dying. You could not have saved her. And had you tried, we might have lost you both."

"I guess you're right." Molly shook herself out of the morbid mood. "Matthew once told me I needed to talk this out, once and for all. He was right. I'm grateful to you, Maya. I feel more at peace with it all."

"At peace?" the sorceress frowned. "With the loss?"

"Yes. And maybe even with the anger. That would be a relief."

"That would be a mistake," Maya corrected. "A terrible mistake. Hate is your shield and your sword. Never forget that."

"For heaven's sake—"

"Listen to me!" Maya's dark eyes left no room for argument. "Control your hate, yes! Control your anger. But never underestimate its power. Some transgressions are unforgivable. Do you understand?"

"I guess so."

"Do you hate this woman called Constance?"

"Yes," Molly admitted quietly. "I always will."

"That is very wise." At that moment Aaric reappeared and Maya stood and touched his cheek. "Teach my niece to summon fire, as I have summoned you, my love. This accursed accident has prevented her development as a witch. It is all clear to me now. It is our place, as her ancestors, to remedy this intolerable loss." Giving Molly one final hug, she hurried into the distance.

Aaric stared after his mistress, confiding softly, "I have never seen Maya in such a state, Princess. So affected by another's plight. She takes her role as aunt so seriously."

"She's so intense about everything," Molly sighed. "No wonder you love her."

"She is not one to nurture, but she is a woman and I am pleased to discover some small maternal instinct in her. Shall I instruct you? Do you wish to learn to call fire from the air?"

"No, thanks. You go take care of Maya. I'm going to wake up for a while. This dream is too exhausting for me."

"Go and rest," he agreed, pulling her to her feet. "Do not think of your mother, or of your champion." Leaning his face down to hers, he kissed her mouth. "Think of the Moonshaker, if you must think at all."

"Aaric!" She glanced nervously about herself. "What if Maya saw that!" Her reddened eyes narrowed. "You love *her!*"

"A man can love two women," he laughed. "You do not share my feelings, and perhaps that is best. Maya is capable of profound jealousy. I simply wish to remind you that you are desirable. If Lost Eagle's son is lost to you, find another mate."

"I don't need another *mate,*" she began, then added half-heartedly, "I can take care of myself."

"I will teach you to summon fire, and then you will have at least one weapon at your disposal."

"Fine," she sighed. "Teach me the spell."

"You need no spell to summon fire," he grinned. "It is always in the air, held at bay by nature."

"By the laws of nature?" Molly echoed, reluctantly intrigued. "I've studied them. That's what science is all about. Are you suggesting I can . . . break those laws?"

"And go unpunished?" he chuckled. "Yes. That is the nature of magic."

"Explain."

"Nature is in delicate balance. You can disturb it, slightly, and the results can be magnificent. First fire, then wind. Then, with practice, you will be able to persuade a vulnerable subject to pursue a desired course."

"By disturbing the balance of nature?"

"Exactly."

Molly smiled. "The historical roots of my science are in magic. Alchemy and astrology . . ." She brushed her hands together. "Okay, let's try. Fire is a combination of oxygen, heat, and combustible matter."

"Oxygen? Do you mean air?" Aaric smiled. "I must remember to teach that word to Maya. Now, look around. Feel what is there. Air, the warmth of the sun . . . As for 'combustible' matter, there are leaves . . ." With a wave of his hand he ignited a nearby bush. "Do you see?"

"Oh, Aaric!" she breathed. "If only Matthew could see this! He'd be so amazed."

Aaric's face hardened. "You have summoned the wrong fire, Princess. You constantly rekindle the fire that burns in your heart for your champion. You will never be able to concentrate unless you forget him, or regain him."

"Are you angry?"

"With you?" He shook his head. "With myself, perhaps. Go and rest. Do not try to summon fire in your world outside the dream until you have had more instruction. A bonfire in your lodge would be distressing."

"True." Rising onto tiptoes, she brushed her lips across his cheek. "Thanks for trying. Goodnight, Moonshaker."

She had overslept, it seemed, but her will to dress and face the world was sorely lacking, and so when she had wiped the sleep from her eyes, she bundled herself in her quilt and sipped tea, wondering what to make of her new "family."

They had the ability to occasionally distract her from thoughts of Matthew, and she was grateful for that, but she wondered at the price she was paying. Could selfish, volatile Maya truly care about her "niece," or was it a form of insurance against being banished from the dream?

The old sorcerer—Maya's own father!—had said Molly had the power to send both Aaric and Maya away forever. Was that the true reason Aaric had kissed her? Was his motive self-preservation rather than affection? Either way, she was coming to recognize that Matthew's instincts had been sound. She was out of her league in her own dream. But Matthew's ultimatum had been unfair, his suspicions had been undeserved and his anger had been unforgivable. And without Matthew, Maya and Aaric were becoming her entire life.

"This is the first skill a witch acquires. Light a spark," Maya demonstrated effortlessly one autumn night, "and then blow it out." A gust of wind served the pleasure of the sorceress's hand. "Kerreya and I would practice for hours as girls, and you dare quit after five attempts?"

"It's no use, Maya. I can't seem to concentrate. I'm not motivated, I guess."

"Motivated?" Maya's frustration flared dangerously. "Aaric, my shoulders ache from trying to teach this stubborn witch."

The warrior's huge hands moved to her shoulders, massaging through the folds of the magnificent blue cape. "Make a spark, Princess," he urged.

"Why? What's the use? Teach me something useful. What else can you do, Maya?"

"I? I am a practiced sorceress, and can perform dozens of marvelous feats, but I started with a spark, as must you, *princess,*" she grimaced, "or not. You must decide what you wish to accomplish. Is it a love spell you crave? I could work one for you, perhaps. Bring Lost Eagle's son here, and I will try."

"Bring him here? Aaric, tell her. Tell her how angry he was." Molly's shoulders slumped. "I don't know how to bring him, anyway. He comes under his own power, or whatever. And he doesn't want to see me—here or in Berkeley or at the mounds."

"He has not returned to the lodge of many weapons?"

"If he's been there, I didn't hear about it. He's probably moved to the mounds permanently by now." Resisting an impulse to complain further, she added, "I'll visit again later. I should go and try to get a little work done on the research project."

"Work? Your work is here! You are woefully lazy, my confused little niece. Aaric, tell her."

" 'Aaric, tell her,' " he mimicked with a yawn. "You two females have been having this discussion for a month of nights, and still nothing is resolved, because the Princess is too accepting of her fate and the sorceress is too *un*accepting of her! You cannot live the Princess's life for her, Maya. And you," he stroked Molly's cheek fondly, "you cannot fight your destiny. Learn to concentrate. Use this time, while you grieve, to educate yourself in our ways. Try them in your world when you awaken."

"Try to make a spark?" Molly sighed. "I'm sorry, Aaric. I just don't see the point. I think I'll wake up and head over to the pool for a swim."

"Swim?" Maya murmured. "Aaric, . . . ?"

"The Princess has no fear of the water," he boasted. "She has played in the sea even as a child."

"Are you insane?" Maya's dark eyes were wide with uncharacteristic fear. "Do you know nothing of your heritage?"

"Aaric told me you believe in some sort of super race who live in the water."

"The water masters," the sorceress confirmed. "Do you scoff at this?"

"Aaric doesn't believe it, either," Molly hedged.

"Because he is fearless. It is one of the reasons I

can never resist him." For a long moment she stroked her lover seductively with her gaze. "Still, you must promise never to swim again. I forbid it." One eyebrow was lifted in cool challenge. "Do you deny my status as matriarch of your family?"

"I appreciate your concern. I'll . . . think about it."

"Think about this: our people were captured and for twenty decades were forced to act as slaves to the water masters. They preferred us, over all the people of the earth, because we are the most balanced and the most agreeable. Do you challenge this truth?"

"I guess not. How did we escape?"

"It is a beautiful tale. Do you remember the pageant, Aaric?" Springing to her feet, the sorceress fluffed her cape and seemed to become transformed by a kind of innocent trance. "There was Kelfire, the water master, and he loved the slave girl, and longed to take her as his bride. And she was neither wise nor strong, but she knew that she must be both if she was to save her people, and so she smiled at Kelfire and warmed his heart and earned his trust and on the day they were to marry she asked for time alone with her people, to say goodbye, and he granted her wish. They had never before been left unguarded, and they escaped through a well that was lined with white clay."

Maya began to sway. "They had not seen the sky in their lifetimes, and the air—the oxygen," her glance toward Molly was sheepish, "burned their chests, and they were in awe of the clouds above and the rocks beneath their feet. When they were only moments into freedom, Kelfire came and would have enslaved them anew, but the slave girl interceded. She offered a lifetime of love to him, in exchange for his abandonment of the pursuit, and Kelfire was consumed with passion, and so he agreed. And our people were free, and Kelfire possessed her body, but it was a cold body and brought him only grief."

"The slave girl killed herself," Aaric translated softly.

"Oh, no!" Molly gasped. "How?"

"Poison." There were tears in Maya's eyes. "She was so brave and selfless! And without magic to aid her!"

"It was before magic came to the land," Aaric supplied. "But it was this very quality—this unselfish bravery—that attracted the twin sorcerers who eventually intermarried with our people and built the mounds."

"It is a special kind of bravery, to act against magic when one has no magic of one's own," Maya announced, adding sharply, "and it is a special kind of foolishness to *have* magic and to fail to employ it."

"Enough!" Aaric thundered. "Princess, make a fire!"

Molly tried to concentrate, failed, and then stomped her foot, more angry with herself than her instructors. "It's Matthew's fault! I can't concentrate."

"Be angry with him," Maya agreed cheerfully. "There is power in anger, so long as you maintain your balance."

"Balance, balance, balance," Molly grumbled.

"Do not underestimate it. Remember, your champion has deserted you because the amulet interferes with *his* balance."

"He didn't desert me. But he did seem . . ." She

turned to the Moonshaker. "Are we sure it's affecting him that way, Aaric?"

"It is obvious. Why else would he turn his back on you?"

"He thinks *I* turned my back on *him,*" Molly reminded him. "In a way, I guess I did."

"You did your best," Maya consoled. "If he loves you, he will come back to you in time." A mischievous smile played across her lips. "If you are impatient, simply take the amulet from him. When does he remove it?"

"Never. It's on his wrist permanently by now. Angela's cousin was going to design some kind of cuff for him."

"Aha!" Maya crowed.

Aaric grinned and encouraged slyly, "What is it, my love? Is that significant?"

"Of course! It is clear now. This Angela is a witch."

"No. It's simpler than that," Molly sighed. "She's just a woman who appreciates him and has never betrayed him."

"Nonsense! Aaric, you see it, do you not?"

"A permanent cuff?" The sorcerer nodded. "I see that now the amulet owns the man, and that is serious enough, witch or no witch."

"And *her* cousin provides it! And her grandmother is like a . . . what did you call it?"

"An encyclopedia?" Molly supplied hesitantly.

"There! I do not even fully comprehend what it is and I know it is dangerous."

The Valmain princess tried to smile, but her concern was growing. Witch or not, Angela *had* thought of the cuff. And hadn't even Lost Eagle eventually needed to get away from the amulet?

Instead, Matthew was chained to it, and living in Angela's home for good measure!

It was time to visit her champion. As a friend. The prospect sent a tremor of excitement through her lonely body.

The cab dropped her at the end of Angela's street and she shuffled through two blocks of leaves, trembling with anticipation. She would see him soon. She would hear his voice. Even if he scowled and complained and ultimately sent her away, it would be worth it. She had missed him so dearly! And if she had missed him with such passion, wasn't it possible that he . . . ?

No! she reminded herself sharply. *You're not here to rekindle romance. You're here to help him, and to guide him, and to be the dream girl who gives him balance, and that's all!*

She hesitated at the screen door of the trim white cottage. What if Angela answered? Was she ready to see just how beautiful an "artist's model" could be? But it was Matthew who appeared out of nowhere and, without hesitation, they were in each other's arms as though both had been starved, almost to death. "I've missed you so," Molly whispered breathlessly.

"You came," he marveled in return. "Finally . . ."

"I was hoping you would come to me," she confessed, dizzy at the feel of him.

Matthew stiffened and pushed her gently away. "In your dreams? Aren't they a little crowded lately?"

"Please, Matthew. I need to talk to you."

"Who is this, Matthew?" a sultry voice inquired

and, to Molly's dismay, a tall, shapely female with perfect cheekbones and an attention-riveting sundress emerged from the house to slide her arm around the Valmain champion.

If Matthew's introduction was awkward, Angela's stare was positively piercing, and Molly found herself retreating down the front steps, instinctively certain that "infliction" was on this woman's list of talents.

"Molly, wait." Matthew grabbed for her arm apologetically.

"It's a little crowded everywhere these days, I guess," she murmured, angry at herself for allowing his blatant infidelity to hurt so much.

"You said you wanted to talk. Where are you staying?"

"I took a cab straight from the bus station. And I guess," she glanced warily toward Angela, "that's where I'm going now."

"Let me drive you. Hold on. We can talk. Angela," he turned and explained hesitantly, "I'm taking Molly to the bus. I'll see you in a while."

"Certainly," Angela muttered. "Take my car. I'll be . . . waiting."

"She didn't look too happy," Molly observed, after the scowling model had disappeared behind the cottage door.

"That's understandable. She knows how serious things were between us. But she trusts me."

How serious things were . . . His use of the past tense silenced her.

"I know this is awkward," he offered lamely, ushering her into a shiny red convertible. Again Molly nodded without responding, and he prodded gently, "You said you wanted to tell me something?"

"Will you listen? With an open mind?"

"If it's about Maya . . ." he warned.

"No! It's about witches."

"Same thing."

"Maybe I should just go home."

"What about witches?" Matthew persisted.

"Well . . ." She had rehearsed this and now considered it her safest approach. "In a way I'm a witch, right?"

"Yeah, if you mean you have powers."

"Right. And it's not an insult. At least, not necessarily. Right? Wouldn't you say it depends upon the particular witch's philosophy?"

"What's going on, Molly?"

Although his cool, direct manner unnerved her, she could imagine his underlying pain and forced herself to continue. "Did you read my letter? About how Lost Eagle decided on his own to get rid of the amulet? Because he felt it affected his judgment?"

Matthew stopped the car and looked at her coldly. "You have this on what authority?" he demanded. "Damn it, Molly! Why are you bringing all of this up now?"

Fighting back the tears his harsh words had elicited, she reached for his wrist, touching the amulet and cuff gingerly. *"This* is why. I'm afraid for you, Matthew. Afraid of the amulet. You have it bound to your wrist. Like a slave."

"More wisdom from my enemies! And what's all this about you being a witch?"

"Not me. Angela. That awful cuff was her idea . . ." The words caught in her throat and she shrank from his enraged scowl—the very scowl that had darkened his face during their dream confrontation. "You scare me when you look at me that way, Matthew," she whispered. "You look like you're going to hurt me."

"Hurt you?" he gasped. "That's great! All I ever wanted to do was *protect* you! You . . . *you* hurt *me!* And I thought you came here to try and make it right, but you're still doing it!"

"You hurt me, too! You left without giving me a chance to explain!"

"I needed a chance to think," he countered sharply. "I couldn't believe you were capable of betraying me *and* Valmain in one insane moment."

"And so you went to Angela?" Molly's voice was raw with pain. "How could you, Matthew?"

"I'm sorry, Valm . . . Molly. I needed someone to talk to. And just for the record," he flushed, "I never slept with her before that night. I never betrayed *you.*"

"You needed someone to talk to? So did I." Molly struggled to regain her dignity. "If all that's in the past for you, okay. This isn't about us. It's about your safety."

"If you're jealous, fine," he countered. "I guess I should be flattered. But I can't let you call Angela a witch. She's like family these days."

"Family? *Her?* Good heavens, Matthew, take a good look at those eyes sometime."

"She's not too crazy about you, either."

Molly studied him warily. "Have you told her I'm a witch?"

"No. All I told them was, you betrayed me." His chuckle was self-mocking. "They think you slept with some other guy. Can you imagine what they'd say if they knew he actually lived in your dreams?"

Her heart ached for him at that moment, but she had to be sure. "Did Angela read my letter?"

"You sent it in care of the motel and instructed me to tear it up as soon as I read it," he reminded her. "Unless that jerk of a motel manager pieced it back together and read it, I'd say your secret's safe."

"Thanks, Matthew. I just don't want Angela and Deborah knowing my business. And," she took a deep breath, "I'm sorry I called her a witch. It does sound a little crazy, I guess."

"Let's just drop it," Matthew agreed. "We're only a couple of minutes from the bus station. Let's try to have a normal conversation?"

"When did we ever have a normal conversation?"

They both forced a smile, but the strain was still between them. His eyes narrowed. "You look good, Molly. 'Prettier every time I see you.' Remember? Are you dating anyone? I mean, besides Aaric?"

That was more than she could bear, and she jerked on the door handle. "I'll just get out here. I'm sorry I bothered you. Sorry I came. There's a lot I could tell you, but I shouldn't have to listen to this!" Tears welled in her blazing eyes. "I'm sorry. I'm not really crying. I'm just so damned mad." Angrily rebuffing his attempt to comfort her, she growled, "Just do me a favor! Take off that damned amulet every once in a while. Just to touch base with the old Matthew. And tell him I said hello. And that I love him." Slamming the car door, she sprinted the last two blocks to the bus without a backward glance.

Matthew drove back to Angela's house in angry silence. Molly's skewed allegiances had changed her so completely, it was as though the calm, balanced, pure-hearted dream girl no longer existed! Her loyalties were dangerously corrupted—or had they ever been sound? Hadn't she resisted her destiny every step of the way?

"What did that bitch want?" Angela demanded when he stormed back into the cottage.

"Don't you start with me, too, Angela!" he warned. "This whole damned thing is getting out of hand. I'm beginning to wonder if maybe I *am* losing my judgment!"

"What do you mean?" she frowned.

"Molly's worried that the amulet affects my judgment." He remembered the genuine concern in the dream girl's eyes and ventured carefully, "What would you think if . . . what if we had your cousin cut off this band, and just put it on a regular chain or something?"

"She suggested that?" Angela's eyes narrowed. "Why would she wish to disarm you? Are you certain she knows nothing of channels and witchcraft?"

Matthew winced. "She's just having trouble with the break-up, I guess. Never mind."

"She knows the story," Angela fumed. "She knows how Lost Eagle was murdered, and yet she suggests you leave yourself defenseless? It's malicious and hateful of her."

"I guess you're right. I mean, that I should keep the cuff. But Molly isn't malicious." He was pacing, suddenly certain that Maya and Aaric were manipulating the dream girl, trying to regain the amulet through her.

"You must be cautious," Angela insisted. "You loved her once, but don't let that cloud your wisdom." Slipping her arms around his waist, she cooed, "You're the wisest man I've ever known. Don't let her fool you. She betrayed you once. Don't let her do it again."

"I won't," he agreed. "It's just that seeing her

again made me think. For one thing, there's the book I've been neglecting."

"We've been working on it!"

"No, I mean the dream legend book. It's more than half written. I should finish it."

"Fine. I will help." She kissed him seductively. "Later."

Matthew grinned weakly. "Yeah, later." His fingers moved to unlace the bodice of her black sundress. "And actually, this is the perfect time for us to travel. Maybe we could start in Egypt."

"Travel? Why?" Angela wrinkled her nose. "I don't like to travel. I'm afraid of planes and ships."

"You'll feel safe with me, I promise. And you'll love it. There's a big world out there, Angela. Let me show it to you."

"What about our world, here, at the mounds? Would you turn your back on this?" She kissed him again and stared searchingly into his eyes as her hand moved to stroke the amulet. "Listen to me, Matthew Redtree. Lost Eagle is buried here. Can you really leave?"

"No. You're right. I'd miss this place too much."

"You can write here. Grandmother can give you a dozen books' worth of legends."

"You're right. You're always right, Angela."

"I love you, Matthew Redtree. More than she ever did . . . better than she ever could . . . more completely." Her hands caressed his shoulders. "You feel more powerful than ever! More than you ever could have with her. More powerful than any man has ever felt. Make love to me now. I'm begging you! Swear to me that you're mine!"

He pulled her down onto the floor, his body aching with desire. "I swear it! We'll stay here forever. Together." Moving his wrist between her thighs, he allowed the amulet and cuff to become drenched, grateful as always that Angela's lust had the power to wash all traces of Molly Sheridan's betrayal from his confused mind.

allowed the gentle and sad imperious discover-
...on... always that vivacin's lust had the spirit
...with all mood of Molly. Sherman's too was too
...be seemed must.

Chapter Twenty-Two

Molly had turned to August Redtree once, almost two months earlier, and had found him to be
a compassionate ally. Now, as she sat on the porch
of his ranch house and told her story, she wondered
if she could expect—if she had any *right* to expect—
compassion. The setting sun was causing the distant
mountains to glow an angry yellow-red, and she
remembered another anger—Matthew's anger . . .

"And so, August," she finished sadly, "that's
what I chose. To reunite Maya and Aaric. Do you
hate me? Maybe I shouldn't have come here, but I
couldn't bear to go back to Berkeley without . . .
without hope."

Matthew's uncle sighed. "You were foolish," he
announced finally. "To bring back Maya! It will
take a long while for Matthew to forgive you."

"Maybe forever. He has a new girlfriend named
Angela. And," she moistened her lips nervously,
"Maya and Aaric think she's a witch."

"Ah. And why does the witch Maya think that
this Angela is also a witch?"

"Angela and her cousin convinced Matthew to
bind the amulet permanently to his wrist."

August frowned. "I don't like the sound of that.

The amulet is a weapon to be controlled by the man, not to control him. What was he thinking?"

"I guess he thought it might be stolen from him like it was from Lost Eagle. But he doesn't tell me things anymore. When was the last time you spoke to him?"

"Not since you and he came here last. No one in the family has seen him. Rita and her boys miss him."

"He hasn't even called?"

"We assumed he was busy with you. Young love. But now his silence concerns me. Has he continued his training?"

"I guess so. No matter where we traveled, even in the midst of all the trouble in Ireland, he still worked out and did his running every day. Of course, now I don't know. To tell you the truth, I have a hard time picturing what it is he does all day, way out there. Maya says . . ." She hesitated, blushing.

The old man nodded. "Maya says he spends all day in bed with the witch? If this Angela *is* a witch, Maya may be right. I have heard stories of their talents in such matters." August noticed Molly's discomfort and smiled gently. "Never mind. I will send for him. He would never refuse me."

"Tell him to come alone."

"No! If this one is a witch, then I want to see her with my own eyes. I can help him. And if she is not," the old man's eyes grew sad, "then she is as welcome in my house as you were." He touched Molly's quivering chin. "Don't cry, dream girl. It has not been so long. Give him time. Destiny is on your side, and it is a powerful ally."

"Destiny and I have never been allies," she lamented, accepting his arm as they walked toward her rented convertible. "Just talk to him. He needs someone he can trust. I think he's in danger."

"And with Maya and Aaric in your dream, you are also in danger."

"They can't hurt me without hurting themselves. Don't worry about me. Just take care of Matthew, and give my love to Rita and the boys. Especially AJ." She reached into the back seat and pulled out the piece of obsidian she had obtained from the weapons dealer. "Give this to AJ. Let him try to shape it into a dagger, like Lost Eagle did. But this stuff is as sharp as glass, so tell him to be careful. And," she thrust the hilt of her own dagger into the old man's hand, "tell him to use this as a guide. And then, give it back to Matthew for me, okay?"

"Matthew wanted you to have this."

"Under the circumstances, I just can't bear to keep it." She choked back a fresh sob, kissed August's cheek, and departed.

"You are fortunate Matthew answered the witch's door!" Maya was outraged at Molly's attempt to reason with Matthew. "This Angela might have killed you had she had you alone!"

"That's a slight exaggeration, don't you think?" Molly sighed, weary from her traveling and distressed over the message that had awaited her on the answering machine upon her return from Los Angeles. Rita had secured Angela's phone number from directory assistance and had contacted her brother, urging him to pay their uncle a visit, but had been politely informed that unless it was an emergency, Matthew was "knee-deep in research" and wouldn't be able to get away for a month, at least. There would be no visit, and Molly found herself again seeking counsel from her dream mentors.

"You are a babe!" Maya wailed. "Ignorant! You have power, but it is useless to you! And you seek help from an old man—a stranger!—instead of your own aunt!"

"But we have learned something vital," Aaric insisted. "Matthew has not only resisted our Princess, but he has since refused to answer the summons of the head of his family. You were right, as always, my love."

"Yes." Maya nodded. "Yes, Angela is not letting him travel from the mounds, because the amulet would lose its power and he would regain his passion for our pretty Molly, and maybe his sense, if he ever had any." Her eyes sparkled. "Now, little niece, you must agree that it is up to us!"

"Yes," she admitted. "When I heard Matthew had refused to come to see August . . ." She straightened proudly. "It's up to us. What can we do?"

"You will summon Angela here. I cannot use my power outside this dream. But once you bring her here, I will attend to her."

"How do I summon her?"

"Concentrate!"

"I don't understand how it's done."

"You claim to love him. Do you?"

"Yes, okay." She closed her eyes tightly. "I'll try my best. What will you do to her?"

"I will kill her, of course. What did you think? Scold her?" Maya mocked. "She *must* die. We know now that she is trying to draw power from the amulet. Combining with Matthew's power, as I did with Aaric's, so long ago."

"But that destroyed you!"

"That was different," Aaric explained. "Angela is

undoubtedly drawing very small amounts. So small
that Matthew is not aware. Her purpose is not the
power that she takes. Her purpose is to learn the
amulet's secrets, so that she can control Matthew."

"The amulet is very powerful," Maya interrupted. "Angela has found a way to tap into that.
Soon she will learn to fully use it and then she will
have no use for Matthew. In the meantime, it gives
her the power to control him. His desires. His pleasure. His every need."

Molly glared. "I get the point. She's great in bed,
right? That's not exactly a reason to kill her, is it?"

"Maya is right, Princess. The witch must be killed
before she kills your Matthew. I have no great love
for him, but I do not want you hurt. So choose
between him and her. Summon her here and let
Maya do the rest."

"What if we're wrong?" Molly sulked. "What if
she's just a harmless bitch? And even if she is a
witch, Matthew likes her. If he ever found out I
killed her . . ."

Aaric shrugged. "He will never find out."

"Aaric! Be quiet!" Maya scowled.

Molly's eyes narrowed. "What? Aaric, what? Tell
me."

Aaric turned to Maya and insisted, in a firm but
gentle tone, "I have told you I do not wish to keep
secrets from the Princess. And she will know soon
enough." Taking Molly's hand, he explained, "Listen to me, Princess. Maya intends to take Angela's
body, after she kills her. It is a perfect plan. Matthew will never even know Angela has gone! And
then you can tell him you have followed his wishes
and have sent Maya away!"

Molly stared at Maya. "You can do that? Take
Angela's place?"

"Yes."

"But what about Aaric? I brought you here so that you could be together . . . Wait! Oh, no. Is that it?" She was almost sick as their plan became clear. "You intend to try to take Matthew's body again?"

"No!" Maya scolded. "Do not be silly. We cannot touch Matthew. Father has seen to that!" Her eyes grew cold. "Once I have left the dream, I will find a suitable body for Aaric in your world, and you will summon him here."

"Summon an innocent man? To be killed? Are you . . . Am *I* going crazy? Can't you see that that's wrong? I can't believe it! And I almost helped you!"

"You have a lot to consider, little niece," Maya glared. "And very little time. Angela grows more powerful by the day. You are waking up now. We will talk later."

Molly struggled from her bed, pulled herself to her bathroom vanity and stared into the mirror. Her head throbbed with indecision. She didn't dare go to Matthew now. Not yet, at least. Maybe Aaric and Maya *were* using her to get to him! Or to Angela—who probably wasn't even a witch!

And even assuming Angela was a witch, if *she* could draw power from the amulet, maybe *Maya* could! Maybe Molly could! If only she could make sense of it all . . .

Matthew had been right all along. There was only one hope. She would call him and agree that if he would leave Angela and come to Berkeley, for just a little while, Molly would banish Maya and Aaric. She would admit she had created an impossible situation and would beg his forgiveness.

Hopefully, the reverence he had carried for so many years would outweigh the lust he undoubtedly felt for Angela—which, in Molly's fevered imagination, was now equated with the burst of hedonistic pleasure that she had experienced during Aaric's impersonation of Matthew months earlier. Her confidence thus subverted, she hurried to the telephone, her fingers trembling as she dialed the number for Angela Clay's residence in Colhaven.

It was Angela who answered, but Molly persevered in as humble a tone as she could manage. "I need to speak with Matthew, Angela. I wouldn't bother him if it weren't urgent."

"He's not here!" Angela snapped. "And don't bother calling back. Ever."

"Wait, Angela," she pleaded. "Don't do this. I don't want to fight with you, I just need to talk to Matthew for one minute."

"He doesn't even remember you exist," Angela assured her. "He's so hot for me it's almost pitiful. You're out of your league, bitch, so just stay away."

"You're a witch!" Molly retorted. "Leave Matthew alone! I'm warning you!"

"You? Warn me?" Angela chuckled malevolently. "I'll tell you a secret, bitch. I *am* a witch, and if you don't get the hell off this line and stay away, I'm going to turn you into the doormat you were born to be." In the face of Molly's silence, she added sharply, "I don't know who you cheated on Matthew with, but when you did that, you lost him. Now he's mine."

"You admit you're a witch?" Molly murmured. "Is your grandmother a witch, too?"

"Her? She wishes," Angela laughed. "How did you come to suspect me, anyway? Did that fool over at the motel open his mouth?"

"No." Molly steadied her voice and insisted, "My aunt is a witch, too. She's the one who gave me the amulet. And if you don't leave Matthew alone, she's going to pay you a little visit."

"Nice try, but you're pathetic. And if you're thinking about coming here in person, think again. If you come within fifty miles of this place, I'll kill you with my bare hands, and I won't need my witchcraft to do it. Now *get lost!*"

Molly's hands were trembling as she hung up the phone. Angela was right, she *was* out of her league. She needed her champion, frustrations and fanaticism notwithstanding. Somehow, he would know what to do. If only she had listened to him before bringing back Maya!

Okay, Matthew Redtree, she accused silently. *You got me into this, when you called me into your office and made me start dreaming again. If you're really my champion, now's the time to prove it. Come back to me . . . before it's too late.*

When Molly pulled her rented Mustang off of the main road and onto the trail that led to August's ranch, a sight far in the distance made her heart ache with memories of her champion. AJ Camacho—ten years of age, exactly the age Lost Eagle had been when he'd chipped a length of obsidian into a dagger for the protection of his descendants—was standing in the hot sun practicing his moves—undoubtedly in anticipation of his next match with his favorite uncle.

"Aunt Molly!" the boy shouted. "Uncle August! Aunt Molly's here!" He raced to the car and demanded, "Where's Uncle Matt? I thought for sure—"

"Hi, AJ," she smiled, trying not to stare into the

gold-dusted eyes that were so reminiscent of Matthew's. "It's just me this time. Sorry."

The boy's deeply tanned face flushed with shame. "I didn't mean I wasn't glad to see you," he insisted. "We just haven't heard from Uncle Matt, and . . ." He waved one hand apologetically. "Sorry."

"I miss him too, AJ. Don't apologize. Hop in and I'll drive you up to the house."

"Okay." He settled into the passenger seat. "Mom'll be sorry she missed you, Aunt Molly."

"She isn't here?"

"She and Robert are home. I'm here because Uncle August isn't feeling so hot. I do the chores and stuff."

"Oh?" She pulled up close to the ranch house and fidgeted with her keys. "Maybe I shouldn't have come."

As if in answer, August shuffled to the doorway and gestured for them to join him. Molly and AJ hurried to his side and helped him back to the sofa. "AJ tells me you're not feeling well, August," Molly murmured. "Can I do anything?"

"You can share news of my nephew with me," August pleaded. "I am heartsick at his refusal to visit."

Molly glanced toward AJ. "Maybe you should go finish your practicing? I need to talk to your uncle alone."

"About Uncle Matt's new girlfriend?" AJ nodded. "I heard all about her from Mom. I don't like her."

"That's enough," August assured him. "Do as your aunt has requested. When she and I have finished our talk, we will all have a meal and visit. Is that acceptable?"

"Yes, Uncle." AJ squared his small shoulders and strode from the house.

"He reminds me so much of Matthew," Molly groaned. "I'm so worried, August."

"AJ is very much like his uncle," August agreed. "Both do what they think is right, and both value family and heritage above themselves. What is the news, dream girl? Have you seen him again?"

"No. I tried to call him, but Angela interfered. She admitted she's a witch, August. I know you want to stay neutral, but I'm terrified. Maya says Angela is trying to take control of the amulet and, once she's succeeded, she'll kill Matthew. I know it's all my fault, but—"

"Your fault?" August mused. "Did you not tell me Matthew met this Angela at the mounds? Am I not the one who sent him there? If I had accompanied him, this would never have occurred. Am I to blame?"

"Of course not. But I brought Maya back."

"And Matthew was angry. His failure to control that anger was his fault, not yours and not mine. Perhaps the witch Angela had already begun to influence him, or perhaps, as you said, the amulet disturbed his judgment. Does it matter where we place the blame?"

"No. We just have to get him away from her. I was hoping you could help, but you're sick."

"Heartsick," he reminded her quietly, "because my Matthew was lost to me. I felt it in my bones. Now suddenly, I see a ray of hope."

"More than a ray," Molly promised. "Matthew wants me to send Aaric and Maya out of my dream, right? Well, if he'll leave Angela, just for one day, I'll do it."

"You will permit me to bring him that message?"

August demanded, his eyes sparkling with renewed vigor. "You agree this is the only way?"

"Absolutely. But maybe we should send someone else . . ."

"There is no one else. Matthew trusts me, and the witch will see no threat in the visit of an aging, powerless uncle. I know how to flatter these witches."

"She's pretty suspicious."

"Don't worry about me. Worry about yourself. Stay away from Maya and Aaric. They will try to draw you into conversation. Be strong."

"But Maya can teach me how to deal with Angela."

"Maya has no love for Matthew," August interrupted firmly. "Our only hope is to reunite you with your champion. You will drive me to the airport and then return here to wait. With AJ."

"With AJ?" Molly shook her head. "What's the point? I'll take him back to Rita's and then fly with you to the mounds."

"I don't want you there. The witch might sense your arrival, and it would endanger our plan, and Matthew's very life. Do you see?"

"I guess so. But AJ—"

"He is a warrior. A descendant of Lost Eagle. It falls to him to protect you."

"August!" Molly's eyes widened in amazement. "He's a little boy."

"AJ's boyhood is a luxury, as was Matthew's. They train for a purpose, not for amusement. If I fail, and Angela gains control of the amulet and kills my Matthew—"

Molly blanched. "Please! I can't bear to think about it."

"If that should happen," he insisted, "you will

turn to AJ. You will tell him everything, and then you will take him to your dream." With a weary smile, he added, "Would you like to see what AJ has been doing these last few days?"

Molly followed him onto the porch and, when he gestured toward a cardboard box filled with sharp black glass shavings, she fell to her knees, examining the half-finished dagger incredulously. "Oh, August . . . AJ did this? It's amazing."

"You have touched his life and given him purpose. And by allowing me to take your message to Matthew, you have done the same for me."

It seemed to Molly that AJ Camacho was much too aware of his "purpose" for his own good, and while she had tried to draw him into light conversation during the silent meal and the long ride to and from the airport, she had been completely unsuccessful. Now, as she sat on the porch to August's ranch house and watched the ten-year-old pace the dusty yard in an endless, flawless imitation of his uncle, she knew August's parting instructions were echoing in the boy's ears. *Take care of your aunt,* the old uncle had said. *She is your responsibility until Matthew and I return.*

"AJ?"

He immediately joined her. "Is everything okay, Aunt Molly?"

She smiled and pushed a dark lock of hair back from his forehead. "I can't stand to watch you worrying like this. Uncle August shouldn't have told you to take care of me. I'm not in any danger."

"He wouldn't have said it if it wasn't true," AJ corrected. "Don't worry, Aunt Molly. I can handle it." Under his breath, he added, "Whatever it is."

"Do you want something to eat?"

"No. Thanks."

"We could watch TV."

"Uncle August doesn't have a TV," the boy reminded her. "Anyway, I'm not in the mood."

"Do you want to throw me?" she suggested, half-teasing.

"No!" He blanched at the thought. "I'm not allowed to throw girls, Aunt Molly." An even more horrifying thought seemed to occur to him. "Did Uncle Matt ever throw you?"

"No," Molly giggled, "and I almost wish he had. Maybe I would have learned a thing or two."

AJ nodded. "Girls can do judo, too, Aunt Molly. I could teach you, if you want."

She smiled at Lost Eagle's worthy descendant and nodded. "Matthew told me judo is all about balance, and using your enemy's momentum against him. Right?"

AJ smiled patiently. "We'll get to all that. First," he took her by the hand and led her into the yard, "you've got to learn how to fall."

Chapter Twenty-Three

She had ached with concern and throbbed with uncertainty for so many nights that it was somehow paradoxically refreshing to be aching and throbbing with good old-fashioned pain that night, courtesy of AJ's lesson. Sleep came easily and soon she was embroiled in a futile attempt to refuse Maya's assistance.

"So you think you and the old uncle and that amulet-drunk Matthew can stop a practiced witch?" the wild-eyed sorceress was jeering. "You are a fool, little niece."

"Stop, Maya," Aaric insisted. "The Princess is trying to do what she thinks is right. As she did when she brought you here to me. I will never forget that!" His tone softened. "Truly, Princess, you touched my heart that day. And I swore to myself that one day I would repay you. Perhaps that day is at hand."

"Leave me alone, Aaric," Molly groaned. "I know you mean well, but I just want to rest. August said he can convince Matthew, and I have to believe him. Please?"

"The old uncle cannot defeat a witch. Let us help you, Princess." His tone grew urgent. "Until we learn the source of Angela's witchhood, we must not underestimate her."

"The source? You mean, like the mounds? Or," Molly's eyes widened, "the lakes? Is that what you're thinking?"

"Any witch, even *with* the amulet, is no match for the three of us," Aaric reassured her. "But we must act quickly."

"Yes, pretty niece." Maya attempted a patient tone. "Bring her here before she kills the old uncle. Concentrate. You can do it."

Molly nodded grimly and tried to imagine Angela's hated face. She could almost see it, and yet, she could not. "It's no use!" she wailed finally. "I can't! I don't know how!"

Maya laughed. "You must keep trying. Catch her while she dozes. Or better yet, *make* her doze off. Do you see her? In the eye of your mind?"

"Yes."

"Good! Keep the image. We are not like Aaric. We cannot snap our fingers and make an illusion. Our power requires hard work. Concentrate."

"It's no use. I'm just no good at it. Tell me how to use the amulet instead."

"What?" Maya shrugged. "I thought you knew. He must wear it tied to his right wrist."

"No! I want to use it like Angela does," Molly insisted. "While it's still *on* Matthew. To make him trust me if I go back there to talk to him again."

Maya and Aaric exchanged amused glances. "So, you have decided to play Angela's game? That is good."

"No. I just want one minute without her interference." Molly shook her head. "I guess you're right. It would be a betrayal of his trust, wouldn't it?"

"You can make it up to him for the rest of his

life," Maya assured her playfully. "For now, listen. Angela must be touching the amulet, and looking into his eyes, and repeating his name. If *you* do that, you can draw a small amount of power, and his trust will be manipulated."

"What are you saying, Maya?" Aaric seemed stunned. *"You* know how to draw from the amulet? How did you learn the method? Why did you never tell me? Or use it yourself?"

Maya was impatient. "Because Lost Eagle knew also. He was wiser about such things than this Matthew! I could never take advantage of it. And when I finally had the amulet myself, I gave it to you out of foolish love." She turned back to Molly. "Remember, Angela uses this power to control Matthew, but that is not her main purpose. Each time she draws from the amulet, it becomes more adjusted to her. Little by little, it becomes channeled to her. Soon she has made a path through which to draw power, even without Matthew's help. It is the nature of this type of charm. Do you understand?"

"I think so. It's already aligned with Lost Eagle's family. She's aligning it to herself?"

Aaric interrupted again. "And when Kerreya had it, for all of those years . . . ?"

"You were a fool to give it to her," Maya glared.

"But do you suppose . . . ?"

"Quiet, Aaric!" the sorceress snapped.

Molly eyed the sorcerer grimly. "More secrets?"

"No!" protested Aaric. "I want to help."

"I can't trust either of you!" Molly accused. "I'm so tired of this."

He grabbed her hand contritely. "Please, Princess. We love you. We will not endanger you or your champion. Trust me."

"Forget her!" Maya commanded. "She is a fool.

Leave her to her conscience. She will realize too late and will come to us on her knees. Come now and make love to me, Moonshaker." The beautiful sorceress strode away proudly.

"Listen, quickly!" Aaric whispered into Molly's ear. "Do you see? I only now learned. *You* can use the amulet! Because Kerreya, for all of those years, *must* have played with it, 'aligned' it, as you call it. Your grandfather must have taught his daughters the secrets of the amulet, and now Maya wants it because she *knows* it has been prepared for Kerreya's kin!"

"It's aligned to me already?" Molly whispered. "Oh, Aaric . . ."

"This explains so much," he nodded. "Now *use* it! I have tried to be worthy of your friendship, Princess. Now I must go to Maya."

He was gone before she could thank him, and as she spread her cape across the grass and prepared to rest, she marveled at the loyalty he had shown her. It seemed he did love her, in his own way, after all, and it was doubly flattering given his lifelong love affair with Maya!

And even Maya, in her very convoluted way, seemed genuinely concerned for Matthew's fate. "Here you go again," Molly chastised herself as she drifted into a much-needed dream nap. "Forget about Maya and Aaric. The only person you can truly trust is your champion, and with any luck, he and August will be here before you wake up. If not, you'll just march right up to Angela's house and . . ." *And hope for a miracle.*

When an unexpected knock sounded on the door to Angela's cottage, Matthew remembered Molly's visit and sighed. What use was there in hoping to see her again? It would just hurt them both, and Angela would have another jealous fit, and Maya and Aaric would probably have a giant laugh at their expense, and so it was best if this was a salesman or delivery boy. When he pulled open the door and saw the frail, ashen-faced figure of his beloved uncle, he stared in disbelief for a long moment before pulling the old man into his arms. "Uncle! I can't believe this! You're here! You're . . ." He pushed him to arms' length and whispered, "You're trembling. And your color . . . Are you ill?"

"I am ill," August acknowledged. "I am old, and sick—dying, perhaps—and yet this is the happiest moment of my life. I thought you were lost to me . . ."

"Lost to you?" Matthew's gasped. "Forgive me, Uncle. Come in. Sit down." His voice was choked with shame. "Let me take care of you."

"Take me home," August countered. "Will you do that for me?"

"Of course I'd do anything for you. I didn't know . . ." Again, his voice almost broke. "I didn't realize you needed me. I've been busy. With the amulet." He drew the old man into the living room and embraced him again. "When you see the mounds, you'll understand. You say you want to go home." His eyes blazed with pseudo-religious fervor. "You *are* home."

"My home is in Los Angeles. Your home is with me. Or in Berkeley, with the dream girl. You must leave this place with me."

"But Uncle, I belong here! Let me show you some of the powers of the amulet. And wait until you meet Angela and Deborah."

"Are they here?"

"No." He eased the old man into a chair. "Angela's on an errand, and Deborah lives off in the boonies. But you'll meet them both tonight and you'll think they're great."

"And what of Molly? The curly-haired dream girl?"

"I loved her. Sometimes I think I still do." He cast a furtive glance, wary of Angela's jealousy even in her absence, and then continued. "What I have with Angela is better than love. I can't explain it, but she makes me happy. She lives where I want to live. She doesn't need anything else. And she'd never betray me the way Molly did."

"I know what the dream girl did. And I know that she loves you. She is worried . . ."

"That Angela is a witch?" He suddenly understood the old man's anguish. "It's not true, Uncle, believe me," he assured him firmly. "I've studied witches and magic all my life. Angela and Molly hate each other and that's my fault, but Molly's going to have to let go! I have, and it hasn't been easy, knowing she's in Maya's clutches. But I can't look at her without seeing our enemies."

"That's why I'm here. She agrees with you now. She wants your help to rid herself of them. She needs you. Her champion."

Matthew's chest tightened with amazement. "Are you sure? It's not just a trick? They might be using her."

"I am sure. At this very moment, she is waiting for you at my ranch. With AJ."

"With AJ?" Matthew caught the twinkle in his uncle's eye and guessed, "For protection?"

"Of course."

"Lucky kid."

"Will you come with me?"

"Yeah," Matthew grinned. "If you're sure Molly's ready, then I want to help her. We can leave as soon as Angela gets back."

"*She* cannot come."

"Actually, she probably won't want to come," Matthew countered. "She hates to travel. But I owe it to her to tell her what's happening. Where I'm going."

"You owe her nothing," August protested. "If we wait for her, she may prevent us from leaving."

"So, Molly has you convinced? Because of the cuff?" He smiled as his confidence rushed back into place. "Listen to this, Uncle. Angela now agrees that it should be removed! We planned on going to her cousin tomorrow. She's there now, arranging it. That's why she's out so late. So you see?" He smiled triumphantly. "There's no danger."

"I see that she is ready to *take* it from you! Are you blind? It's gone farther than we'd guessed."

"What?" Matthew moistened his lips nervously. It didn't make any sense, and yet . . .

August spoke with renewed urgency. "Matthew, I have been a good uncle to you. Almost a father. Now I'm asking you, do this for me. Now! No questions. Leave with me this minute."

"All right, Uncle, I'll do what you ask," Matthew agreed quickly. "We'll leave now. I'll call Angela later. But you're wrong about all of this. I swear it."

"Wrong about what?" Angela's voice from the doorway was sweeter than ever. "Who is our company, Matthew?"

August bowed graciously. "I am August Redtree. Matthew's uncle. I have missed him these many weeks. I hope you do not mind my impulsive visit to your lovely home?"

"Not at all," she beamed. "I'm Angela. Matthew

speaks of you often. Matthew," she slipped her arms around her lover's waist and brushed her lips across his, "where are your manners? Go and get our guest some tea. I'll keep him entertained."

"Uncle?" Matthew eyed August sternly. "Will you be okay?"

"Of course. I will enjoy the chance to talk with this enchantress."

Matthew grinned, relieved to see that August intended to behave. Still, it wasn't wise to leave them alone together for too long and so he hurried to the kitchen, hoping Angela would indeed be "enchanting" and August would realize that Molly's fears were the product of jealousy.

His pulse quickened as he recalled August's news. Had Molly finally come to her senses? If she actually wanted to rid herself of Maya and Aaric . . . If she was willing to allow him to be her champion again . . . In spite of the majesty of the mounds and the outlandish success of his sexual relationship with Angela, he had felt a loss, so deep it sometimes frightened him, at being estranged from the dream girl and her quiet strength.

With a fresh tray of tea and cake, he hurried back to the living room only to see a not-so-enchanting Angela holding a knife to the throat of the man who had indeed been almost father to him. In that instant he was transformed by a heady rush of amulet and adrenaline so strong it seemed to propel him into a murderous rage. "So it's all true!" he roared. *"Let him go* or I'll kill you, Angela."

"But I can kill *him* also! Notice the knife and relax, my love. We will wait for my cousin, whom I have just finished calling." She batted her long, dark eyelashes flirtatiously. "As soon as he gets here, you can both be on your way to your precious Molly."

"She will never let us go!" August interrupted. "Destroy her! Use the power of the amulet! I am dead either way."

Angela's playful mood vanished. "Shut up, fool. Matthew, tell this old fool to shut up!"

"Uncle, please. Let me do the talking." He forced himself to assume a reasonable tone. "Angela, you can't hope to get away with this."

"Who's going to stop me? Once I have the amulet, I'll be able to kill you both with my bare hands if I wish. But of course I wouldn't. Not after all we've been to each other." She was cooing again. "Dear Matthew. So in love with me."

"I was never in love with you!"

"Oh?" Angela's smile was icy. "I suppose it's still the little Molly bitch? She's a joke. Be glad you had a chance to know a real woman." She glanced impatiently through the window. "Where is my cousin? I have *never* gone so long without sleep. I feel so drowsy! I won't be able to enjoy my new toy if I don't sleep soon."

August's head snapped up. "You should sleep, too, Matthew. If this witch is to let us go, we will have a long journey tonight. You will need your strength."

Matthew nodded slowly. August was telling him to sleep. To get to Molly that way? Could she really help? Was she even dreaming? With the amulet, he could do almost anything, but he had to make the right choice. The sight of that knife at August's throat . . .

Even during the worst of it with Aaric, he had never felt more intimidated or vulnerable. He would try to get to the dream. The dream girl. The only true source of strength in this world gone mad.

"Give me your word, Angela," he suggested quietly. "If we don't resist—if we cooperate fully—will you let my uncle leave unharmed?"

"Of course, my love," she smiled. "I am hardly a murderess."

"Then we'll wait quietly for your cousin. It's a fair trade. The amulet for my uncle's life." He sank onto the sofa and pretended to stare through the window, willing himself into a wary sleep.

The first thing he noticed was the color—the most vibrant green in the world. More beautiful than at the mounds themselves. And the Valmain Princess was sleeping peacefully on her cape. Looking prettier than ever, he noted ruefully as he knelt beside her and took her into his arms.

Chapter Twenty-Four

"Matthew! Oh, Matthew . . ." Molly melted, savoring the feel and smell of her champion. "I've missed you so." Only with the greatest effort could she add, "You have to go away. Please? You feel so good, but we have to meet *outside* the dream. Maya's scheming!" Clinging to him, she admitted, "You were right. I can't control her! I love her, but she's so powerful . . . You have to meet me at August's ranch. That's where I am right now."

"Forget about Maya," Matthew murmured, burying his face in her soft, sun-streaked curls. *"Angela* is the threat right now. She has my uncle. She has a knife." He pushed her away reluctantly and stared into her eyes.

"Oh, Matthew, it's my fault. I sent him!"

"It's no one's fault. And you tried to warn me about her. She wants to cut the amulet from my wrist tonight, and," he smiled grimly, "I doubt she intends to be very careful how she accomplishes it."

"Oh no! That means she can fully control it! We can't let her get her hands on it, even now while you sleep. I'll have to bring her here!"

"Bring her?"

"If she sleeps, I can do it," she insisted with weak

confidence. "Maya taught me. I've been trying off and on all evening."

"Maybe it's working," Matthew nodded. "She says she's drowsy. Maybe now that she thinks I'm cooperating she'll let down her guard."

"Shh . . . let me concentrate."

"But what should we do when she gets here?" Matthew worried. "I've never had to fight a woman."

"Give me the amulet now," Molly instructed briskly. "I'll fight Angela myself. And you get back there before she tries to take it from your wrist while you sleep. And you should get back before Maya comes around anyway."

"How can I give you the amulet . . . ? Oh! I forgot. Here it's just tied with thread." He loosened the silver knot carefully. "I guess it makes sense for you to hold it, but how can you use it? You're not descended from Lost Eagle."

"Aaric thinks I can use it. He's on our side, for now." Tying the amulet securely to her wrist she blushed, "Don't look at me like that. I think we can trust him. But Maya . . ."

" 'But Maya' what?" The sorceress's voice was cold.

Molly took a deep breath. "Maya! You're back!"

"So, this is Matthew Redtree. We meet at last." Her dark eyes surveyed him methodically, taking in the bronzed limbs, simple tunic, and ornate headband with a knowing gleam. "You resemble Lost Eagle, I see. Where is your amulet? Do not tell me that Angela . . . oh, I see! Molly!" Her pride in her niece overcame her annoyance. "You surprise me! You intend to use the amulet to fight the witch?"

"I'm going to bring her here and stop her."

"You cannot mean *kill* her? A sweet princess like you?"

"Okay, Maya," Molly groaned, "I admit you were right about some things. But Matthew's going back to kill Angela's body, just in case you have any ideas about taking it over."

"You do not even know what you are talking about!" Maya glared. "How can you stop something you do not understand?"

"I know enough. You can't hurt me. Somehow your father saw to that. And he made sure you couldn't control me, didn't he?"

"Go on."

"Once Angela is dead, I'm going to banish you. Forever. Back to wherever you came from. I can do *that,* too. Especially with the amulet."

"You can, but you will not. You need me to train you. And what of the Moonshaker? Will you send him away?"

"Aaric can stay, or go, as he wishes."

"No!" Matthew interrupted. "Send them both. Now!"

"Matthew, please."

"He helped you once, Molly. Okay. Be grateful to the guy. But can't you see their kind never changes for long? He'll get bored. Ambitious. He'll think he's entitled! *I'll* kill him before I go back."

Maya laughed. "Without the amulet?" Once again her gaze traveled over Matthew's lean, bronzed body. "Now you *definitely* remind me of my old lover Lost Eagle!"

Throughout the discussion, Molly had continued her efforts to summon Angela. The sudden appearance of that witch, dressed in a dull gray cape, startled even Maya, who watched with some amusement as the foe's eyes widened in recognition of her plight.

"Welcome, Angela!" Maya grinned. "My little Molly has been waiting for you. And so have I."

"Stay out of this, ancient one!" Angela struggled to maintain her bravado in the face of Maya, magnificent in her flowing blue and gold cape, and Molly, humble yet stunning in silver and white. "This is between your pitiful offspring and myself."

"Not so pitiful. She brought you here, did she not? And she has the amulet."

Angela shrugged. "She can't use it. I'll take it from her!"

"She *can* use it, and with it her power is far stronger than yours."

"But not stronger than ours together, ancient one," Angela cajoled. "Let us overpower her! I will give you the amulet if you help me!"

Maya laughed again. "Amazing. Even *I* see the wrong in that! She is my flesh and blood. My only niece. And she wants to fight you. To the death."

Angela advanced grimly toward Molly, who intended to stand her ground in spite of her terror. Matthew stepped forward to separate them, but a glance from Maya sent him reeling.

"You can't fight me, little bitch," Angela taunted, circling Molly. "If you had any talent you would have used it before now. Can you do even the simplest of tricks? Can you make a fire?"

Concentrate and do it, Molly commanded herself briskly. *You have the amulet now. Maybe . . .* She tried and failed and Angela howled with laughter.

"I'm sorry, Maya," Molly sighed. "I tried."

"As you have so often observed," Maya replied sweetly, "you have never seen the usefulness of these skills, and so you have never mastered them."

Turning to Angela, she added haughtily, "Do not toy with my niece. It is clear to me that your power is weak and derivative. My niece is a dream sorceress. She will surprise you."

"She's helpless," Angela corrected gleefully. "She'll be a pleasure to kill."

"I brought you here!" Molly fumed. "I have the amulet and I have Matthew."

"Shall I break her heart, Matthew?" Angela grinned toward the still-dazed warrior. "Shall I tell her how ravenous you were for a real woman after weeks of her tame little bed?"

The Valmain princess fought for control as jealousy and hatred simmered in her heart, spilling over, in the form of fury, into her very soul. She needed to save August . . . She needed to purge the world of Angela's brand of witchcraft for Matthew's sake and the sake of others . . . She needed revenge on this woman for the hurt, perhaps irreversible, that she had inflicted on her love affair . . .

Then she became aware of Angela's struggling. The witch was trying to pull free of the dream power. To go where? Molly wondered. Without Matthew, or the amulet, what true harm could she cause now? Maya had said Angela was weak. Wouldn't she just disappear and never bother them again? Could Molly justify killing a harmless human being? Shouldn't she just send Matthew back to free August, and then allow Angela to depart?

Then Angela jeered, "I don't need the amulet. I'm leaving, but not for good. I'll go to the lakes!" She tossed her head and insisted, "The amulet is a child's toy compared to the powers of your ancient enemies, and they'll gladly assist me in destroying you and all traces of the mounds! I'll tell them you possess the dream power, and they'll hunt you down and destroy you again!" Summoning all her strength, she raised her arms high above her head and shrieked.

The movement, and its accompanying surge of energy, almost broke Molly's hold, but the threat had been too chilling and the permission to kill too heady to resist. With her own angry shout she tackled the hated witch to the ground.

"Fool!" Angela screamed. "How I hate you!" Pinning Molly's shoulders to the grassy earth, she spat, "How I hate your weakness! Pitiful, whining fool . . ."

"And I hate you!" Molly gasped, allowing visions of Angela and Matthew—naked and writhing in carnal ecstasy—to flood her brain until an almost mindless need to kill infected her. *"Whoring bitch!"* She wanted to scratch Angela's eyes from their sockets, to rip her hair from her head, to exterminate her . . .

And the power was there! It jolted her, like megavolts of charged adrenaline, feeding on the amulet and the look of fear in Angela's widening eyes. Hatred gave the Valmain witch the power and concentration she needed to manipulate her magic, but the skills—of fighting and witching—were few.

Angela, on the other hand, was biting and scratching like an angry cat. The two adversaries struggled, rolling and screaming in chaos, until Maya could apparently stand it no longer. With calm authority she pointed her finger at Angela and commanded, "You must die now, unworthy one." In an instant, Angela's body was engulfed in flames.

Molly stared in horror, then remembered Maya's plan and tore her eyes from the burning corpse, fixing her concentration on her aunt and holding her in place in the dream.

Maya beamed with delight. "I see there is hope for you, my pretty niece. Perhaps, with a little time and practice, you will become a sorceress worthy of this dream power."

"Do you understand, Maya?" Molly whispered. "I just can't let you have her body. I can't take the responsibility."

"Poor niece." Maya drew the stricken girl into her arms and cooed, "Of course I understand. My father would be proud of you, and so am I." Peeking over Molly's curls, she informed Matthew, "You have been cruel to my favorite niece. Now you must pamper her. Take her to the place she calls Paris and make love to her."

"My pleasure," Matthew murmured.

Molly pulled free reluctantly. "I have to banish you, Maya. I'm sorry, but there's no other way."

"Shall I send myself away?"

"No, I'll do it."

"Very well. Tell Aaric I will be waiting for him."

"Wait, Maya. Let us thank you." Matthew seemed surprised by the sound of his own voice thanking this ancient enemy. "You helped us when you could have cooperated with Angela."

"Her? Never! Her power was really quite weak."

"You called it derivative," Matthew remembered. "What did you mean?"

"Through some charm or spell, her mother's womb gave her the ability to steal from our mounds, but in pitifully small amounts. She was no one until she met you. Now," the sorceress grinned, "she is no one once more." Stroking his cheek, she added, "Farewell, son of my old lover. Take care of my niece. And, Molly," Maya's tone softened, "if I have caused you pain or distress in your life, I truly regret it. I did not know you then. Forgive me for your loss and take care of yourself."

"I love you, Maya," Molly sobbed. Then, with her teary eyes tightly closed, she concentrated—as Maya herself had taught her—and wished her away in a flash of blinding blue light.

Only Maya's stunning cape remained, lying in soft folds on the sweet green grass. Molly picked it up and stroked it against her cheek sadly. "Would it really have been so wrong," she whispered, "to have let her live again as Angela?"

Matthew gathered his shaken dream girl into his arms. "You had to do it, Valmain. I wish I could tell you it's all over now, but I can't. I have a duty, as your champion." He reached for her wrist. "I need the amulet now."

"No. You'll use it against Aaric. I'm going to send you back to August now."

"Not so fast, daughter of Kerreya," a cheerful voice boomed. "You will spoil all of our fun."

"Aaric!" Molly groaned. "Oh no. Why couldn't you have stayed away?"

"Away? I was right here all along. I saw the hilarious fight. *And* I heard this one's boasting. So, Matthew, you think you can defeat me again?"

"I think I have to," Matthew replied coolly.

"Maybe so. With Maya gone, I will want your woman for my own again." His royal blue eyes were twinkling wildly. "So? How shall it be? Myself and my powers against you and your amulet? It might be allowed. Or," he glanced impishly toward Molly and added, "shall we fight as two men who are in love with the same woman?"

Matthew grinned. "No powers. No amulets. Just my fists . . . and your face."

Molly backed away, less horrified than frustrated. Again! Would this never end? She tried to summon August, but he was not sleeping and there was no sign of intervention by her "grandfather." "Stop. Please. Both of you!" she tried valiantly. "How can you say you love me and then torture me like this?"

"Now, Princess," Aaric teased. "You have had your fun with Angela. Let us have ours. And look at my future! If I lose, I get Maya. If I win, I get you! Has any man ever been in so tantalizing a battle?"

"Walk away, Molly," urged Matthew. "There's no need to watch."

"No, I'll watch. And remember, I still have the amulet. And," her eyes locked with Aaric's, "I know how to banish you."

The sorcerer nodded. "I understand. You are saying that I go to Maya either way? Still, I need no reason to fight Lost Eagle's son. And who knows . . ." he winked, "maybe you will find you do not wish to send me away."

Matthew assumed his fighting stance, a relaxed posture that belied his total concentration. "Any time you're ready, Moonshaker."

"I no longer hate you, Son of Lost Eagle," Aaric taunted cheerfully. "You are not nearly as cowardly as your sniveling ancestor was."

"My ancestor? The one Maya couldn't get enough of?" Matthew jeered. "Just like your 'Princess' can't get enough of *me?*" He grinned when the remark clearly hit home. "The men in my family always come out on top—in bed with *your* women."

Molly winced. It was merely hyperbole—war talk—but it was less than flattering. "Leave me out of this, both of you!" she instructed from her resting place.

"Out of respect for the Princess, I will not tell you of the praises she moaned in my ear when I took her."

"Shut up!" Matthew growled.

"You had neglected to introduce her to certain sensations—"

"Bastard!" The Valmain champion's kick cut short the boast, shattering the Moonshaker's ribs. Before the sorcerer could recover, Matthew had leapt away and was dancing gleefully. "How old *are* you, anyway?" he quipped, heady with adrenaline.

When the sorcerer lunged, it seemed indeed as though the moon itself might shake from the force of his blow, and Matthew momentarily reeled, gasping for air. When the two men resumed their circling, however, Matthew appeared unharmed, while Aaric's eyes blazed with feverish agony.

Molly understood the warriors more clearly now. Just as she herself had drawn on images of Angela and Matthew in a lustful embrace to fuel her jealousy and thus her single-mindedness, Matthew Redtree was now allowing himself to be consumed by jealousy, focused against the Moonshaker. He was using it as a weapon—controlling it, exploiting it—and the results were impressive.

Perhaps Aaric also was drawing upon the flames of jealousy to consume his age-old enemy. Perhaps Maya had been right to counsel Molly to value hatred as dearly as love. It was indeed a powerful weapon.

Would Molly ever need such a weapon again? Against the lakes, perhaps? If, as Angela claimed, they still existed, what could Molly do against them? Without Maya or Aaric to teach the age-old skills . . .

But she would have Matthew Redtree and,

watching him now, she almost believed he could be enough. A one-man army—her champion—destroying anyone or anything threatening his dream girl. He was tireless in the face of the Moonshaker's superior size, landing punch after kick after punch with almost legendary prowess.

And Aaric's skills—without weapons or magic— were no match for those of the cross-trained fanatic who now confronted him. While he wrestled mightily, and landed his own jabs with repeated success, he was tiring more rapidly, and his mouth, although still grinning, was a profusion of blood and raw tissue. Molly was almost certain that beneath his battered ribs his insides were in similar shape, and she finally abandoned her neutral posture, approaching the fray with mournful determination. "Aaric?" she called gently. "It's time."

When the sorcerer threw her a parting glance and disappeared, Matthew roared, *"Why did you send him? I was so close. I wanted to prove—"*

"You had nothing to prove!" Molly caught his bloody face between her hands, gentling him with her kiss. "I always knew you were the stronger. Which means, you know, that you are even stronger than Lost Eagle was!"

"Yeah?"

"Yes. You're my hero, like I said before. But I couldn't stand to see Aaric suffer."

"I suppose maybe you did the right thing." He wiped the blood and sweat from his brow and tested one swollen wrist gingerly. "They did help you, he and Maya. They seemed to feel real loyalty toward you. Which shows they weren't all bad. And," he slid his hands under her cape and around her waist, "it shows how really good you are, that you could touch them like that. Strong and pure of heart. I've missed you. Come here."

"Mmm. I've missed you, too," she breathed.

He interrupted their kiss to tease gently, "You called Angela a whoring bitch."

"What's your point?"

Matthew grinned. "It was awesome. I didn't think you had it in you."

"Well, I guess I'm not as pure of heart as we hoped."

"Sure you are. She threatened your whole culture. She threatened you with ancient enemies and you responded with some kind of primal group-preservation instinct. It was incredible."

"But ineffective. Maya had to finish it." Her eyes twinkled. "Don't tell AJ what a failure I was."

"Failure? You fell like a real pro. Did he teach you that?"

"I'm black and blue all over."

"Because you're a lover, not a fighter." He slipped a rough hand under her lacy petticoat. "Let's make love."

"What about August? Shouldn't we check . . . ?"

"August will handle it all there. He's fine. I know it. And . . ." Matthew nuzzled her neck in anticipation, "once we wake up, we're hours from our reunion. And here, you're wearing the amulet. I always wanted to make love with a superwoman."

"I thought that was Angela's allure."

"Let's just say I now prefer benevolent superwomen."

"Better for your health," Molly agreed, pulling away gently. "But you have to go to August. He'll be worried. Bring him safely to his ranch and then take me home to Berkeley." She was trying to be casual, hoping that her champion, the great love of her life, would not realize why she could not be comfortable making love here in this seemingly-deserted meadow.

"One more thing, just in case we can't get back here." Matthew removed Molly's cape and studied the stitching carefully.

"More Lost Eagle stories?" Molly smiled.

"No. I'm looking for information about the lakes. That threat of Angela's really hit home." His brow was creased with concern.

"Aaric and Maya told me a little about them," Molly admitted. "Hopefully, they're as scarce as mounds witches."

"They told you stories? Details? Great! As soon as we get back to my house, I'll debrief you. We'll tape every detail while it's fresh."

"Matthew," she groaned. "I don't want to live *there.*"

"We *have* to live there. It's practically a fortress." He confronted her squarely. "When will you ever learn? I can't protect you unless you cooperate with me!"

"I don't want to live in a fortress. I want our children to have a normal life."

"Our children?" he grinned. "Does that mean you'll marry me? Right away?"

"Yes, Matthew. And," she smiled hopefully, "can we have our honeymoon in Paris?"

"Paris?" he scoffed. "It's overrated, Molly. You know where we should go?"

"Where?"

"Boston. Your dad can give you away and little Nicole can be our flower girl."

"Never!" Her eyes flashed. "Leave it alone, Matthew Redtree. I'll never forgive them for what they did to my mother." She caught her temper. "Listen

to us. We've gone from recurring dreams to recurring arguments." Draping her arms around his neck she smiled seductively. "I'm a lover, not a fighter, remember?"

"Yeah," he grinned. "August and I'll be on the next plane to LA. Get rid of your little warrior nephew and meet us at the airport."

"It's a date. I love you, Son of Lost Eagle."

"You proved it," he nodded proudly. "You sent Aaric away. I know that was hard on you, Valmain, but I'll make it up to you for the rest of our lives." With a confident wink he was gone from the meadow.

Molly sighed and glanced around herself, knowing, deep inside, that Aaric would never send himself away from her forever. Matthew believed Molly had done it, and she hoped it would never become necessary to tell him otherwise. She could lose him, and she couldn't bear that. She couldn't bear to lose either of her champions.

Epilogue

Deborah Clay stood and stared, in muted horror, at the lifeless body of her only grandchild. There was no pulse. There was no sign of Matthew Redtree. Most importantly, there was no amulet! The old woman moved slowly, conducting a painstaking search of the tiny cottage as her worst fears became her reality.

"Angela! Angela!" she mourned. "My ambitious foolish beauty. Have you failed me? Am I never to taste power?"

Her eyes blazed with hatred and envy. Molly Sheridan and Matthew Redtree—*they* had done this and would pay dearly. There was not a mark on Angela's body, but from the expression of terror on her face, her grandmother knew the truth. Death had not come from Matthew's physical prowess or an old uncle's interference. Death had been inflicted by magic.

The old uncle was one of Lost Eagle's descendants. He was a source of wisdom and knowledge, but not magic. That left only one player in this murderous drama: Molly Sheridan. The amulet had been in her family for years. It had seemed to be so charming a coincidence, until somehow, from a distance of over one thousand miles away, she had killed Angela. How was that possible?

There was only one explanation and it was so staggeringly simple that the old woman cursed herself for not having recognized it sooner. Hadn't Matthew asked, that very first night, for information concerning Maya's sister? He had even known the girl's name—Kerreya. And Deborah had thought nothing of it, so wrapped up had she been in the story of Aaric's travel through the centuries. Now the truth was staring her in the face through the dead eyes of her only granddaughter. Maya's sister had run off with a stranger, unable to bear being second best to Maya. But some had said the old sorcerer father had been so distraught at the idea of being separated from his younger daughter that he had gifted young Kerreya with the dream power, so that he could visit her from time to time in her new homeland. And if Matthew knew of Kerreya, when he was otherwise so ignorant, and if Molly Sheridan could kill from a distance of over one thousand miles . . .

How she hated them at that moment! They had outsmarted her, and they would pay. Deborah would find the lakes, despite the awesome danger they posed, and would give them the information necessary to destroy the mounds once more. The high lake wizard—if he still existed, and Deborah had no doubts along these lines—would be aghast to hear that a mounds witch with the power of dreaming had come forth after so many centuries!

The wizard would be told of the amulet, and of the vulnerability of the witch's champion when he was far from the mounds. He would also be told of the silver spoon, which Deborah had used to charm the womb of her daughter-in-law so long ago, resulting in Angela's lovely yet eventually ineffectual witchhood. That silver spoon bore the marks of the mounds, as did Matthew Redtree's accursed amulet. All of this would be told to the lake wizard. In return, Deborah would demand raw power . . .

Demand? From a lake wizard? A long, cold shudder racked Deborah's frail body. Did she dare pursue such a course? Was there any true alternative? She was almost a century old. The day was fast approaching when even the most powerful magic would not be able to rejuvenate her stiff, dry body. She had to act now if she hoped to gain life for herself, vengeance for Angela, and death for the daughter of Kerreya.

My powers are from another time, Molly reassured herself over and over as she stood at the airport gate and prepared to greet the Valmain champion and his uncle. *We may someday need an adviser from that other time. And maybe, from now on, I can control it all better. Maya had confidence in me, and that alone is incredibly encouraging. Maybe I can have it all. My balanced Matthew away from the mounds, my powerful Matthew close to the mounds, and Aaric, in my dreams. Advising, amusing, adoring. And if it becomes necessary to banish him—if he becomes too bold or ambitious—I'll at least have had a chance to thank him and to kiss him goodbye. He deserves that, at the very least.*

She hoped it would never become necessary for her to use her magic, but understood the importance of being prepared. She had no real choice but to embrace her relentless destiny and allow Aaric to transform her into a mounds sorceress.

Not that she would abandon her career, of

course. She would pursue her studies, become a research toxicologist and devoted mother and loving wife and mounds sorceress . . .

In other words, a benevolent superwoman, or a basket case, whichever comes first, she teased herself, but when Matthew Redtree appeared, his knapsack slung over one shoulder, his black hair tousled and his eyes of gold twinkling with reverent anticipation, all thoughts of the lakes, the mounds, and the recurring arguments faded and she moved eagerly into destiny's embrace.

A Dream Embraced
by Kate Donovan

Life should have been perfect for Molly Sheridan Redtree—blushing bride, fledgling sorceress, and almost immediately, expectant mother. But her Matthew is still Matthew—ever restless, ever questing, and Molly finds herself turning again and again to the sorcerer Aaric, who loves his "Princess" with a passion Matthew seems to reserve only for cosmic duty.

Aaric knows that, due to his dream imprisonment, he can do little but comfort, train, and advise. The real protection must come from the Valmain champion. But when evil wizards brutally attack Matthew, stealing his precious amulet and robbing him of his memory, Aaric *must* find a way to escape from the dream and rush to Molly's aid.

Now Molly must once again choose—between the sorcerer who loves her and the husband who seems forever beyond her reach . . .

Coming soon from Pinnacle Books!